KINGDOM KEEPERS

DARK PASSAGE

BOOK SIX

ALSO BY RIDLEY PEARSON

RIDLEY PEARSON

KINGDOM KEEPERS

DARK PASSAGE

BOOK SIX

DISNEP • HYPERION BOOKS

New York

The following are some of the trademarks, registered marks, and service marks owned by Disney Enterprises, Inc.: Adventureland® Area, Audio-Animatronics® Figure, Big Thunder Mountain® Railroad, Disney®, Disneyland®, Disney's Hollywood Studios, Disney's Animal Kingdom® Theme Park, Epcot®, Fantasyland® Area, FASTPASS® Service, Fort Wilderness, Frontierland® Area, Imagineering, Imagineers, it's a small world, Magic Kingdom® Park, Main Street, U.S.A., Area, Mickey's Toontown®, monorail, New Orleans Square, Space Mountain® Attraction, Splash Mountain® Attraction, Tomorrowland® Area, Toontown®, Walt Disney World® Resort.

Buzz Lightyear Astro Blasters © Disney Enterprises, Inc./Pixar Animation Studios

Toy Story characters © Disney Enterprises, Inc./Pixar Animation Studios

Winnie the Pooh characters based on the "Winnie the Pooh" works by A. A. Milne and E. H. Shepard

Printed in the United States of America

First Disney • Hyperion paperback edition, 2014
10 9 8 7 6 5 4 3 2
V475-2873-0-14189

ISBN 978-1-4231-6523-1

Library of Congress Control Number for Hardcover Edition: 2012035597

Visit www.DisneyBooks.com
www.thekingdomkeepers.com
www.ridleypearson.com

SUSTAINABLE FORESTRY INITIATIVE
Certified Chain of Custody
Promoting Sustainable Forestry
www.sfiprogram.org
SFI-01054
The SFI label applies to the text stock

Dedicated to the crew, stewards, cast members, actors, singers, officers, and staff who make the Disney Cruise Line unlike any other cruise experience out there.

Hats off.

KINGDOM
KEEPERS

DARK PASSAGE

BOOK SIX

1

THE CONSTELLATIONS GREW DIMMER, the night sky swallowing them whole. These were no normal stars—they were red, blue, white, green, yellow. Nor were they strung in familiar patterns. Instead, they formed long, straight lines, the stars symmetrically spaced.

It was only as white, foaming clouds rose to challenge the stars, dousing Finn Whitman's face with salt water, that he realized the lights weren't stars at all.

But neither was he a boy.

Not exactly.

"Help!" A girl's cry. Finn fanned the water, turning around as the ship's wake arrived, bobbing him higher. Just before plummeting into another wave trough, he saw a girl flailing to stay afloat.

Willa. He remembered now: the two of them jumping from Deck 4 of the *Disney Dream* cruise ship, leaping into the darkness to avoid a pack of mad hyenas on their heels. Leaving their fellow Keepers back on the ship.

The *Disney Dream* was on a celebration cruise to inaugurate the opening of the new locks of the Panama

Canal, while also promoting the onboard installation of the Kingdom Keepers' hologram DHI guides. The dangers that had arisen on and off the ship during the cruise's first stop at Disney's private island, Castaway Cay, had happened less than a day earlier. It felt more like a year.

The speed with which the *Dream* now receded surprised and frightened Finn. As a passenger he'd had no idea how fast they'd been moving. As he watched the cruise ship shrink away at an alarming pace, he understood that in a minute or two it would be just another flickering light on the horizon.

Another wave from the ship's wake caught Finn, lifting him like a cork. He saw Willa riding the top of the adjacent crest, looking toward the ship.

"Over here!" Finn shouted.

Treading water, Willa turned to face him.

Then she sparkled and vanished.

Finn pulled hard, bodysurfing down the rolling wave and swimming strongly toward Willa. Stretching to extend his freestyle stroke—amazed by his own strength—he saw his hand and forearm dissolve into glitter, a sparkle of light washed away by the hungry spray.

An instant later, Willa reappeared—and so did Finn's arm.

The phenomenon would have stunned, even frightened, an ordinary person. But to Finn it made perfect sense. He and Willa were holograms, three-dimensional projections of light generated by a computer server on board the disappearing *Dream*. The farther away from the ship, the worse the projection. Being low in the water as they were, the two holograms were subject to additional interference from each wave. Riding the crests, they came into clarity. But it wouldn't last, and once their projections failed, Finn would have no way of finding Willa. The audio stream, being a narrower bandwidth, might last slightly longer, but it wasn't a risk worth taking.

"Here!" Finn shouted a second time. Kicking ferociously, he propelled his hologram down from the wave's crest, through the trough, and up the other side, cutting the distance between them in half. Their holograms sputtered, a result of distance from the ship. Any farther, and they would dissolve altogether.

He and Willa, along with several other high school kids now aboard the *Disney Dream*, had once modeled for the roles of Disney Host Interactive (also known among Disney Imagineers as Daylight Hologram Imaging) teenage Park hosts, holograms that guided families around the Disney parks. And now the cruise ships.

Undisclosed at the time (some would say "unknown") was a side effect that allowed the DHIs to "cross over" in their sleep, becoming their hologram replicas. Finn and his friends often found themselves inside a Disney park while their bodies, their human selves, slept at home. They'd quickly discovered that their holograms had been engineered by Disney's Imagineers to do battle with certain Disney villains—the Overtakers—whose one desire was to take over the parks and ruin them.

The OTs, as the Kingdom Keepers referred to the Overtakers, dreamed of a darker experience for Park guests than the one Walt Disney had envisioned. That same dark force, in the form of Maleficent, the Evil Queen, and Cruella de Vil, was currently aboard the *Dream*—and intent on turning it into the *Nightmare*.

This time, the Overtakers had stolen a historic journal once belonging to the Disney Imagineers— or perhaps even Walt himself. The Overtakers had infiltrated the ship, and smuggled Tia Dalma and Chernabog—a mysterious and monstrous creature from *Fantasia*—aboard at Castaway Cay. The addition of a witch doctor and the most evil of Walt Disney's creations didn't bode well. Where Maleficent went, trouble followed.

Which accounted for the man-eating hyenas that had forced Finn and Willa to jump overboard in the first place, and had put them in their current predicament.

When a hologram's projection failed, it fell into what the Keepers called DHI shadow. The result was invisibility, which in certain instances could be a good thing. Not so much when you were nearly drowning, and the only hope for survival was steaming away at eighteen knots.

"Your hand!" Finn called, reaching for Willa. "Before we're gone!" Then, when she didn't react instantly: "Come on!"

Again, he amazed himself by how strongly he swam. A Florida boy, Finn was no stranger to water—but since when could he swim like a lifeguard?

Willa's hologram had lost its density and was porous, like sand spread loosely over a floor. It had lost its third dimension as well; she looked like a pixelated, digitally enlarged photograph. The final stage before invisibility.

"Reach!" Finn shouted. His voice sounded like a bad radio signal, scratchy and popping with static. Desperate, he plunged his face into the sea and called out, "Starfish wise, starfish cries!" a phrase he'd been given to summon King Triton, who'd saved Finn once before.

Striking out blindly in the water, Finn felt his hands

catch Willa's. Finn squeezed hard, then walked his fingers up to Willa's forearms so that they held each other's wrists—a stronger "fireman's" grip.

"You okay?" he said, but it came out, "oo . . . ay?"

Finn turned his back to Willa and pulled her hands around his neck so that she rode on his back like a cape. She held tight; he felt her soft cheek pressed against his neck. He swam. Swam hard. Kicking and pulling through the sea, more like a machine than a man. Finn supposed this crazy strength had something to do with his exposure to a massive jolt of electricity just before he'd jumped. He'd been in the ship's engine room. A world away from here.

But he didn't much care about the source of his power, only its efficacy.

Finn's progress was admirable, his churned wake joining the wide white strip of aerated seawater thrown out by the ship's propeller. The water sparkled and fizzed like a freshly poured soda. Viewed from overhead, Finn and his passenger were invisible, not even a speck in a strip of sea paved flat by the passing of a hundred and thirty thousand tons of steel.

". . . invis . . ." Willa said. Or tried to. "D . . . sh . . . dow."

Finn didn't bother trying to answer, saving his energy for his breaststroke. If he could get close enough to the *Dream* for his hands to start flashing, however faintly, his voice would likely return.

But that was the problem—as hard as he was swimming, they weren't catching up. Not even close. Granted, Finn had slowed the rate with which the *Dream* pulled away, nearly matching the ship's forward progress. But he wasn't gaining on it. Not an inch. And if he eased back at all, the ship visibly pulled farther away.

He knew what had to be done. Knew the one chance they had. The likelihood of drowning was slim, given the state-of-the-art software upgrade running their projections—DHI 2.0. But it hardly mattered. If they remained invisible, lost at sea, their human bodies would stay asleep on board, unable to awaken. They would be locked in what the Keepers called "Sleeping Beauty Syndrome," or SBS—a hologram no-man's land where their sleeping bodies never woke, and their hologram projections could not be reached.

King Triton's code offered the promise of rescue, but Triton's agents could not rescue what they could not see. He and Willa had to move closer to the *Dream*. But how?

"F . . . thhh," Willa said. Choking Finn with her left forearm, she tapped him on the shoulder with her right hand, forcing him to look back. He saw something no thicker than a tree branch sticking out of the water, moving quickly toward them, cutting a fine wake to either side.

A fin? A shark? The object sparkled as it caught starlight from a dazzling sky. A pipe. A periscope—an old, rusted periscope moving very fast and coming right for them.

Captain Nemo? Finn wondered.

Finn uttered a series of wet burps and patted Willa's arms, indicating: *Hold tight.* Then he swam hard—straight for the periscope, now eight to ten yards to his right. He had to time it perfectly; he could ill afford to undershoot or overshoot his target.

The approach of the periscope—its sudden appearance out of nowhere—seemed to suggest it was part of a rescue attempt. Arranged by Wayne? How could he know of their predicament? They'd only been in the water a matter of minutes. Had the sub been following the *Dream* all this time?

Or was this a result of his calling for King Triton's help, as he'd been instructed?

Finn calculated his position, adjusted with a swift backward flutter kick, stretched forward, and grabbed the briskly moving periscope with both hands. His arms felt like they would tear from his shoulder sockets. The submarine was moving much faster than he'd imagined.

With Willa holding on to his neck for dear life, the

two surfed and coughed for air. Somewhere in the deep recesses of his mind, Finn understood that as a hologram he didn't need to concern himself with breathing; but instinct dictated otherwise.

During the next gulp of air, he saw the *Dream*'s lights as distinct strings. The sub was pulling closer.

Finn's hands suddenly appeared, clasped around the periscope. They flashed and pulsed light—then vanished. Finn ducked into the water and closed his eyes. With the next lifting of his head, he clearly saw the hologram images of his arms. He was visible again. Willa, too.

"Return!" she said, gargling the word.

The suggestion hit Finn as a beacon of hope. Philby, a fellow Kingdom Keeper, or Storey Ming, a shipboard ally, would be attempting to cancel their current hologram projections and "return" them to their sleeping selves, on board ship. Having failed to accomplish the task immediately after Finn and Willa jumped, hopefully they had not given up altogether. With Finn and Willa back in range, it was imperative the Return be attempted again.

But how to signal them?

The sub continued to gain on the *Dream*; the ship's stern loomed ahead, black paint glistening. An oversized Captain Mickey, sprawled on a plank slung from the upper deck, had been installed on the stern. Mounted next to Mickey and the yellow letters that spelled out DISNEY DREAM were three large Disney brooms and pails from *Fantasia*.

The sight reminded Finn of a near-deadly conflict Maybeck and Charlene—the final members of the Kingdom Keepers team—had had a week earlier backstage at Disney's Hollywood Studios. *If those brooms come alive too . . .* Finn thought.

He and the Keepers didn't have a credo, per se, but if they did it might have been: *Nothing is as it seems; take nothing for granted.* Park attractions came alive at night. Disney characters turned out to be real—and the Disney villains, dangerous. Turns out that magic pens, evil curses, puzzling stairways, corrupt villains, secret passages, and dungeons all existed within the parks. All for real.

Part of Finn was ready to get back to being a normal high school student and leave all of it behind. But in that order. He didn't want to leave it all behind by drowning.

"You see what I see?" Willa choked out.

At that exact moment, the sub veered off course, steering well to port of the massive ship. The periscope began slipping through Finn's hands; the sub was submerging. He would have to let go in a matter of seconds or be sucked under.

To signal Philby and Storey for the return, Finn and Willa needed to be spotted from the ship—but without drawing undue attention. Finn needed passengers to notice, for the word to spread quickly, and for it all to be considered a big mistake a few minutes later. He could not invite lifeboats and alarms without drawing attention to the Keepers' "misuse" of their holograms—an action that might get them locked up for the remainder of the cruise, and prevent them from stopping the OTs.

Finn spotted a romantic couple leaning on the rail of an upper deck, and remembered all the fuss the night of the Sail-Away party.

"Hang on!" he called to Willa, and let go of the pipe just as it sank beneath the surface. Again, Finn sank his face into the water and spoke the Triton code in a loud bubbling voice.

"Starfish wise, starfish cries."

Willa let go and treaded water.

"NO!" Finn called out, aware of the physics involved. The two were instantly the objects of opposing forces: the concussion of the sub's propeller wash and the downdraft of currents caused by its rapid descent. Willa was swept back, hands and legs held awkwardly in front of her as though she were crawling. Finn, slightly to the side, was caught in the downdraft, sucked deeper and deeper as he watched Willa zoom away.

For him and Willa to have the best chance for a return, they needed to be together, and they needed to be on the surface. Finn didn't trust the projection strength underwater, even this close to the *Dream*. He kicked furiously as he was pulled deeper still. He could feel the water pressure squeezing him smaller, compacting him. He had no idea if even a 2.0 projection could survive such pressure.

His hand struck something hard and slimy. Finn yanked away and kicked out instinctively, spooked by the unyielding darkness of the depths. A shark? It had to be!

The creature impaled him with its snout, striking him in the center of his chest. An instant later, he was struck again, then snagged under both arms—*two* sharks, not one?—and driven higher. Finn wrestled to be free, but the force of the water and speed of his escorts pinned him to their slick, snot-like skin.

Only as Finn pulled toward the surface, where the moonlight and starlight penetrated, did he finally get a look at his captors. Not sharks. A different nose. Sleek bodies mottled gray and white. Spotted dolphins, fast as lightning, streaking for the surface.

The Triton code, answered—again.

Finn rolled and hooked on to the dorsal fin to his right, carried now by a single dolphin. The animal responded to his willing participation immediately, bursting through the surface, arcing through the air, and plunging back into the sea. It chittered playfully while airborne. Finn gave a spontaneous cry of joy.

"Ooooo-weeee!"

But it was a girl's voice he heard, not his own.

To his right, between his dolphin and the ship, Willa was straddling her dolphin like a pony, one hand on the dorsal fin, one high in the air like a bucking-bronco rider. The dolphins closed ranks, side by side, diving beneath the surface, then busting loose in high, acrobatic flight.

Glancing up, Finn saw the ship's port rails filling with spectators. This was what he'd hoped for: word spread quickly aboard the *Dream*, especially around whale or dolphin sightings. If their fellow Keepers were still looking for them—and Finn had every reason to believe they were—there was no way they would miss this.

Equally important, however, was that not *too many* passengers see the two kids riding the dolphins. Better that the sighting seem like the ramblings of someone who had drunk too much, or be taken as a Disney special effect. The Panama Canal cruise had been designated a Kingdom Keepers cruise, after all—excuses could be made.

Finn leaned down to his pilot, having no idea where a dolphin's ears were located. "Stay under!" he called out.

Having no idea what Finn had just said, the dolphin rose and leaped again. Finn saw that the flippers by his legs aimed upward as the dolphin dove; he reached out and held the flippers up, then let go. The dolphin got the message, diving deeper. Finn pulled the flippers to horizontal—using them as an equestrian would reins. The dolphin responded, leveling off. Its companion dolphin, carrying Willa, caught up, staying abreast of the leader, both submerged.

Willa's short hair streamed behind. She glanced over at Finn, eyes white with exhilaration.

The passengers on deck would be scouring the waves, hoping. But by now the crowd would be growing. Finn didn't need witnesses comparing notes: *Did you see the two kids* riding *the dolphins?*

The dolphins sped forward, racing through the water like torpedoes. Willa and Finn held tight. Thirty seconds underwater . . . Forty . . .

How long until the Keepers heard about the sighting and communicated with the Radio Studio to attempt a Return?

Willa motioned a thumb up, toward the surface. Finn, in weighing exposure to the passengers against the chance to return, had neglected the needs of the hard-working dolphins, who were mammals and required fresh air. He pressed the dolphin's flippers down, holding them there briefly. The dolphin responded, raising its head, kicking its fluke, and exploding into the night. Water sprayed from its blowhole, fresh air filling its lungs.

Finn heard shouts as viewers called out to one another.

Then his arms tingled. He looked over at Willa, but it was like looking at her through a shower curtain; her image was faded and dull. She reached for him, and he for her. Their fingers wiggled, trying to touch. They connected.

Finn woke in an empty stateroom. Bone dry. Panting. A dream? A nightmare? Or had he returned? Nearly always the same sensation—mystical, mysterious. Awash in disbelief and not trusting his own powers of observation, he briefly wondered if he'd imagined everything.

Or had he lived it?

Where did the potency of possibility give way to the power of persuasion?

2

FROM THE MOMENT Finn and Willa had jumped off the deck, the situation on board the ship had gone from bad to worse.

As he'd leaped, Finn had thrown a small object back onto Deck 4. It had been spotted by Amanda and Jess, two girls with unusual abilities who had joined forces with the five Keepers. The "sisters" had been crossed over onto the ship hours earlier as holograms at the instruction of Wayne's daughter, Wanda. Wayne supervised all the Keepers' activities and missions; he had the final word on everything.

The four hyenas in pursuit of Finn had seen it as well. Nasty creatures intent on reducing Finn to a midnight snack, the hyenas were homicidal maniacs. The lead hyena was so determined to catch Finn that it misjudged the traction on the slippery deck and plowed headfirst into the metal railing, knocking itself unconscious. The second beast bounced off the rail, but recovered. Hyena number three aimed for whatever it was Finn had tossed behind, and snapped it up in its frothing mouth.

Maybeck arrived on deck wearing a kitchen costume: white pants and pullover shirt. "Don't ask," he said to the bandaged Charlene at his side. The ship's doctor had patched her wounded shoulder.

A big kid for his fifteen years, and fearless to the point of stupidity, Maybeck dove for the hyena but missed. None of the kids knew exactly what the hyena had stolen, but Finn had tried to save it, which made it important.

Maybeck's effort was commendable if unsuccessful. He tried for the animal's rear leg. But this model hyena came equipped with the full package, including backup sensors; it spooked as Maybeck dove, avoiding his eager hand. Like a trained seal, it tossed the small object into the air, opened its maw wide, and appeared to swallow the thing.

Charlene lunged to stop the hyena. It veered, heading straight for Jess.

As sisters who weren't really sisters, the enigmatic Amanda and Jess were known to the Keepers as "Fairlies"—fairly human, but with unique powers. Amanda possessed telekinesis (the "supposed" power to move objects with her mind); Jess, clairvoyance (the "supposed" power to see events in the future). In fact, there wasn't anything "supposed" about their powers, except that the U.S. military was confounded by them and continued to study kids like Jess and Amanda at a facility in Baltimore, an institution from which the two girls had escaped before meeting the Keepers. Currently, they lived with a number of other "strays," charges of a foster mother called Mrs. Nash, whom the girls referred to as Mrs. Nasty.

Now the hyena aimed at Jess, who reacted defensively and reached out to block it. She grabbed its hind leg. The animal squealed, rolled over, and bit Jess, whose hologram was solid at that exact instant.

Jess cried out and let go. She balled up in pain, rolling onto the deck.

An injury a Keeper sustained as a DHI ended up as part of their real body when he or she returned. This bite was a bleeder. Jess was in serious trouble.

The hyena scrambled back to its feet and charged up Deck 4's jogging track toward the bow, the other hyenas trailing close behind.

Maybeck started out in pursuit but quickly lost ground. He snatched up a shuffleboard cue, smacked it on the deck, and broke its U-shaped head from its broomstick-like rod. He hoisted the rod to shoulder height and launched it like a javelin. He would claim later that it had been a protective instinct to defend Jess, a combination of anger, frustration, and the urge to play action hero.

A wild shriek echoed down the deck—the lead hyena was hit, the spear dragging from its flank. The animal slowed but continued toward the bow. The spear wiggled loose and clanged to the deck. The hyenas disappeared into the jogging track's bow tunnel.

Charlene and Amanda stooped over the fallen Jess.

"What's happening to her?" a frightened Amanda said.

"She's . . ." Charlene studied Jess, trying to understand what they were witnessing.

The girl's hologram grew translucent, then disappeared altogether. As it reappeared, it sputtered and wouldn't hold. Each time it faded, Jess squirmed and cried out in pain.

". . . form-shifting," Charlene continued. "Her fear and the pain of the wound are switching her from hologram to mortal. She's in limbo, flashing between the two."

The bite was ugly. It was on the top of Jess's right thigh, two curved lacerations—a frown and a smile. It bled heavily.

Philby arrived from the Radio Studio through the deck's center doors. He spoke with a slight British accent, having spent some of his childhood in England, and had a crop of red hair and a sparkle to his eyes that signaled his uncanny intelligence.

"What about Finn?" Amanda called out to him.

"Storey's on it. At the moment, everyone's on the port side because someone claimed he saw two kids riding dolphins."

"No way!" Charlene said.

Philby grinned at Amanda. "Storey returned the two of them. So for the moment," he continued, "we should be alone here, but it won't stay that way."

He took in Jess's injury and her form-shifting.

"The ship's doctors can't find her like this! They'll try to medicate her hologram and who knows how that will affect her real body."

"Well, she can't return like this," Amanda said firmly. "No way we can deal with the wound at Mrs. Nash's, not to mention that we'd have no way to explain what's happened."

"So she can't stay here and she can't go back," Maybeck said. "Someone have a plan?"

Philby caught Charlene's eye. He said, "We have to—"

"Hide her."

"Yes."

"How?" Charlene asked.

"Even if she could walk," Maybeck said, "which I doubt—it's not as if anyone's going to miss *that*."

He was pointing at Jess's bloody leg.

"And we need to find that hyena," Philby said, "and whatever it stole from Finn."

"The bee suits," Jess groaned to Amanda through clenched teeth.

All eyes fell on Amanda.

"What are you talking about?" Philby said.

"One of her dreams," Amanda explained. "She sketched out two guys in beekeeper suits carrying *her*. You know: big, baggy suits and netting for a helmet?"

Philby said, "Not beekeepers. Hazmat suits. Hazardous materials. Coveralls." He addressed the wounded Jess. "Is that right? Suits? Goggles? Masks?"

Jess nodded.

"Rubber gloves," she said. "I thought it was bee-keepers."

"They call 'em protein spills," Charlene said. "Kids puking. Passengers who get cuts and bleed. Protein. Get it?"

"That's disgusting!" Maybeck said.

"Better than Puke Patrol," Philby said. "Any guesses as to how many people get seasick on a cruise ship? And if it's a bug instead of seasickness, they have to make sure it doesn't spread."

"They dispatch teams," Charlene said. She turned to Maybeck. "Did you read *any* of Philby's background notes for this trip?"

"I . . . ahh . . ."

"Three suits," Charlene proposed. "One, to hide her. Two more to hide whoever's carrying her."

"Take Maybeck with you. More suits, if you can. A protein spill team can follow the blood trail."

"That would be us," Maybeck said, understanding what Philby had in mind. If they could get four suits, they could divide into two teams of two—one team to get Jess to a stateroom; the other to follow the hyena's spilled blood.

"I'm all right," Jess said, lying. She struggled to get up.

"Let's get her to the bench," Philby said, "before anyone sees her. We'll hide her leg—"

"With my bandana," Charlene said, untying her Cast Member neckerchief.

"Here we go," Philby said. "You two . . . hurry!"

3

Having fainted when she'd seen the gaping gash in her leg, Jess felt the warm salt spray across her face. Warm as the sunshine that pelted down. Which was technically impossible, as it was currently nighttime. But dreams—especially Jess's dreams—were unconventional and surprisingly convincing. Only in a dream could you be absolutely sure something was happening that was not.

A warm breeze was happening. Sunshine was happening. But then it was dark again, and there was something soft and squishy beneath her feet: sand. Sharp twigs belonging to bushes and shrubs scratched her calves.

Sand. Prickly shrubs. The sound of the ocean, or was it wind? She followed a group of dark shapes. Not kids. Adults. Five? Four? They stopped periodically as if to listen for anyone following. Like her. She stopped, matching them. Stayed low. Alert.

Rocks and shadows. A cave. The others followed the leader—a woman.

Jess followed, running the long way around to avoid being seen. She crept up to the slanting corner of the cave's opening, where a huge gray rock formed the ceiling, and sand the floor. The rock was smooth. Paper wasp hives hung from the rock like warts. Dozens, maybe hundreds of them. A few wasps flew to and from the nests, their tiny legs dangling like landing gear.

Jess stayed hunched as she crawled inside. The group ahead of her was after something. They were hunting.

And now she was hunting them.

* * *

Finn awoke in one of the few interior staterooms that had not been booked for the cruise. Storey Ming had made it available, so the Keepers had somewhere to sleep when crossed-over as holograms. Ever since his own mom's loyalty had come into question, he'd been bunking in with Philby. But here, there was no one. He reached for the Wave Phone and saw a text message was waiting.

r u there?

It had been sent from Storey Ming's stateroom phone.

here

It took several long seconds for a new message to appear. Anxious seconds.

j in trouble. deck 4. willa ok?

Finn felt thickheaded, like he'd had no sleep. It took him a moment to process "j" as "Jess." His feet were already moving as he texted:

on way

He knocked on the stateroom door where he expected to find the returned Willa. Looked in both directions. Some passengers, but no stewards or crew members. He knocked louder, and the door opened. Willa heaved a sigh of relief at the sight of Finn.

"Oh, it's you!" She opened the door. Finn rushed inside.

"Hurry. Jess is in trouble."

"Where?" Willa asked.

"Deck four. Starboard."

"Where we jumped."

"Yeah."

"The hyenas?"

"Way ahead of you," Finn said.

"Don't be such a jerk, okay?" Willa was in his face, up on her toes. "For one thing: you are *never* way ahead of me." She trembled there, about to lose her balance.

Finn nodded. "Point taken."

"We nearly drowned," she said.

"Sort of."

"Close enough for me."

"I got us out of it," Finn said.

"You?"

"Sorry . . . *We* got us out of it."

"Better."

"I may have spoken the Triton Code," he added. "Twice."

It took Willa a moment to allow herself to grin. "And I thank you for that," she said.

"No charge."

"Jess," she said, reminding them both of their mission.

"Yes. And quickly."

* * *

As one of the five prettiest girls in ninth grade, if you counted Marsha Coleman—and it was hard not to— Charlene had the attention not only of most juniors but even a few seniors as well. She was "popular," which often translated to "hot." She was checked out in the hallways. To girls who were jealous of her, she was an object of derision, the recipient of far too many text messages; and she even received a few anonymous gifts from time to time, not all of which were appropriate.

She had a lot to be thankful for—but at the same time, not so much. Boys wanted to get to know her, but not in a way she had any interest in. She kept tabs on a couple of them, but the more she learned, the less she liked.

Except when it came to Terry Maybeck and Finn Whitman, two of her fellow Keepers. Terry, who wasn't exactly Calvin Klein eye candy. Terry, who considered himself to be God's gift to girls. Terry, who came from a broken home, had few close friends, and worked every day after school to help his aunt Jelly. Terry, who Charlene couldn't stop thinking about. She'd been warned about falling for the bad boys. No one could put Terry in that category. Not bad, just different. An artist. Someone who wasn't afraid to express himself.

As a cheerleader and freshman starter on the school gymnastics team, Charlene was expected to date athletes. Varsity athletes. Her friends were constantly trying to match her with Kaden Keller, the star soccer player, or Josh Brewer—or any boy with a number on his back. But while she liked them as friends, even good friends, the jocks didn't satisfy her romantic ideals. She wanted someone thoughtful, funny, interesting, and interested in things other than the obvious stuff boys were always interested in.

She glanced over at Maybeck, wondering once again

if he fit any of her requirements. And if not, then why was she always thinking about him?

"Keep up!" he hissed at her.

"You look like a psycho in a hospital ward," she said.

"The costume was handy. Okay? Or should I be running around in a towel?"

That hardly brought her mind back to business.

The trick was to look like you were walking while moving close to the speed of running. The *Disney Dream* was more than three football fields in length. Getting from amidships to the bow, and moving from Deck 4 to Deck 1, one covered a good distance.

"Storey's going to meet us," Maybeck said, checking his phone.

"Because?" They were stride-for-stride in the port side Deck 4 hallway, the Buena Vista Theatre to their right.

"She has the all-access crew-member card," he said.

"Uh-huh," said Charlene. She'd had about enough of everyone's fascination with Storey Ming. She appreciated the help, but not the noise.

They reached Deck 1. Despite the added distance she'd had to cover from Deck 14, Storey Ming had arrived first. Without introduction, she said, "I can get the Hit Man's trolley—that's what we call Mr. Mop, 'the Hit Man'—but it'll only have one suit. Two at the most. There must be others in Costume—

Laundry—which won't be too hard to get, but it'll take a few minutes. So what da ya want to do?"

"I'll take the trolley," Maybeck said. "That way, when the real guy comes looking for it, we can stall him. Charlie will hang here and wait for you." He addressed Charlene. "You'll get the other suits up to us."

Charlene nodded.

"You'll need to wear a suit," Storey cautioned. "If Uncle Bob sees you on video with the trolley, he'll know something's up. We all know the Hit Man, and he's not you."

"Okay. So go. We gotta hurry!"

Storey took off through the Crew Only door that led to the I-95 corridor.

"How is this possibly going to work out for Jess?" Charlene asked softly.

"You'll see," Maybeck said.

"And what about you?" she said. "If you're caught in that suit . . . If you're stealing—"

"Borrowing!"

"—gear that belongs to the crew . . . they'll throw you off the ship."

"We gotta do what we gotta do," he said. "If they take Jess into the ship hospital, she'll end up in SBS, and then we're *all* in a big-time jam."

"You're going to look stupid in that suit."

"Me? Seriously? I don't think so."

* * *

The Hit Man's suit was made of clothlike disposable paper. There were four suits on the mop cart, not the two that Storey had predicted. Paper hoods and heavy-duty gloves as well. Only a single set of goggles. The suits closed up the back with Velcro: they were one-size-fits-all. While Storey was off attempting to collect additional goggles, Charlene and Maybeck arrived at the Deck 4 promenade in the ill-fitting suits.

"Finn," Charlene said excitedly. "Willa!"

The spare protein spill suit went to Jess's hologram. The group collected around her as a visual barrier while Amanda and Willa helped her into it.

"She can hang on to the cart," Maybeck suggested.

"We'll get her to one of the empty rooms," Philby said, "and treat her there."

Maybeck worked the gloves awkwardly to get a spray bottle and cloth from the cart. "I'm going after the other wounded."

"Someone else was bitten?" Finn said.

Philby answered. "Maybeck hit a hyena with a javelin. Stuck him pretty good. Left a trail." He pointed toward the bow.

"I'm with you," Finn said, claiming the fourth suit.

"Then you'll man the defibrillator," Maybeck said, indicating the emergency box mounted to the ship's wall.

Finn, already on the bench struggling into the last suit, looked puzzled. The girls almost had Jess into hers.

"We need some kind of weapon," Maybeck said. "I'm taking the shuffleboard spear, but a homemade Taser wouldn't hurt."

"I'm supposed to paddle them?" Finn said.

"You're supposed to shock the one that stole the Return."

"It's not the Return," Finn said. "It's a thumb drive from the Overtakers' server."

"Their hologram data," Philby said as all eyes turned to him for an explanation. "If we can get that drive back, even if the OTs launch another server, I can write a search-and-replace program that will effectively shut down their DHIs. Each time they try to cross over, the network will reject the data. They'll never get projected."

Finn glanced over at the defibrillator. "Philby, you're going to have to tell me how to work that thing."

* * *

Dressed in the white paper coveralls, hood, and rubber gloves, Finn carried the defib kit with the red broken heart on the side. Maybeck held a spray bottle, rag, and the blood-tipped shuffleboard cue handle. At each spot of spilled blood they paused to spray disinfectant and wipe the area clean. They quickly approached the bow, where the promenade entered a metal tunnel and continued to port, creating a jogging loop used by runners and walkers.

They worked quickly, not wanting to lose the trail. But at the same time, they had to look the part. They couldn't pass up blood spills.

As they entered the tunnel, Finn felt a shiver.

"You smell that?" he said.

* * *

Greg Luowski had done as he'd been told. As the biggest boy in his class since second grade, Greg didn't take orders easily. They were to him as vinegar was to oil, or water to fire. To say Greg challenged authority was to give him too much credit. He was more of a bumper car at an amusement park; he went in the direction he was pushed, crashing and forcing his way, rarely mindful of the consequences. He'd been recruited by the Overtakers through a YouTube video someone had e-mailed him. He didn't remember clearly what had happened after that, but his eyes were green now—not that his mother noticed; she didn't notice anything about her son—and instead of being told *not* to make trouble for other kids, he was encouraged to do so.

Ordered, if he was honest about it—which he was not.

He got cool stuff in return, like a Disney cruise. Even if he'd sneaked aboard and was currently a stowaway. So what? He was still on the ship, wasn't he?

So when the order came to stop the hyena, when he was authorized to use the Taser he'd been given, Greg jumped at the opportunity. How cool to shoot off a stun gun! He'd only seen it done once, in the back of a ceramics shop. This big lady had fallen to the floor like the stuffing had come out of her.

Greg knew there'd be nothing to it. Aim. Fire. Big deal.

But then things changed. Then this new world of his began to fray at the edges. There were limits, even for Greg Luowski.

And what these people were asking him—*ordering* him to do . . .

For the first time since becoming an OTK, Greg Luowski felt like a rat in a maze, looking for a way out.

Any way.

* * *

The smell was at once metallic and dangerous; it struck a primeval chord in Finn that told him to run.

"I'm not liking this," he said.

"I hear you."

"Maybe we should turn around."

"We need that thumb drive," Maybeck reminded him.

"I'm the one who got it in the first place," Finn said, wiping up the spot Maybeck had sprayed. The quantity of spilled blood had increased. Neither boy mentioned it, but neither missed it either.

"Where'd it go?" Maybeck said, his goggle-covered eyes trained on the deck. The blood trail had been regular and predictable—every eight to ten feet—until here, at the forward section of the jogging track, where it vanished.

"Weird," Finn said.

"You think it was magically healed?"

"Nah. Maleficent doesn't have that kind of power."

"Tia Dalma might." Maybeck sounded worried. "I don't put anything past her."

"You think it's Tia Dalma who's running the OTs?" Finn asked. For years there had been speculation that Maleficent was not the top Overtaker. "What about Chernabog?"

"Anything's possible."

"Exactly."

"But if we could capture Tia Dalma . . ." Maybeck said.

"Yeah. I'm with you."

"Whitman!"

Maybeck's shout stopped Finn cold. Finn tugged back the paper hood in order to see where Maybeck was pointing: the jamb of one of the closed doors carried a red smear. Blood.

The door's sign warned:

DANGER:
CREW MEMBERS ONLY
BEYOND THIS POINT

Maybeck muttered a curse word.

Finn's family had a rule about not using such language, and though he never admitted it to his friends, he didn't like hearing them. "You think?" Finn said.

"I think," Maybeck answered. He tried the door handle. It moved. The door opened a crack. He reached for the light switch.

"No lights," Maybeck said. "You think someone took care of them?"

"If that was the case, we'd be nuts to go in there."

"No doubt."

"But we're going in anyway?" Finn said, tentatively.

"You're the leader."

It had never been voted on. But Finn didn't deny it. "We need the thumb drive," he repeated.

"No argument from me."

Maybeck hungered for such adventure; he listened to jacked-up music and flaunted his independence. The rest of the KKs tolerated conflict; Maybeck seemed to thrive on it. Maybe it had to do with anger over his living situation—none of the Keepers knew whether something had happened to his parents or if they'd bailed on him. Or maybe he was an adrenaline junkie. Finn wasn't in any hurry to rush into something simply because Maybeck wanted to.

Through the door, they found themselves in a mostly open area where the anchors and docking lines were neatly stored. The wind carried with it salt and the sweet scent of the sea. But mixed into this were other, disgusting odors, like an outhouse in the sun, like garbage cans set out on the curb, like a mouse that had been under the couch for the past week.

Something dead.

Finn faltered. Maybeck cursed under his breath.

"Whoa," he muttered.

"I know," Finn said.

There were two inverted rowboats strapped tightly to the deck. A fiberglass rescue launch was slung overhead, looking like a miniature tugboat. Twin spools the size of small cars were loaded to full with twisted steel cable as thick as a man's forearm. Each played out to a monstrous chain neatly ordered on the deck, leading to one of the ship's two anchors, weighing four tons—eight thousand pounds of iron. The rowboats and the darkness blocked the sight of the forward deck. Something crunched beneath Finn's leather deck shoes.

"Glass," Finn said.

"The lights."

"We could report the broken lights," Finn suggested. "Whatever we're smelling . . . whoever came looking . . . they'd find it."

"And that's a good thing?"

Maybeck and Finn stopped at the exact same moment, compelled to do so by the sudden stench.

"On three," Maybeck said.

Finn wasn't waiting. He used the face of the phone to cast a green pall across the deck.

He retched.

Maybeck blew his cookies onto the inverted rowboat. He cursed again.

Before them, lying on the deck atop the neatly ordered coil of chain, was a hyena, cut open and eviscerated. Maybeck turned away from the gruesome sight. Finn tried to make sense of it. *A ritualistic sacrifice.* Something a Creole witch doctor would do?

"Psst!" Finn caught Maybeck's attention. By moving

the light from his phone away from the horror and incrementally to his right—starboard—he illuminated a line of thin S's on the painted deck.

Maybeck picked up on it and nodded, wiping spittle from his lips.

Bloodred S's, from the edge of a rubber-soled shoe stamping an ever-fainter line of color along the deck. Finn turned away, not wanting to make a big deal out of it.

The line led into the dark shadows between a pair of steel girders on the outer hull that supported the overhead deck.

Someone was hiding there.

Finn suppressed the urge to scream, to charge into the shadows and attack whoever had slain the hyena in this horrid manner. Retribution.

"We need to tell someone," Maybeck said, louder than necessary, loud enough to be heard by whoever was lurking a few yards away. He leaned against the opposing rowboat, as did Finn, their backs to the girders.

Finn took notice of the coveralls, realizing whoever it was would believe them to be crew members, not kids impersonating crew members. For a moment both he and Maybeck had forgotten their roles.

"You mean to help us clean it up," Finn said.

"Ah . . . yeah. Of course," Maybeck said, catching on. "Disposal. Easiest thing is to toss it over the side, but they'll want to incinerate it."

"They'll want to explain it," Finn said.

"No joke. Since when are dogs allowed on board?"

"That's one ugly dog," Finn said. "You see the neck on that thing?"

All the while he'd been unpacking the defibrillator while signaling with his gloved hands, pointing first to the wall behind them, then counting down by putting up one finger at a time.

When Finn's third finger lifted, Maybeck spun to the far side of the rowboat; Finn stayed on the bow side and charged the dark, lugging the defibrillator along with him. He dropped the main business of the thing, extending the wired stickers out like a weapon.

Two guys jumped out of the dark. No matter that Finn had been expecting something like this; he startled and tripped on a deck-mounted cleat and went down hard. Defending himself from the fall, he let go the defibrillator's electronic stickers. Suddenly defenseless, he rolled into the ankles of the two boys and knocked them down.

Maybeck took the bigger of the two, while Finn rolled on top of the other one. But Maybeck jumped back as a steel blade flashed in the low light.

"Back!" Greg Luowski said, lunging with the knife. "Off him!"

Finn paused, then let go of the other kid.

The only light—and there wasn't much of it—came from the open door to the jogging track. The light played across Luowski's sullen face in patchy scabs. Finn was no stranger to the bully, but he'd never seen him like this. The boy's dull Cro-Magnon eyes were alight with energy, like the eyes of a guy on a street corner talking loudly to the passing traffic. Luowski looked unsure and unstable. If anything, it made him more dangerous.

The other boy wasn't a boy at all. He was in his thirties, maybe, with a bony, pinched face and unfocused eyes set close together. He wore all black, a stagehand's costume, and a name tag that Finn couldn't read because of the angle.

"No problem, Greg."

"Shut up, Whitless."

Judging by Luowski's blood-caked clothes and hands, they were looking at the hyena's killer.

"He swallowed it," Maybeck said, figuring it out. "The hyena. They made you go after it."

Luowski said nothing, but he didn't have to: he was horrified by what he'd done.

"Nice people you're working with," Maybeck said.

"Shut it!"

"They're not people," Finn said.

Luowski waved the knife in Finn's direction. "I said—"

"Yeah, yeah, we got it," Maybeck said. "Let me ask you this: after what you just did, how can you possibly wave a knife at us? Fellow human beings. You gonna cut us open like that?"

Luowski's knife hand lowered. He was breathing hard; he looked sick. "My advice: get off this ship before they carry you off. I'm telling you, she's not going to let anything stop her."

She? Finn thought. Which witch? What woman? What girl?

"From doing what?" he asked.

Luowski almost looked ready to tell him. With his hand lowered, Maybeck could have jumped him, but he thought better of it.

"Tia Dalma? Maleficent? The Evil Queen?"

"I have no idea," Luowski whispered. "I don't want to know." His body shook from head to toe. Finn sensed that the real Greg Luowski was held in a spell.

Then it occurred to him: the other guy was likely under some kind of spell, too.

"We can help you," Finn told Luowski.

Maybeck's questioning look threatened Finn.

"Get out of here before I hurt you," Luowski said, brandishing the knife.

"I'd listen if I were you." The unnamed man spoke in a gravelly monotone. Definitely drugged, drunk, or under a spell.

"You're not us," Maybeck said.

Finn stepped back carefully. Maybeck matched him step for step, but reluctantly; he wanted a fight.

Finn said, "We need the USB drive, Greg. Its contents, at the very least. Make a duplicate. Who's going to know?"

"I'll know," the man—Dixon—said. Finn could finally make out his full name tag.

"Who that matters is going to know?" Maybeck said, making sure to direct this at Dixon.

Luowski spoke in the same grinding whisper. "Get off the ship. All of you. Get off and stay off. I'm telling you: they mean business."

"Better listen to him, *boys*."

Finn felt gooseflesh ripple across his skin. He spoke directly to Greg, doing his best to ignore Dixon.

"Come to us. Anytime. Anywhere. We can help."

"Someone will die," Luowski said. "One of you—you'll die."

He blurted it out like he was divulging a secret. For a moment they all stood still as statues.

Then Finn stepped back until he reached the door to the promenade. He and Maybeck never took their eyes off the two men as they retreated. Luowski still held the bloody knife.

Someone will die, Finn thought.

One of you.

4

IT WAS SOMETHING OF a Keepers convention in stateroom 816. Finn and Maybeck shed their coveralls and joined the other Keepers—Willa, Philby, and Charlene—along with the hologram of Amanda and the real-life Storey Ming. Jess's sputtering, sparking hologram lay on the bed, the leg wound sometimes bleeding, sometimes not, depending on her current state.

"What a mess," Charlene said.

"Keep calm," said Philby.

Finn tried to catch Amanda's eye, but she wouldn't look his way. To say they'd been more than friends for the past year was an understatement. It was something special, and they both knew it. But things had noticeably cooled off since Finn had accused her of leading the Overtakers into Typhoon Lagoon, a conflict that had left Finn's mother under the Overtakers' power. He'd been stupid. It had come out of his mouth all wrong. He wasn't sure if Amanda would forgive him. The possibility of that loss left Finn with a sickening feeling in his gut. Only one thing had eclipsed this reaction: that moment when he'd looked at his mother behind the wheel in the Typhoon Lagoon parking lot and had seen his mother's bright-green eyes.

She had been born with blue eyes.

That moment had been paralyzing. Terrifying.

Finn's mother was somewhere on the ship now. If he'd been successful in threatening Tia Dalma, she'd be his mother, not some lady under a spell. Finn was itching to find her and make sure she was okay; itching to have Amanda relent and allow him back into her world; itching to get Jess taken care of so he could figure it all out.

But as leader, he knew he had to stay focused on the task at hand. He knew to put the needs of the group first and his own desires last, no matter how frustrating and painful.

"We need to fix her leg, make sure Amanda is returned first, and then get Jess safely back," he said. "Philby, you need to get to the Radio Studio, so only Amanda goes on the first Return."

"Why did you come, anyway?" Willa asked Amanda, somewhat accusingly. The question hushed the others.

"I told you, Wanda. Jess's dream about Maleficent and the Evil Queen capturing Charlie—*Charlene*," Amanda corrected, knowing Charlene only liked the boys to use her masculine nickname. "The bee suits. Her dreams, her visions—whatever—get all tangled. Wanda wanted us here as backup."

"Let's stay on point, please," said Professor Philby. "What matters is *right now*."

"Once she returns, Jess is going to be in some serious pain," Charlene said. "Amanda, you're going have to be ready for that. She may cry out."

"Ice," Willa said. "We can numb the wound here. When she returns, it'll still be numb."

"Numb or not," Maybeck said, "that thing's going to hurt."

* * *

Amanda scratched and clawed at the darkness like she'd had a blanket tossed over her. Pulled herself up and out of a nightmare in which Finn tried to kiss her good-bye and she put her hand up to his face, stopping him like a traffic cop. Pulled at the fabric of her unconscious as it bunched at her feet, still allowing no light to penetrate. Just then, a sound. A thin electronic whine that she knew well but couldn't place. No, wait! It was their roommate's CD player, an ancient portable thing that the girl used to listen to "massage music" to help her sleep.

Amanda was returning.

She opened her eyes, threw her legs off the upper bunk, and jumped to the floor, arriving at Jess's side as her sister sat up in pain, her startled eyes wide. She grabbed for her leg. Amanda covered Jess's lips and signaled quiet. Jess squeezed her eyes shut and nodded, tears running down her face.

Amanda carefully peeled back the bedding and winced. Even in the dark, she could see the stain on the sheets and the open wound on Jess's leg. She checked repeatedly to make sure their roommate was sleeping. She helped Jess out of bed, and together they went into the hallway bathroom. Amanda locked the door behind them and ran warm water.

"The bandages didn't return," she told Jess.

"I sort of figured that out. The ice didn't work so great either, I'm sorry to say."

Amanda touched around the wound. In fact, it was incredibly cold—the ice treatment *had* worked— which meant it was only going to hurt worse as it warmed up.

"There's ointment here," Amanda said, checking the medicine cabinet. "I'll wash it. Then we'll bandage it again."

"I'm going to be fine."

"It's nasty."

"It's like a few cuts all together. No big deal."

"It is a big deal, and you know it."

Jess bit her lips as Amanda washed the wound with soap and water.

"You're a lot braver than I am," Amanda said.

"We need to get back on the ship."

"Chill. We need to get you healed."

"I had almost the same dream again. Maleficent and the Evil Queen. Someplace dark. A cave, I think, same as last time. But this time I was inside, and if it was Charlene, I don't think she was alone. It looked like her from the back, but when she turned . . . there was a scarf wrapped around her. Maybe a *rope* around her neck. I couldn't see her face clearly. I don't know exactly what was going on, but if it was Charlene, I think they meant to kill her. We have to protect her. We have to tell the Keepers."

"I can send Philby an e-mail. You stay still."

"It doesn't feel right. We need to be on the ship with them."

"I know, but we're not. And you're in no condition to go anywhere."

Amanda's phone vibrated. It was insanely late to receive a text or a call. Driven by curiosity, she checked the device.

"It's from Wanda. A text."

"Saying?"

Amanda read, "'Sorry to hear about current situation. Text me back when you two are able to TAKE A NAP.' She capitalized that last part. What's with that?"

"She probably thought you wouldn't get it until tomorrow morning."

"So?"

"So someone wants us to cross over."

"Well, that's not going to happen! You're injured!"

"Amanda, she knows that. They wouldn't cross us over if we couldn't handle it. They must need us."

"Need *you*, you mean," Amanda said, emphasizing Jess's importance. For years it had been the same: everyone wanted what Jess had. Her ability to dream the future was more precious than money.

"I'll probably feel better crossed over. So if you're worried about me, don't. Write her back and tell her we're going to sleep now."

"It's not right."

"It's Wayne. It's Wanda. It's right. They'll have us back by morning. Remind them of that in the text—that Mrs. Nash will check on us if we're not down for breakfast."

"As if you'll get downstairs like that," Amanda said, the phone suddenly heavy in her hand.

Amanda awoke beneath a superstructure of metal beams on an open-air, circular tiled terrace. It took her several seconds to recognize it as the base of Mickey's Sorcerer's Hat at Disney's Hollywood Studios.

She studied her hand's peculiar quality—a luminescence that she wished was hers. It was, in fact, her hologram's. She'd crossed over.

Jess was to her left. Amanda wore the boxer shorts and spaghetti-strap tank top that she always slept in. Jess still wore the clothes she'd been wearing when she was injured on the ship. Her bandages were blood-soaked and nasty.

"How are you?" Amanda asked.

"I don't think it hurts as much."

Amanda took Jess's hologram hands and began dragging her awkwardly into the shadows. In that moment, a voice called out.

"Willow?"

A red-haired girl in a purple clamshell bikini top approached. Amanda froze. It was Ariel!

Recalling Willa's stories about Ariel saving her here in the Studios, Amanda smiled and called back.

"Friends of Willa's. I'm Amanda. This is Jess."

"Ah!" Ariel's eyes grew larger as she took in Jess. It

was obvious she didn't see the injury, or chose to ignore it. "The sorceress, Jezebel!"

"Hardly a sorceress," Jess said, sitting up, but unable to stand.

"We owe a great debt to you and the others," Ariel said.

"It's the other way around," Jess said. "We all—everyone who comes to the parks—worship you guys."

"Guys?" Ariel said curiously.

"Characters," Amanda. "You, the characters. We were sent here by—"

"The Imagineers," Ariel said. "The Elder."

"Wayne," Amanda said. She'd never heard him called that.

Jess couldn't contain her curiosity. "Is our coming here connected to the theft of the journal from the library?"

When Ariel smiled, the terrace filled with a soft light. "I believe you may be familiar with my friends." She gestured into the shadows. Three silhouettes appeared, two of them distinctive. Tigger and Pluto. As they came into the light, Amanda and Jess saw that the sultry female form was Megara, from *Hercules*.

None looked exactly like their film animations, but again, each was unmistakable.

"We wish to help you," Megara said in a silky voice. She looked directly at Jess's leg. She was possibly the most beautiful of all the characters the girls had ever encountered in person. "Telephus, son of Hercules, is here in spirit."

Amanda looked around the area. The Engineering Base was only a few hundred yards from where they stood. "You're exposed here. We know our enemies to be in the area."

"You forget," Ariel said in an eerily calm voice. "Long before you and your friends came along, my friends and I were battling these same forces. Every night for decades. Yes, it is more serious now. Yes, the evil ones have organized in ways we never believed possible. But we are quite aware of the dangers."

"The battle for Base."

"Has subsided, at least temporarily."

"The Keepers were told only days ago the final battle was imminent!"

"The darkness appears to lack leadership."

"We know where the leaders are. But there's a technology that could allow them back here at any moment."

"I do not know this word *tek* . . ."

"It's . . . a form of magic. It comes from the power of lightning. We are trying to prevent the leaders from appearing magically." Amanda ran her hologram arm through a wooden kiosk stand. Ariel was clearly impressed by the demonstration.

"You see, Amanda," she said, "once upon a time— forever, actually—the evil ones' imagined superiority over one another has prevented them from working together effectively. They have battled each other, rather than us. This gave us an advantage. Now it is different. They have come together unexpectedly. This is why your friends like Willow were summoned. It is why all of you are here."

Ariel's calm, lilting voice affected Amanda.

It is why all of you are here.

Tigger jumped up and down. Pluto nuzzled Amanda. She petted him.

Megara approached Jess, knelt by her side, and kissed Jess on the forehead.

"You have sacrificed and suffered much, my dear. We wish to thank you." As Megara ran her hand directly above the wound, she whispered, "The oracle of Delphi once said, 'He that wounded, shall heal.' Do you know what this means?" As she asked, she pulled out a small leather purse sack and loosened its drawstring. She reached inside.

"I suppose," Jess said through clenched teeth, the pain tightening her throat, "I need to heal this myself?"

Megara chuckled. "Not exactly, child. To the contrary, it means all one needs is the source of the injury to end the effects of the injury." She pulled out two small white teeth from the bag. "Hyenas are part cat, part dog. Did you know that?" she mused to herself as Ariel passed her a knife and Megara scraped each tooth with the blade. She collected a tiny amount of tooth dust in her palm.

"You mustn't fear this, child," Megara said. She rubbed the tooth dust into the open wound.

It was as if two different photos of Jess's leg had replaced each other: one showing the wound; one, without.

"There," Megara said. "That should feel better."

The rip remained in Jess's pant leg, but the wound was closed and clean. Jess flexed her leg effortlessly. "No way . . ."

Megara grinned serenely. "They have not defeated us yet, my child! The magic lives, I assure you. There is still much to fight for."

"This is why Wanda . . ." Amanda muttered, her eyes brimming with tears, unable to contain her joy at the healing miracle.

"We are a team," Ariel said. "Megara's powers . . . well, this is child's play for her."

It might be child's play, but Megara looked tired

and drained. Clearly the healing had taken something out of her.

Ariel continued, "We ask that you come to believe in us. To rely upon us. We are at your disposal. We ask that you tell the others: you are not alone. You will do this for us? You will tell them about the power of our magic, please?"

"Yes!" Amanda said.

"Of course!" echoed Jess.

It is why all of you are here.

5

FINN MET STOREY MING outside the Radio Studio just after three that same morning, the sun far from being even a pink smudge on the horizon.

Finn had sneaked out of his stateroom, feeling a bit like a traitor for leaving Philby behind.

"This seems a little cloak-and-dagger to me," Storey said. "Aren't we basically going behind Philby's back?"

Her concern about Philby made Finn wonder about her motive. Was she interested in Philby?

All things girl confused Finn. Specifically, Amanda confused him. They hadn't had a chance to talk the night before. Finn wanted so badly to get things right with her again, but he had no idea how to rewind and reset his life.

And was he more interested in Storey than he'd admitted?

Storey challenged him with a take-no-prisoners look. "He put this call through last time, right?"

Finn hoped the heat he felt in his face wasn't showing. "Right."

Now he got it. She wasn't suggesting that she

and Finn liked each other and were cutting Philby out. Storey feared that Finn was betraying the other Keepers by asking her, not Philby, to connect him with Wayne.

"It's just . . . like a phone call," he said. "Think of it as a phone call."

"But then why couldn't Philby do it?"

"Is this about Philby?" Finn said, wondering who had made those words come out of his mouth. What a stupid thing to say!

"Is *what* about Philby?" Now Storey was blushing. "I'm not complaining. Am I whining? It's early, if I'm whining—"

"You're not whining."

"There aren't a lot of guys I would get up early for, Finn, if that's what you're asking. People," she said, attempting to correct herself. "Not a lot of people."

"I guess we should do this," he said.

She stepped to within an inch of him, their faces almost touching. The landing outside the Radio Studio had felt chilly until that moment. "You think?" she whispered. "Me too."

If he dropped his chin or leaned forward they would kiss. Until then Finn hadn't realized how phenomenally perfect her eyes were. They seemed oversized and bottomless. He wanted to dive in there and swim around inside her thoughts and discover what she was really thinking.

Storey reached up and stroked his neck and ear. He felt shivers rip through him. "You are an incredible person. You know that?"

"You're the one who keeps saving us."

"I mean as a person. How you care so much about everyone. Think of them first. Put other people first all the time."

"That's not exactly me . . ." How could she smell so good so early in the morning?

"And you're modest, on top of everything else."

"You have me confused with a secret agent who looks an awful lot like me."

"And funny."

This was it. He was supposed to kiss her now. Everything inside him was telling him that; everything but his brain, which was screaming for him to turn an about-face and scram.

The elevator dinged.

Storey swiped her crew member ID badge to the left of the door and the Radio Studio unlocked. She grabbed Finn's hand and pulled. She eased the door shut. *Click.* She paced her index finger in front of her very full lips and kept him quiet—though Finn hardly needed to be told; he couldn't think, much less speak.

Soon, Storey had made contact with Lou Mongello of WDW Radio, whose Web-based radio show served as an interface to shipboard communication with Wayne. Lou, who sounded enthusiastic despite the early hour, patched them through. Soon Finn heard Wayne's scratchy voice come through the headphones.

"We have managed to encrypt the transmission this time," Wayne said. "No need for code speak."

"O . . . kay. Is that why it sounds like you're on the North Pole?" Finn said.

"Actually, I'm much closer than that. Much."

"You're on the sub!" Finn said.

Storey's eyes went wide. Then she put on her own set of headphones, and Finn could hear she'd cranked up music so as to not eavesdrop. He thought all the more of her for doing that.

"I cannot confirm or deny my current location," Wayne said. "What I can tell you—because we haven't much time—is that your situation has taken a precarious turn."

"As in dangerous." Finn told him about the hyena attack on Jess.

"I'm sorry to hear about Jezebel," Wayne said, using a name the girl had once been given by Maleficent. It struck Finn as an odd choice for Wayne; he did not question it. "But I was actually referring to the incident on Castaway Cay. Ship radar has confirmed the landing of a plane."

"Yes! Chernabog," Finn said. "They've brought him on board."

"Then you must find him. You must work with Bob—Uncle Bob, they call him. Security."

"I've seen him around."

"He may not believe you. That may pose a bit of a problem—"

"You think?"

"But now Tia Dalma's presence there makes much more sense."

"Because?"

"She's . . . clever." It wasn't often Wayne was at a loss for words. "She's powerful and cunning and, as you found out, no one to tangle with." He paused. "To resist her power is futile. With her you must lose yourself to win."

"What does that even mean?" Finn asked.

Finn heard noises in the background. Wayne rushed his next words. "How's your mother?"

The question hit Finn as awkward. "My *mother*? I . . . ah . . . haven't seen her. I afraid she may have . . . vanished."

"No, actually, she hasn't. Worry not. Certain factions loyal to our cause have hidden her. They are taking care of her." Wayne often spoke cryptically. Whether to overdramatize or to motivate, Finn wasn't sure. But it bothered Finn because it worked. His heart sped up.

"You won't see much of her on this voyage," Wayne continued, "if at all. But don't let that worry you. She's resting. Recovering. She's going to be fine."

Finn knew better than to argue, but couldn't help himself.

"If it's all the same, I'd really like to see her," he said.

"It's not advisable. We have concerns. Threats . . ."

"We always have concerns," Finn countered. "She's not involved."

"But she was seen as being part of it. She drove you to your meeting at Typhoon Lagoon. That *made* her part of it."

"I want to see my mom."

"And put her at risk? At additional risk? You saved her, Finn. Leave it at that for now. Allow her to fully recover."

Finn didn't want his mother to be any part of this. As much as he wanted to see her—needed to see her—he wouldn't forgive himself he put in danger again.

"We have more pressing matters," Wayne said. "First is the Base. We have signs that our friends are regrouping, possibly for a major offensive."

The Overtakers had been attempting a siege on

Disney World's Engineering Base for some time. Seizing control of Base would give them not only full control of the attractions and electronic security at all the major parks, but access to the DHI servers, which had recently undergone a software upgrade. DHI 2.0 eliminated bugs and exponentially increased hologram performance. Like going from a bicycle to a Porsche. Loss of the Base would cripple Wayne and the Imagineers in their efforts to keep the parks functioning as usual; it might also put the Keepers out of business for good.

"We doubt very much," Wayne went on, "that any attempt will be made until the leaders are off the ship. But there's a catch: if they're able to restart their own holograms, all bets are off. Their DHIs could lead the battle for the Base while their bodies sleep on the ship, Finn."

"I understand."

"That must be prevented at all costs: they must not get a server restarted."

"We lost their data." Finn blurted it out for Wayne to digest. "It was . . . messy. We had it, and we lost it."

"All the more critical, then," a troubled Wayne said.

"I understand."

"I hope you do."

Wayne rarely scolded Finn, but Finn felt horrible

nonetheless for letting him down. The old man didn't speak for several long seconds; Finn could have sworn he heard the hum of engines in the background. Again, he thought: *The sub*. He marveled at the idea that King Triton might actually have saved him by summoning Captain Nemo, and that Wayne could possibly be on the *Nautilus* with him. As much as Finn was ready for his role as a DHI to end, for life to go back to normal, moments like this made him want it to go on forever.

"More pressing for the moment is this plane. You tell me Chernabog is now on board the ship. You must find him."

"It's why they're on the ship, isn't it?" Finn asked. "Something to do with Chernabog. The journal. Tia Dalma being a witch doctor."

"I warned you before that the mission may involve resurrecting the beast. You have to understand, Finn. How do I put this? His powers, should they ever return, should they ever be at the level Walt originally imagined . . . You see? *Fantasia* was as close as Walt ever got to showing us just how bad . . . to what degree this character is possessed by evil. You cross the Minotaur with a Central American bat god, and you get not only the most hideous, powerful physical features of both, but the power of two cultures as well. The Greeks. The

Mayans. One had active imaginations, the other horrific practices and backward beliefs. Should the intention be to return this beast to its full abilities? Well, God help us all."

"So, we find him . . . and then what?"

"So confident."

"I'm trying. All I'm saying is we'll try."

"And I thank you for that. Okay. First? Let's say you find him prior to whatever they have planned for him. To the awakening—if I'm right about that. In that case, Bob may have a hold that can contain him."

"This ship is made of steel," Finn reminded Wayne. "Of course it can contain him."

"I see. You're suddenly the expert?"

"I didn't mean—"

"Finn, you lost the DHI data. And now you're not listening. If Chernabog regains his full cognitive and physical abilities, nothing you have—nothing anyone on that ship has—will stop him."

"You're kidding, right?"

"You will recall your encounter at Expedition Everest, please. Even at twenty-five or fifty percent of his potential, he's still many times the strength and evil of anything you and your friends have encountered."

Only Amanda had managed to save Finn from Chernabog. "But . . ."

"*Any . . . thing, any . . . one* you have battled. Maleficent is a mere pawn in comparison."

Finn felt a chill.

"*Chernabog* is the embodiment of evil and lethal force. We haven't seen the half of him."

"So . . . ?"

"They may have cut off their noses to spite their faces," Wayne said. "They've brought him on board in order to transport him somewhere the cruise is going. I doubt seriously the awakening, if that's what's at play, is to take place on the ship itself. They could have awakened him on Castaway. But they've chosen to take him out to sea. If you can find him, if Bob can contain him—perhaps drug him—before he's fully conscious, it's at least possible that he might be drowned. Bats do not swim. If you can drown him . . . The ship may be our one chance. But once on land . . ."

"You're scaring me."

"Good. Then I'm accomplishing something."

"And Base?"

"We may need the five of you on a moment's notice. It depends what develops. Check your phones. Check back here with me as often as possible. It's fluid, Finn."

The connection ended.

Storey was rocking out, virtually unaware of Finn. He pulled off his headphones, his vision blurring. He'd wanted to ask her about 2.0, about Wayne's apparent favoritism of Philby, about the rumor that the present Keepers would be retired in favor of "new models" once 2.0 was fine-tuned.

He wanted to ask a lot of things.

But not now. At the moment, he couldn't get a word out.

6

In the wee hours of the morning, Luowski climbed a steel ladder inside the ship's forward funnel. Pausing once to look down, he decided never to do that again. It was a thirty-foot drop to a metal deck.

He probably should have considered an invitation to meet with Maleficent some kind of honor. But since it was delivered as an *order*, he felt uneasy about the whole thing.

The interior of the stack, including the ladder he climbed, trembled from the vibrations of the ship's motor. The claustrophobic space was overly warm, noisy, and dark. The higher he climbed, the more it felt as if there might not be a way back down again.

Reaching a ladder, Luowski pulled himself up through the hole and stepped out onto a catwalk's metal grate. He gripped the handrail, mopping sweat off his face. A pale guy dressed like a pirate blocked his way—a henchman for the Overtakers. The man was most likely a crew member in costume, but Luowski wasn't about to insult him.

"And who might you be, lad?" the pirate said in a deep-throated rasp.

"Greg," the boy said. "Luowski."

The man shone a blinding light into his eyes. "Open 'em wide."

Luowski did as he was told, revealing the deep-green irises. For a while he'd worn green contacts because Maleficent had told him to. Then, one morning he'd woken up and they weren't contacts anymore. From that day on, he hadn't felt like himself.

A voice behind him said, "Arms up. Feet spread."

Luowski startled as he was patted down from behind. He didn't look back.

"Clean," the unseen man said in a fake Jamaican accent.

Sheesh! "Is this happening or not?" Luowski said, impatient despite his better judgment. He knew to keep his mouth shut, yet like so many things in his life, his brain said one thing and his actions came out the exact opposite.

"Chill," said the one in front of him. Definitely not a pirate.

A blindfold was pulled over his eyes. Tightened, it covered his ears and dulled the sounds as he was guided forward. Straight for five paces. Left. He tried to memorize their movements in case he needed a quick exit.

"Up!" said the fake Jamaican, prodding him from behind.

"You're kidding!" he said.

But it was no use. Luowski climbed a ladder blindfolded. Not easy. Six rungs up. A turn right. Two steps. Left, three. Left again. He was losing track, already forgetting the turns they'd made. It grew noticeably colder, and the whirring of fans made it loud.

"You have it for me." Her voice, like cracking ice.

The character of Maleficent in *Sleeping Beauty* was a tall, green woman in a pressed cape and nice clothes. The Maleficent Cast Member was nearly identical. But the Maleficent Luowski heard—he'd never actually *seen* her—sounded like an old, menacing hag, like the nastiest grandmother in the neighborhood, the one with thirty cats in her house and a brown, overgrown yard.

There was yet someone else standing nearby, someone previously unaccounted for. Luowski resisted turning in that direction. The person was a mouth breather—a long-time smoker, maybe—and he/she gave off strange odors—moss, mud, human sweat. The smells didn't fit with what he thought about Maleficent. This was someone else. Someone . . . unforgettable.

Wanting it all over with, Luowski reached into his front pocket, withdrew the blood-and-guts encrusted USB thumb drive, and held it in his open palm.

Cold fingers plucked it away.

Maleficent needed the cold.

"Well done, young man," the dark fairy said. "Well done, indeed."

"It . . . we had to kill it."

"Yes. Pity. The hyenas are so helpful."

"Had to gut it."

"Spare me the whining."

"Yes, ma'am."

The dry-throat breathing sounds came from his immediate right now. Luowski could *feel* whoever it was sizing him up.

"There is more to be done," said Maleficent.

The other one wouldn't speak.

"We need you to collect one of them for us."

"Collect," Luowski repeated.

Now it was Maleficent holding her tongue.

"One of what?" he asked.

"Not what: whom."

"You want to run that by me again?"

"Are you deaf?"

"No, ma'am. Your Excellency. Whatever . . ."

"Never mind that for now. But we will speak of this again." A shiver swept through Luowski. "Presently," she said, "there is a task at hand. Once on Aruba . . . you will be joined by an associate. Perhaps we will send Dixon. Perhaps Victor. It is hard to say. It is an important task. Of the utmost importance. To fail is . . . *unacceptable.*"

"What task is that?"

"I'm beginning to regret my choice of you," she said. She muttered something. Luowski couldn't hear the words—they sounded like a gibberish, like a foreign language—but there was a soothing chantlike quality to them as well. He felt overwhelmed, like a blanket had been pulled over him. Pleasing, but disturbing. Something he knew better than to trust. Yet he welcomed it.

It was hard to think, like in the moments just before sleep. Luowski's thoughts were flat and soft. He saw arms wrestling the electrically stunned hyena onto its back; he saw the blade glint above his head. He shuddered as the camera of his imagination pulled back and he recognized the arm holding the knife as his own. He'd killed the poor thing. He couldn't think, couldn't grab a single thought. It was as if . . .

"You will do as I say," spoke the cracked-glass voice. "You and your accomplice will get in and out with no one the wiser. Including the police. *Especially* the police. To fail is to disappoint me. I advise strongly against that.

"Now, you will listen, and you will listen closely, and

you will remember everything I tell you as clearly as your own name."

Greg Luowski had no comeback because he had no thought. What he heard, he knew to be the truth. What he was told to do had to be done. And he would do it. Just like the hyena.

He hated this woman—this fairy—for making him do whatever she wished, and in the same breath he loved her for it.

"I'm listening," he said.

7

HAVING SLEPT FEWER THAN three hours, awakened by Mrs. Philby (who didn't want the boys sleeping in), Finn and Philby sat cross-legged on the stateroom's bed, the Disney journal between them.

The notebook, dating back more than fifty years, had once been part of a private collection in a library kept by the Disney Imagineers at Disney's Hollywood Studios in Florida. Some Disney historians believed the journals had belonged to Walt Disney himself.

Maleficent, the Evil Queen, and Cruella De Vil had been seen stealing the journal, making its return critical to the Kingdom Keepers. Finn had, in fact, gotten it back; he'd kept it locked up in the stateroom's safe.

They thumbed ahead to the author's notes about the creation of Walt Disney's most fearsome villain: Chernabog. It was in among those pages that a beautiful watercolor had been drawn—faded by time, but still striking.

The next page in the journal was left blank except for four doodles, one in each corner, done in pen and ink.

The last of the three pages was no better, holding only the inscription:

"LIFE IS BECAUSE OF THE GODS; WITH THEIR SACRIFICE THEY GAVE US LIFE. . . . THEY PRODUCE OUR SUSTENANCE . . . WHICH NOURISHES LIFE."

The boys spun the journal back and forth between them like a pinwheel.

"What the . . . ?" Finn said.

"There is a good and a bad to this," Philby said.

"I'll take the good first," Finn said. "I had about all the bad I can take last night."

"The good and the bad are the same thing," Philby said. "Whatever this is, it seems highly unlikely the OTs have figured it out yet." He cleared his throat. "The bad news is: we have no clue what any of it means either."

"Way to cheer me up."

"I do what I can," Philby said sarcastically. "Whatever it is, whatever it says, it's why they're on board, why Chernabog's on the ship."

Finn thought back to his secret conversation with Wayne. "We don't know that absolutely, but I suppose it makes sense."

"It makes tons of sense." Philby ticked off each point on his fingers. "They've spent months battling for control of Base—still a work in progress; they steal the journal; they board the *Dream*; they smuggle Chernabog onto the ship—no easy task; they bring in OTKs like Luowski. They are trying to *kill* us. They may want to kidnap Charlene, according to Jess. They're taking huge chances. It has to be for huge rewards."

"Again, with the cheering up," Finn said.

"Why?"

"Why what?"

"Try to kill us?"

"We can be very annoying," Finn said.

Philby smiled. "We can, can't we?"

"But I see what you mean. What happened to this being a game?"

"Exactly. It's as far away from a game as it can get."

"It's us," Finn said. "The fact that we exist at all. Before, it was the villains against the princesses and princes, the fairies versus Mickey and Minnie. There was a balance of power. Wayne brought us in as DHIs to make sure the balance didn't tilt too far toward the villains. But maybe by doing so, it upset things."

"The balance of power," Philby said.

"That's what I'm talking about."

"You're saying *we're* the problem."

"I'm saying we may have started things going wrong."

"Escalation. So they've brought in OTKs," Philby said. "They're attacking the Base. If we win, they lose—"

"Which is probably different from when both sides won and lost, but not all the time."

"More permanent."

"Permanent vacation," Finn said.

"And now that we're winning some of the time, they bring along Chernabog. Though, granted, he's sleeping or in a spell or something. They see a chance for real victory, not the give and take that's been going on after hours in the parks for decades. The only thing is, we're in the way. As long as we're alive . . ."

"Cheery thought."

"So their mission has two parts: get rid of us, and bring Chernabog to power."

"And the journal's part of that," Finn said.

"This journal's important to them. This journal is why they're on the ship in the first place."

"We don't know that!"

"Let's assume it," Philby said. "The kind of detailed planning that went into the Chernabog pickup? This thing's on a whole new level."

"Agreed."

"We need the others," Philby said, pointing to the journal. "We're better at figuring out stuff like this when it's all of us. The sooner we crack the code, the better chance we have of stopping them."

8

AT BREAKFAST, the cafeteria-style food stations in the Cabanas restaurant teemed with hungry passengers. The Keepers' quest for privacy put them at a corner table, where they spoke in soft voices.

"We couldn't risk bringing the actual journal," Philby said, "but we photocopied the important pages."

He passed them around—the painting of the stone steps, the coin-sized designs, the line of text:

"LIFE IS BECAUSE OF THE GODS; WITH THEIR SACRIFICE THEY GAVE US LIFE. . . . THEY PRODUCE OUR SUSTENANCE . . . WHICH NOURISHES LIFE."

"We don't know if the OTs have solved it or not," he said. "Regardless, we have to figure out if it means anything. Whatever's going on with Chernabog must be connected to the journal."

"Can I mention something bizarre?" Charlene said.

No one answered, but she continued anyway. "Philby asked me to photograph the hyena Maybeck and Finn found." She cringed. "Which, I'm happy to say, was gone by the time I got there. But anyway, I'm heading up the jogging path and I'm practically speared by a *hummingbird*!"

"That's not possible," Philby said. "They can't survive at sea. They're land birds."

"But I saw it."

"You're sure it was a hummingbird?" Willa asked.

"One hundred percent."

"So we have a monster that doesn't belong on board," Finn said. "And a species of bird that has no business being here."

"Can we talk about this later?" Philby said, pushing back his hair impatiently. "This meeting is about the journal."

Charlene shrugged, put off but unwilling to start a fight.

"When we work together, we're good at this kind of thing. The Stonecutter's Quill. 'Under the Sea' in AK."

"Maybe Jess's dream about caves has something to do with these stairs," Willa said, nudging the drawing. "I mean, they're stone. They look old. Maybe we should copy the actual journal and e-mail it to her."

"Too dangerous," Philby said. "The journal has to be locked up. We can't risk losing it a second time."

Willa passed the sheets to Storey Ming.

"Pictographs," Storey said. "Not Egyptian. I've studied those in art class."

"Interesting," Philby said.

"Not really," Maybeck quipped.

Philby ignored him, always the best tactic in the face of Maybeck's cynicism. "Caribbean?"

"The Mayans were highly civilized," Willa said. "They had a written language, a lot of which still hasn't been translated."

The others stared at her. Even Philby.

"What? I suppose none of you gets National Geographic Channel?"

"I get it," Maybeck said, "but I don't watch it!"

"What if we combine the Jess cave thing," Charlene said, "with the steps and the symbols?"

"There are famous caves on Aruba," Storey said. "One of the *Dream* excursions goes there."

"Our next port of call. As in, tomorrow morning. So maybe the symbols are in one of the caves," Finn said. "Maybe we still have time to figure this out!"

"Yeah, and maybe they lead to buried treasure, too." A jaded Maybeck wasn't buying any of it. But when he picked up the page with the symbols, his tone changed.

"Hey, is this how they look? I mean, arranged like this?"

"Yes. As close as we could get it," Philby said.

"Then there's something missing. See? The blank space between the four corners? It's like they were framing something." The artist in Maybeck was adamant. "But whatever was there isn't there now."

"More interesting," Philby said, as if about to vote on it.

"The OTs have it," Charlene said. "Whatever it is!"

"We don't know that," Philby said. "Maybe they do, maybe they don't."

"We need to figure out what the glyphs mean," Storey said.

"The computers on Deck Two," Willa said. "We can search the Web."

"A good place to start."

"Trouble is," Storey said, "there are something like ten thousand characters in the Mayan language."

"My nana presses flowers," Charlene said, pointing at the page with the symbols. "The thing in the middle of the frame? It could have been a pressed leaf or a flower or something like that."

"Nice!" said Maybeck. "That makes so much sense."

No one commented on the fact that lately Maybeck liked anything Charlene said.

"But wait a second!" he continued, his frustration revealing itself as a tightening of his fists and lips. "Are we insane? How could some journal entry written in Florida fifty years ago have anything to do with a Caribbean cruise that wasn't even around back then?"

"It doesn't," Philby said. "It can't. Obviously. So it has to do with something else, something Walt Disney and his animators were working on: *Fantasia*. Chernabog."

Mention of the monster sobered the group.

"He's half Minotaur, half bat god," Finn said. Wayne's words echoed in his ears, and he shivered. "The most evil villain Walt Disney ever created. There are descriptions of him being the 'embodiment' of evil."

"The Minotaur was no picnic," Willa said.

Again, the group turned to her.

"History Channel," she said. "What? I watch a lot of TV! In Greek mythology—and I'm not talking Percy Jackson—the Minotaur ate people."

"Lovely." Maybeck pretended not to be interested, but he clearly was.

"He was horrible and did horrible things. You know how stuff found in one culture is often found in others?" Willa's eyes were wide. "Let's assume the old Imagineers found references to a Minotaur-like demon, like a Caribbean Bigfoot. You know? Including some lore, some pictographs or whatever, that supposedly told you—"

"How to wake it up," Philby said.

"Not good." Charlene sounded panicked.

Maybeck moaned.

"That would interest the Overtakers," Storey Ming said. She used the term with familiarity, Finn noted.

"See?" Philby said. "We're much better at this when we do it together. I think we're getting somewhere."

"Charlene's hummingbird!" Willa said suddenly, sitting up straighter.

"The Animal Channel, I suppose?" said Maybeck.

"Yes, as a matter of fact. Torpor." Willa spotted several blank expressions and sighed. "You *guys* are such duds. Wayne explained it to Finn, who told us all about it. Anyone remember?" She waited. Sighed again. "Hummingbirds have this insane metabolism. Like drinking-six-lattes-an-hour kind of thing. So they don't actually sleep; they enter a state called torpor. It's like hibernating, but for a matter of minutes or an hour. Some bats use torpor as well."

"Bats. As in bat gods," Philby said.

"Tia Dalma," Willa said.

It was like just the two of them in the room now.

"A witch doctor."

"They smuggled some hummingbirds onto the ship

so she can practice her magic. She puts the birds into torpor. She wakes them up. One of them escapes—"

"—and tries to spear me," Charlene said.

"Whoa!" Finn said.

"No kidding." Maybeck was suddenly a convert. "This is making way too much sense."

"They're missing something," Philby said, "or they'd have taken Chernabog out of torpor and taken over the ship already."

"Something from a cave," Finn said.

"Something the glyphs describe," Storey added.

A tattooed arm reached over Finn's shoulder and dropped a folded piece of paper on the table.

Finn spun around, trying to see whoever it was, but Cabanas was mobbed. Dozens of people were milling around the food and drink stations. Another dozen stood with trays, looking for open tables.

He searched for an arm with a tattoo—a thin arm, a girl's arm, he thought. In his random search, he caught a flash of red-streaked hair.

Her again? A girl with similar hair had helped them in the past few days, showing up exactly when needed. Philby would discount the coincidence, but Finn had little doubt it was the same girl. Had to be!

"Did anyone get a look at her?" Finn asked.

"Who?" Maybeck asked.

"No one?"

Blank looks.

Finn unfolded the note and read:

k'an pet ch'en

Instead of reading it aloud—he had no idea of its significance, and with the OTs, you could never be too careful—Finn passed it around. It moved hand to hand across the table.

"So? What's that about?" Maybeck said, breaking the unbearable silence.

"We have friends working for us," Storey proposed.

"Or enemies trying to trick us," Finn said.

Professor Philby said, "Deceit typically involves subtlety. Dropping a note on a table is not terribly subtle."

"So let's be positive," said the cheerleader, "and figure out what we do with everything." Charlene cleared her throat. "I saw the hummingbird on Deck Four forward. The hyena was killed up there, too."

"Interesting," Maybeck said.

Charlene smiled widely.

Willa said, "Storey and I can Google the pictographs and the words on the mystery note."

Finn lowered his voice. "The thing is, if she's leaving us a clue, she's got to be on our side. So why not just talk to us?"

Maybeck said, "Because we're radioactive, Whitman. We're nothing but trouble. She wants to help, but not get involved."

"But if she's helping us, then Wayne sent her."

"Most likely," Philby said. His face tightened. "Which is odd."

"Odd that we weren't told," Finn said. "Maybe she's part of the 2.0 upgrade. Maybe it isn't rumor."

"Maybe she was a hologram," Willa said, silencing the group.

The rumor about 2.0, begun by Finn's making assumptions about things said by Storey Ming, was that the Keepers might be facing early retirement. It seemed possible that, unbeknown to them, Wayne and the Imagineers were testing out the beta phase of 2.0 before fixing bugs and installing it onto a new set of DHIs—bigger, faster, stronger.

"That's hardly critical thinking, Willa," cautioned Philby. "There's nowhere near enough empirical evidence to bring us to any kind of conclusion. It's pure speculation. Speculation can be dangerous."

Willa looked crushed. He'd blurted it out in typical Philby fashion; now he looked as if he wished he could take it back.

"Whatever," Finn said. "We need to make plans to spy on the OTs."

"Say, what?" Charlene said.

"We have to follow them," Maybeck said. "We have to know what they're doing. Same with the OTKs. If they leave the ship in Aruba, we need to leave the ship. If they stay on board, we stay on board."

"How can we follow them if we don't know where they are in the first place?" Charlene said.

Philby said, "I have access to all the shipboard camera feeds now. We're not without assets."

"Speak English," said Willa, irritated.

"Let's assume Jess's sketch of the cave is accurate," Maybeck said. "We know there are caves on Aruba. In her dream, there were women in the cave. Women—as in witches and dark fairies, maybe."

"Maybe," Philby said, emphasizing the word. "We don't know any of this to be fact."

"Shut up a minute. Let's assume it's fact. Okay? If so, we need to know what they're doing in that cave. Right?" Maybeck answered himself: "Right. So . . . Thanks to Philby's cameras, we can cover a lot of the ship. The problem is getting off the ship at the exact same time as the OTKs, so we don't lose them."

"Forward following," Philby said.

"Say, what?"

"Now you're just talking nonsense," Willa said, her irritation showing again.

Group meetings had gotten way too complicated, Finn thought. Clearing his throat, he waded in, determined to break the tension.

"Willa, Philby's saying that we don't need to follow the OTs *off* the ship. There are probably only a couple of caves this could be. We can narrow it down using Jess's drawing. Then we let them come to *us* for a change, by getting to whatever cave it is *ahead of time. They* walk into *our* trap."

"Nice," Maybeck said.

"We'll have to check out the island tourist information for caves. I'll bet one will match up pretty closely with Jess's drawing."

"I can do that," Storey said. "Being a Cast Member, I can get a look at all the excursion stuff."

"It could be at one of the other stops," Philby reminded them.

"Aruba is known for its caves," Storey said. "Not so sure about Costa Rica and Mexico."

Philby took in the faces staring at him. "Fine. Charlene and Maybeck will get off early and, providing Storey's found a match, go to the cave and hide. I will use my hack of the shipboard security cameras to keep an eye on the various gangways off the ship. If I see Luowski or any OTs leaving, Willa and Finn will follow them." He added, "I should be able to get us all walkie-talkies."

"Meanwhile," Finn said, "we're keeping an eye out for the girl with the bright red streaks in her hair."

"The Girl with the Dragon Tattoo," Maybeck said.

"Ha. Ha." Finn wasn't amused.

"But, Finn, if she wants to be anonymous, shouldn't we let her be?" Charlene said.

Finn studied the people in the busy breakfast room. "She can help us," he said. "But most important . . . the most important mission of all . . . Before we reach Aruba tomorrow, we need to find Chernabog. If we find him, if security locks him up, then it won't matter what's in the journal. We won't have to do any of this." He thought back to his communication with Wayne. "We get Chernabog, and we spoil their plans, whatever they are. He's the key."

"It's not like they can hide him just anywhere," Maybeck said.

"Well, he's no longer in the box under the stage," Willa said.

"But how far could he go without being seen?" Finn said. "Something like that? There are passengers, crew, cameras. Someone would have seen him."

"So maybe he's still backstage somewhere. There's a lot of room there," Storey said.

"Tonight, during the orientation, *we'll* be

backstage." Philby's voice rose with excitement. "We're part of the program."

"You remember what happened last time we were in the theater?" Maybeck asked. "As in: chaos?"

Maleficent had made a video appearance at an evening show that had resulted in thorny roses raining down on the passengers.

"But that's the point, isn't it?" Philby said. "What if the OTs are counting on us being too scared to go backstage?"

"They'd be right," Willa said. "It's a miracle no one was hurt the first time!"

"We'll appear in the orientation as scheduled," Finn declared. "But we'll arrive backstage twenty minutes early—as a group. That'll give us extra time. We meet at the stage door, starboard side. They're not going to make us wait out in the hallway. They'll let us backstage, and that's our chance."

"I like it," Philby said.

As if I care, Finn nearly said. But the truth was: he did care. He not only needed Philby's support, he wanted it.

"Willa and I can say we need a place to work on our makeup," Charlene said. "That'll get us separated into two groups, once inside. Two are better than one."

"Nice," Philby said.

"Boys take the backstage area," Finn said. "Girls: the salon, costumes, and the other rooms downstairs."

"There's no way Security missed him," Maybeck said. "Has anyone thought about that?"

"Depends on how well the OTs hid him," Finn said. "And *why*."

"Meaning?" Charlene said.

"Maybe the OTs don't want Chernabog found because they haven't figured out how to wake him out of this torpor thing yet. Maybe Tia Dalma isn't doing so well with waking up her hummingbirds. Who knows? Maybe they're worried about how they'll control him."

"The stuff in the journal," Willa said, her voice a whisper.

"What if it's more like an owner's manual?" Finn said.

"You have to do it right. And then whoever wakes him . . ." Philby said, speculating.

"Yes!" Finn said. "Whoever decodes the journal properly and applies it to Chernabog as he comes out of torpor ends up in control of him."

Maybeck coughed. "Us? Control Chernabog?"

"I like the sound of that," Professor Philby said.

9

WILLA HAD DONE HER HOMEWORK and was eager to share what she'd found. The first to arrive in the unremarkable companionway outside the starboard stage door to the Walt Disney Theatre, she waited for the others. Impatiently. Overcome by the hallway's dullness. Drab walls. No artwork. Several unmarked doors. At the end, the backstage entrance: CAST MEMBERS ONLY PLEASE.

In all likelihood, a monster lurked on the other side of that door. Where else would the OTs have hidden something Chernabog's size? The engine deck seemed like the only other decent possibility, but something that huge making it down there without being seen? *Impossible.*

Wayne's concerns about the balance of power were warranted. The OTs were dangerous enough, strong enough, without such a force on their side. With Chernabog, they'd be unstoppable.

Chernabog was the worst, Willa thought, feeling her gut twist. Evil incarnate. Both the Minotaur and the Mayan bat god, Camazotz, were said to have devoured their prey. Alive.

Finn was next to arrive. Willa fought to keep the disappointment from her face.

"Hey," she said.

"You were hoping for Philby," Finn said.

She shrugged. "We're not exactly seeing eye to eye."

"I don't think you have to worry about him and Storey."

"I don't want to talk about it, Finn. Okay? Besides, he's not coming with us anyway. He's watching the cameras." Willa waved at a hemispheric plastic globe in the ceiling, but it was a churlish gesture. "So, Finn. News alert: I may have deciphered the code."

"Seriously? Already? Did Storey help you?"

"No," Willa said tersely. "I had some extra time at the computers. *Ka'n* is 'gold.' It's also the symbol in the upper left. *Pet* is 'island,' upper right."

"Gold island?"

"Patience! *Ch'en* is 'cave.' Lower left. I haven't figured out the fourth one yet."

"That's huge!" Finn said. "So maybe it is a treasure map. Gold. Maybeck will love this."

"Whatever it is, it's buried in a cave on an island."

"And the only island remaining on the cruise is Aruba. Tomorrow morning."

"We'd be stupid not to follow the OTs, not to

do everything we can to find out where they're going and why."

"That's genius work!"

"That's Google," Willa said.

"You never let anyone compliment you," Finn said. "What's that about?"

"Thank you for the compliment," Willa said, effectively ending the discussion.

"You're welcome."

"What's with you and Amanda, anyway? Or is it you and Storey, too?"

"Me and Maleficent is more like it."

"Who do you think is more powerful? Maleficent or the Evil Queen?"

"I put Tia Dalma above them both."

"Seriously? Because?"

"She's a witch doctor. She practices black magic. And she's more in this world—our world—than any of the others. She doesn't wear a costume. She doesn't play a role. She throws bones and stabs dolls with pins, and who knows what else?" Finn's eyes were haunted.

He's remembering his mom, Willa thought. She didn't know what else to say.

Next, Maybeck, then Charlene arrived to join them. Willa caught them up quickly on what she'd learned.

"So as promising as that is," Maybeck said, "we're

still hoping to find Chernabog and end this before it starts, right? Trouble is, no one ever said what we do when we find him."

"We call Security," Finn said. "Wayne said we can trust Uncle Bob."

"As if," Maybeck said. He had issues with authority and didn't trust anyone in a uniform.

"We pretend we didn't see anything and call Security. No heroics. Got it?"

"Hey, you and I are paired up, Whitman. No heroics. Agreed."

"Same for you two," Finn said, mostly to Willa.

"Way ahead of you," she said.

Charlene looked at Maybeck and he looked back at her, and for a moment Finn thought he was going to be sick.

"Let's do this."

* * *

The Aruba orientation in the ship's Walt Disney Theatre began with a welcome to the audience from Christian, the director of entertainment. He stood alone on the huge stage in his ship whites, pressed and sharp. He cracked a joke about the ceiling falling while a slide-show of Aruba played behind him on a screen bigger than most houses.

Finn and Maybeck heard him clearly over the backstage speakers, and caught the blinding white of his uniform out of the corners of their eyes.

Charlene and Willa separated from the two boys upon entering backstage—two performers looking for the beauty salon. They descended the stairs leading to where Chernabog's crate had been found earlier, empty.

Upstairs, Finn pushed the walkie-talkie's button. "Clear?" he asked Philby, adjusting the iPhone earbud in his right ear.

"Yes. I don't see anyone." Philby was monitoring the backstage cameras, running interference for both search parties.

Maybeck led the way, cutting across the back of the deep stage behind the giant projection screen.

Backstage areas were separated by drops—thick fabric curtain dividers. As Finn and Maybeck approached, they saw the metal hull walls stacked with well-organized groupings of stage furniture and show props, all of it tied down and secured. Neon tape designated safe walking lanes. To his credit, and to Finn's astonishment, Maybeck remained inside the yellow.

They passed giant alphabet blocks used in a *Toy Story* show, pieces of a disassembled castle, jungle vegetation, and a pushcart from *Beauty and the Beast*. They carefully searched for a possible hiding place for an eight-foot-tall half-breed monster with flaming eyes.

"Nothing big enough," Maybeck told Finn in a whisper.

"Agreed."

They passed a ten-foot tower of stacked tables, all fitting together like a puzzle. "But this is cool, right?" Finn said.

"Totally."

"How about inside one of the alphabet blocks?"

"I guess it's possible," Maybeck said, "but he'd be squished."

"Maybe he doesn't care if he's in torpor. We could try to move them. Test how heavy they are."

"Solid."

The boys reversed direction just as Philby spoke into Finn's ear. "Red alert!"

"Hide!" Finn hissed.

The two boys slipped behind the alphabet blocks as two stagehands walked past the prop storage, silhouettes against the big screen. Their gait was stiff-legged, like robots or soldiers.

Maybeck sneezed, causing Finn to jump. One of the stagehands turned.

Finn spun away and slapped his back to the wood block. Maybeck's face glowed bluish in the dark; he looked thunderstruck by his mistake.

"Dust," he said.

"Not good," Finn said.

* * *

Willa and Charlene huddled at the bottom of the backstage stairs. Every surface of the hallway was painted black and dimly lit by blue neon to keep stray light from infiltrating backstage.

Male voices echoed throughout, giving little hint as to their source or direction. To the right, the hallway dead-ended in a T; to the left it ran straight, clear across the area beneath the stage and to the other wing.

The girls knew from their earlier attempt to find Chernabog that two of the rooms off this corridor accessed substage service rooms, where the elevator lifts from the stage's three trapdoors were loaded and unloaded. But there were other doors as well. Chernabog could be in hidden on the other side of any of them.

Twenty feet down the corridor, the sounds became clearer.

"We are walking *toward* the voices, Willa," Charlene hissed.

"I've got that," Willa said. She tried a door. *Locked.* She waved the crew member ID card supplied by Wayne. *Unlocked.* They stepped inside and switched on the light.

Four green-metal electric panel boxes on the wall, each the size of a washing machine, produced a loud humming. They carried stickers warning of electric shock—the stick figure lying down apparently symbolizing death. Metal conduits crisscrossed the ceiling. The room was small and was absurdly hot. It was not even close to being big enough to hide Chernabog.

The next door would not open to Willa's credentials. It was labeled SERVICE BREAKERS—NO ADMITTANCE. They took it at face value.

A door to their left was familiar to them both as the larger of the two substage service areas. Some of the voices were clearly coming from within this room. Willa shook her head, but Charlene moved the lever anyway; the door opened. Charlene poked her head inside.

"Oh!" she said, feigning surprise. "Sorry; I'm looking for the washroom."

Four guys wearing the all-black uniforms of stagehands, each holding a water bottle, sat on upturned crates.

"Two doors down," said a potbellied. "On the right."

Charlene took a mental snapshot of the space. The lightbulbs were turned down lower than candlelight, the blue neon painting the room in an otherworldly way. Chernabog's smashed crate was nowhere to be seen. As before, the space was immaculately clean and tidy— shipshape—despite the dozens of props and pieces of furniture it contained. Every square inch was thought-fully organized and accounted for. If Chernabog was still in here somewhere, it was far from obvious where he might be hidden.

"Your entrance isn't for another twenty." The man who spoke had sharp, angular features like a mouse's; narrow-set, suspicious eyes; and the weight of distrust in his voice. He checked a clipboard. "Greenroom's at the top of the stairs, starboard."

"Go easy on her, Dixon," the heavy guy said.

"There's a washroom off the greenroom," said Dixon. "But you know that."

The subtext: What are you doing down here?

"Got it! Thanks!" Charlene said. She pulled the door shut.

Willa looked upset. Charlene made a face as if to say: *So shoot me, I had to look!* They had a mission to ful-fill, and Charlene was more a field agent than an analyst; she liked action.

Not much bigger than a kitchen pantry, the next room smelled of engine oil and was filled with machin-ery. Again, no room for something Chernabog's size. This was the trouble for the Keepers: any space identi-fied as backstage and therefore away from guests was filled and utilized; there wasn't an unused or unoccupied square inch on the ship.

"Trouble following directions?" A man's voice.

They turned to see Dixon, the rodent-faced stage-hand, blocking their way.

"Funny, this doesn't look like the girls' room to me," he said, his voice void of inflection.

"We . . . ah . . ."

His eyes didn't seem to focus. He stared past them in a daze. "Best if you come with me, please." He produced a wooden billy club from out of nowhere and slapped his left palm with it. "We can do this peaceful-like, or not so peaceful."

"You're not going to hit a girl," Willa said.

"No, I'm going to hit two girls. If I have to. Your choice." That same dreadfully calm voice.

A spell? Willa wondered. The idea was chilling: a thousand crew and Cast Members traveling on the ship, with some of them acting as undercover OTs? She didn't like those odds.

Charlene faked a cough to cover her saying, "On three." Willa nodded.

Charlene patted her leg once, twice . . . Her third strike was accompanied by a front handspring and a one-eighty-degree pivot back handspring directly into the face of the zoned-out crewman. He flew off his feet and across the hall without having gotten the club to shoulder height.

Willa took off down the hall, running away from the room full of men, heading to port. The sound of the stage's public-address system played from small speakers. Some kind of scientist was being introduced. She went to speak to Charlene, but she wasn't there.

Willa stopped and looked back.

Charlene had knocked the club from the skinny guy's hand. She hooked a knee around his neck and leaped to her side, flipping the guy like a beached fish in some kind of MMA move Willa had never seen. Charlene tugged free a length of rope the man had tucked into his belt—rope meant for tying up two girls?—and bound his hands behind his back like she was a policewoman. Lacking a gag, she pulled his shoe and sock off and stuffed his dirty sock into his mouth. She waved for Willa to come help her.

Willa couldn't move.

Charlene gestured a second time, more desperately. Her eyes said, *Hurry!*

The man kicked Charlene in the chest, sending her airborne across the room.

"Uhhf!" Charlene grunted as the wind was knocked out of her.

The man stood and reared his leg back to kick her while she was down.

He fell flat onto his face. With his hands tied

behind his back, he couldn't protect himself. He was knocked unconscious. Willa looked down. She held his bare foot in her hand; she had upended him.

Charlene regained some breath. "Way to go, Willa. Nice move!"

Willa helped Charlene to her feet. Together, they dragged the unconscious man into the machine room and pulled the door shut.

Charlene tried to steady her breathing. "Next time, remind me to come as a hologram. For the record, this is way too difficult."

Willa laughed. The girls fled down the hall.

Upstairs, the audience broke into applause.

* * *

"Hey," Finn said, innocently, lowering his voice for the sake of the lecture going on. "We're looking for the greenroom."

"Sure you are," a clean-cut Joe College–type guy said.

The two crewmen moved closer to Finn.

"What are you doing hiding back here?" the second man said. Built like a weightlifter, he was short but solid, with a young face.

"We . . . ah . . ." Maybeck was fast on his feet, but not always with his thinking.

"We weren't hiding. We had this bet," Finn said, "about what letter was on the other side of the bottom block. I said it was an *R*. My friend here, a *B*."

"We had the same blocks when were kids," Maybeck said.

The two guys separated. Neither Finn nor Maybeck liked the look of that. The stocky one moved toward the blocks while Joe College faced them.

"And what was the letter?" inquired Joe College.

Finn and Maybeck exchanged slightly panicked looks in the flashing light from the slide show, which was continuing on the big screen above.

The weightlifter leaned in to look at the back side of the alphabet block.

Maybeck shook his head ever so slightly, like a pitcher shaking off a catcher's signal; he didn't want to make the guess.

Finn took in the visible letters on the existing stack of blocks.

"It's *E*," he said.

He and Maybeck watched as the short guy nodded to his partner.

Maybeck shot him a look that said, *How could you have known that?*

"So. We should be getting to the greenroom," Finn said.

Joe didn't move. He rocked his head back, eyes on the ceiling. "So . . . what exactly are we going to do with you?"

Maybeck had had enough. "Look, man, you can join us in the greenroom. That's where we're going."

"I don't think so," Joe said in a menacing voice. "We hear your two girlfriends are poking around downstairs where they don't belong. What is it you kids are looking for? Witches? Monsters?" His tone was mocking. "Grow up."

"Just the letter on the block. Really," Finn said.

"Uh-huh. Right. Now, there should be five of you. Where's the other boy?"

Finn didn't like how much Joe knew.

"Schedule says five of you. Where's the fifth? Huh? Hiding somewhere? Like you two?"

"We weren't hiding," Finn said defiantly. "I told you, we were—"

"Yeah. I got that the first time." He stepped closer. "Must be coincidence, all of you just happening to arrive early."

"Don't trouble your brain," an annoyed Maybeck said. "You must have a microphone to go plug in or something."

Finn scowled at him. *Cool it!*

"Stage manager would like to speak to you.

Downstairs. We'll go this way." Joe College indicated the port side of the stage.

The strongman remained a few paces behind Maybeck, squeezing the boys between himself and his partner.

"Actually, we're going to meet the girls. Wouldn't want them to worry," Finn said.

"Boys," Philby said into Finn's and Maybeck's ears, "I can throw a breaker, killing the lights but not the presentation. Emergency lights will kick in. You might get a second or two."

"We'll make sure the girls join you. Trust me." Joe had a hungry glint to his eye.

"Yes!" Maybeck said, a little loudly given the presentation taking place a matter of yards away. Finn saw his hand on his radio; Maybeck was signaling Philby.

The backstage went black.

Maybeck attacked the strongman, diving blindly into his legs and knocking him down. He drove an elbow into the back of the man's neck, stunning his spine and briefly paralyzing him.

Finn had kept his eye on Joe, knowing it would be dark by the time he attacked. He shoved the guy, hoping to knock him down.

The emergency lights flashed, went dark, and came on again for good. As the sterile white light strobed like something on a dance floor, Finn saw Joe College halfway across the backstage area, just getting to his feet.

Had he done that? he wondered. In years past, when the other guys on the baseball team hit triples, Finn could only manage singles. He was fast and agile, but he wasn't exactly muscleman material.

Had the guy taken off in the dark, slipped, and fallen? If so, why the look he was giving Finn—one of both anger and . . . respect?

Joe charged. Finn's knees went to rubber. But as the lights flickered off and then on for good, Finn balled his fists and connected on an upswing with Joe's chin. Joe looked like he'd hit a patch of ice.

"Sorry," Finn said, forgetting himself for a moment.

He stared at his own hands. *Did I do that?*

Willa and Charlene appeared from the right, running frantically.

Maybeck lay faceup on the stage floor where he'd dived. Finn offered him a hand, and *with one arm* lifted Maybeck onto his feet. Reminded of his explosive swimming, Finn wondered what was going on. A spell?

"Quickly," he said.

Maybeck looked dazed.

"I'm okay," Finn said, thinking that was the source of his friend's bewilderment.

"Piñata," Maybeck said in a harsh whisper.

Just the one word: *piñata.*

* * *

The four Keepers passed behind the projection screen. The reversed image showed what the speaker called a "ceremonial arch."

"Carved into the stones of the arch you can see pictographs and glyphs. These are an example of the ancient Mayan language, which is not dissimilar to glyphs found in Aruban caves. Historians and archeologists speculate that there was much trade and cross-cultural exchange within the Caribbean during the Mayan and Aztec dynasties."

Finn led the team around to the far side, aware that their opponents would be fast on their heels. As they hurried, a close-up of one of the pictographs appeared on the screen, now fifteen feet high.

"This is *janaab*, the Mayan symbol for 'flower,'" he said.

"Seriously? That's number four!" Willa cried. As a group they arrived at stage left. "That's the Mayan character I couldn't find: flower! So it's gold, island, cave, flower."

Charlene said, "Gold island, flower cave."

Her rearrangement of the words made it a kind of game; a game the boys weren't interested in. Their attention was fixed on the backstage area, where Philby had restored the blue light.

The two zoned-out stagehands were up and moving.

"Island cave, gold flower."

Both girls gasped and repeated the words in unison, voices rising in excitement: "Island cave, gold flower!"

* * *

Dixon appeared at the top of the stairs, blocking the stage-door exit. The other two, Joe College and the weightlifter, approached from backstage.

"We're talking OT sandwich," Maybeck said. "And we're the PB-and-J."

The two stagehands closed fast. Joe walked with an angry limp.

"Not good," Finn said.

"Grab hands," Willa said, "and get ready to smile."

"What?" Maybeck said, incredulously. But before he

112

could protest, Willa took his hand and led the Keepers out onto the stage—the one place the stagehands could not follow.

A wild cheer arose from the audience. The speaker wasn't sure how to handle their early entrance.

Behind them, the stagehands divided; the weight-lifter crossed backstage, reappearing on the opposite side, trapping them.

They were a Kingdom Keeper short—no Philby—but the audience didn't seem to care. Many were on their feet, giving the group a standing ovation.

Maybeck spoke to Finn through a fake smile. "Like a piñata."

Finn had no idea what he meant. "You must have hit your head pretty hard. You're talking nonsense."

"I'm telling you: a piñata."

The audience stomped and cheered. The stage floor vibrated. Christian crossed toward them, waving to the crowd.

"Ladies and gentlemen, boys and girls, your very own Kingdom Keepers!"

Another loud cheer from the audience.

Finn glanced back to see the *janaab* image. *Island cave. Gold flower. Island gold, cave flower?* While he waved to the audience, his mind worked through the various combinations and tried to throw a piñata into the mix. He couldn't make sense of any of it.

Christian did a nice job of covering for their early entrance. The lecturer looked dazed. Didn't know where he was.

At that moment, the three stagehands suddenly rushed the stage from both sides, carrying wireless microphones. They'd found their excuse. And each held a second item, obscured by the mikes. It took Finn a moment to process what those items might be.

"Look out! Tasers!" he cried, tripping Willa into Charlene and intentionally sending them toppling. He pulled Maybeck down by the arm.

The stagehands fired their Tasers nearly simultaneously, but missed.

Missed the *kids*.

The lecturer collapsed; Christian caught him. The audience laughed and applauded as the stagehands retreated, passing Philby, who was arriving late. He drew more applause. A new group of stagehands rushed onstage and dragged the fallen lecturer into the wings. These guys, Finn realized, were the real stagehands, not Maleficent's zombies.

"Ladies and gentlemen, boys and girls, please give a big *Disney Dream* welcome to the Disney Hosts Interactive!" Christian had little else to say, so he tried again, making out that this was all part of the act. His eyes flashed to Finn, demanding an explanation for the attack. Finn just shrugged. What could he say?

The Keepers, led by Willa, followed the script they'd been given for the orientation. Willa picked up perfectly on Christian's second introduction, reciting her memorized lines. The other Keepers followed her lead. The spoke about all the fun they were going to have on Aruba, the interesting places to sightsee, and how to take full advantage of the excursions being offered.

A slideshow of the island's features ran behind them while high seas adventure music provided background. Despite the awkward beginning, the orientation ended well.

Surprising Christian by going off script, Finn led his friends into the audience. There, surrounded by admirers, the OTs had no shot at them.

Minutes later, the theater doors swished closed behind them. The Keepers divided into two groups; Maybeck with Charlene; Finn with Philby and Willa. They would meet in 816, by prior arrangement.

Climbing the stairs two at a time, Finn was deep in thought. *Piñata. Gold island, cave flower?* What did it all mean?

10

FINN HELD OPEN the backstage door for Philby and Maybeck, who slipped through quietly. He followed them inside. It was two in the morning, the ship plying the waters for the final push to Aruba.

Maybeck had argued against a return backstage on the same night as the orientation, but Philby was determined to follow through on Maybeck's mention of a piñata.

"The idea that the OTs have hidden Chernabog inside a Buzz Lightyear parade balloon backstage is just insane enough to make complete sense! If he's in torpor, as Willa believes, he will require almost no oxygen. Maybeck, it's possible you're right. Well played."

"I hope not," Maybeck said.

The three boys crept across the backstage area, holding close to the backdrops. Together, they shared an anxious inhale as Maybeck led the way to where he and Finn had encountered the two stagehands.

The only sound was a slight hum of electricity and the whoosh of forced air.

They were directly below several character balloons

secured to the ceiling: Buzz, Bolt, and the five members of the Incredibles family.

Maybeck pointed to himself, then up.

Philby nodded.

Maybeck climbed the ladder strapped to the wall.

* * *

From up close, the Buzz Lightyear balloon was all color and clear plastic. Maybeck didn't know whether he was looking into the guy's side or his arm, but what he saw caused his heart to leap in his chest.

He panicked, a rare and unnatural state for him. Throwing his feet to the outside of the rungs, he slid down the ladder like it was a firehouse pole. His sneakers squealed against the metal. He landed on the stage with a loud thud.

"Sheesh!" Finn reached out to steady Maybeck.

"We're out of here!" Maybeck said. He took two steps.

"Who's there?" A man's voice carried across the stage. "Hello?" It came from their left.

Philby waved for Maybeck and Finn to follow him. The three boys hurried away to a set of dark stairs leading to the theater auditorium.

They were cornered. If they went through into the theater, they'd be seen; if they stayed where they were, they'd be caught.

Finn wasn't going to stand around. He yanked open the door and dove beneath a seat in the first row, crawling forward and tucking his legs into a ball. Philby and Maybeck followed. The three boys lay on the auditorium floor beneath three side-by-side seats.

Footfalls pounded out onstage.

"Anybody there?" The man's voice was incredibly present and close. "Answer me! Who's there?"

More footfalls. One, maybe two more people.

Finn used the loud sound to cover his rolling onto his back and wiggling forward to beneath row three.

Philby had the nerve to grab hold of him to try to stop him. Finn shook off his hand a little too harshly, pulled himself to sitting, and peered through the spaces between seats.

He saw a squat but wide-shouldered stagehand looking up into the dark where Maybeck had climbed. Finn sensed the other man before he ever saw him, a man standing as still as a predator cat, only the whites of his eyes ticking left to right as he searched the auditorium. Finn didn't so much as blink. *The man was looking right at him.* He held his breath; fought to keep from moving.

At last, the stagehand turned away. A second later he could be heard descending the stairs.

Finn finally rested his eyes, relief flooding him.

The stage stood empty.

The boys gingerly extricated themselves from under the seats and moved quietly into the aisle. They crept toward the back of the theater and the glowing exit signs.

"You! Stop!" The sneaky stagehand had tricked them.

"Don't show them your faces!" Finn told Philby and Maybeck as the three ran.

The stagehand jumped and took off after the boys, supernaturally fast.

"Go!" Finn shouted to Maybeck and Philby as he skidded to a stop and turned to face the man coming for them.

Finn possessed a confidence acquired over time by being the unanointed leader of the group. But usually it was Maybeck or Charlene, not him, who stuck around for the battles. Without thinking now about what he was doing, he dropped to one knee, grabbed hold of either side of the aisle carpet, and pulled. Pulled hard.

Nothing happened. What the heck had he been thinking?

The stagehand drew closer. Anger and frustration overcame Finn. He gave the carpet one ferocious tug. To his surprise, this time it tore loose and rose like a wave, rippling powerfully as it pulled free. The wave surged beneath the stagehand—a magic carpet—dumping the man flat onto his back and knocking the wind out of him.

The boys ran out the theater's main doors reaching Mickey's Mainsail shop in record time.

"What was that, Whitman?" Maybeck asked.

"No clue."

"Since when do you go for the Superman stuff?"

"Since never." Finn panted. As if to prove it, he was out of breath.

Then, arriving down the opposing hallway alongside White Caps, came the second stagehand, the one with the shoulders of a weightlifter. He glowered at the three boys.

"Well," he growled, "if it ain't the Three Stooges."

"Split up!" Philby shouted as the three boys took off.

Finn and Philby headed aft; Maybeck peeled off and bounded down the amidships stairs.

The stagehand ignored Maybeck, increasing his odds by going after two of the kids.

Though he tried to focus on fleeing, Finn couldn't help wondering what had happened back there. That surge of strength . . . was it a fluke? Something he could learn to do? He glanced over his shoulder.

No question the man was after him, not Philby. Time to act.

Finn bumped Philby, sending him tumbling.

The stagehand ran past Philby, just as Finn had surmised.

Finn put his newfound power to a test, ascending the Atrium's grand staircase. He huffed and puffed as usual. Was slow, as usual.

The man labored behind him.

Finn was running on fumes by the time he headed through the Vista Gallery, ran down the long port companionway leading to the District, and then through the warren of nightclubs. He needed oxygen. He needed a paramedic.

When he looked next, the stagehand was nowhere in sight. Finn climbed the aft staircase, feeling like he was a hundred years old.

He stopped at Deck 8, his lungs ready to burst, wanting desperately to find out what had happened.

To find out if he could ever do it again.

* * *

"It's him!" Maybeck rarely sounded frightened.

He, Finn, and Philby were outside on the veranda of Finn's stateroom.

"Chernabog?" Finn worked to keep disbelief from his voice.

"He's inside the Buzz Lightyear balloon."

"You saw him." Philby swallowed so hard it looked like he'd gulped a mouse.

"Most of the balloon is colored. I saw an eye, and part of a horn." Maybeck allowed this to sink in. "An extremely, unbelievably big eye."

Maybeck was no chicken. Just the way he'd bailed down the ladder told Finn he'd seen something horrific.

"So we report him to Security." Philby sounded disappointed.

"You realize, this could be the beginning of the end for the OTs." Finn sounded stunned. "No Chernabog. Security realizing something big is going down. That we're not a bunch of lunatic kids."

"You and I go to Security."

"What about me?" Maybeck complained.

"You hang back. If Security detains us, we may need a jailbreak."

* * *

"Let me get this straight," Uncle Bob said to the two VIPs. "You've demanded to speak to me at three in the morning because you say Chernabog, who is a Disney character who has *never* sailed with us, is hidden inside the Buzz Lightyear inflatable backstage in the Walt Disney Theatre."

"Correct." The redhead, Philby, was bright-eyed

despite the late hour. The other boy, Finn, seemed more quietly confident, like a person in charge.

"And how did this monster get aboard?"

"A plane landed on Castaway Cay. He was the cargo."

Bob said nothing, revealed nothing in his face. He'd been told of guests having seen a plane landing. At the time, he'd not believed it.

"I saw it," Philby said. "I was there."

"And how did everyone else miss this event?" Bob purposely didn't reveal that some had in fact reported similar happenings.

"The fireworks," Finn said. "They were used as a diversion. The plane didn't turn on any lights until seconds before it landed."

"So the sound was covered by the fireworks," Uncle Bob said, trying not to appear interested. He faked a laugh. "Okay. This is part of your show, right? The late-night video dump? I thought you weren't supposed to know about—" His expression changed dramatically. "Listen. Sorry. Okay? We'll look into it."

Finn didn't understand what had just happened. Uncle Bob had gone from suspicious and confrontational to apologetic and chummy.

"By 'show,'" Philby said, his tone confrontational, "do you mean our role in the parks or something? Look.

We're not asking you to believe any of the stories about us, sir. We only ask that you inspect the Buzz Lightyear balloon's contents."

"We are in the process of that as we speak," said Bob, now a different man. Finn and Philby exchanged perplexed glances.

"We're serious." Finn had a sense Bob was not.

"As am I. I have a man on the way there now." Bob worked the radio at his waist. "Yup. He's on his way."

"What did you mean just now by the 'video dump'?" Professor Philby said. When Bob shot him a look of ignorance, Philby continued. "I'm aware that the ship uploads the larger data packets to the satellite at night when the guests are asleep and there's more bandwidth on the satellite link. But isn't that mostly for the media tours or the special events?"

Bob looked as if Philby had tricked him, as if his brain was trying to catch up. That expression gave way to one of impatience, and finally, determination.

"I was referring to the three-six-five you're shooting for Disney Channel. The director uploads after hours." A Disney 365 was a two-minute video publicity piece that ran on the Channel.

Finn was having trouble focusing, his brain too tired. He understood Philby's concern about high-volume video dumps: the transmission of DHI data required enormous bandwidth—that was how the Imagineers had been able to track the movement of the Overtakers' server to a possible ship at sea. This ship. This sea.

If the ship performed a video dump at night, sending the 365 to the company's studio, the huge bandwidth requirements could diminish the quality of Amanda and Jess as DHIs. Philby was trying to figure things out in order to avoid complications.

Bob touched his ear. "Did not copy!" The man listened intently. "Roger that."

He looked at the two boys quizzically. "Okay, so what's going on?"

The boys offered only puzzled expressions.

"If it was an accident, I need to know that right now. If it's found to be vandalism and you're trying to pull my chain, heads are going to roll."

"We don't have a clue what you're talking about," Philby said.

"Don't mess with me."

"Not happening," Finn said. "No clue."

Bob studied them. "The condition of the Buzz Lightyear balloon the last time you saw it? And I advise you to think carefully before giving me your answer."

The boys stared at each other, dumbfounded.

"If I'm hearing you," Philby said, "you're telling us something's happened to the balloon?"

"The longer you mess with me," Bob said, "the deeper the hole you dig."

"We're not messing with you," Finn said. "Give us a lie detector test or whatever, but when we last saw that parade balloon it was inflated and secured to the ceiling backstage."

"Why?" Philby said. "Your guy found Chernabog?"

"My guy found a deflated balloon, cut—not torn—from one end to the other with a sharp object. That's a five-thousand-dollar prop. As in *dollars*," Bob added for their benefit. "You're trying a clever plan to pretend someone else did this and get yourselves off the hook."

"So we dreamed up Chernabog," Philby said, allowing fatigue and anger to color his voice. "We dreamed up a plane landing on Castaway. Yeah!" he said, sarcastically. "We did that to make sure you wouldn't bust us for popping your Buzz Lightyear balloon."

"You be careful with that mouth of yours, son."

"We're in danger here, *Dad*. You're under attack and in trouble, and we're apparently the only ones trying to keep your ship from being overtaken by people—by *things*—you will not believe. When you finally do, it'll be too late."

Bob's face was scarlet.

"We were told we could work with you," Finn said.

"Wayne Kresky told me you were the one person we could trust."

Mention of Kresky's name stood Bob up a little taller. The rogue designer, the man accused of running a secret agency within the Imagineers. Who were these kids to tell him about Wayne Kresky?

"You will answer for the damage to this balloon," he said.

"Seriously? You think we're *that* clever? To turn ourselves in at three in the morning in order to take suspicion *off* of us?"

"I wish we were that smart," Finn said.

"Return to your rooms. You'll hear from me."

"Chernabog is gone," Philby said. "You guys have got to find him!"

"I acknowledge that you and your friends are special guests aboard this ship, young man"—Bob directed this at Philby—"but I will determine what I have to do. Not you. Now get out of here before I change my mind."

11

A BOY WALKS DOWN *a dark tunnel. A shadow climbs the wall to the left, runs along and rolls down the rocks like a snake. There are sounds—his feet? Someone else's?*

The sound of rapid breathing suggests danger lurking. The boy is afraid, deathly afraid. Yellow light leaks into the confined space.

The boy continues through a square tunnel of some kind. A park attraction? There are no lights, no music, no sounds other than water splashing.

Something is chasing the boy. It's monstrous. It makes hideous, guttural sounds that drive the boy forward, deeper down the tunnel.

Whatever is back there, whatever is coming—it means business.

It means to kill him.

Jess's eyes snapped open. She was looking at the underside of a mattress, held up by wire mesh. Her natural instinct at such moments was to reach for her sketchbook, switch on the battery-operated book light, and take the pencil out from the binding. She did just that and started to draw the image of a frightened boy in a square stone tunnel, knowing that Amanda was so attuned to her process that at any second her head would come over the edge of the upper bunk.

And it did.

Amanda knew better than to speak. Nothing could come between Jess and whatever images lurked in her thoughts. The dream needed to be preserved. Jess's premonitions contributed to the Keepers' efforts like information from a spy. The more detailed and accurate her drawing, the better.

Amanda lowered her head to her pillow and stared at the ceiling. Three glow-in-the-dark stick-on stars gave her dull green images to focus on. Patience was everything. The persistent scratching of pencil point on paper was all she heard . . . and the occasional dull rubbing sound of the eraser.

The eraser meant a lack of confidence; it was the sound of Jess changing her mind or not liking the way something had come out. Amanda knew her to be an expert illustrator. Her crude drawings of a year or two earlier had evolved into sophisticated realism.

The sounds of sketching finally stopped. Jess sighed, as if she had held her breath for the past ten minutes— an unintentional signal. Amanda slipped off the top bunk.

"Can I see?" she whispered, painfully aware of Jeannie Pucket sleeping only a few feet away.

"I'm not sure what was going on. A boy."

Amanda knew not to force her. "Any hints as to who it was?"

"No."

"A shadow," Amanda said, studying the superbly sketched image.

"Yes. A boy."

"It's a cave."

"More like a tunnel," Jess said. "See the square walls?"

"We need to get this to Finn."

"We will."

"I mean right now."

"Why the hurry?" Jess asked.

"Because the *Dream* docks in Aruba this morning. They're heading to the caves."

"I'm not so sure this is a cave."

"Doesn't matter." Amanda couldn't take her eyes off the sketch. "They need to see it."

"I don't know. It doesn't feel complete. I heard water, but I didn't see any."

Amanda felt sorry for Jess, who bore the burden of her dreams and the messages they contained. Jess occasionally rebelled against the significance Finn and

Philby attributed to her visions. To her, they were just dreams, sometimes accurate projections into the future, sometimes not. She didn't like her friends basing their plans—or worse, risking their lives—on something so ephemeral.

Amanda said, "I'll get this to Philby, make sure he sees it before they leave the ship." She forced her eyes off the page. The edge of the window casement was glowing yellow with the flush of dawn. "I hope we're not too late."

12

IN THE EARLY HOURS of Thursday morning, Clayton Freeman, a handsome African American man who shaved his head to a spit polish, found himself heading backstage in the Walt Disney Theatre. He blamed the two Kingdom Keeper boys for making him lose sleep. But he also found himself at least slightly believing what Bob had told him.

Maybe it was because he was younger than Bob. Maybe it was due to inexperience. Maybe it was because he'd come through college on the fringe end of Harry Potter, and he still had a thing for Artemis Fowl, Percy Jackson, and Legend, but he didn't immediately dismiss the improbable the way his boss did.

Certainly what the boys reported seeing backstage was a stretch. Clayton Freeman would rank it as highly unlikely. But impossible? He worked for Disney; was anything beyond the scope of imagination?

Clayton had heard the stories from fellow security personnel within the Disney World parks, stories that Bob had no time for. He'd seen the damage inside the It's a Small World ride—dolls broken off the scenes, others floating in the water; he'd heard it called vandalism. He'd also heard rumors that the dolls appeared to have broken free of their platforms, as if marching like an army. Clayton didn't know what to make of any of it.

He approached the backstage prop storage, his mind weighed down by the disappearance of a second Mickey Mouse who had been spotted on board; the vandalism done to some security cameras during the Castaway Cay stop; and Maleficent's unscheduled video just before the lights sparked and shattered.

Too many unanswered questions . . .

Clayton stopped. As they'd been told, the Buzz Lightyear balloon lay on the stage floor, deflated, collapsed. It was his job to inspect it. Indeed, it appeared to have been cut open with a sharp blade.

Like Bob, he wanted to fob this off on the two boys who reported it. *They goof around backstage, a bit of mischief leads to vandalism. The boys—both VIPs!—report the incident as something much bigger.*

But the balloon had not popped by accident. It had been cut open intentionally. Try as he might, Clayton couldn't see the boys doing that. Physically, it would have been nearly impossible.

He kneeled and inspected the cut seam. There was a bead of dried glue, implying it had been opened previously and then repaired.

The boys claimed the Buzz Lightyear balloon had contained Chernabog. *The creepy thing from* Fantasia? *As if!* Clayton nearly laughed aloud.

Then he discovered a five-inch length of coarse hair. Animal, not human. Thick and inflexible. *A whisker?*

He found another, and another, all stuck to dried beads of glue.

Impossible!

The evidence supported the boys' claim. Clayton collected the hairs. No choice but to show them to Bob.

No choice but to consider this a legitimate investigation.

13

PRIOR TO LEAVING the ship for the day, the early risers met on the deck of Cabanas for breakfast before sunup.

Philby, Storey, and Finn listened as an excited Willa explained to Storey and Philby what the other Keepers had figured out the night before.

"*K'an* is gold, yellow, or precious. *Ch'en* is cave. *Janaab* is flower. *Pet* is island. We have nearly all the pieces of the journal's second clue."

Philby said, "Yes. Finn told me last night."

"But?" said Willa, contesting him. The friction between them was palpable.

Finn answered, trying to keep the fireworks to a minimum. "Philby points out that now that the OTs have the flash drive with their DHI data, all they need is a new server, since I fried their other one."

"If I were them," Philby said, avoiding eye contact with Willa, "I'd replace it in Aruba. After Aruba we have a day at sea, then the Panama Canal passage, then another night without a stop. It's several days before anyone gets off the ship again."

"Today is the final *island* stop on the cruise," Storey said.

"'Island' is one of the four words from the journal," said Willa. "Not 'computer.'"

Ouch, Finn nearly said. Instead he tried to keep them focused. "Let's consider the four words—"

"Twenty-four different combinations," Philby said proudly, and made an unpleasant face at Willa, who winced and blinked.

"Actually," she snapped, "it's three times that when you consider the two added definitions for *k'an* of yellow and precious."

Philby looked crushed.

"In my opinion," Willa said, "the most promising is: island cave, gold flower—or maybe yellow flower. I don't see 'gold cave' or 'gold island' or 'island flower' or 'precious flower,' though who knows?"

"Okay, so let's start there," Finn said hastily.

Philby glanced down below the edge of the table where he held a printout of an e-mail sent by Amanda. It showed a shadow on a wall of what might be a cave. He nearly showed it to them, but looking across at the defiant Willa, he shook his head, refolded it and slipped it into his pocket. "I think we should consider their need for a server."

Finn said quickly, "So . . . island cave, gold flower. Any luck with the look of the caves?"

Storey slid an excursion brochure across to Philby, followed by some computer printouts of Aruban caves.

"None are an exact match with Jess's drawing, but what's interesting is the similar formations and the surrounding landscape. She was definitely dreaming of a cave on Aruba."

Philby compared Jess's drawing to the various photographs. "Agreed. So we're in the right place at the right time, and we know what they're looking for." He fingered the vacant space framed in the copy of the journal page and glanced up at Willa. "You're going with *flower* because of this."

"Yes. There was a pressed flower in there, like Charlene said. Has to be."

"And the OTs have it," Philby said.

"Could have it. Might not," Willa said.

"We are outnumbered once again," Philby said. "Forward following could work, should work, but it won't if we're watching the wrong cave." He turned to Storey. "There are what, five important caves?"

"Yes. And many more up and down the northeastern coast," Storey said.

"Divide and conquer," Finn proposed.

"No other choice," Philby said. "Five caves. Six of us, including Storey. Not to mention the need to cover the computer stores."

"Then let's not mention it," Willa said, and drew a scornful look from the boys.

"What if you stay behind and watch the cameras for a computer box being brought aboard?" Finn suggested to Philby. "We'd know where to look, who to go after."

"Hmm."

"There are two others we could ask to help us," Storey said, somewhat tentatively.

Dillard? Finn wondered. He was fairly certain his neighbor, who'd helped the Keepers in the past, was on the ship, but how could Dillard possibly know Storey? And how could he possibly find the kid anyway? He kept quiet.

She said, "Their names are Kenny and Bart. I work with them."

"Not for fieldwork. I could use them as lookouts," Philby said.

"Done."

Philby, apparently satisfied with Finn's solution to the computer problem, mellowed. "The rest of you . . . four will each take one of the famous caves. The fifth—maybe we give this to Maybeck?—will be our control: he'll show the Jess sketch to a taxi driver and see where he's taken. Maybe it overlaps with one of you, maybe not."

"Maybe we should all do that," Finn said. "I like that idea."

"It puts too much faith in the sketch," Philby said. "Better to cover as many bases as possible."

"Jess's drawings have never been wrong," Willa said.

"But if you talk to Amanda, that's not the case." Philby looked Willa in the eye. "Jess gets confused now and then. We have to stay objective, be as statistically accurate as possible. Of the five most popular caves, we cover the top four. Maybeck acts as our control."

No one looked sold.

"The stolen journal started this," Philby insisted. "The journal tells us it's an island cave. This is the only island stop after Castaway, and there aren't caves on Castaway. Right place. Right time."

"And if Luowski or another OTK leaves the ship?" Finn said.

"They won't trust him or anyone to do whatever it is they're planning. You want something done right, you do it yourself." Philby squinted, deep in thought. "Okay. A compromise. Maybeck and Willa leave super early. You and Charlene leave next," he told Finn. "Storey goes last. If an OT or OTK is seen leaving the ship during that time, maybe we change plans. If not, each one of you takes a different cave and I watch for a computer coming back on board." He paused and said, "Is everyone good with that?"

No one objected—unless you counted Willa's rolling eyes.

* * *

A blade of bloodred arched above the horizon, absorbed in spots by cumulus clouds, all of it dripping with foreboding. The smells and sounds of land had awakened Greg Luowski as the ship docked; now he climbed down to the deck, peering over the rail to see dockhands and shore workers busy below.

The shiver that ran through him had nothing to do with air temperature; it was instead the recollection of his meeting with Maleficent—the Ice Queen—and how she'd told him he had to "collect one" for her.

"One what?" he'd asked.

But he'd known the answer. Another shiver. He knew "what." He knew "who."

His contempt for Finn Whitman knew no bounds. Whitless was the kind of boy Luowski lived to hate: clever, brainy, fast-tongued and slow-footed. His feelings of ill will were multiplied by Amanda's obvious adoration; she wouldn't give Luowski the time of day as long as Finn Whitman existed.

Focusing on the task at hand, Luowski attempted to collect his thoughts—a bit like picking up three dozen apples without a basket or bag: the more he gathered, the more he dropped. And so it was that his plans spilled out of his head and over the ship's rail like confetti, lost to the whims of the wind.

First, he had to get off the ship. He'd deal with the rest later.

Maleficent had made fun of him—something no one got away with. He would show her: he'd pull off this assignment flawlessly, return with the computer she needed. He'd use his accomplishment as a bargaining chip. Let someone else do the other thing. Luowski was no killer. She'd treated him like a thug. She'd see.

Twenty minutes later, he wore a ship hand's blue coveralls over a pair of NBA shorts and a World of Warcraft T-shirt. A Disney Cruise Lines ID badge hung from a lanyard around his neck. His hands and forearms looked like those of an engine room worker who'd failed to get all the grease off. Crew members were disembarking to the docks. The process of resupplying the ship was well organized and executed: everyone had his or her assignment; they worked in concert. A single player like Greg Luowski was, to the security team scanning the crew as they disembarked, just another player. His ID was legit. He was scanned off and disembarked.

Luowski stepped onto the sands of Aruba and inhaled deeply.

There was work to do.

14

IN THE BALCONY SEATING of the Buena Vista Theatre, Storey Ming was met by Kenny Carlson, a tall, freckled kid. His sidekick, Bart, looked like a surfer dude.

"They still don't know?" Kenny said.

"Actually, now they do. You've done an excellent job of laying low. But that's changed. They need lookouts. You'll be on Wave Phones reporting directly to Philby."

"Cool," Kenny said. "We're ready."

"This isn't a game."

"I know that."

"You're high schoolers."

"Acknowledged."

"So act like it."

"Roger that."

"Which means don't use radio speak when I'm sitting next to you."

Kenny blushed.

"You're excited. I get that. It's exciting work. But their *lives* depend on our doing a good job. You understand? Their *lives*. No exaggeration. So get the giggles out and man up."

Kenny nodded. Bart looked a little confused.

"Explain it to him," she said.

"Will do," Kenny said.

"And don't mess this up!"

Kenny leaned away from her.

"Now you're getting it." Storey appraised them both. "Cast Members. That's all. You are Cast Members, helping out."

Not knowing what to say, Kenny said nothing. Storey left the balcony, but not without one last menacing look to drive home her point: they were answering to her.

And she meant business.

* * *

With Maybeck and Willa long gone, the disembarkation of Luowski and then Dixon set off a flurry of Wave Phone texts and conversations that resulted in Philby's leaving his post.

With a bird's eye view from Deck 11, Kenny reported that Luowski had bypassed the excursion buses and was headed into town on foot. A man—or a big kid—followed nearly the same route, about five minutes later.

Philby closed the distance but lost sight of Luowski behind some massive oil tanks. Kenny reported that he was heading west on the street closest to the docks. "Just below the blimp."

A miniature blimp, about the size of a car, maneuvered overhead. It bore the Disney Channel logo in bright yellow. Following in the general direction of the blimp, Philby spotted Luowski entering a Quiznos sandwich shop. So far, so good.

Finn left the ship and headed to the taxi queue on schedule. As he was about to climb into the backseat, he heard a report through his earbud that a small boat had just pulled up on the opposite side of the ship from the dock.

"I'm on it," said Storey's voice.

"No time," Philby told her.

"I'm taking the express lane," she replied.

* * *

Storey Ming opened a watertight door marked CREW ONLY. It was an exterior deck area where a number of cables as thick as her leg ran through portholes and secured the ship to the dock. These spring lines tied the ship tight to the dock while allowing for, and self-adjusting to, the ship's subtle movements.

She stuck her head out oval porthole and gulped. It was a long way down.

She located a short length of chain and threw it

over a cable, taking hold of the chain at either end. Storey sat on the sill of the open porthole, watching the dock activity, awaiting her moment. Then she slid off.

She flew down the line, a tiny speck of girl amid the oversized world of the *Dream*. There were several spring lines securing the bow. She'd chosen the farthest forward line. A second line, set just below hers, gave her a way to break her descent.

Storey raced toward the huge iron cleat on the dock, counting down in her head. At the last second, she let go of the chain, tucked into a ball, and rolled across the dock in a somersault. She scraped both her knees and elbows, but didn't break any bones.

"Hey! You there!"

She took inventory: the ship behind her, stretching a thousand feet to her left; the empty pier and taxi stand to her right.

She took off at a sprint. No dockhand was going to catch her.

As Storey cleared the terminal building, she spotted a pair of umbrellas and behind the umbrellas, two men, all climbing steep stairs from a small boat. She reached for her Wave Phone to report. Gone!

She checked for her wallet: still in her pocket.

When the umbrellas were collapsed, allowing their

holders to board a parked taxi, they revealed two women, one small and dark, the other tall and thin.

Diving into the back of another waiting taxicab, Storey yanked the door shut. The driver spun around, a wide smile on his face.

"Welcome to Aruba! Where can I take you?"

She'd always wanted to say the words she said now.

"Follow that car!" Storey cried.

* * *

A sad-looking sandwich sign on the sidewalk advertised an ATM. A tired, darkly tanned man in a loud shirt stood by a dilapidated former school bus, now painted in outrageous colors reading FANTASY ISLAND TOUR. Neon lights flashed in various shop windows: GOLD! JEWELRY! SOUVENIRS! T-SHIRTS!

Philby kept his eye on the door of the Quiznos, his palms sweaty.

The stagehand Dixon entered, obviously to rendezvous with Luowski. Moments later, the two left the shop. Philby followed, keeping a good distance back.

Quickly, the upscale street, Arendstraat, gave way to a seedier side street. The crumbling sidewalks and low concrete-block buildings made Philby feel unsafe. The drone of the overhead blimp grabbed his attention. It was like an annoying insect circling his head.

When he refocused, he'd lost Luowski and Dixon. Philby panicked and studied each of the shops.

Next to Peggy's Yarn Shop, a store window: Bytes, Bits, and Beyond.

A computer store.

Philby crossed the street at a run. The shop's window was filled with gear, some of it switched on and working. One monitor displayed a live video of Philby looking in. To the right was another monitor divided into four video quadrants.

A handwritten ad read:

Security Special! Package includes 4 wireless cameras and software!

In the lower-right quadrant, two dark shapes were crouched below the counter. Philby wondered how Luowski could be so dumb.

A police siren grew steadily louder.

And closer still.

At first, Philby assumed Luowski had tripped a silent alarm, and was delighted at the idea of the bully getting himself locked up. Then he considered his own position.

Not good. He could easily be mistaken for a lookout. An accomplice.

Tires screeched. A police car slid through the turn onto Jolastraat.

Philby took off running, realizing too late that this was a stupid thing to do. People who ran from cops appeared guilty. Car doors slammed behind him. The dying siren crawled up to a scream again as the police car peeled out.

Cursing under his breath, Philby cut left onto a dirt track. The police car slammed on the brakes, backed up, and took a sharp left, now immediately behind Philby.

Fence, Philby's brain cried.

The wooden fence was eight feet high, with lumber bracing halfway up. Philby headed for it.

At that same moment, Luowski and Dixon emerged from the shop's back door cradling large cardboard boxes.

For a split second Philby hesitated: he'd led the police directly to the thieves. That had to be a good thing!

But as the police car slowed and the passenger door swung open, dispensing a woman cop who ran straight at Philby, he knew he was in big trouble. If arrested, he would not only miss the ship's departure but he'd look like an idiot to the others—all brains, no brawn, though that was far from the truth.

Wayne had recruited Philby in part for his rock-climbing skills; he'd ended up as the group's techie only after Maybeck shirked the responsibility. Now—unbeknown to the others—he seemed to be being groomed to lead the Keepers, a role currently all Finn's. Wayne treated him special, gave him secret responsibilities. An arrest would sabotage all he'd been working toward.

Philby scaled the fence like he was flashing a new climbing route, crossed the street, and tried to lose himself in a stand of trees.

The lady cop fell awkwardly into the dust. When she looked up, the tall kid was gone.

* * *

If Dixon hadn't reacted the way he had, Luowski might have frozen in place. At the very least, Luowski would have dropped the stolen computer before running. But Dixon reacted calmly. He wasn't afraid. It gave Luowski strength.

Dixon took off without looking back.

Within seconds Luowski was following him across a busy street amid a flurry of protesting car horns.

The police car's siren cried behind them, but at a distance now; they had the jump on them, and Dixon and Luowski shot though a narrow gap between buildings, knowing a police car would not fit. The driver should have followed on foot. By pursuing in the car, he'd lost his advantage.

Dixon and Luowski seized it.

15

MAYBECK AND CHARLENE had disembarked at seven when Cast Members were allowed off the ship. They'd headed for separate taxis and left for separate caves.

Ten minutes out of the city, Maybeck's driver drove him onto a road of sand no wider than the car. After a long, bouncing drive, the taxi arrived at a turnout where three boulders blocked vehicles from entering a weed-infested, trodden-down footpath lined with cactus and discolored by litter. Maybeck told the driver to wait for him.

Maybeck passed a boulder; decaying wrought iron bars blocked access to a dark hole where rock met sand. Hoping that wasn't the cave in question, Maybeck hurried up a path that climbed a small hill, now facing a smooth rock formation that rose unexpectedly out of the sand. Giant boulders lay atop one another at odd angles, creating dark spaces between them. The path led under and through the boulders, revealing shaded spaces, but not exactly caves.

Bugs swarmed around Maybeck's head.

None of the spaces matched the copy of the sketch

he carried in his back pocket. The path continued through more of the partial caves and broke out again into sunlight.

A bust.

Back in the taxi, he described the cave in Jess's drawing to the driver.

"The cave I'm looking for is on flat ground." He passed the driver the copy of the sketch. "The cave opening is like a mouth about to smile."

"A poet," the driver said.

"Artist, actually."

"You draw this?"

"A friend."

The driver dragged his hand over his face, stretching his skin.

"I might know this place," the driver said. "Not so popular. A ways from here. Cost you twenty florins."

Maybeck calculated the conversion. Eleven dollars. It seemed like a lot. "And if you wait for me maybe an hour and take me back to the ship?"

The driver considered the proposal. "Thirty florins to return, then the meter back to the ship."

"Twenty-five," Maybeck said to the driver. "Then the meter."

"I wait one hour," the driver said. "You have the money?"

"U.S. dollars," Maybeck said.

"Show me."

Maybeck didn't like the idea of showing a taxi driver he was carrying a bunch of cash.

"No problem." He struggled to pull a single twenty from his pocket. Waved it toward the front seat. The driver nodded and took off so fast Maybeck's head snapped back.

Five minutes into the ride, Maybeck turned on his charm.

"This cave? You know anything about it?"

"This island got nothing but stories, mister."

"Any stories about the caves?"

"Guadirikiri, where you're going, has two parts. Holes in the roof of the cave let in the light by day. Let the bats out by night. Thousands of 'em. It's said that they're souls of all them slaves flying each night, trying to find eternity."

Maybeck felt a chill. He leaned back.

"Slaves?"

"Aruba's first settlers were Indians—natives, like me—escaping other tribes like the Carib. Then the Europeans came, in the year of our Lord 1499. But unlike on the other islands, the Europeans didn't try to grow nothing here. Instead, they packed up the natives and sold them, sent some of them poor souls back to the country their ancestors first escaped from. The bats of Guadirikiri . . . are souls that stayed behind on the island, even though their bodies left."

Maybeck swallowed back a knot of anger and frustration.

"You okay?" The driver asked.

"My ancestors . . . they were slaves." Maybeck's stomach felt tight, his throat dry.

"That why you look for the Guadirikiri Cave? You look for their souls?"

"Something like that."

* * *

Seeds carried by the wind and washed ashore by storm tides had found purchase on the island's shores and randomly rooted in clumps, like a poorly planned obstacle course. Maybeck now lay beneath the shade of one of these bushes. Surrounded by a thicket of stickers, engulfed by the unrelenting heat from a steadily rising sun, he kept his eye on Guadirikiri cave. Its similarity to Jess's drawing was unmistakable.

He was glad he'd chosen to be dropped off up the road. Another taxi waited in the sand parking lot. Maybeck had already jumped to the conclusion that this taxi had brought the Overtakers—to Guadirikiri, a cave not on the tourist list of the top five sightseeing attractions. But Maybeck was here; his moment had arrived.

Bugs swarmed him, landed on his arms and neck. He fanned them away, but they drove his impatience to a barely controlled restlessness. He could not stay hidden much longer. He was going to have to move.

The cave entrance was concealed within a towering set of rocks, accessed by a concrete staircase that, unfortunately, looked nothing like the painting of the steps in the journal. Other outcroppings of rock rimmed the area, like spaceships that had crashed in a sand-swept desert.

Maybeck swatted away the black bugs, rose, and ran to the next clump of shrubbery and thorn. As he moved, he saw a person, crouched and running toward him. He tightened his fists and fixed his feet squarely, so that even squatting, he'd have a firm base for fighting.

Storey Ming slid in next to him.

"How did you—?"

"It's a long story," Maybeck said. "Later."

"They're in there!"

"I kinda figured," he said. "How many?"

"Two women. Two guys," she said.

"Are those steps the only way in?" Maybeck asked.

"Yes. There are these erosion holes up top, but I

don't recommend them. They're way too high. We'd make a scene."

"You've been watching?"

"I heard them talking. The women, not the guys."

"What were they saying?"

"Not sure. It was weird, like old ladies arguing."

"Can we get in there without being seen?" Maybeck asked.

"We can try."

With his attention moving between the parking lot, the steps, and the cave entrance, Maybeck shielded his eyes from the sun.

"The driver?"

She said, "Asleep, with his seat laid back."

"Good. Okay. So, I'll check out the entrance. You chill. If it looks good, I'll signal you."

"Fine, but we go in together," Storey said.

"You realize how stupid that would be?" Maybeck said. "If I'm caught, I need you to get me out."

"Strength in numbers."

"Battle tactics," he countered.

"It's a deep cave with a bunch of rooms. If you don't signal me to join you one minute after you go inside, I'm going to drop in."

"You said that would make a scene."

"Yeah, I did, didn't I?" Storey said proudly.

16

THE STAIRS HAD BEEN CARVED out of the rock that formed the cave. Maybeck stopped near the top, made himself flat against the stone, and edged closer to get a look inside.

Storey Ming had hinted to Finn that the 2.0 upgrade was beta testing for a second generation of DHIs, that Finn and the others were about to be "retired" and replaced. Standing there, about to enter a cave infested with bats that supposedly embodied the souls of dead slaves, Maybeck saw a miniature Disney Channel blimp in the distance and was reminded how much he liked being a Keeper. Being part of Disney had made him famous, had given him a sense of real purpose. The idea of returning to his "normal" life really wasn't what he hoped for.

Pushing the thoughts away, he slipped around the rock and into the mouth of the cave.

Dark. Cool, almost cold.

He heard the voices that Storey had mentioned, but they were a long way off.

The awful smell hit him immediately: bat guano.

Shafts of light streamed through the overhead holes. It was like entering a slab of Swiss cheese; he'd gone from daylight to dusk. It was hard to see more than a few yards in any direction.

Maybeck cautiously continued inside, dodging stalagmites that rose from the sand floor like melted candles. If Storey jumped down onto one of those, she'd be killed.

He hurried back to the entrance and signaled. She joined him a moment later. Together, they crept quietly forward toward a second "room." *Darker. Colder.* The sickening smell grew more intense; Maybeck's sandal squished into a deep pile of guano. He thought he might puke.

They followed the cave wall slightly to the left and lower, the darkness swallowing them. The overhead holes emitted marginal amounts of sunlight, barely penetrating the gloom.

Maybeck steered Storey away from a cone of this faint light, moving them deeper into the dark. He took the long way around this second room, ducking under stalactites that hung down like stone icicles.

As the ceiling grew progressively lower, the distant voices grew progressively louder. Here, the stalactites reduced the clearance to five feet, forcing Maybeck and Storey to weave in between. With the eerie gray light, it was like trying to see through smoked glass.

But there was enough light to see the shapes of two women.

Storey touched Maybeck's arm and turned him. She pointed to herself and then at the two women who were crouched, talking.

Before Maybeck could register if she was asking or telling, Storey was on her stomach, crawling through the sand and guano. She reached the far side of the "room" and held to its edge, trying to get near enough to overhear what they were to up to.

Maybeck felt worthless, like he should do something to help. He didn't appreciate Storey's tricking him like that, but he knew better than to follow. There were other words for guano, after all.

He carefully dodged the rock icicles that hung from the ceiling, moved to the nearest wall, and placed his back against it, wishing his eyes would adjust to the light. After another thirty seconds of watching Storey, who was nothing but a dark, slithering shadow, he realized his eyes *had* adjusted—there just wasn't much light back here. It was about one birthday candle shy of pitch-black.

Storey got closer still.

Whatever was being said by the two women sounded like gibberish, all grunts and chants. Maybeck couldn't tell who it was. Maleficent? The Evil Queen? It might have been a couple of tourists, for all he knew. Maybe he and Storey had gone to all this trouble over a pair of old ladies from the ship!

That was when he spotted a second moving shadow. This one was standing almost upright and moving through the stalactites *across* the cave in the direction of where Maybeck had last spotted Storey.

The new shadow paused. It, too, vanished a moment later, a trick of the low light. Maybeck dropped to his hands and knees and, despite the bat guano, crawled toward where he'd lost the standing shape only moments before. His fingers sank into the gooey stuff, unleashing the worst smell—a combination of outhouse and puke. He held his breath and tightened his throat to keep from hurling. Trying to see between the stalactites was like trying to see with a comb in front of your eyes; they created optical illusions of impenetrable walls; they looked like spears, knives, icicles, and snakes. Maybeck didn't want to run into the shadow-shape guy—if it even had been a guy. Maybe it was nothing but an illusion.

Pulling into a squat, Maybeck slowly stood, an inch at a time. A blob of darkness moved, only feet from him. It moved again, toward where he'd last seen Storey. With her attention on the two women, she wouldn't see this man—if that's what it was—coming for her.

Maybeck took a step forward. What he'd been look-ing at *was* a shadow.

But to his left, less than three feet away, stood a man.

Looking right at him.

* * *

Up close, Maybeck could see that the guy was Joe College, the one who'd helped attack them backstage. One of the zombified Overtakers. Blond, tall, and fit, he had the clean-cut look of a Cast Member and was dressed as one, in khaki shorts and a white polo.

The guy swung a club up and into his grip, a string loop holding it to his wrist. He handled it in a con-trolled, practiced way, striking Maybeck on the shoulder and dropping him to one knee.

Maybeck's shoulder was numb. He found himself unable to move his arm.

The club was raised again. It was coming for his head.

And then Joe College was hit from behind and knocked off his feet, revealing Storey, suspended from a pair of stalactites, which she'd used as handles in order to elevate and kick.

From the recesses of the dark cave came Maleficent's crackling voice.

Joe College got to his feet again, directly between Maybeck and Maleficent, raised the club—and turned into a huge, hairy crab.

He'd intercepted Maleficent's transfiguration spell.

The crab, easily the size of a cafeteria tray, landed on its back.

"Ew," Storey said, now on her feet.

She scooped up sand and guano, packed it into a snowball, and flung it at Maleficent, forcing the dark fairy to duck out of its way. But not before Maleficent lit a fireball in her hand.

The cave came alive with a million shadows thrown by the stalactites. The floor and walls shifted in a disorienting dance of darkness and light.

To Maleficent's side stood Tia Dalma, shorter, darker, and holding a tiny rag doll in her hand. She stabbed the doll.

Maybeck screamed and twisted.

Tia Dalma stabbed the doll a second time.

Maybeck roared and buckled over, holding his stomach.

Storey grabbed on to him. "Run!" she said.

He limped forward. She steered him through the maze of ceiling spears. He buckled again. His right leg dragged behind him, stiff and unusable.

Then, as quickly as it hit him, he recovered. He was

more surprised than anyone. "I'm good!" he gasped.

"Not so good," Storey warned.

All around them the stalactites transformed: no longer calcified stone but a thousand snakes hanging by their tails.

Maybeck's pain had disappeared because Tia Dalma had changed tactics, casting a curse that endangered both of them, not just Maybeck.

Storey was lifted off her feet. She was hanging by her throat, a snake coiled around her neck. The snake constricted, lifting Storey higher, choking her more fully. Leaping up, Maybeck forced his fingers between the snake and Storey and pulled. It was like trying to uncoil a steel cable. Storey's face bulged like an overinflated pool toy. It was no use—the snake wasn't going to let go.

Maybeck took hold just behind its head. The snake didn't like that. It flexed and pulled. In doing so, it loosened its hold on Storey, who drank in a gulp of much-needed air. Maybeck pulled hard, twisting the snake's head at the same time as he unwrapped it from Storey's neck. It came free.

Storey fell to the sand, coughing. But breathing.

Maleficent, holding the burning orb, marched steadily toward them.

Storey and Maybeck crawled away, keeping low to avoid the dangling snakes.

"Oh, please!" Maleficent called out. "Are we so limited in our thought?"

A hundred snakes dropped to the sand, writhing and coiling. Maybeck started dancing from foot to foot, shifting wildly, terrified. Storey grabbed him and tried to climb up him to get her feet higher.

Maybeck eased her back to the sand. "Hang tough." He knew this was one of those defining moments, his chance to prove himself. He sucked it up and shook off his outward fright.

"Perplexing, isn't it?" Maleficent said.

Maybeck dove, took hold of one of the snakes, and threw it at Maleficent—more out of fear than heroics, but he wasn't ever going to admit that.

Maleficent threw a transfiguration spell. The snake became a harmless length of rope, and she caught it with her free hand.

Tia Dalma strode up behind Maleficent.

"How you feel now, me boy? Eh?" She stuck the doll with a pin.

Maybeck twisted, moving in inhuman ways that seemed sure to break his limbs.

"Stop it!" Storey shouted.

"Now?" Tia Dalma said, delivering more of her voodoo.

Maybeck folded backward, screaming. Storey

feared the next pin would break him in half.

"Run out of fire, old lady?" A girl's voice echoed through the cave.

"Charlie?" a tortured Maybeck whispered.

Charlene dropped through a ceiling hole in the next room, sticking a perfect landing. Irate, Maleficent wound up and threw the fireball in Charlene's direction. Charlene cartwheeled. The fireball missed and ricocheted off the cave's ceiling in a shower of sparks.

In that moment, two things happened:

The fireball caused the snakes to release and slither away, clearing a path to the exit. And as the fireball exploded into the ceiling, ten thousand bats took flight.

Maleficent, blinded by the swarm, spoke a curse that turned a thousand of the feckless bats into rats.

Tia Dalma cursed at Maleficent. "Rats? You make the rats?"

"Children hate rats."

"I no like the rats, neither, you lizard-skinned fairy!"

"You shut your trap, or I'll turn you into one yourself."

"You talk like that, missy; I give you the gift of pain. Pain like none you felt."

For Maybeck, Charlene, and Storey, escaping the

cave was like trying to run underwater. The churning, screeching, flapping bats were like windblown leaves, batting against faces and arms, making it hard to see, to breathe. The rats crawling on the floor only made matters worse; no foothold was secure. The three teens held their breath, squinted, and dashed for the entrance. Maybeck hollered as he ran. Charlene and Storey covered their faces, peering through the cracks between their fingers.

Gasping for air, they followed the bats out the cave, bursting into the sunlight. There, twenty feet away, a Japanese tour group that had gone off-map cowered back from the black wave escaping the cave. Without noticing Charlene, Storey, and Maybeck, the tourists ran for their mini-bus. The kids headed for the street and Maybeck's taxi.

"Where did you come from?" Maybeck asked Charlene. Looking at her, he couldn't help the huge smile breaking out on his face.

"My first cave was no good, but my driver recognized the sketch. Sorry I was late."

"Me, too."

They dove into the cab and slammed the door shut. The driver came awake, banging his head against the steering wheel and sounding the car horn.

Looking back, Maybeck saw Maleficent at the

mouth of the cave, bats flooding out past her. She swiped her cape up, posing for the running tourists.

The taxi sped away.

"So?" Maybeck asked Storey.

"It was some kind of ceremony or ritual," Storey said. "Tia Dalma was crouched over a pile of bones. She was burning a bird's nest, or maybe twigs? I couldn't see that well in that weird light. She was chanting and kind of half-singing, and Maleficent said nothing. Just stood there, watching her."

The driver was turned, listening to Storey.

"Drive!" Maybeck shouted. "Fast!"

The taxi driver sneered. The cab gained speed.

"And there was this yellow flower," Storey said. "It seemed like that was what the crazy lady was focused on."

"A key flower?" the driver said, his eyes locked on theirs in the rearview mirror. "You actually saw a key flower?"

"Yellow," Storey said. "The only flower I saw."

The driver nodded. "You are special, missy. And so very lucky! A key flower! Imagine!"

"I take it, it's special," Maybeck said.

"Special?" The driver scoffed. "Only blooms between a new moon and a full eclipse. You tell me, mister. Special?"

"They picked it," Storey said. "They did their little ceremony, and they picked it."

The driver's eyes filled with terror. "They killed a key flower?"

He sounded horrified.

"What?" Maybeck said.

The driver shook his head, refusing to answer.

* * *

Finn and Willa reboarded to the ship after Philby, but before the others. While Philby returned to his stateroom to review the ship's security video for Luowski and the stolen computer, Finn and Willa watched for their friends on the dock over the stern rail of Cabanas restaurant.

"Have you kissed her?" Willa asked.

"W . . . h . . . a . . . t . . ?"

"Amanda. Have you guys kissed?"

"We barely even talk anymore. Why are you asking me this?"

"Conversation breaks the tension. We all need conversation."

"You need your head examined," Finn said.

"It's a simple enough question. Have you kissed her?"

"Yeah. I guess so."

"You *guess*!? Was it that bad? Seriously?"

"I didn't say it was bad." Finn felt like jumping over the rail.

"You don't sound too impressed."

"I've kissed her. Okay, Willa?"

"It was just okay?"

"Stop messing with me." Finn peered over the edge at workers sitting on a plank suspended by ropes, washing the hull.

"I'm sure it was more than okay for Amanda. Same for Charlene."

"What's Charlie got to do with this?"

"Are you that blind?"

"She likes Maybeck."

"You got that right. She *likes* Maybeck."

"Get your head in the game," he said.

"There's one checkpoint, Finn. How difficult is it to watch one checkpoint?"

There was a moment of awkward silence.

"The silent treatment is killing Amanda," Willa said. "You know that, don't you?"

"That's ridiculous. She's barely even spoken to me lately."

"What's she supposed to say? 'Hey, Finn, I'm crushing on you big-time, and the way you gawk at Storey and the way you treat me leaves me in tears and unable to sleep at night'? That?"

"Oh . . . come on!" Finn said.

Willa rolled her eyes at him. "Seriously? Get . . . a . . . clue."

The Disney Channel mini-blimp passed over the ship for maybe the sixth time. Passengers waved up at it.

"Do they have any idea," Finn said, "that it's a drone? That it's way too small to carry even a pilot?"

"They probably think it's filming them," Willa said, scoffing.

"Yeah, right. Boneheads."

"You should say something," Willa said. "To Amanda. And it should start with 'I'm sorry.'"

"For what?"

"Take your pick. Hurting her feelings? Not speaking to her? Being a boy?"

"Good one."

They stood there for a long while before Willa spoke again.

"What do you suppose it means if they get a computer on board?"

"That the OTs become impossible to stop. Or nearly impossible."

"Because of 2.0."

"Yes."

"But if Amanda's 'pushing' tires her out when she's

crossed over, doesn't that mean Maleficent's powers would tire her DHI out, too?"

"No. Pushing tires Amanda anytime. Don't confuse that with Maleficent throwing spells. We need to accept that with Maleficent in 2.0, there's basically nothing we can do to stop her."

Willa hesitated before speaking. "You don't suppose the Imagineers *want* the OTs getting hold of 2.0, do you? Like, what if they want to test how invincible or how vulnerable 2.0 makes you? It's not like we're going to attack each other, right? There's really no way to test that side of the upgrade without giving us a 2.0 opponent."

"Do not say that stuff."

"I'm just wondering."

"Wayne would never do that. We're not guinea pigs."

"Are you sure?"

A boy stepped up alongside Finn and leaned against the stern rail.

"There's a Cast Member making the rounds that I don't trust. He'll be here any minute."

Finn looked over at the boy.

"Dill!"

Dillard looked older and more serious than normal. He also looked *thinner*. A *lot* thinner. Maybe he'd been wearing baggy clothes the last time he'd seen him, but the change was drastic.

"You should get going."

"It *was* you at the Sail-Away."

Dillard smiled at Willa. "Hi. We met before." He offered his hand, and the two shook.

"Yes," Willa said.

"Wayne sent you," Finn said.

"Wanda. As your guardian angel."

"Alone?" Finn asked. Storey had already told him about Kenny and Bart; now he was beginning to see a pattern to Wayne's bigger plan to protect his team of Keepers.

"Alone. Listen, the aft staircase is safe. Head over to the starboard side of the restaurant. The guy's searching the port side."

"Ah . . ."

"You can thank me later. I'll stall him," Dillard said. He left, heading for the restaurant. A moment later they heard a crash. Someone's tray had spilled.

"We'd better get out of here," Finn said.

17

SHOOTING A DISNEY CHANNEL 365 while on a moving ship containing three thousand passengers is a study in "controlled chaos." In this case, the chaos was controlled by the film director, Andy Meyers. The handsome, dark-eyed man was joined by Jodi Bennett, the Disney Cruise Line executive, a kind-faced woman whose managerial and organizational skills rivaled those of an army general.

Andy won the attention of Charlene and Willa with "Hello." This was the fourth Disney Channel 365 the Keepers had shot; Charlene and Willa both had barely disguised crushes on Andy.

Maybeck, forever a thorn in Andy's side, catered to the fans who gathered around, turning a deaf ear to direction while offering autographs and smiling for photo ops. Finn reluctantly tried to help Andy keep the group under control, while Philby busied himself with studying the camera and lighting gear and interacting with the five-person film crew.

The location of the morning sun required them to shoot on Deck 12 aft, starboard side. A half-dozen tripods connected by dozens of thick black cables awaited the Keepers.

Andy barked out instructions to Finn, Willa, and Charlene, speaking loudly enough for Maybeck and Philby to hear him.

"The first scene we're going to shoot is where the five of you are talking excitedly about everything cool on the *Dream*."

"Remember," Jodi said, "not 'the *Dream*,' but 'the *Disney Dream*.' Very important."

Andy continued. "Near the end of the shot, Maleficent is going to make a cameo appearance behind you. You guys will freak out, she'll throw a spell—" He paused. "Then I think Charlene, you will catch Willa as she faints. Finn, you run toward Maleficent as she hurries off screen."

He stared at Finn's long face.

"What?" Andy asked. "We're going to turn Willa into a bouquet of flowers in post-production. Charlene ends up catching a bunch of flowers. It'll be good, you'll see."

"Maleficent?" Finn said.

"Oh, come on! The big evil fairy? You're talking to a guy who deals with special effects on a daily basis. You're going to try to sell me that the Imagineers have figured out how to allow your brain function to control a hologram while you're *asleep*? Uh-huh. Look, I'm in on the gag, Finn. Don't worry, it's safe with me."

"But Maleficent," Finn said, realizing Andy was a lost cause.

"I'm shooting an interstitial for the Channel. I've got a casting call for Maleficent, who is currently down in wardrobe and styling, and as much as I'd love to play along with the whole"—he drew air quotes—"'Keepers thing,' we're burning daylight. 'Kay? So let's get in a couple run-throughs before the talent arrives."

"The talent. Right," Finn said. He'd lost Maybeck to the adoring crowds, and Philby to the lighting grip, but he addressed Willa and Charlene. "The Green Machine is scheduled for the next shot."

"Green Machine?" the lighting man inquired, overhearing. "Those smoothie drinks? Blue Machine. Red Machine. They got a green one now?"

"Something like that," Finn said as his eyes met Willa's.

Jodi overheard Finn, saw the troubled look in his eyes, and consulted her clipboard. "Andy . . . this character appearance . . . she wasn't in the final script."

Andy looked up from his clipboard of notes. "Yeah, I know. But she's in the sides now, so we're shooting it."

"I should have heard about this," Jodi said, approaching him.

"Reach Storey Ming," Finn whispered to Willa. "Have her check the break room, make sure we're getting the Cast Member character, not . . . our friend."

"I'm on it."

He asked Charlene to get Maybeck away from his fans.

"Philby!"

Philby joined Finn. "I know my lines. I'm good," he said.

Finn told him about the addition of Maleficent to the scene. "We need to think fast."

"We've got nothing!" Philby said. "We're totally exposed out here."

Indeed, with the passengers held back from the film shoot, it left the small film crew and the five Keepers isolated in an empty area of open deck with nothing but some tripods, lights, and cameras to hide behind.

Charlene returned with Maybeck.

"Guys," Maybeck said, "if she throws a fireball, we're toast. As in, crispy. She misses us? She's going to hit *them*." He indicated the dozens of fans and their parents, held back by crew members.

"We're aware of the situation," Finn said.

"Storey's heading to the break room." Willa wore her concern openly.

"Okay everyone!" Andy called out above the sound

of the wind from the moving ship. "Places! Let's do a run-through ahead of the talent!"

"The 'talent,'" Willa whispered. "Now, that's just precious."

* * *

Storey Ming reached the bulletin board in the I-95 crew corridor and read the day's itinerary. Her plum-colored painted nail traced across the matrix of boxes, stopping at the column labeled "Character Calls."

Chip and Dale (BR3M, A, 8:00am) . . . Belle (BR 3F, MM, 9am) . . . Maleficent (BR11A, D12aft, 8am). Break Room 11A, Deck 12 aft, 8am

This appearance accorded with the video shoot now under way. Confirmation of a Cast Member playing the Maleficent character lowered Storey's anxiety—it seemed less likely this was a sneak attack by the OTs.

She texted Willa:

on way to break room. M appearance confirmed.

In the break room, she swiped her ID card over the reader, pushed the lever, and banged her face on the door. It hadn't opened. Storey swiped her ID a second time. The small light on the card reader: *red.*

She knocked loudly. The door had to be privacy-locked from the inside. No answer. She knocked again. And again.

A DHI could lock the door from the inside and then step *through* it, leaving the room sealed along with whoever was inside, like the Cast Member Maleficent, Storey thought.

DANGER!

Her fingers hovered over the Wave Phone's keypad. How far did she dare to go?

Malef possible DHI

* * *

"Code red from Storey," Willa whispered to Philby, being sure to keep her lips still. She didn't want Andy screaming at her.

The five Keepers were lined up against the starboard rail, a pale trace of sun skimming off the waves. It was too tranquil a setting for the suggestion of any kind of danger.

"The shot is this," Andy said. "First, Finn's line about how every day is a beautiful day on the *Dream*—"

"The *Disney Dream*!" Jodi called out.

"The *Disney Dream*," Andy repeated. "Okay.

Charlene, you come back with 'magical'; then Maybeck's line; Philby checks his watch—we're going to use some CGI there to make it glow or something—and then Willa, you spin your head around to see Maleficent. Finn, you give the line about running for it. Philby hoists the *Return*"—a film crew member handed Philby the prop— an automobile remote—"and then hold positions. In post we're going to fade you out like holograms. Got it?"

"This is just a walk-through?" Finn said.

"A run-through. Yeah."

"No Maleficent yet," Willa clarified.

"You're trembling, I suppose?" Andy was an incredibly nice guy. He just didn't get it.

"Yes, as a matter of fact," Willa said. She held her hand out; her fingers shook.

"You're safe with me!" Andy cracked himself up. His crew laughed with him.

The Keepers practiced their lines and moves four times, with small adjustments made by Andy after each new pass.

"If she's back there by the time you turn around . . ." Finn said privately to Willa.

"Yes. It'll be too late."

"Can Storey Ming get up here?"

"And do what? She thinks Maleficent may have crossed over."

Finn looked dumbstruck. "This is not good."

"Okay, everyone! This time's for real!" Andy shouted.

The makeup artist, Nichole, rushed into frame, touching up hair and patting noses with white sponges.

"You guys are sweating like you just ran a marathon," she said.

"No need for nerves," Andy said, playing the coach. "You've done this dozens of times."

If you only knew, Finn thought.

Philby caught Finn's attention and pointed to two tripods supporting light panels. His hand signal told Finn to take the panel to the left. But take it where? How? Finn wondered.

"The blind leading the *blind*, eh, Andy?" Philby called out to the director while looking at Finn. He was trying to communicate something. Finn shook his head; Philby pantomimed the motion of twisting something. "On the back," he mouthed, hoping Finn could read his lips.

"Stand by!" Andy said. "Roll cameras."

The two cameramen called back, "Speed!"

"Action!"

That word jogged Finn's thought: Philby hadn't been clowning around with the lighting crew; he'd been figuring out how to operate their equipment.

Light panels. Turn knob. Blind leading the blind.

Finn understood.

"Action," Andy called out. Finn faced the camera.

"Hey, guys! Every day's a *Disney Dream*, every meal a banquet when you're cruising with the Disney Cruise Line!"

"A *Disney Dream*?" Charlene said on cue. "It's *Disney Magic*."

"Or," said Maybeck, "a *Disney Fantasy*. From the Caribbean to the Mediterranean, you've never cruised like this."

"It's time," Philby said, checking his watch, "to welcome you aboard!"

That cued Maleficent to enter the shot. Willa turned simultaneously.

"Oh, no!" she said, reciting the memorized script. "Look who's here!"

The five Keepers looked back at once.

Maleficent stood at the rail, her black and purple robes swirling in the wind, her green index finger pointing skyward into a stunningly blue, serene sky.

Finn spotted at once what was missing. Maleficent had no handler. All Cast Members playing Disney characters were accompanied by a fellow Cast Member guide whenever appearing in public. The fact that Maleficent lacked a handler suggested she was not a Cast Member playing her character. She was the real thing. Or a 2.0 hologram of the real thing.

Willa and Finn took off for the lighting panel nearest the railing. Maybeck and Charlene dove for the tripod closest to them.

Willa aimed the panel higher while Finn found and twisted two knobs on the back. Light burst from the panel, like a car switching to high beams. Maybeck and Charlene did the same. Maleficent cried out, trying to shield her eyes.

As much as Philby had annoyed Finn lately, the idea of blinding Maleficent was a stroke of genius. Even holograms had to see.

"What the—?" Andy managed to say as the Keepers ran toward him. Charlene hooked Andy's arm and dragged him with her. Each of the Keepers snagged other members of the film crew.

It sounded like a jet had broken the sound barrier somewhere up in the clear blue sky. Maybeck looked up and over his shoulder.

He hollered, "Hit the—"

An explosion rocked the deck as a bolt of lightning struck. Sparks flew from the film crew's gear.

Maybeck shoved the cameraman aside to safety, crossed through the smoke, and threw a football block on Charlene and Andy just as a second spike of lightning struck.

Maybeck screamed and lay flat. Gray smoke swirled.

Passengers in the ship's swimming pools cried out. Parents grabbed their children and ran for cover.

As he was knocked off his feet by the concussion of the lightning strike, Finn looked in the direction of Maleficent. She was gone.

Returned, he thought.

His head thumped against the deck, and his eyes found a piece of the staircase that led to the AquaDuck—the world's first enclosed waterslide on a cruise ship. He saw bare feet running up the stairs. He stared at the steps for a good long time, finally making the connection to the illustration in the journal.

Something nagged at him: stairs? steps? bare feet? He couldn't place it.

He also spotted something else, something more sinister: a black crow on the rail of the upper deck from which the fireworks were launched. Diablo, Maleficent's sidekick.

The crow lifted its beak and cawed shrilly.

What happened next made Finn's blood run cold. He'd seen such scenes in movies: the boy and girl high on a skyscraper roof, the bad guys coming after them and then, from out of nowhere, helicopters surface from below, rising high, searchlights aimed at the bad guys.

But this wasn't helicopters. And no bad guys were chasing the Keepers. It was frigate birds—long-winged black seabirds with white necks and heads. The birds' five-foot wingspans were oddly angular, like something attached to a stealth fighter. First, there were five or six, then twenty, then fifty or more, rising into view from below the deck.

Diablo cawed twice, sharply. In unison, like a squadron of aircraft, the frigate birds angled up, catching the ship's wind and racing skyward.

Finn called out loudly, "RUN . . . FOR . . . IT!"

The others had rolled and tumbled in reaction to the lightning strikes. Finn spotted and crawled to Maybeck who lay still on the blackened deck. Finn shook Maybeck, but the boy was unconscious—*or worse.*

A crew member, a college aged boy, knelt by Finn. "I'm trained in CPR! I've got this!"

"You sure?"

The boy pointed up. "Take cover!"

Finn saw the frigate birds poised to strike.

"FOL—LOW ME!" Finn shouted, rising to his feet as he searched for someplace safe from the birds. The obvious choice was the nearest door—the door through which Maleficent had come—but something told Finn that was what he was supposed to choose, that Maleficent had made sure it would not open, leaving the Keepers exposed as frigate food.

Instead, Finn crossed the deck toward . . . the stairs

to the AquaDuck. Where better to avoid a bird strike than inside an acrylic tube? He glanced back: others followed, including Andy and his crew.

The frigate birds dove in concert, as if something—or someone—were controlling them. They tucked their wings back as though they were diving for a fish in the ocean, increasing their speed tenfold, their black, beady eyes trained not on fish, but on the heads of the four teenagers.

"DOWN!" shouted Philby.

The kids and the film crew all ducked at once. The first wave of frigates arrived. Several missed their targets, crashing into the deck in an eruption of feathers. A beak grazed Finn's right shoulder, tearing his shirt, opening up his flesh. He grabbed the bird's wing and flung the creature away. It spun in a loop and splashed into the pool.

Charlene was down, a bird tangled in her blond curls. The frigate pecked at her scalp, the blood turning her hair pink. Finn grabbed the flapping bird and choked it with his bare hands until its talons released the knot of blond hair; he threw it into a wall with enough force to send feathers floating in the air. He and Charlene pulled another frigate off Willa, as Andy suddenly turned hero, waving his arms and fending off the next wave of diving birds like a one-man antiaircraft gun.

"Go!" Andy roared. His arms bled from taking direct hits, but he stood his ground, knocking the birds out of the air like it was a video game.

"Come on!" Finn hollered. Andy's crew, Willa, Philby, and Charlene bounded up the stairs. Andy went down behind them. Finn stopped and hurried back. He fought through the flapping wings, found the man's hand and grabbed hold. Finn pulled Andy out from beneath the cloak of black feathers and sharp beaks.

Finn took a shot to the head. Another to his shoulder. Andy steadied him, the man's face pecked and bleeding. Together they entered the covered part of the stairs that climbed to the starting platform for the AquaDuck waterslide. It sounded as if they were suddenly inside a kettle drum as the birds collided outside. Finn looked back to see scores of the black birds dropping to the stairs and cartwheeling down lifelessly.

For a moment it felt safe. They caught their collective breath.

"Thanks," Andy said, gasping as he bent to grab his knees.

"You saved us," Finn said.

"Not the way it felt when I was under that pile."

The lights went out. At least that was how it seemed to both Finn and Andy. But the AquaDuck's stairway was lit only by natural light. Light now blocked by a thousand beating wings.

If the first two waves of frigate birds had seemed like an attack, this was an invasion. This was a dam bursting. No longer dozens, but hundreds—thousands!—of the enormous black birds came at Finn and Andy like a wall of white-headed hatred. Beaks outstretched, the flock filled every gap of fresh air.

"RUN!" the two men cried, taking two stairs at a time.

They reached a landing that carried a bunch of signs and climbed the next set of stairs, already shouting. "GO! GO! GO!"

"You can't do that!" an adult's voice called out, his words drowned by splashing.

Finn made the mistake of looking back: ten thousand black eyes coming at him at sixty miles an hour.

"Dive, man! Dive!" Andy called out to the Cast Member whose job it was to distribute the ride's inflatable rafts. There was no time for rafts, though, as Willa and the others had demonstrated, entering headfirst into the slide's acrylic tube. Though completely against the rules—rules the Cast Member was there to enforce—Andy glanced up to see a wall of pointed beaks heading up the stairs at him, and dove into the waiting tube.

Finn and Andy followed, facedown like they were

bodysurfing. The water was warm and moving incredibly fast. They flew out *over* the ocean, twelve stories below, and then shot in a straight line for the huge screen on Deck 11. Birds collided with the clear plastic wall of the water tube. The wall of frigates behind them hit a dead end on the upper platform, self-destructing as they piled into one another.

The water course suddenly dropped out from under Finn, then pushed him up an incline and sent him into darkness as he traveled behind the Funnel Vision screen. Another turn. Daylight. A straightaway. Birds dropped from the sky, imploding on the plastic tube and falling dead to the deck below. Finn tucked into a ball and managed to ride feet first the rest of the way. The AquaDuck spit him out into an open trough where Andy's crew, Willa, Charlene, and Philby were just climbing out, soaking wet.

"VIPs or not, you're not going anywhere!" shouted a Cast Member. "You're all barred from using the AquaDuck for the remainder of the cruise. Hand over your room cards this instant!"

The water had washed the blood from Finn and Andy. Neither was as badly injured as it had appeared.

"We'll have to do that later," Finn told the man.

"Back to Maybeck!" he shouted to his fellow Keepers. They took off running—also not allowed.

"They're calling it blue-sky lightning," Philby said. The Keepers had gathered in the ship's Health Center—its hospital. Maybeck was stretched out on a table wearing a blood pressure cuff and other sensors. He remained unconscious. The Keepers had been left alone with him. They were supposed to be shooting more footage for the 365, but Andy and his crew were off, trying to pull together their damaged gear and explain to the Disney Channel execs what had happened.

"What's that supposed to mean?" Willa said.

"It's a weather phenomenon. Weather clouds just over the horizon. The lightning can travel more than twenty miles—including through clear blue sky."

"Come on!" Finn said. "That was no blue-sky lightning. That was Maleficent."

Charlene stood off to the side, biting her hand and trying hold back her sobs. Willa wrapped an arm around her shoulders, unsuccessfully attempting to calm her.

"And they're calling the frigate bird attack a virus," Philby said bitterly. "Like when whales get messed up and beach themselves."

"I'm sure," Willa said.

"They need to explain this, both to themselves and the passengers. They can't very well say Maleficent is out to kill us and that some raven is using seabirds as its air attack force."

"I'll bet they just happen to mention that this is a Kingdom Keepers cruise," Willa said. "You watch, they'll make it sound planned."

"Well, it was planned," said Philby. "Just not by us."

Maybeck twitched and shifted on the table.

Charlene finally spoke, calling for the doctor.

"Hold that arm!" the doctor directed Finn. Together, they held down the unconscious Maybeck.

"Hope!" the doctor shouted. "Restraints!"

Hope, a kind-looking nurse with sandy hair, entered carrying nylon straps. Together, she and the doctor strapped Maybeck down.

"That's awful," Charlene said. "He won't like that!"

"This happens," the doctor explained to the Keepers. "Vivid dreams during a coma. Best if we keep him from rolling off the table and further injuring himself."

"How long is he going to be like this?" Charlene blurted out. She broke out sobbing before the doctor could answer.

"Fifty people die of lightning strikes each year," Philby said calmly. He won the harsh scrutiny of everyone in the small exam room, including the doctor and nurse.

"Which is why," the doctor said, "we should be

glad it wasn't a direct strike. I'm told the lightning hit a tripod next to Terrance. Melted it. The deck being metal . . . Terrance being so close . . . but it wasn't a direct strike. He's in trauma. His body took a heck of a jolt. People recover from comas every day. Sometimes they're two minutes, sometimes two days. The body has to convince the mind it's safe to come out again. You all being here, talking to him, talking near him, that's got to help. He can hear you—at least we believe he can."

"He's going to come around," Finn said.

"We're not done here," Willa said. The others nodded.

The doctor seem poised to say something, but did not speak.

"He's going to be okay," he said finally.

"You can't promise that!" Charlene said.

The doctor eyed her sympathetically.

"What if he's not awake by tonight?" Philby asked.

The doctor considered each of the Keepers individually. "I'm not going to sugarcoat it. The sooner, the better. It gets . . . more delicate . . . the longer he stays asleep."

"And if he's not conscious by the time we reach the canal?" Philby said.

"Let's take it one step at a time." The doctor and nurse left the exam room.

"What was that about?" Charlene asked. "What did he mean?"

"They'll take him off the ship if he's not better."

"No way!" Charlene said, her eyes glassy. "What? Some hospital in Panama?"

"Better than an exam room on a cruise ship."

"We are not leaving him behind!" Charlene shuddered. "That is not happening."

"We're going to do what's best for *him*," Finn said. "Whatever gives Terry the best chance."

"No . . . way . . ." Charlene muttered.

"Like the doc said," Philby said, "one step at a time."

Charlene grabbed Maybeck's hand and squeezed. "Wake up, you idiot! Wake up right now!"

Tears poured down her cheeks.

* * *

A day at sea presented Uncle Bob with his first real chance since sailing from Aruba to follow up on what the two Kingdom Keeper boys had told him. He wanted someone held responsible for the damage to the Buzz Lightyear balloon; and he wanted to pursue the stowaway he and his team believed was linked to the trouble on board.

Determined to get his ship in order, to explain the improbable lightning strike, the bird attack, the reports of a plane on Castaway, he intended to put his security team to the test.

Having briefed the captain, having put them off to random chance—bad luck, something no captain wanted to hear—Uncle Bob now doubted his own explanations. It was one thing to say that blue-sky lightning had struck the *Disney Dream*; but combined with the bird attack, the boys' explanation made more sense than he wanted to admit.

The DHIs had an underground reputation for trouble—company-wide, the various security heads were regularly updated about their activities. Bob knew that there had been skirmishes *of some sort* outside the Engineering Base in the Studios; he had been told these involved the DHIs.

Accepting the reports as factual was another matter.

And yet, coincidence was no longer a viable explanation. It seemed quite possible, even probable, that the Kingdom Keepers were under attack.

Bob couldn't explain it; he didn't want to think about it. He felt foolish for even considering it. But he had no choice. Maleficent's video warning on the first day of the cruise seemed to be coming true. Who would have thought?

The sighting of two Mickeys at once—impossible! The likelihood of a stowaway? It was all fitting together.

The duplicate Mickey had been mean to several kids—an attempt to discredit the character.

As far as Bob was concerned, his ship was not getting taken over by anyone. If he had to give credence to what the boys had told him, then so be it.

Find the stowaway, interrogate him or her, and maybe, just maybe, he would get his ship in order.

To this end he dispatched every available member of this team. Bob had far-reaching powers aboard the ship. With the captain's blessing—and he had it—he could deploy a veritable army.

Members of his security team were sent to once again search areas of the ship for Chernabog or "anything else of a suspicious nature." All Cast Members and crew were reminded to keep watch for unusual activities or individuals. No one was beyond reproach. Uncle Bob wanted this trouble over with.

"What about working with laundry?" Clayton Freeman had come up quickly through the ranks of security. At twenty-four, he was the youngest deputy director in the cruise line's history. Bob had come to trust the young man's "out of the box" ideas.

"I'm listening," Bob said.

"Two suggestions. First, we ask laundry for a full inventory. It's all computerized anyway. What's missing? What sizes? What gender? We know that's probably a big list on any given day, but with the new incentives to turn in your dirty laundry—"

"I like it," Bob said. "They can also tell us who hoards their laundry. If we take those people off the list, maybe we get a missing costume or two, and at least that would tell us the kind of outfit the stowaway could be wearing. What's the second idea?"

"All our costumes and uniforms carry RFTs." Radio frequency tags were tiny computer chips used on the *Dream* to track everything from small children to laundry. "If we add the RFT identification numbers for all missing laundry to the Cadet Monitoring System . . ."

Bob gasped. He got up, walked over and shut the door to his office.

"What you're suggesting . . . It's a violation of privacy."

"Actually, it's not. The Oceaneer cadets already wear wristbands that contain RFTs."

"I know. But we do not employ the Oceaneers."

"So? An RFT is an RFT," Clayton Freeman said. "We reprogram the computer with the laundry codes."

"We would end up with thousands of data points of our crew and Cast Members moving around the ship. So what? It'll just be a pile of useless data. Besides which, the CMS sensors are only on a couple of decks where the cadets spend time. Mainly, Deck Five."

"Yes, but there are others as well: Six, Eleven, Twelve. And don't forget, the monitoring points record the time. Each Cast Member, each crew member can be tied to a particular costume. Those costumes are *only* supposed to be on a given deck when those people are on duty."

Bob looked as if his eyes might pop out of his head. "Someone who's wearing a stolen costume or uniform would have no way of knowing what hours that laundry belongs in service."

"Bingo," Freeman said. "And the system would catch them. At which point, we could track them, and we'd have our stowaways."

"Can we do this, Clayton?"

Freeman looked back at his boss as if to say, *Would I have brought it up if I didn't think we could do it?*

"I want this on the QT," Bob said. "The crew gets wind that we're tracking their movements around the ship, and the union will have my head."

"Understood."

"I like the way you think, Clayton. Fine work."

"Thank you, sir."

"Catch me that stowaway, and I'll put in a good word for you with the people upstairs!"

"Trust me, he's ours!"

18

W ITH THE KEEPERS CONFINED to their staterooms because of Kingdom Keeper DHI activities onboard, Finn and Philby were victims of cabin fever—they took room service breakfast in the stateroom and were basically prisoners until noon, while their Disney hologram guides entertained passengers.

With the advent of the 2.0 upgrade, the Imagineers had rolled out a two-server system. Currently, a company-sanctioned Disney Host Interactive server projected the kids as guides and entertainers in version 1.6; a second, 2.0 cloud-based server was used to project the Keepers during missions. While the two might be able to operate over the same projectors simultaneously, it had never been tried. With their Disney DHIs out on deck, the kids could not be seen. Company policy forbade two of any Disney character to exist at the same time.

Finn opened the stateroom safe and removed the Imagineer journal. He sat on the bed; Philby leaned back on the couch, his laptop out, his feet up on the coffee table.

"When the lightning hit," Finn said, "I was thrown

down, and I ended up looking at the AquaDuck."

"So?"

Finn ignored Philby's rudeness. Philby was tired, as were all the Keepers. Maybeck's condition and their inability to help had put them all in bad moods.

"The AquaDuck stairs, to be more specific." Philby liked things exact, so that was how Finn served it up.

"Is this going somewhere?"

"The stairs in this drawing," Finn said, referring to the journal, "are not stairs. They are steps. There are three of them: as in, three steps."

Philby looked up from his computer. "Okay. I'm listening."

"It was never about buried treasure in a cave. It was about a flower. A key flower, right?"

"Right."

"This part of the journal is an owner's manual."

"To wake up Chernabog. We all agree that's a big possibility."

"The picture is saying: 'There are three steps.'"

Philby set the laptop aside and joined Finn on the bed. He studied the artwork for a long moment, and then shook his head.

"It's too simple."

"This is Walt's journal, don't forget. For the Imagineers, before they were called that. Walt studied magic. If he discovered an ancient way to raise their gods, what would he do?"

"He'd make it simple, but difficult."

"Three steps."

"And you're the reincarnation of Walt, I suppose?"

"That would be Wayne."

They laughed. Philby reached out for the journal; as he did so, a folded piece of paper popped out of his pocket. Philby tried for it, but Finn's arm moved with inhuman speed and seized it.

"What's this?" Finn said.

"It's . . . How did you grab that so fast?"

Finn ignored the question. "This is an e-mail from Amanda."

"Yeah."

"To you, or *us*?"

Philby didn't answer.

"A Jess sketch."

"Correct."

Finn studied it. "A cave, looks like." He turned it slightly; his eye found the date stamp at the top. "Hey! This was sent at 4 a.m. the morning *before* we docked in Aruba."

Philby, being a redhead with a light, freckled complexion, had no chance of disguising a blush.

"She says it's Charlene in the drawing. Again! That

Charlene's the target!" Finn said. Philby jutted out his chin. "Why didn't we see this *before* we went cave hunting?"

"I didn't think it was relevant."

"Is that right? A drawing of a cave, with notes at the bottom about Charlene being hung by a rope. Not relevant?"

"Not a cave. More of a tunnel. We needed all of us."

"What is it with you, anyway?" Finn said. "All the secrecy. The attitude. The lying!" He held up the e-mail as his evidence. "Charlene's obviously their target!"

"Three steps," Philby said. "I like it. Simple. Easy to interpret."

"Don't change the subject," Finn said. "Explain the secrecy."

"I have no idea what you're talking about."

"You have something going with Wayne. Something the rest of us aren't included in."

"You're paranoid."

"It has to do with 2.0," Finn said. "What they have planned."

Philby pursed his lips. "Storey said more than she should have. She does that sometimes."

"Is the mystery girl with the tattoo and red-streaked hair part of this?"

"I don't know her or her role. Honestly, I don't. Neither does Storey."

"But you know Storey Ming." Finn paused. "Did you know her before this trip?"

"We may have met."

"Through Wayne," Finn said.

"You don't have to see it as a conspiracy."

"Don't I? Don't we? Me and the others? You've been acting totally weird, Philby. Like you're running things."

"When we started out—can you remember that far back? We all thought Maybeck would be the techie. But look how things turned out."

"Sure. You're the techie, and you're saying that things change. Big surprise. Are you telling me that the leadership of the Keepers is changing, too?"

"Calm down. Look, who's going to interface the most with the Imagineers and Wayne? Hmm? The techie, right?" The hint of a British accent came out most when Philby acted superior. "Wayne invented the crossover. They'll be studying this stuff for a hundred years. He can put our dream state into a hologram projection. Think about that! That's totally sci-fi, right? But we do it! You, me, the others. It's nuts! Insane! But it's real! You know it. I know it. So, yes, Wayne consults me from to time on technology issues. So sue me."

"Technology issues . . . like 2.0," Finn said, trying to measure Philby's reaction. He saw nothing. The guy was chill.

"Like 2.0."

"Because we're being replaced."

"Have you stopped to think about the ramifications of 2.0? The control that the new software gives us? Remember back when we had to use every ounce of strength to hold off our fear in order to stay *all clear*? But now we don't give it a second thought."

"So?"

"So, the five of us. Now picture fifty. What about five hundred?"

"An . . . army." Finn gasped. "The military wants this?"

"Everyone wants this, Finn. Not just Maleficent and some has-been witches. *Everyone.*"

"The OTs want Chernabog to lead an army?"

"You're not thinking big enough. Let's just say that encrypting 2.0, keeping it safe, is the most important work any of us can do. For now, we need to keep 2.0 protected, and we need to make absolutely certain Maleficent doesn't get her hands on it—or on any one of us."

"She's working for someone?"

"Don't worry yourself with this stuff."

"There you go again," Finn said, "acting so smug, like you know everything."

"If Wayne swore you to secrecy, what would you do?"

Finn thought long and hard. He felt hurt that Wayne had not included him. Hurt . . . and envious.

"I'd worry," he said.

* * *

Charlene and Willa remained by Maybeck's side during the remainder of their confinement for DHI activity.

Maybeck slept. And slept.

"What do you think?" Willa asked.

"About Terry?"

"About the blue-sky lightning," Willa said. "Chernabog being smuggled on board. Maleficent's warnings. All of it."

"What do you mean, what do I think? I hate it."

"I mean: why is it all happening?"

"I don't care. I just want Terry to wake up."

"So you two are for real?" Willa said.

"As real as you and Philby."

"Then you're *not* real." Willa smirked, winning a grin from Charlene. "Philby and I are nothing right now."

"It's all crazy, isn't it?"

"I thought you liked Finn."

Charlene looked over at the sleeping Maybeck. "Yeah? So what?"

"But you like Maybeck better."

"I like Terry different."

"You don't want to kiss Finn."

"I didn't say that."

"You do want to kiss him."

"I didn't say that either."

"Kissing is gross," Willa said.

"You say this because . . . ?"

They both burst out laughing.

"Boys are so weird," Willa said.

"I like boys," Charlene said, "but not that way. Not that way at all. I just like them better than girls. Less drama. They like to do stuff. They like sports. Working out. Stuff I like to do."

"Philby and I think the same way," Willa said. "That's . . . refreshing, I guess."

"'Refreshing,'" Charlene said. "See? That's just not a word I would use. But you and Philby would."

"I suppose."

"That's why you like him."

"I guess," Willa said.

"It's okay to like him," Charlene said. "To want to go out with him."

"I don't want to go out with him. I don't want to like him. The five of us . . . it's like we work together. Right? It's totally consuming, this DHI stuff." Willa hesitated. "To tell you the truth, if this stuff about our being replaced is for real, I won't be complaining. I mean, I love you all. You know that. But these past couple of years, I've had four friends and no life."

"We get free cruises," Charlene said.

"With our parents."

"Hey," Charlene said. "My mom doesn't expect to see me. She knows I'm working and that when I'm not working I'm in Vibe. She's loving this trip, believe me." Charlene paused, and brushed her hand gently across Maybeck's forehead. "For the record: we are not leaving him behind in Panama,"

"The passage is tomorrow morning. We'll reach the Pacific, the Panama side of the canal, at the end of the day around sunset." Willa stared at Maybeck. "Whoa!" She sat forward.

"What?" Charlene asked excitedly.

"How stupid can we be? I mean we've done it before, several times!" Willa was talking to herself. "No reason we couldn't at least try."

"Try *what?*"

"What happens when we're asleep, Charlie?"

Charlene didn't answer.

"We cross over."

Charlene still wasn't getting it.

"Maybeck's *asleep!*" Willa reminded her.

"*O . . . M . . . G!*"

"If Philby turns on the 2.0 server, maybe his DHI appears and we can find him and talk to him. Maybe we can get through to him. Get him to wake up." Willa took a moment to think it through more carefully, and then nodded decisively. "We need to call a meeting."

* * *

At noon, with their DHIs on break for an hour, the Keepers met up in Vibe, the teen-only lounge. They sat off by themselves, wary of OTK spies.

The discussion began with Finn's excitement over the concept of the three steps. This prompted a response from Willa.

"Before I talk about Maybeck, there's something we have to think about," Willa said. "In my Web searches, I read that Aztec priests believed 'a great ongoing sacrifice sustains the Universe.' That almost matches the line in the journal about the gods: 'with their sacrifice, they gave us life.'"

"The OTs are looking to perform some kind of sacrifice?" Philby sounded deeply concerned.

"Three steps," Willa said. "At Castaway, they got a

witch doctor. On Aruba, a key flower. And that leaves a sacrifice. It says it right in the journal."

"'One of you will die,'" Finn said, quoting Luowski—admittedly not the most reliable of sources.

"That's comforting," Storey snapped sarcastically.

"The person sacrificed was often a young woman," Willa said. She looked directly at Charlene.

Finn looked over at Philby, who said nothing.

Finn said, "We received an e-mail from Amanda." He made a point of not indicting Philby in front of the others. "Bottom line is—"

Philby interrupted in a whisper. "It had to do with Aruba, and Aruba's behind us. We will work in *pairs* from now on. We stay out in public—no crew corridors unless absolutely necessary."

Finn boiled. "No, it had to do with Charlene. It showed Charlene in trouble. So we have to at least consider the possibility that she is the one who is meant for the sacrifice."

"We don't have near enough to make that jump," Philby said.

"Tell them about Terry," Charlene said to Willa, attempting to deflect attention from herself—a rarity. But everyone looked at her intently just the same. "Seriously," she said. "Philby's right. Been there, done that. We made it through the cave drama. Let's move on."

206

A long silence settled over the group.

Willa offered her theory about crossing **Maybeck** over while in a coma.

"That's brilliant!" Philby said.

"If we can explain his situation to his **hologram,** then maybe when we return him he can try **harder to** wake up."

"If he were here," Charlene said, "he'd **tell us that's** a stretch."

"It's worth a try," Finn said.

"So, as soon as the ship's DHI server is **down, we** light up 2.0 and try to find Maybeck's DHI."

"We can't afford to wait," Charlene said.

"I think she's right," Willa said.

"Are you kidding?" Philby protested. "**With our** Disney DHIs in use most of the day, we can't **risk trying** to cross him over. It's never been done. It's **too risky.**"

"If there was ever a time to take a risk," **Charlene** said, "it's now."

* * *

The search for Maybeck's DHI began in earnest **the fol-**lowing morning, the first chance Philby had to **switch on** the 2.0 cloud-based server. It was Panama **Canal Day,** meaning the Keepers' DHIs and the Keepers **themselves** had a bunch of separate appearances to make.

As a precaution, the Keepers had all adopted disguises, some more convincing than others. They hoped to move around the ship unrecognized.

"Remember," Philby reminded them, "by noon we have to be out of the disguises for the ribbon cutting."

Finn and Charlene (he didn't want to let her out of his sight) headed to the Atrium photo alcove, where before dinner, families posed in front of various backgrounds. The photo alcove, one of two locations on board the ship that DHI crossovers occurred, had been chosen by Philby to render Maybeck's hologram.

Waiting there, Finn could see worry on Charlene's face—about her own situation or Maybeck's? he wondered. He said, "Even in a disguise, you're way too pretty."

Charlene had her hair up in a bun tucked beneath a *Disney Dream* ball cap. She wore no earrings, and no makeup. She felt ugly.

"I can't say the same for you," she said. "You look *different*."

Finn's disguise consisted of a stupid-looking hat, a Band-Aid on his left cheek, and mirrored sunglasses.

"Isn't there something you can do to make yourself at least a little less pretty?" he asked her. "Don't girls have ways to do that?"

His sincerity caused her chest to tighten. "You really think I'm pretty?"

"Honestly?" Finn said, "you are . . . you look . . . I think you're more *you* without all that stuff on your face."

"Duh. Hence the expression 'natural.'"

"As in: way hotter." Finn blushed. The elevator doors opened; he stepped out and walked away.

Maybe everything was getting better. Charlene didn't believe that a person could change overnight, but in that last meeting, something about Philby seemed different. Like he'd lost at least some of his aloofness and bossiness. The tension between him and Finn had subsided as well, almost wasn't there. She assumed it all had to do with Maybeck's being in trouble. The team came together when in crisis mode.

Finn and Charlene awaited Maybeck's DHI. When it failed to cross over, Finn tried texting Philby but didn't get a reply.

They headed back to stateroom 816.Charlene recalled Willa's words about not "having a life," and frowned. Belonging to something felt good to her.

As they were admitted into the stateroom by Willa, Philby called out.

"So?"

"Nothing," Finn said. "I texted you."

"Texted me? I don't even know where my phone is. My laptop froze. It took me until maybe a minute ago to cross him over."

"Well, we were halfway back here by then. So he crossed over without our being there."

"Terrific!" Charlene said in frustration.

Philby's freckles were covered with foundation; baby powder in his hair turned it a milky strawberry blond. Even without the baseball cap, his own mother wouldn't have recognized him.

Looking up from his laptop, he saw Willa for the first time. She'd been in the room for the past ten minutes.

"You look . . . wow," said an astonished Philby.

"What about Maybeck?" Finn asked. No one seemed to hear him.

"Wow as in good, or wow as in bad?" Willa asked, setting a trap most boys Philby's age would have had no idea was waiting. But Philby was smarter than most, by a long shot. He seemed to understand immediately: if he said she looked prettier, it implied she didn't normally strike him that way; if he said she looked older—which she did—then he was telling her she looked girlish the rest of the time.

"As in, no one will recognize you. That's the point, right? You did a good job."

"Earth to Philby!" Finn said. "What about Maybeck?"

"The fact is," Philby said, "if Maybeck crossed over, no one was there when it happened."

"Because you didn't answer my text."

"It doesn't matter why," Philby said. "It just is."

"Well, if I crossed over feeling like he's probably feeling," Finn said, "the first thing I'd do is look for a place to hide. He couldn't have gone far."

The girls looked toward Philby, expecting him to counter Finn or object as he'd been doing for months.

"Go on," Philby said, acquiescing.

"There isn't a lot of choice of where he can go," Finn said. "He's not going to drag himself up that staircase. And he's not going to get very far across the Atrium without someone seeing him, without someone trying to help—only to find out their hands go right through him. At that point Security's called, I think, and it's Uncle Bob's problem. If Bob spots any of us, or gets hold of Maybeck's hologram . . . He has the authority to shut us down completely. At that point, we're toast."

"They'll shut down our server," Philby said. "We do not want that. Our one chance to defeat the OTs . . . they can't harm us."

"So," Charlene said, recapping, "no stairs, no Atrium. If he sticks to the wall, he could get down to the Shore Excursion Desk. Maybe hide back there—"

"That place is occupied every living second of every living day," Philby said.

"The Royal Palace," Willa said. "It's huge. It's empty a lot of the time. There are waiter stations, tables, a ton of places to hide."

"Great idea!" Philby said, nodding.

"They close up between meals. I know that for a fact," Finn said.

"All the better for hiding," Willa said.

"All the trickier if we're supposed to go looking for him," said Charlene.

"Yes," said Finn, "but we're arriving at the locks— the ceremony. *Everyone* will be out on deck, even the crew."

19

DAZZLED BY RAYS OF SUNSHINE streaming out through a few stray clouds like Hollywood searchlights, the sound of an off-key brass band, and the snap of flags in the wind, the *Disney Dream* crept forward into the waiting mouth of the new locks of the Panama Canal. Governors and politicians had been brought aboard for the inaugural ceremony. A canal pilot controlled the ship while the dignitaries occupied a forward deck just below the bridge, standing with Captain Cederberg in his starched whites, as well as Captains Mickey and Minnie, both dressed in festive south-of-the-border costumes and sombreros.

Over three thousand passengers and crew jammed every available stateroom balcony and open deck on both sides of the eleven hundred and fifteen feet of painted steel. Miniature flags—U.S. on one side, Panama, the other—waved from the ship and ground. Cameras flashed. Video rolled, professional and amateur alike. Tens of thousands of locals cheered.

Among those celebrating was a sturdy girl with dark hair that carried a few streaks of bright red highlights.

While the other passengers were fully focused on the crowds below and on the spectacle, Mattie Weaver was on a mission. It was no easy task studying every face, every profile. She moved like a spy, her arm raised and waving, her eyes never straying from the passengers surrounding her. She moved slowly, one end of a deck to another. Deck 4 to Deck 11. Then 11 to 12. The sports area. The stern. Somewhere she would find him. The allure of the celebration would prove too enticing. He would not have the willpower to resist.

* * *

"We've got him!" Clayton Freeman informed Uncle Bob. The men sat thirty feet below the water's surface in the air-conditioned confines of the Security offices.

With Bob's attention jumping from one closed circuit camera image to another on the five hi-def television screens, with his earbud carrying the voices of twenty members of his staff and crew working to protect the *Disney Dream* on a historic day in foreign waters, with five recent e-mails from the FBI warning of threats to the ship, Bob failed to hear his right-hand man.

"Sir!" Clayton Freeman said, trying again. "I've got the stowaway!"

"What?!" Bob said, practically falling out of the chair as he lunged forward. He pressed a button on a wire and spoke into the radio microphone. "Stand by all for redeployment." To Clayton, he said, "Go!"

"The RFT, sir. The laundry. You remember—"

"I remember!" Bob said. "Tracking the stolen laundry electronically . . . blah, blah, blah . . . As you can see, Freeman, I'm *a little busy* trying to keep my passengers and ships safe from terrorist threats, fake or not."

Thankfully, the FBI listed all five "threats" as "Reduced Risk." The company would not have gone forward with the inaugural had there been any "Legitimate Risk" cautions. Bob rubbed his forehead wearily.

"It's just that—"

"Not now."

"Yes, sir."

"If you can handle it on your own," Bob said, capitulating. He knew Freeman wanted the stowaway as badly as he did—though the timing couldn't have been worse. "So be it."

"Yes, sir! Thank you, sir!"

"Now that you've interrupted me . . . what exactly *do* we have?"

"Vibe, sir. Whoever is wearing that stolen costume entered Vibe five minutes ago."

Bob directed a camera image from Vibe onto the upper right corner of the second screen. The club was empty. He switched views to Vibe's outside deck. It was packed with so many kids that they looked like a single tanned body with several dozen heads.

"Looks like if you hurry," Bob said, "you've got your boy."

"Or girl. Yes, sir."

"Well? Get the lead out!"

"Yes, sir!"

An elated Clayton Freeman hurried from the office.

* * *

Finn and Charlene descended the empty amidships stairs. Everyone was outside. The Keepers were due to be on shore with the captain as the ship reached the lake, about two hours away.

"Storey should be there by now," Finn said, slightly out of breath.

"With Philby and Willa. In the galleys."

"Yes."

Deck 7 . . . a landing . . . Deck 6 . . . another landing . . .

"I lost a bracelet," Charlene said, repeating the excuse they intended to use if caught.

"Correct."

"As if I would ever wear a bracelet."

"What?" he asked.

"I'm not a bracelet girl. Forget it." She kept up with

Finn easily. "They're going to tell us they turn everything in to Lost and Found."

"Yes, and we're going to politely ignore them."

"You think he's hurting?" Charlene asked.

"Maybeck?"

"No, the Pope!"

Deck 5 . . .

Finn stopped abruptly. Charlene bumped into him. For a moment they were extremely close, both breathing heavily, eye to eye. Finn stepped away.

"Yes," Finn said. "I mean, I would think so. Just as I assume Jess was hurting when she returned."

"You can't stop thinking about *her*, can you?"

"Who?"

"Yeah, right," Charlene said.

"Charlie!"

"Don't call me that," she protested. "The others, sure. But not you, okay?"

"Because?"

"It makes me sound like a boy. I don't want you thinking about me as a boy."

Finn swallowed. "O-kay."

"Not ever," she said, closing the distance between them.

"Maybeck," Finn said.

"I *know*," Charlene said breathlessly. She led the

way down to the next landing, then further, to Deck 4.

On Deck 3 they kept their heads down in case there were cameras watching. They moved through the shops toward the Atrium, sticking to the starboard side of the ship. Less busy here.

As they faced the wide-open expanse of the lavish Atrium, Finn threw his arm out like a gate. Not a person in sight. Not a sound or vibration. The ship's propeller was barely turning.

"What?" Charlene said, much too close to his ear. His skin rippled with gooseflesh. *Think!* Finn chastised himself.

"I don't know," he said in a hush.

"Well, that's convincing."

"Something's . . ." he said. "Something's wrong."

"It looks fine to me."

Finn slipped his Wave Phone out of his pocket. He sent a text to Philby:

trap! search is all yours
we forgot about obvious
Char and I on way to med center

"We are?" Charlene said, reading over his shoulder.

"The OTs know Maybeck is down," he said, waiting for her to connect the dots. Searching her eyes. When

218

she failed to look as if she understood, he added, "The DHI appearances are printed in the *Navigator* every day, meaning the OTs know when our holograms are making appearances. That means they also know when we aren't allowed out of our staterooms."

"I still don't—"

"You and Willa were hanging with Maybeck earlier. You were protecting him. But now . . ."

"There's a nurse with him at all times."

"The OTs may be slightly afraid of us. But a nurse? I mean, come on!"

Charlene's face bunched.

Finn nodded. "That's what I'm talking about. This is the perfect time to kidnap him."

Charlene took off running. Finn hurried to catch up, but was no match for her speed.

* * *

Mattie Weaver found Vibe's interior empty except for a Cast Member behind the bar. The outside deck was another matter.

Bodies were crowded together so tightly, you couldn't slip a piece of paper between them.

She drew a deep breath, knowing he was out there, knowing what had to be done.

It was never easy for her. Harder than anyone

knew. That blast of energy, draining and filling her all at once. Like a strobe light flashed in her eyes from an inch away. Like a slap in the face, or a punch in the gut.

Worse, it wasn't so controllable. That's what the freaks who controlled the Fairlies were trying to figure out. How could she harness it? How could they *use* her? At parties for foreign diplomats? In train stations where they suspected a bomber? At political functions? To manipulate the stock market? They *needed* her, and by now they would be looking for her, big-time. For now, Mattie felt safe—though at every port, she panicked, terrified that they'd board, looking for her.

She shook her head clear. She had work to do. The fact that she couldn't control her powers meant that in a flesh jam, like the one out on Vibe's deck, she might experience a dozen connections. More! It would feel like being spun in the dark wearing a blindfold, only to peek out every few seconds. It would make her sick. It would be frightening.

But when . . . if . . . she found *him*, it would all be worth it.

* * *

From Deck 11, passengers waved at the Panamanians greeting them. Crowds estimated at more than ten thousand lined up along the first lock alone.

Cheers rose over the Disney music blaring from shipboard speakers. Disney characters waved down to the crowds.

Both sides shot video and took pictures of the historic event.

Robotic tugs crept forward, matching the ship's crawling speed, keeping it centered in the new, wider canals.

A miniature Disney blimp—an unmanned drone—hummed above the scene. There were many hours yet to go, but if the rest of the day lived up to the start, it was going to be one of the greatest celebrations ever.

* * *

Storey Ming led Philby and Willa down the I-95 corridor, having instilled in them the importance of walking with purpose. If a Cast Member looked lost, he would be easily spotted as an outsider. To give the impression they were old hands, the three carried on a conversation, complaining to one another about not being topside enjoying the festivities. They passed no officers, only other Cast Members who paid no attention to them. Eventually, Storey Ming directed the two into a companionway of steep stairs.

"This is where I leave you. You go down two

landings." She continued with directions to the bakery, from which they could make their way to yet another companionway leading to the ship's stores—the ware-housing of the dry goods.

"I know my way from there," Willa declared. She remembered a visit to the galleys a few days earlier.

"Up to the galley," Storey said.

"Yes."

"The main galley serves both the Royal Palace and the Animator's Palate. You don't belong there, so if someone stops you, tell them Herman sent you on an errand."

"Herman?"

"One of the chefs. No one messes with what Herman wants," Storey said. "He . . . Willa? What's wrong?" The girl had gone an ashen pale.

"Nothing," Willa said, clearly lying.

Philby placed his hand on her shoulder. "It won't happen again. I promise." He explained to Storey, "She and Finn were attacked by doughboys the last time she was in the galley."

"Doughboys?"

"Giant doughboys," Willa whispered. "Freaky doughboys."

"But you all," Storey said, "have been attacked by all sorts of creatures, right?"

"The doughboys are creepy," Willa said. "You know

how some people don't like snakes? Give me a snake any day over a doughboy."

"Everything's good," Philby said encouragingly. He briefly repeated the directions to Storey, making sure he had them right. He thanked her.

Together, Philby and Willa headed down the steep metal stairs. A moment later, they faced the door to the bakery.

"You okay?" Philby asked.

"No," Willa answered, "not really. I mean, of all the places, it had to be the bakery, right?"

"We can't look scared," he said.

"You mean I can't look scared."

Philby said nothing.

"But I am. They were . . . creepy." She paused. "And huge."

"We have to look as if we belong."

"As if."

Voices arrived behind them—someone coming down the stairs.

"Now or never," he said.

"Never?" she asked.

Philby opened the door.

The ship's bakery was all stainless steel and white tile. Large commercial kitchen appliances crowded the interior. A petite woman and a large man, both in uniforms, white aprons, and chefs' hats, looked up from their duties.

"Herman wants us," Philby said, pointing across the room.

"Sorry to bother you," Willa said.

"Not bother," said the man in a foreign accent. He smiled. He was missing a front tooth.

Willa was fidgety, remembering the twin six-foot doughboys that had attacked her and Finn with butchers' cleavers. Philby held the door for her; they passed into the galley—a vast space of preparation tables and, along the back wall, huge ranges and ovens. Willa had been here before; but for Professor Philby, it was like a research field trip—he was instantly fascinated by the size and scope of the ship's kitchen. Then it struck him: they had work to do.

"Empty," Willa muttered from behind him. "They're all up on deck for the inaugural."

Philby tried not to sound surprised. "As expected."

"You wish."

"It makes sense they'd be given a few minutes to join the celebration."

"Leaving us *alone* in here."

"All the better."

"You wouldn't think that if you'd been here with Finn and me."

Philby withheld comment.

They had a long way to go to reach the waiter entrance to the Royal Palace. The galley was divided into cooking and preparation areas for all the different aspects of a meal: main courses, salads, desserts, beverages, all connected by a waiter-collection area—an endlessly long stainless steel counter with warming shelves above and storage shelves below. Philby and Willa walked this pickup area atop spongy, slip-proof, black-rubber floor mats.

"It was at a place like this that we were attacked," Willa said flatly.

"Yeah, thanks. Good to know," Philby whispered back. His eyes zeroed in on all the knives, cleavers, and other weaponized kitchen gear.

They both stopped at once, frozen by the sound of . . . ruffling.

Philby pointed to their right: an area filled with five-foot-tall square carts, used for keeping salads fresh. Salad leaves did not make the sound they had just heard.

Willa waved her arms like a bird and mouthed, *Diablo?*

Philby's mind worked like a precision instrument. His head was like the cockpit of an F-16. He was the Top Gun of brainiacs. The sound of the ruffling wings had barely stopped by the time he was moving *at a run* for a hanging rack of strainers. He climbed atop a prep table to reach them, grabbed two, and started back for Willa.

The raven took flight out of the cart area, appearing just to Willa's left, a piece of lettuce clamped in its beak.

Philby launched one of the two giant strainers at Willa, who caught it one-handed and swiped the air like a lacrosse player, narrowly missing Diablo.

"He'll tell Maleficent we're here!" Philby said, leaping over the pickup counter and landing out in the line ahead of Willa. "Can't . . . let . . . him."

Diablo reversed directions at the sound of Philby's voice and flew at him. He nicked Philby's forehead with his beak before Philby could raise the strainer like a butterfly net. Blood trickled down into Philby's eyebrow.

The raven's feet latched onto Willa's hair and pulled a clump loose, knocking Willa over backward; she cried out with pain. As she fell, she threw her strainer at the bird and, surprise of surprises, hit Diablo in the tail feathers. The bird's flight faltered. It careened into a stainless steel post, fluttered, and fell to the floor.

Willa crawled quickly to her fallen strainer. Philby vaulted over her and slapped his strainer down to trap the crow. But one of Diablo's black eyes caught a reflection of a polished spatula; the bird threw out its talons, clawed onto the pole, and flapped its way straight up, avoiding Philby's trap.

Diablo screeched, and pecked at Philby's face, tearing a gash in the boy's nose.

Philby reacted instinctively, defending himself by raising his right forearm to protect his face and eyes while attacking with his left hand. He took hold of Diablo's wing and yanked hard. The crow was hurled across to the preparation counter, crashing there like a plane in a failed landing.

Willa jumped up and slapped her strainer over the bird, trapping it. She used both hands to hold the strainer down atop the table.

Diablo bounced and fluttered and fought to be free, but it was no use.

"You okay?" she asked, not taking her eyes off her captive.

"Yeah, I suppose," Philby answered, touching his wound.

She stole a glance in his direction. "OMG! You look . . . you're bleeding."

"Head wounds," said the professor. "They bleed a lot. Looks worse than it is, I'm sure."

Philby found a kitchen towel and mopped up his wounds.

"What do we do with this . . . thing?" Willa asked.

An angry Philby looked around. "You ever heard the term: eat crow?" His eyes were fixed on the rows of ovens.

"We can't do that!"

"Says who?"

"Me," said Willa. "No matter how much I hate the Overtakers, I'm never going to be reduced to their level."

"They'd kill us in a heartbeat."

"That's what I'm saying: we have to rise above that."

"Because?"

"I shouldn't have to answer that."

"We put him in one of the ovens," Philby proposed, "but we don't turn it on. If someone else happens to turn it on to preheat it . . . so be it."

"That's the same thing as us killing him."

"He's Maleficent's spy. He has to be dealt with."

"Listen to you! Do you hear what you're saying? There!" she said, pointing.

"A microwave?"

"You don't start a microwave without opening it."

Philby nodded. "And a microwave is vented, so he won't suffocate."

"Maybe they won't use it for a day or two."

"Maybe they'll use it tonight."

"Either way, it won't matter." She added for the sake of Philby's obvious hunger for vengeance, "She's going to freak when she can't find him. Have you ever lost your dog or cat?"

"I lost Elvis, my cat, one time," Philby said.

"Find a cookie sheet. We need to move him."

"We run the microwave for two minutes and he cooks from the inside out."

"You need your head examined."

"True story."

* * *

"From the moment we use our Cast Member cards to enter," Finn told Charlene, poised in front of the CAST MEMBERS ONLY door on Deck 1 that accessed the I-95 corridor, "both Security, and possibly the OTs, will know we're in. And if they know we're in—"

"—the OTs will know we're headed to the hospital."

"And any advantage of surprise we might have is blown."

"The OTs could be waiting for us."

"That's what I'm saying. Yes." It did not escape him that Maybeck could be the bait and Charlene the ultimate prize. *The sacrifice.* He felt responsible for her; he had to protect her.

"It's not like we have a choice," she said.

"Actually," Finn said, "I think we do. That is, I think we have to consider that this could be a trap.

That while one of us goes in, the other could hide here, alongside the stairs."

"Oh, no, you don't!"

Far more agile and quick than he knew himself to be, Finn shoved Charlene *and* unbuckled her ID lanyard at the same time. As she fell off balance, her lanyard came loose from around her neck. *No ID card, no access.*

Charlene grabbed the lanyard, but couldn't hold on as she fell.

With her ID already in hand, Finn unlocked the door, slipped through, and pulled it shut, locking her out.

Charlene raised her fist, about to pound on the door, but stopped herself. To bring attention to Finn was stupid.

"I hate you!" she hissed at the closed door. Then she stepped back and stomped her foot. "Not really," she said.

* * *

This is so cool! It's boiling out here. I forgot my suntan lotion. I'm so bored.

The thoughts in Mattie Weaver's head were not hers. Instead, she heard a loud tangle of expletives, happiness, frustration, malcontent, desire, joy, elation, hunger, apprehensiveness, and angst. They came to her in whispers and shouts, complaint and celebration. Like something from a nightmare. It made her so dizzy that she had to stop amid the press of human flesh on Vibe's deck and collect herself.

A large brass band was performing in front of a five-story hotel with a vast terrace restaurant on ground level and a balcony restaurant on the roof. People, both on shore and on the ship, were clapping in time. Banners read:

WELCOME, *DISNEY DREAM*!

and

DREAMS DO COME TRUE!

and

PANAMANIACS ♥ DISNEY

By her watch, they were still forty-five minutes from the ribbon-cutting ceremony at the second lock. The morning's *Navigator* had implied that the second ceremony might be considered the most important of the four.

While Mattie considered the best deck from which to view the festivities, she took her eyes off the crowded deck outside Vibe. When she looked again, there he was: wide shoulders, pink skin raw from the sun, a stubble of hair atop an enormous head, ears like a cartoon

231

character's puffy cheeks, piggish eyes. Greg Luowski, as they'd described him.

It was a risk worth taking, but a risk nonetheless. Some people could feel it. The experience went back as far as the New Testament. If he had that kind of sensitivity, she would be in big trouble. Big, as in six-feet-one, one hundred and eighty or ninety pounds. Seriously big. The kind of big capable of picking her up like an oversized pillow and launching her over-board.

No sound whatsoever now; everything in slow motion, driving her right shoulder between kids as she worked her way toward him. Heads, hair, and shoulders bouncing in unison—something beyond the rail had excited the gathering all at once. Mattie never took her eyes off the man-boy's freckled neck. His height made him an easy target.

Closer now. Only a yard to go. The crowd jostled, crushing her. She fought against the invasive voices, resisting them, holding them back as best she could. But it was like trying to fight off a fire hose with a napkin. The voices rose from the depths of the silence.

"Stop shoving!"

"That hurts!"

"My foot!"

She willed them out of her head, out of her

thoughts. She had to focus. To concentrate. She was interested only in him. It would take more than brushing up against him. Full contact. What she thought of as *a lock*. Only a lock would do. Ten to fifteen seconds at a minimum. More, if she could manage.

The moment was upon her. She squeezed past one more girl. The man-boy towered in front of her. Much scarier up close.

Mattie rose to her toes, trying to appear as though she were stretching to see over the rail. Her hands hovered briefly alongside the boy's upper arms, and then she took hold, as if losing balance.

It was a good, strong lock.

The boy's head turned. *He feels it!* she thought.

"Sorry!" she said, not letting go. She closed her eyes to prevent him from seeing them roll into the back of her head. Images flashed through her brain like a high-speed slide show. The boy's voice filled her ears, foreign at first, then owning her. The same every time.

Mattie's having a seizure! Mattie's speaking in tongues! For so much of her childhood even her own mother had seen her gift as an illness. Doctors always giving it names. Labels. Her parents mumbling behind her back. Packing up. Sneaking out. Running away.

The rush of impressions from the boy pushed the memories away.

The closest thing Mattie could compare a successful lock to was a computer download. Data flow. Other people couldn't understand, except maybe the few who felt it happen.

One of the images caused her knees to sag. It happened too quickly for her to know exactly which image—was it one of the boy's thoughts?—but Mattie lost the lock on the way down to her knees, sliding between the crush of bodies.

Her eyes fluttered open; the boy glared down at her. *He knows!*

* * *

On hands and knees to avoid being seen by a pair of waiters, Philby and Willa crept through the Royal Palace restaurant in search of Maybeck's DHI. Circular low-wing walls divided the large dining area into sections. White columns lent it the feel of a castle. Philby, in the lead, used the low walls as screens, moving to the center of the room where a hub held six or eight dining tables. They paused, their backs to the wall, studying the room's perimeter.

Where would he hide?

Willa cupped her hand and whispered softly into Philby's ear. "A waiter station."

Yes, Philby thought. Strategically placed throughout

the Royal Palace were high cabinets where the food could arrive on trays and be sorted, where drinks like tea and coffee were prepared, and tableware and extra dishes stored. The cabinets had shelves, but if Maybeck had control over the 2.0 software, he could fit in there, shelves or not.

"Or the columns," Philby whispered back. "If he stepped into one of those pillars, he'd be in DHI shadow. You can't see what isn't there."

"There must be twenty pillars in here. Eight or ten waiter stations."

"If we had waiter uniforms, this sure would be easier," Philby said.

"Think about it," Willa said. "The waiters don't get involved in the ship activities. It's possible that they might recognize us—"

"But doubtful."

"Yes. So instead of trying to hide from them, we should confront them. Put them on the defensive."

"Take charge."

Their eyes met. A recently unfamiliar energy exchanged between them. "Exactly!" Willa said, trying to dismiss the excitement she felt.

"You first," Philby said.

"Right." She nodded. *Back to business.* "Here goes."

Willa crept around the arc of the low wall and stood,

approaching the two waiters with confidence. Philby trailed behind by a few steps.

"Hello?" she called out, her voice steady. "Excuse me?"

The two looked up.

"I'm Willa. This is Philby. We're Cast Member guides who've just joined the *Dream*." She paused. "Do you know about us?"

The man's name tag read *Omar from Somalia*. The woman's said *Giuliana from Peru*. He looked puzzled. She looked vaguely aware of what Willa was talking about.

"I am afraid not," said Omar.

"The picture people," said Giuliana.

Willa had never heard the term before. Both she and Philby suppressed grins.

"That would be us," she said. "We are . . ." She froze. *We are . . . what?*

"Designing a game." Philby stepped forward. "You know: hide-and-seek? It's like that. One of us hides and the kids—the passengers—have to find him—"

"On their way into dinner," Willa added. They had a flow going now.

"Something to make the Royal Palace as much fun for the younger passengers as Animator's Palate is."

Both waiters nodded at once. Waiters moved from

dining experience to dining experience with the guests they served. They didn't need any reminders about how popular the Animator's Palate was.

"So one of our friends is hiding in here now," Willa said.

"And we're going to look around to find him," Philby added.

"You're welcome to join us if you like," Willa said, inviting them.

"You are kind to make this offer," Omar said. "We have jobs we must complete."

They made no effort to stop the two kids from searching the room.

"Shouldn't take long," Willa said.

They turned and separated, dramatizing their searching. Willa reached a waiter station and opened a cabinet without looking back for approval. Philby picked up on her lead. They were making good progress, having covered a full quarter of the vast dining room. Now a third. Half.

By this time, the two service staff no longer knew they existed. They finished setting up a table; the next time Willa looked back, they were gone. This should have made her feel victorious; instead, the size and emptiness of the Royal Palace sunk in. What if Maybeck wasn't the only one in hiding?

She struggled to rid herself of the memory of the doughboys swinging meat cleavers, but to no avail. Then her spine tingled as she passed a row of painted portraits along the far wall. Each portrait depicted a particular princess: Aurora, Belle, Cinderella, Snow White. Aurora's eyes had just moved.

It's a painting, Willa reminded herself. *The eyes of paintings don't move.*

"And the dolls in It's a Small World don't come alive," she muttered to herself cynically.

Aurora was the princess in *Sleeping Beauty*. The villain in *Sleeping Beauty* was the dark fairy, Maleficent.

Willa worked her way over to Philby, who was currently knocking on the columns and then cupping his hands and speaking to them; if anyone saw him they would lock him up in a straitjacket.

"Over my shoulder," she whispered, "very carefully. The eyes in the Aurora portrait."

"Got it," he said, waiting several long seconds before changing columns and stealing a look in the direction of the far wall.

He passed Willa a minute later. "Those peepers are creepers."

"Moving."

"Yup."

"It's the OTs."

"Not necessarily, but I'm not sure that it matters exactly who it is. That painting is watching us."

"What do we do?"

The professor glanced about. "We've got it *covered*," he said, softly. "First, we locate him—if he's even here. Then, we'll take care of Miss Crazy Eyes."

"I'll start over there," she said, "and work to the front."

"We're almost done."

Willa headed to the farthest corner of the dining room, an area removed from the rest of the dining area and one where an especially large waiters' station had been built into the wall, wisely placed so as to be invisible to virtually all of the dining passengers.

Twice the length of any of the others, it also contained twice the number of cabinets.

Willa opened up the second of these. It appeared filled with an oddly formed stack of table linens. But something made her reach inside and feel around behind them, pulling them out onto the floor.

"Terry?" she hissed, leaning fully into the cabinet.

"Willa?" Maybeck's voice whispered weakly.

Philby heard her talking to herself and abandoned the pillar that he was speaking to. He worked his way toward her, keenly aware that the Aurora painting could be watching him. Thankfully, unless it could see around corners, they were safe. Squatting, he helped Willa up and studied the empty cabinet.

"He spoke," Willa gasped.

"Can you hear me?" Philby said.

After a moment, a groan issued from the cabinet.

Philby searched the ceiling and walls for possible security cameras—the devices most commonly used to project their DHIs.

"He's in DHI shadow," Philby said to Willa. "Nice place to hide, man," he told the empty cabinet.

"Maybeck, you were struck by lightning," Willa said. "Your body is in a coma in the ship's hospital."

"Tired," the DHI said. "Hurting."

"You have to wake up," Willa said. "You have to work really hard to wake up."

Maybeck said nothing.

"Maybeck!" Philby said more loudly.

Maybeck groaned again.

"When I return you, you'll be back in the ship's hospital. You know that jolt you feel when you're returned?" he asked rhetorically. "You need to harness that jolt. Use it. Let it wake you *all the way awake.*"

"They're going to take you off the ship otherwise," she said. "No one wants that."

"We want to get you out of here," Philby said. "But we need your help. Are you hearing us?"

"I hear you."

"The Return," Philby said. "Use it."

"Repeat it," Willa said.

"Wake . . . up," Maybeck said.

"Or get left behind." Willa knew Maybeck well; he would not want to be miss anything.

"Got it." Maybeck already sounded slightly less traumatized.

"It's going to happen soon. Willa's going to stay here with you as long as possible."

"Don't go back to sleep," Willa said. "Fight to stay awake."

"Easy for you to say." That sounded more like the Maybeck she knew.

With the two waiters gone, Philby threw a table-cloth over the Aurora portrait on his way out. He texted the others that they'd found Maybeck and that the OTs may have been watching. That he, Philby, would return Maybeck within a matter of minutes.

The rest was up to Maybeck.

* * *

The I-95 corridor stood empty, the result of the Canal celebration up on deck. Finn held his head high and his shoulders square, attempting to express a confidence he didn't feel. The ship's hospital was up ahead on his left.

Not long ago, Finn had headed into the dark tunnels of Fort Langhorn to literally catch the Overtakers napping. It seemed only likely that they would attempt to repay the favor—to try to capture the comatose Maybeck when he was defenseless.

When will any of this end? Finn thought. How do we break their hold for good? Does Wayne know? Does anyone? How do you stop a fifty-year war?

Finn wondered if they were just pawns, foot soldiers in some tiny battle in a war now older than their parents. Had they escalated things by bringing in technology? Hadn't everyone been better off when there was little more going on than after-hour pranks between the villains and heroes?

These seeds of doubt grew roots as Finn drew closer to the hospital. He questioned the point of it all, including his leading a bunch of friends into life-threatening situations time and time again. He knew what he'd face when he passed through the door ahead—no better time to try to capture Maybeck than now. Determined to reduce their numbers and spread the concern Finn was now experiencing, Maleficent would take advantage of the Canal celebration; she had proved herself an experienced tactician.

Normally, Finn would approach such confrontations as a DHI, able to use his transparency to his benefit.

Perhaps this was part of her plan as well: force him into the open, exposed him as mortal flesh, a physically vulnerable young man, not a projection of light and mirrors.

Looking back at the still-empty corridor, Finn wished he hadn't tricked Charlene; he could use the company and support. If you wanted anyone in a confrontation, it was Charlene: levelheaded, nimble, and fast. What kind of stupid jerk would *stop* such a teammate from joining a potential battle?

His Wave Phone vibrated in his pocket. Charlene, no doubt trying to talk him out of going this alone. And while he'd just been thinking the *same thing*, he had no desire to argue the matter. He left the phone in his pocket.

The iridescent glimmer of unnatural light beat down uniformly from the ceiling fixtures overhead, causing a dreamlike shimmer on the walls and floor. It looked strangely like a ship's version of the gates of heaven, or wherever people went when they were no longer people. Was this to be the end of it all?

It was only a single vibration: a text message, not a call. That might be anyone. He slipped his hand into his pocket. *Chicken!* his conscience called loudly. He was stalling, using any excuse not to open the door and confront whatever evil lay on the other side. He released the phone and let it fall back to the bottom of his pocket.

He pushed down on the lever and leaned his shoulder into the metal door.

* * *

Mattie Weaver huddled on a toilet seat in Vibe's restroom—the only place she could think of to be truly alone. Maybe he hadn't recognized the Caller ID on his Wave Phone. Couldn't he assume it was from a friend if the number came from stateroom 816? She typed the message a second time, struggling with the antiquated system for text entry the phones used.

Her thumb hovered above the SEND key below the phone's tiny green screen. She was about to reveal herself in a way she had hoped to avoid. She was about to enter someone else's fight. A favor for a friend was about to turn into volunteering for a team she knew little about.

Her thumb pressed the key.

one of you is going to die

* * *

"Oh, hello." Finn was met by a ship's crew member, Maybeck's nurse. "I'm—"

"I know who you are." She was twenty-five and quite beautiful. He thought he'd seen her around the ship.

"A friend . . . of Terry's."

"Yes."

"And I . . . Well, how's he doing?"

"Same, I'm afraid. No metabolic changes, no motion or activity."

He's suspended in SBS, Finn wanted to say. *He'll be returned in a matter of minutes, and I need to protect him until then.* Instead he made the proverbial offer that could not be refused.

"I plan to be here for a while. If you wanted to go up on deck for a few minutes and catch the festivities, I'd be happy to text you if there're any changes."

She studied Maybeck's still form, then Finn.

"You sure you don't mind?"

"Not at all."

"Someone has to be here at all times."

"I understand."

"Don't mess with that," she said pointing to a syringe on a stainless steel tray. "That's to sedate him if he wakes up too violently. It happens."

"Of course not."

"I'll be five minutes, tops."

"No problem."

"Are you sure about this?"

"It's incredible up there. Awesome."

"This is really nice of you."

"Not at all."

"You know, on second thought . . . you mind turning around?"

"I . . . ah . . . Of course not."

"I shouldn't leave any meds out."

But as Finn turned, he found himself facing the polished frame on the back of the interior door—the *mirrored* frame. The nurse carefully put the tray bearing the syringe into a cabinet, which she then locked. The card key was returned to the drawer on the right of the cabinet.

"Five minutes," she said, pinching his shoulder in a friendly gesture.

"Sure."

She pulled the door shut behind her.

Finn searched the room for what he needed. Was it all here? Would it be enough? He started collecting items necessary to his plan. While he was at it, wanting to let Philby know that Maybeck could be returned now, he withdrew his Wave Phone. His chest tightened at the text message waiting there for him.

one of you is going to die

He spun around, facing the unconscious Maybeck. "Not you!" he said. "Not going to happen!"

* * *

Clayton Freeman stood by the door of Vibe, his iPAQ mobile device in hand. By his estimation there were about a hundred kids out on the club's small deck; he had little hope of finding the one he was after. The way he saw it, he had a choice to make: he could stay where he was and monitor the iPAQ to tell him when the radio frequency tag inside the stolen laundry tripped the sensor on its way out, or he could go looking for the kid. Both choices had benefits and risks.

The relay to the iPAQ would lag—the wireless system could be delayed anywhere from ten to forty seconds . . . *or longer.* But there couldn't be many kids wearing Cast Member laundry—specifically, a white polo T-shirt, size extra-large. Even so, he didn't want to mix it up with the kids and risk the stowaway slipping past him.

The better solution, he decided, was to wait outside the club entrance for the tagged shirt to pass him.

The spider weaves the web and waits.

"So close," Clayton told himself.

Catching this stowaway was certain to make him a star in the eyes of Uncle Bob and the company. Clayton

Freeman was hungry for advancement. This stowaway was his ticket to be director of security on a ship of his own.

He bit back his impatience and waited for the electronic web to signal a catch.

* * *

It took Finn a minute to realize his mistake: by trying to protect the comatose Maybeck, he had also set him up for trouble; by giving the nurse a moment off, he had invited an attack. The Overtakers had been watching the ship's hospital, waiting for just this moment. And now Finn had put himself and Maybeck in harm's way.

The door from the companionway to the Health Center waiting room groaned open. Maybeck's room was to the left, and the person entering eased open the door, slowly, silently. This intruder saw the back of a person sitting in a chair facing Maybeck: a narrow-shouldered white medical coat, a man's bald head.

A robed figure stepped into the examination room. She wore a golden crown. A starched white collar rose up from her shoulders behind her head, hiding her face.

"*Haame-lo-lo,*" spoke the woman.

The head and lab coat shrank to less than half their original size, the head bouncing on the floor and splitting into brains, ears, and nasal passages.

A plastic head. A physician's demonstration human skull Finn had found on the counter and mounted to look like Maybeck's guardian.

Finn stepped out from behind the partially open door, the twin fabric patches from a HeartGo defibrillator raised like a weapon. He pushed them against the Evil Queen's left arm and fired an electric shock. She literally flew across the small room and rammed into the counter. The device hummed, regaining its charge. Finn came forward; remarkably, the Evil Queen wasn't down, only stunned.

What is this creature? he thought. The beeping defibrillator's main box dragged on the floor behind him. He willed it to reach full power—one more shock, and the Evil Queen was going down. They could lock her up; it would be a big setback for the OTs!

Struggling to hold herself up, she hooked her elbow on the countertop and turned to face Finn. Her eyes were either bloodshot or glowing. She looked like she was in pain.

Finn took in her beauty, and his breath caught. He tried to look away, but couldn't. His hold on the patches loosened. He wanted to touch her face, to kiss her ruby lips. He felt himself drawn into her eyes; iron shavings to a magnet. Who could harm a woman so lovely? So . . . perfect?

He pulled closer to her, easing the wired patches lower. The battery box continued its low-toned beeping, not yet charged.

The Queen's lips moved.

Finn thought himself privileged that one so precious would bother to speak to him at all. It never occurred to him that she was attempting to cast a spell.

The box emitted a single piercing beep. *Fully charged.*

The Evil Queen knocked the patches to the floor.

Finn suddenly saw her for what she was. A witch, drunk, or sick, half asleep.

She reached with long fingers for Finn's throat and locked her hands around his neck. He wrestled to break free, throwing her against the near wall as he managed to turn his back to her.

She pushed him into the cabinets, smashing his face into the safety glass. It cracked into a spiderweb but did not break.

Through the glass, Finn spotted the syringe on the metal tray.

Finn pushed her back, stunned as she threw him forward, his head smacking the glass for a second time. He managed to pull open the drawer, fingers groping for the key card to the cabinet. Only then did he realize he'd watched the nurse in a reflection, a mirrored image. Wrong drawer. He knew what it meant: he had to endure yet another blow to the head.

He heaved back.

The Queen shoved forward.

Finn cracked the cabinet's safety glass for a third time. He pulled open the drawer to the left, and there was the key card! Seizing hold of the key card, still wrestling with the Queen as she managed to get his neck fully in her grip again, he swiped the card next to the cabinet. It unlocked.

After the three collisions with the glass, Finn's head was beginning to go spongy. Colors floated before his eyes, blinding him. He felt his knees give out. He sank lower as his left hand found its way into the cabinet.

"I came for the other, but you are the prize! You will do nicely for our little sacrifice, my friend!"

"I don't like to be overlooked." Maybeck's voice. A hand appeared on the Queen's shoulder and spun her around.

The sound of Maybeck's voice gave Finn strength, a strength so unfamiliar, he was still learning how to use it. He stood, broke her grip, and looked Maybeck in the eye. He'd come out of the coma; Philby had returned him!

The Evil Queen looked as if she'd seen a ghost. She tried to speak, but her eyes rolled back in her head, flickering open just long enough to see the syringe still inserted in her arm. She spoke, but her words came out at half speed.

Maybeck sagged, losing strength.

The Evil Queen fell to the floor, weakened but still conscious. He would not be able to capture her.

What is this creature? Finn thought for a second time. The dose was meant for Maybeck, who weighed a good deal more than this slight woman, and yet she remained partially awake. She'd said, *I came for the other.* Had she meant Maybeck, or had Finn, by using Charlene's ID tag, led the Queen here?

His plan to kidnap her foiled, Finn took Maybeck's arm around his shoulder and helped him out of the exam room and into the companionway, leaving the Evil Queen groaning and cursing in some strange language while a plastic doctor's model of a human head, its brains missing, stared back at her.

20

CLAYTON FREEMAN'S IPAQ signaled that the radio frequency tag in the unaccounted-for laundry had left the lounge. He was back on the trail.

A minute later he was following a wide-shouldered boy with buzz-cut red hair.

The level of sophistication of the boy's violations suggested more organization than a high school kid was capable of. More sinister as well. It would be pretty stupid to step on a single ant only to realize too late he'd missed the colony. Freeman intended to stay with him.

Freeman was the wizard of *Disney Dream*'s security office. When Uncle Bob had given the Imagineers a wish list of security upgrades for the new class of ship, all the technical ideas had come from Clayton. These included the use of radio frequency tags for passenger identification, stateroom entry, the Oceaneer Club, tracking laundry inventory, and the inventory of security-sensitive equipment, including closed-circuit video surveillance—CCTV. The ship possessed four highly-encrypted private WiFi systems. Night-vision imaging on certain decks.

In the end, Clayton Freeman wanted a safer ship, but not a ship that invaded anyone's privacy—all of which required a great deal of forethought, compromise, and planning. With the upgraded wireless networks came the ability to transmit security video to the handheld devices, a functionality he finally got the chance to test now, as he dropped back from the subject yet remained able to follow.

When the suspect entered the forward tunnel, which enclosed the jogging track, Foreman hurried. He'd lost the boy here once before.

No sign of the two. Nada. Nothing. Zilch. Zero.

Vanished. Same as last time.

Freeman could envision three explanations: 1) He'd used the CREW MEMBERS ONLY door immediately to Freeman's right; 2) Their hideaway was right here under Freeman's nose; 3) He was a hologram and had walked through the wall.

This last possibility came under the heading *Top Secret.* He and Uncle Bob had, for several days now, realized something extraordinary was happening on their ship. One thing seemed clear: if he went to Uncle Bob with only theories he'd be laughed at. The older man was starting to question, but he wasn't sure. Clayton Freeman would need proof. Hard evidence.

Freeman opened the CREW MEMBERS ONLY door. Nothing.

He pulled it shut and paced the jogging deck.

He was in the exact location at which the cameras had lost the double Mickey the first time. All he saw was a line of stains where some passenger had spilled soda.

There was a hiding place here.

Something he was missing.

* * *

There was barely time to celebrate Maybeck's coming out of the coma. Standing in a crowded area by the gangway on Deck 1, Charlene attempted to hide her relief at having him back.

Finn and the others felt a sense of hope. They had not exactly defeated the Overtakers, but they had caused them to fail, and that was almost the same thing.

Just before noon, a security officer quieted the thirty people gathered.

"Passage ceremony personnel are now cleared for disembarkation. Please have your identity cards out to expedite the process."

Led by Captain Cederberg, who was followed in succession by officers of rank, a parade of VIPs crossed the temporary gangway. The Kingdom Keepers brought up the rear behind Captains Mickey and Minnie.

Maybeck was in decent shape. They'd teased him about being well-rested.

But once on Panamanian soil, Philby and Finn stood on either side of Maybeck, ready to help prop him up if he needed it.

The Keepers understood the honor of being part of the inaugural festivities, of being in the presence of the cruise line executives. The event had been carefully scripted, so it surprised everyone—most of all the Keepers—when the biggest cheer, bigger even than for Mickey, arose as they crossed the plank.

Mickey came back and patted each Keeper on the head, winning ever louder applause from the crowd.

The president of Panama spoke briefly, followed by Captain Cederberg. There seemed to be more journalists and photographers than Panamanians. Cameras flashed. Photographers signaled the ship's representatives to look one way, then the other.

Jodi directed Captain Cederberg with hand signals. Andy and his crew were among those filming.

"Excuse me . . . you can't . . ."

A security man on the ship side of the gangway was trying to stop a robed woman from disembarking. Laughing horribly, Maleficent walked *through* the man's outstretched arms.

"Red—"

"Alert," said Philby, finishing off Finn's thought.

"Hologram," said Willa.

Seeing the dark fairy, the crowd cheered all the more loudly—everyone but the ship contingent. Jodi and the other company executives and ship's officers stepped out of Maleficent's way.

All but Captain Cederberg, who, judging by his expression, had had enough of Maleficent and her intrusions.

"I'll ask you to leave," Captain Cederberg said.

"Here, catch," Maleficent said.

Finn saw it in slow motion but reacted in real time. A ball of fire formed in Maleficent's hand; it left her grasp; Captain Cederberg's natural reaction was to put his hands together in order to catch something thrown to him.

Finn covered his face and took the ball of fire in his chest, immediately diving to the patch of green grass—sod, laid just for this event. He did so two feet in front of the captain, sparing the man a third-degree burn.

Finn scrambled to his feet, the front of his shirt burned, his skin pink. The crowd on the decks of the ship and the shore was in a frenzy. The chant of "King . . . dom Keep . . . ers!" started up.

It occurred to Finn: *How do the Panamanians have any idea who we are?*

Security men rushed to tackle Maleficent, but ran smack into each other, knocking themselves to the ground.

Maleficent wasn't there. Only her hologram, which continued to cackle evilly.

Captain Cederberg first looked to Finn, then saw his men collide.

"Blind her!" Finn called.

Too late. Maleficent walked up to the lectern. With no way to pull her off, they had no choice but to listen to her.

Only Philby saw a way around this situation; he took off for the soundboard under a small white tent to the left.

"This is indeed an historic moment!" Maleficent turned back to Finn as if he were part of her plan. "We inaugurate not only a ship's passage through a territory once believed to be inhospitable to man, but the passing from the old to the new. The old canal"—she waved vaguely over her shoulder—"and the new." She indicated the *Dream*. "The old, weary mice"—she pointed to Mickey and Minnie; Mickey put his hands on his hips indignantly—"for the almighty Cherna—"

The name died in the air. Philby had yanked the

microphone cord from its socket. Fury burned in the eyes of Maleficent's DHI. She raised her hands high overhead.

A cloud formed above them in the center of the blue sky, growing outward, darkening, and becoming increasingly ominous at a phenomenal pace. Within the boiling gray cloud an image appeared. A face. Part Minotaur, part bat.

"This is not within her powers," Willa cried.

Spinning around, the four Keepers scanned the ship for someone . . . anyone . . .

"Two o'clock," said Maybeck weakly.

Tia Dalma was positioned on a flat roof near the back of the ship, an area off limits to all but the crew. She, too, held her hands toward the sky; but the expansion of the cloud appeared synchronized with her movement.

Chernabog's ghoulish maw yawned open as he licked his chops. His slit eyes squinted.

"Everyone back on the ship!" Finn hollered.

Chernabog blew down on them.

A wet, foul smelling wind stirred the trees. Slowly at first—just a breeze—it increased in force. The clouds rolled, casting crazy shadows on the ground. Tia Dalma summoned a lightning strike; the bolt slammed directly onto the lectern, and it exploded into flames.

In the midst of the chaos, Bob and Finn exchanged a look. Bob's eyes seemed to say, *Okay, so now I believe you about the blue-sky lightning*—though perhaps Finn was imagining his capitulation.

Bob herded the group toward the gangway, making sure that the top executives and Captain Cederberg were at the front. But the captain stepped aside, calmly ushering others on board ahead of him.

"Just a small squall," he said. "We get them all the time. Shame to rain on our parade. . . . Watch your step. . . . Grip the rail. . . . Mind the gap!"

In a surprisingly orderly manner, the thirty *Dream* representatives returned to the ship as the crowds scattered in an alarming mob scene behind them. The president was rushed to a waiting limousine as two more lightning bolts struck with earthshaking force. Raindrops the size of golf balls fell; pieces of tents and flags went airborne, smashing to bits against the stands that had been set up for the event.

Then, as the gangplank was hauled aboard and the hatch was just about to shut, the storm stopped. The clouds melted from the sky like hot wax.

It was over, leaving what looked like a war zone behind.

"I want answers!" Finn overheard Captain Cederberg shouting to his team as they huddled past security.

Finn knew the truth: there were no answers Captain Cederberg would like. Even fewer that he might believe. If Chernabog's rise to power had already happened, why had the Queen been in pursuit of Maybeck or Charlene only minutes before? Maleficent had seized an international media stage to make her statement, reaching the biggest audience possible, perhaps signaling other Overtakers around the globe that their time had come; but the Chernabog in the sky—a mile across by a mile high—had been nothing but an image conjured by Tia Dalma. If the real Chernabog had been empowered, why not have *him* make an appearance?

The answer seemed obvious: Chernabog remained in torpor, awaiting the sacrificial offering.

If they could protect Charlene—and they had to!—perhaps they could prevent the bat-god from gaining power.

* * *

A meeting was hastily arranged later that night when a handful of texts from Amanda demanded that she be crossed over to the ship ASAP.

For Finn, it was a collision of confusion. At the time, he'd enjoyed the flirting with Charlene. It had been harmless enough. But he'd soon felt bad about it. He wouldn't have told Charlene she looked pretty if Amanda had been present. But Amanda hadn't been present, and Amanda hadn't been nice to him for a while now. Was it wrong to flirt with Charlene when Amanda wouldn't give him the time of day? He knew the answer when he felt guilt-stricken at hearing Amanda was coming aboard.

The rendezvous, the companionway outside of Animator's Palate, was always busy around mealtime. But not late at night, which was why it had been chosen.

After midnight, the ambience aboard the *Disney Dream* changed dramatically. Bands of older teens and small groups of barhopping adults roamed the ship. Romantics sat in a deck chairs observing the night sky and the moonlit highlights on the water. It was a restful, quiet time. An officer might be seen in crisp whites, strolling, hands behind his or her back, contemplative— the close of another long sea day.

Charlene took up sentry duty in the long port-side corridor leading to the restaurant. She lay down on the recessed frame of one of the many large porthole windows that ran from the Atrium all the way aft to Animator's Palate. Willa took watch on Deck 2, just below the rendezvous, while Storey Ming took the same location on Deck 4.

All four sentries had entered their location in a text message to Finn ahead of time, ready to send with the push of a button; this would tell him from which direction the trouble was coming, and therefore in which direction to flee.

Philby took command in the Radio Studio, controlling the 2.0 server that would allow Amanda to cross over, and to return her if necessary. Their Disney DHIs had been discontinued at ten o'clock, following the stage show in the theater.

Finn liked creeping around the ship at night, just as he enjoyed being inside the Disney parks after the gates closed. He remained keenly aware that security cameras were watching, and that crew members who served as security personnel might recognize him. Being recognized—which, he'd come to find out, was the price of fame—was not always such a good thing.

Although most of the passengers had gone to sleep, the crew had not. Finn approached from Deck 11, the warm Panamanian winds blowing across the rail. The ship had passed through the new canal without another incident; the captain had come over the public address explaining and apologizing for the "freak squall." The open deck area that featured swimming pools by day was lined with pool furniture facing the Funnel Vision screen. Everything shipshape, neat and tidy, not a soul in sight.

Finn moved slowly between the wood cabinets that

housed fresh towels, using them as screens. He felt exposed and at risk out here. He'd already gone over the rail once. He had no intention of ever doing so again.

A tall figure passed far on the starboard side of the ship, heading forward. Finn recognized the man's clothing as that of a Cast Member—khaki shorts and a white polo shirt. It felt strange that the Cast Member didn't acknowledge him, didn't look in his direction, not even once. Typically they were so outgoing. He wanted to say this guy was just at the end of a long day, but it didn't feel right; he found himself looking back at the man and walking faster.

Deck 11 had been a stupid choice. It required him to go through an empty Cabanas restaurant to reach the stern stairs. Being inside the closed cafeteria gave Finn chills. He saw OTs jumping out from every shadow. By the time he finally descended the aft stairs, he was a nervous wreck. He caught the eyes of Storey Ming at the landing of Deck 4—only the eyes, peering out of the shadows. That didn't help things any.

When he arrived on Deck 3 he found himself alone. It took him a minute to settle down. Animator's Palate occupied most of the stern. The landing on Deck 3 formed a kind of room, with closed doors to the restaurant to starboard and a narrow corridor leading to bathrooms and the restaurant's main entrance to port. He waited, checking his Wave Phone for the time.

One of the port-side doors opened. The girl with the red highlights appeared.

"In here," she said.

Finn hesitated. *A trap?* The plan had been to stay on the stairway landing, giving them plenty of options for escape.

"I'm waiting for someone," he said.

The girl swung the door open wider, revealing Amanda. Amanda smiled a bit uncertainly at Finn. For a moment, his Charlene-guilt overwhelmed him. He wanted to run to her, to apologize for something that she didn't even know about. But he caught himself. *Not the time.* He looked around—how could he tell the others they were going off plan? He entered the dark restaurant. The girl eased the door shut quietly. It clicked into place.

Animator's Palate was cleverly divided into a dozen smaller areas almost like rooms, each with several large hi-def televisions mounted on the walls. The televisions were the only source of light: they were like windows into the sea around the ship; blue bubbling water with schools of animated fish and the giant sea turtle "dude," Crush, swimming about.

The three sat at a table relatively near the side door.

Finn and Amanda said with their eyes what both

of them had wanted to hear: they'd missed each other. Finn felt like he could breathe again. He drank in a deep lungful of air and felt stress dissipate. Amanda didn't show anything more—just that one look, but she couldn't take it back!

"This is Mattie Weaver," Amanda's hologram said.

"You *know* her?" Finn asked.

"We're friends from Baltimore," Mattie said, extending her hand to Finn. They shook.

"A Fairlie?"

Mattie nodded.

"Jess and I asked her to be on the ship. To help you guys out."

Finn looked at the two girls. "You know each other," he repeated, feeling stupid for having done so.

"When Jess and I realized we could only be here as . . . this . . ." Amanda said, indicating her hologram, "we thought—"

"How is she?" Finn interrupted.

"Is something wrong?" Mattie asked Amanda.

"An accident," Amanda said. "We haven't much time; let's keep to the point."

"Which is?" Finn found himself pulled to the action in the television screens. The peacefulness there belied his internal tension.

"I've been . . . watching you all," Mattie said. "As

Jess and Mandy asked. Trying to help where I could."

"The journal. And the note." He considered the various times she'd been spotted. "But how could you possibly . . . Do you realize we thought you might be an Overtaker?"

"We asked her to stay in the background," said Amanda. "We didn't want any chance of her being associated with you, with the Keepers. She's of more value to us all that way. The only reason we're even meeting tonight is because . . . because . . ." Amanda's hologram seemed about to cry; Finn wasn't sure that was even possible.

"How much do you know about Baltimore?" the girl asked him.

"The Fairlies? A little, I guess. Not much."

"How much of what you do know do you believe?"

"Let me put it this way: a couple of years ago I would have thought Amanda and Jess were psycho. Seriously damaged goods. But, you might say circumstances have changed. For me, I'm talking about. For the other DHI models. Meaning that there isn't much that can shock me anymore, not that I would dare try to explain any of this to a normal friend"—he thought of Dillard Cole—"for fear someone would have me locked up. But the Fairlies? Honestly? You guys are way easier to believe than most of the stuff we see. Some kids born with weird powers or whatever you want to call it? Seriously? I mean, I had to read about the Salem witch trials in middle school. Am I supposed to freak if some girl can move a book across a desk without touching it? I don't think so!"

"Do you know the word *empathy*?" Mattie asked.

"Like *sympathy*. Sure."

"Not exactly."

"Feeling bad for someone."

"Actually, it's feeling *the same*. An ability to share a feeling with someone. Like something you have in common."

"I guess I don't get what you're saying."

"By now, half the U.S. military is probably looking for me," Mattie said, "because they don't get it either. But they'd like to understand it better."

"You're empathetic?" He heard her masking her concern with humor, and was reminded once again about all the risks everyone was taking.

"I am."

"I'm sorry . . . I get the empathy part . . . but what's it mean, exactly?"

"You know fortune tellers?"

"They're all crazy ladies."

"Most. Nearly all. But not absolutely all."

Crush, the turtle, stopped and stared at them

through the fish tank of flat panel displays. Something about that bothered Finn. *Come on.* He couldn't believe he was getting bad feelings about an animated turtle. He was really tired. Maybeck's illness and the fight with the Evil Queen had exhausted him.

"What's one of the first things a fortune teller does with a client?" Mattie sat forward, her eyes fixed intensely on Finn.

"How would I know? I've never been."

She reached across the table, her hands asking Finn for his. But he wasn't playing. He moved his hands into his lap.

The turtle swam away.

"They touch you," Mattie said.

"Wait a second . . ." Finn gave her a sideways glance.

"That's right: that's all it takes. I touch someone, and I hear them. The longer the contact, the further back the 'conversation' goes." She drew air quotes.

"That must get kind of creepy."

"You have no idea. I wear gloves. Long pants when possible. Any skin contact . . . *presto* . . . all your secret thoughts."

Finn was glad his hands were in his lap. Especially with Amanda in the immediate vicinity. He contemplated the power this kind of insight gave Mattie, and a chill went down his spine.

"A spy. The government wants you as a spy."

She smiled. "You know them. They see all sorts of uses for me. Trouble is, they don't seem to care what I'd like to do."

Like Amanda's and Jess's, Mattie's "gift" was more of a burden. Finn felt bad for her, felt worse that she'd been drawn into their intrigues.

"And you're here tonight because . . . ?" Finn looked over at Amanda.

Amanda didn't answer. It was Mattie, instead. "Because I connected with the big guy. The bulldog."

"Luowski. When?"

"This afternoon, during the ceremonies. He was out on Vibe's deck."

Finn felt a nagging need to look back at the flat-panel aquarium. He reacted without meaning to: a shark's wide head filled the screen, its jagged teeth showing.

"Now, *that's* ugly," Amanda said.

Finn lowered his voice. "You know how this place works, don't you? Animator's? Crush talks in real time to people at the tables. The guests have conversations with a flat panel. They can do that because the Imagineers have *hidden cameras* all over the place. *Hidden microphones*. Making this the worst place in the world for a secret meeting. Why don't we take it outside?"

He didn't add that the Keepers were in position to help protect them outside but would be of little help in here.

"Mattie is about to tell us about Greg Luowski."

"I'm just saying . . . maybe in the hallway?" Finn's eyes pleaded with Amanda's hologram. What did she have to worry about? he thought. It's not like her DHI is vulnerable.

But am I?

Finn had felt different ever since his hologram had been shocked by electricity in the *Dream*'s engine room. For days now, he'd been feeling stronger and faster than before, a power that came in strange bursts of adrenaline that left him exhausted and confused. He'd also started having dreams that seemed terrifyingly real. In that moment, sitting in Animator's Palate, he added prescience to his list of new qualities.

Only seconds after he'd voiced their vulnerability, two chefs appeared across the dining room. Even from a considerable distance, two facts were apparent: the chefs had bright green eyes, and each was carrying a boatload of knives and cleavers under his arm.

Without thinking, Finn heaved up the table, forming a barrier, and pulled Mattie behind it. A Chinese cleaver slammed into the table and stuck.

A carving knife passed through the chest of

Amanda's hologram; had she been present in the flesh, it would have killed her.

"You know what color this palate is missing?" called one of the men in a thickly Slavic accent.

"Red!" his pal answered.

"We can call it Dead Red. A nice addition, I think."

Finn peered around the edge of the upright table. A knife whizzed past, removing a clump of his hair. Strands floated to the carpet.

"To the door," he said, gripping the table. "All together."

Thwack! A knife lodged in the carpeted floor to either side. Finn crouched, waving Mattie and Amanda over to him; he had to keep the table low or risk having his feet diced.

"This is mine," Amanda said.

"No," Finn objected.

"They can't hit me," she reminded him.

"Just don't try anything . . . else," Finn hissed, looking at her. They both knew what he meant—use of her ability to "push" would weaken her substantially, perhaps resulting in the failure of the hologram's immateriality.

"Don't tell me what to do!"

Amanda stood. A cleaver flew through her head and clattered into the far wall. The harsh sound of breaking glass filled the room—one of the flat panels.

"Amanda, no! Stop!"

But Finn was too late. Amanda picked up a chair like a lion tamer.

She has to be solid to touch it! Finn thought, hysterical fear surging in his chest. And if she was solid, that meant—

Knives banged against the chair as Amanda marched steadily toward the two chefs.

"Go on!" she shouted. Reluctantly, Finn and Mattie moved toward the exit doors, the table held before them like a shield. With all attention on Amanda, only one knife flew in their direction. It slammed into the wall by the doors, and hung there, shivering violently.

Amanda crouched and called out loudly, "I'm counting to three. You will put down your knives or pay the price."

"Oh! Listen to her! I'm terrified!" one of the chefs said to the other.

"One . . . two . . ."

Finn knew the timing was meant for him and Mattie more than the chefs.

"Three!"

Amanda dropped the chair and shoved her open palms at the two chefs. The men were lifted off their feet and crashed into the wall. One was nicked by a flying cleaver. Blood streamed down his neck.

"Criminy!" the other chef called out in an Australian accent.

"Go!" Finn said, shoving Mattie out the door.

He then surprised himself by picking up the table and throwing it as effortlessly as a Frisbee across the dining room. *Like pulling the carpet in the auditorium.* Again, the demonstration of strength shocked him.

The chefs saw the table coming fast, aiming to decapitate them, and slipped down flat on the floor. The table struck, punching a hole in the wall over the chefs' heads.

"Such sweet children!" the Aussie said. He and the other man scurried on hands and knees back into the kitchen. Amanda limped for the door, drained of energy by her use of her powers. Finn reached for her—she'd lost her hologram—and helped her through the doorway.

He texted an emergency code.

In seconds, Charlene and Willa converged, rounded them up like Secret Service agents handling diplomats, and rushed the three upstairs to Storey Ming who, pointing to starboard, led the way. They were in the District, the ship's warren of nightclubs and bars. Unlike the orderly layout of the rest of the ship, the District's few hallways were curved, and clubs phased into each other, further confusing the visitor. The kids ran past a grouping of single-occupant restrooms. Storey

274

skidded to a stop and ushered all of them into one. She closed the door and locked it. It was a small, crowded space. Storey kept her ear to the door and a finger to her lips. She held up her palm, like a traffic cop.

Footsteps could be heard. Then the thunk of a nearby bathroom door closing and locking. Storey nodded, as if to say, *Okay.* Quietly unlocking and opening the door, she checked both ways and signaled for them to follow.

Hurrying through the 687 Lounge, they drew immediate attention. All the ship's bars were Adults Only. A Cast Member with unfocused eyes and an awkward gait approached from the far side of the lounge, clearly intending to intercept them. Another OT zombie.

As a group, the Keepers jogged into the neighboring District Lounge. Having violated the age rule there as well, they had two crew members after them—one zombie, Finn thought, one not. It was too dark to determine the color of the crew members' eyes, but the Keepers weren't sticking around for any close-ups.

Finn could no longer hold on to Amanda's hologram arm, but realized as she jogged beside him that she was back to full power. They reached the District's forward entrance where, unfortunately, they encountered a third crew member.

"We're going!" Storey called out to the lady guard.

"Hold on a second!" the woman shouted. "We . . . want . . . to . . . talk—"

She took off after them. The kids broke into a sprint.

"Why are we running?" Willa panted.

"What are we going to do, tell them a couple chefs were practicing their knife throwing on us?" Finn said. "That would go over big."

Rule #1: Kids are faster than grown-ups.

Rule #2: Disney crew members aren't grown-ups, in the grown-up sense.

"I know who you are!" shouted the crew member, now only a matter of yards behind them.

"You . . . don't . . . know . . . who . . . *I* . . . am!" Amanda charged the woman.

Finn and the others kept running. The crew member crossed her arms in preparation for a full-speed collision. Amanda's DHI passed through her.

Slack-jawed, the woman stared at the hologram in disbelief. "Wow."

"Pretty cool, huh?" Amanda stepped through the wall and out onto the jogging track. She waved back at the gawking crew member from the far side of one of the hallway's large circular windows.

The woman's fellow staff members arrived, out of

breath. Two of them looked down the empty hall, and saw the kids were gone.

"Must . . . pursue," one of them said in a strange monotone—like someone who'd been hypnotized onstage during one of the magic shows.

"For the record?" the woman said to the two. "I don't even care about losing the kids. What I just saw? That was totally worth it."

No one acknowledged her. The two men took off in a bizarre, stiff-legged run that made them look more like puppets than people.

* * *

The Cast Member beauty salon was like a prop shop for a horror show. Along the tops of the cabinets that surrounded the room and the six well-padded salon chairs were plastic heads wearing wigs—Snow White, Cinderella, Belle, and a dozen others—as well as latex prosthetics like noses, ears, chins, cheeks, and bald caps. The salon was a special effects laboratory possessing the theatrical cosmetics and technology needed to turn an ordinary Cast Member into an extraordinary Disney character—one who looked nearly identical to the character's image in a Disney film.

Dillard Cole and Kenny Carlson entered the empty salon on top secret orders, received from Wanda Alcott by encrypted e-mail. They'd been told where to find the salon: forward on Deck 2 through a locked Cast Member–only door; the salon was part of the Walt Disney Theatre's lower-level backstage area, shared by the stage productions and the character appearance groups. They'd also been advised of the safest time to be there: one hour past the conclusion of the Canal celebration, a rest time for the dozens of characters involved.

Dillard stepped through and locked the door from the inside.

"Find a hiding place. I'm going to put a chair by the door. If it opens, we'll hear the chair slide. We hear that, we hide."

Kenny found a closet of hanging crinoline petticoats; there was space enough to tuck in behind. It was the best spot in the small room for a boy so tall. Dillard was able to squeeze into a dark area under the makeup station farthest from the door; thus hidden, he was nearly invisible to the naked eye. A risky spot, but one he liked because it afforded him a view of the room.

With their hiding places planned, they followed procedures outlined in YouTube videos showing various techniques and practices of people working in salons. They'd memorized most of it.

The hair was not the problem. Both boys had previously booked appointments in the Senses Spa and

Salon and brought magazine photos of the haircuts they desired. It was nothing new to the experts in Senses to work from such photographs—kids often wanted to look like their favorite film, television, or rock star.

The challenge was the choice of, and application of, the latex prostheses that would transform their faces as Wanda had requested. They tried a variety of different noses and cheeks, finally gluing them into place, each boy serving as the other's beautician. Dillard had to shave off his eyebrows and use stick-ons to match color and shape; Kenny was able to use his freckles and red hair to his advantage. Twenty minutes passed. Thirty. Bit by bit, the boys saw themselves slowly transform. The coloring and application of makeup was a different matter.

"This is way harder than it looked in the video."

"I don't get how much time this must take for girls every morning. What do they do, get up at four or something?"

"I don't think they're as slow as we are."

"You look like some ninety-year-old geezer with bright red cheeks and fake eyelashes."

"You're the one doing this to me."

"And I'm really sorry about that, but you look ugly and ancient and a lot like a girl."

"Get it together, would you?"

"I'm trying."

"Try harder."

Dillard had done a good job on Kenny, but the reverse was not true. No matter how many times Kenny cleaned up Dillard's face—itself a time-consuming job!—and reapplied the cosmetics, Dillard looked only slightly better, and still nothing close to the person he was supposed to resemble.

"It's going to work, but I need more practice," Kenny said.

"Yeah, you're pretty pathetic at this." Dillard couldn't keep it in any longer. "We should tell Finn what we're doing."

"Wanda said not to." Kenny tried adjusting Dillard's latex nose.

"He needs to be told."

"You worship that guy," Kenny said.

"Do not."

"Do too."

"We're neighbors. I've known him since first grade."

"So what? You are so weird about him. It's like he walks on water or something."

"Shut up."

"You shut up."

"He's the leader. He should be told."

"Wayne's the leader and Wanda's his daughter, and she says no."

They left the salon ten minutes later, still arguing.

* * *

The new Keeper stateroom, 9603, was another unoccupied room that Storey Ming had found. An internal cabin, it had no windows to the water. But the Imagineers had once again outdone themselves: a high definition circular porthole on the wall played live video of the view as would be seen through any other stateroom window on the ninth deck. The result was a sense of the horizon and the weather; you didn't feel like you were locked up in a windowless room.

But the cabin was small, and with the five Keepers crammed into it, smaller still. The two girls sat up against the bed's headboard. Maybeck was stretched out sideways at their feet. Finn and Philby stood. Amanda's hologram sat on the floor by a recycling can. Mattie Weaver sat on a plastic trash basket turned upside down. She looked uncomfortable, knowing only Amanda well.

"I know where he's hiding," Mattie said, speaking of Luowski. "And I know what he was told to do."

"You see their memories." Professor Philby studied her like she was something under a microscope for him to pick apart with stainless steel probes.

"Their thoughts, sometimes their *feelings*. I get glimpses, because some people think visually. I get pictures in my head."

"Like Jess," Willa said.

"Except she sees the future. Not me. I suppose I see the past some, but mostly it's the present thought, I think. I don't know exactly. I get feelings. A sense of things."

"And what about Luowski?" Finn shifted foot to foot like a runner getting ready for a race. Nerves.

"Turmoil. Worry. Concern. He's horribly conflicted. If I touch someone who's happy, I'm happy. When I touched him I nearly passed out. He's this angry jumble of mixed-up emotions. He is to get one of you for them."

"The sacrifice," Finn said.

"Who?" Willa barely got the word out.

Mattie shook her head. "He doesn't know, but he knows it means death. A horrible death. He sees a knife dripping with blood."

Silence, followed by Maybeck. "The hyena killing."

"I don't see the past," Mattie reminded them all. "He fears that knife. The blood. He's terrified. He was out there on the deck, but none of his attention was on the celebration. He's worried, for himself, and for one of you."

"Sacrifice," Philby repeated, making it sound like a homework assignment. He said to Willa: "The journal."

Finn addressed Amanda's hologram. "Jess's drawings."

Amanda met eyes with him but said nothing. She looked frightened.

Mattie said, "The guy is haunted."

"Think how we feel!" Maybeck said. Everyone but Philby laughed.

"Any images?" Philby asked.

"There were metal stairs. Darkness. But I wouldn't put too much into it."

"We have to protect Charlene," Maybeck said.

"And Willa," Philby added. "It's girls they want. Willa, you said so."

"That was fifteen hundred years ago, FYI." Willa contemplated the gathering. "It could be any of us."

"I think he's afraid it may be him," Mattie said, winning their attention. "That he betrayed them somehow."

"When he warned us," Maybeck said, reminding Finn again.

"Could be," Finn said. "If Maleficent found out—"

"That other guy was there," Maybeck reminded them.

"Dixon."

"And he's a total zombie," Charlene said. "He was one of the stagehands Willa and I ran into."

Philby waited for the resulting chatting to settle down. He addressed Mattie. "Can you make contact with him again?"

Mattie said, "Some people sense when they're touched. It's like when you go cold all of a sudden for no reason. Luowski felt me doing it." She looked first at Philby, then the others. "The more times it's done, the more the person can sense it. I'm basically stealing their thoughts. They feel it."

"And Luowski knew," Willa said. "Could that have been what he was afraid of?"

"I don't think so," Mattie said. "It's possible, I suppose."

Finn withdrew the printout of Amanda's e-mail and passed it to Mattie. "Did you 'see' anything like this?" He passed it to Mattie.

"No. But as I've said, I don't see the future the way Jess does."

"We thought it was Aruba," Finn told her. "Even though it came a little late."

"It doesn't look like a cave," Mattie said of the drawing. "More like a tunnel. The walls are straight and smooth."

"But that doesn't fit with whatever you saw."

"No. I'm sorry." She passed it back. Finn returned it to his back pocket.

"We're scheduled to guide the zip line group tomorrow," Maybeck said. "It's the perfect place for more blue-sky lightning."

"Do you want to stay behind," Charlene said, "after what happened to you? We've got no problem with that."

The Keepers all mumbled agreement.

"I didn't say that. What I meant was—"

"We know what you meant," Philby interrupted.

Finn said, "Charlene, it's you who should stay behind."

"Safety in numbers," Charlene said. "And besides, I'm probably safer off the ship than on."

"If I signed up for the zip line," Mattie said, "if I could move through the passengers on the excursion, I might sense something."

"You have no documentation," the Professor pointed out. "Besides, those excursions were fully booked a long time ago."

"The gathering spots," Finn said. "All excursions meet as a group on the ship and leave from there. Mattie could cruise among the passengers, passing out pencils or something so she has the excuse to touch them."

Philby nodded. "Could work."

"But the problem is, we don't know if Luowski's orders have anything to do with the zip lines. He could be planning to toss one of us overboard, for all we know." Finn moved to stand next to Philby, addressing the others. "Our rule has always been to pair up. That's kept us safe so far. So we'll pair up, but everyone keeps an eye on Charlene. Anything weird, and we get her to the bus, or whatever. We keep her safe."

All the Keepers nodded.

"Okay," Finn said, "so we'll pair up where possible. Mattie, you'll let us know whatever you find out."

"Where do we find you, anyway?" Charlene asked. "Where are you sleeping?"

"If you need me, just stay after one of the movies in the Buena Vista. When you're sure the theater is empty and the Cast Members have left the projection booth, call out, 'Mad Hatter.' I'll meet you in Shutters Photo Studio a few minutes later."

"And if you don't show up?" Philby asked.

"Then I'm either out trying to make contact with other people like Luowski, or . . ." She hesitated. "Or something's happened."

21

THE SHIP'S D LOUNGE, the gathering place for the Costa Rican zip line excursion, was known for its night-club decor, dim lighting, and dance floor. But under full light at seven in the morning, it was home to a large group of guests wanting to hang in a harness and fly across steel wires in the mountains of a foreign country.

"Something's different about Finn," Charlene said to Willa. "And Philby, for that matter."

"It's seven in the morning. We said we'd pair up, and they're paired up. We also said we'd stay away from each other, and they're staying away from us."

"Does Philby look taller to you?"

"He's across a room filled with a hundred people. How should I know?"

"He looks taller to me," Charlene said. "And Finn looks . . . heavier." She paused, then said, "I don't get why you and Philby aren't going out."

"It might be because we're barely speaking."

"'This, too, shall pass.' You need perspective. We could ask Maybeck about perspective. He's the artist." Charlene scanned the room.

Charlene was looking forward to the excursion. She loved a good adrenaline rush. Like the others, she'd seen Jess's drawing, but unlike the others, she didn't think it looked anything like her. She knew she was a cute—some might say adorable—older teen who would make for a terrific sacrifice; she just didn't happen to believe even someone as cruel as Maleficent would resort to murder. Everyone was taking this thing way too far.

"We stay in pairs," Willa reminded her, ever the one to go by the rules. "And the pairs stay apart."

"You ever notice the boys make the rules?"

"Not always."

"Just about."

"I hadn't thought about it."

"You should," Charlene said. "Because they listen to Amanda and Jess, but not so much to you and me."

"You think?"

"I *know*. Come on, Willa, when do they ever actually ask us for our opinions?"

"Why are you doing this? We're a good team, the five of us."

"It's not a team if two or three people make all the decisions for everyone else." Charlene rose to her toes.

Maybeck entered the lounge in big strides, his

shoulders square. A rock star. Wraparound sunglasses. Storey Ming at his side.

Charlene's full attention fixed on Maybeck and Storey, who now held the attention of at least half the room. Younger kids recognized Maybeck and broke away from their parents to adore him. He loved every second. Storey held her own, playing the part of Maybeck's sidekick and possible girlfriend—a role Charlene saw as belonging to her.

"Who put her in charge?" she asked Willa.

"Down, girl. We all have roles to play. Don't blame her for doing hers well."

"Oh, but I do."

"Maybeck is taking the attention off us."

"Off of *me*," Charlene said bitterly. She didn't like being the one babied.

"It's what he does," Willa said.

"Yeah, well, Storey doesn't have to look so into it."

"Of course she does. Relax. We're acting out roles here. Nothing more."

"Tell that to Storey," Charlene said. "She hardly looks like she's working! She's enjoying this!"

"Hi!" A young girl with bouncy brown hair and so much suntan lotion her skin shone addressed Charlene with trepidation.

"Hi."

"You're Charlene, right?"

"Yes." Charlene offered her hand and the girl shook it, clearly thrilled.

"My friend saw you guys on TV." Keeper fans blurted out this kind of thing all the time. Tongue-tied and believing Charlene a celebrity, a kid would say whatever came to mind. "She e-mailed me about it."

"I'm glad," Charlene said, unsure how to respond. Although the Keepers had shot a Disney 365 a year earlier, it seemed unlikely the Channel would be airing it again. It was an odd comment to be sure. "We have a lot of fun shooting those three-six-fives. We're shooting another on the ship."

"I don't think it was a Disney three-six-five. She said it looked really scary and awesome. Anyway . . . I think you guys are great."

"Thank you."

The girl asked for an autograph and offered Charlene a pen to sign her T-shirt.

The group organizer called out a greeting and then ran through the logistics of getting off the ship and into the bus. Legal forms had to be signed because of the risks associated with that activity. Everything seemed to be going smoothly. Charlene and Willa took their place in line, and Charlene found herself looking back at the fan.

"What was that? Since when are any of our three-six-fives scary?"

"I wasn't listening."

"That was a bizarre thing to say."

"Maybe they're running some kind of new ad or something. One we haven't seen yet."

"We see everything before it goes out," Charlene said.

"I suppose."

"No supposing about it." Charlene followed the girl with her eyes, wanting to catch up and ask more questions. But right then a leader shouted out to the group and the room went silent.

* * *

Greg Luowski was bothered by the low lighting in the D Lounge. The faces of the two boys were already shaded and hidden by ball caps and sunglasses. Not right. If this was going down, Luowski wanted to look Finn Whitman in the eye.

What he was about to do wasn't easy. And it wasn't safe. So he did a gut-check and then walked right up behind the two when the opportunity presented itself.

"Don't turn around, Whitless. You either, brainiac." The boys' shoulders tensed. He knew he had their attention. "Listen to me and listen good, 'cause this is the only time you're gonna hear it. I don't like you, Whitless. I never have. You're a jerk and you're too cool for school and jerks like you deserve what they get. But I draw a line, okay?"

Philby started to turn his head. Luowski smacked him.

"Stay, Dog Breath. Do not move! These people . . . sheesh, they aren't even people. I don't know what they are. But they're taking this too far. You understand? Too far. And it's bad. Real bad. You . . . the five of you . . . *all* of you . . . *none* of you can get off this boat. Not ever. And if I was you I wouldn't leave my room either. One of you . . . I don't know how it's going to happen or when, but it's going to happen. You got that? *It's going to happen unless you keep it from happening.* If you don't disappear, they're going to find you and make you. Okay? And I'm talking, like, forever."

He'd worked himself up; he was shaking. His low voice trailed off in a dry whisper.

"As in: *forever.*"

He turned and hurried into the crowd. It wasn't hard in such an excited group. He just kept his head down and didn't stop walking until he reached the long corridor outside the District.

Once there, he pushed his back against the paneling,

shaking like a baby. Something had happened to him out on the deck during the canal passage. It was like a drain plug had been pulled and some of the bad had drained out. He didn't know what it meant, or how it worked.

But another part of him knew that whatever these *things* had planned for Whitless and his gang, it would be much, much worse for him if that green thing came to understand he had warned them.

It's the last time, he told himself—the two voices inside him battling for control.

If this kept up, he was going to go insane.

A girl with a red tint in her dark hair swept past him. Why did she look so familiar?

* * *

The air-conditioned bus bounced down a dirt road on the last leg of the forty-five-minute drive. Instead of jungle, the Costa Rican landscape on either side was brown, sun-baked grass and shrubs interrupted by the occasional copse of trees and outcropping of rock. A power line hung loosely between concrete poles, looking like it would come down in a strong breeze. The bus slowed and passed through a fence and gate delineating the Mountain Aventura Resort and Campground. The name was painted in black as a subtitle beneath bright green Spanish words.

"I'm in second-year Spanish," Willa said to her seat mate, "and I have no idea what that says."

"I still don't get why he won't even look at us," Charlene said. In an effort to ignore Maybeck and Storey, she'd spent the ride fixated on Finn and Philby, who sat two rows from the back of the bus.

"Chill," Willa said. "By now Terry's freaking because you've barely looked at him once."

"They're never like this. And I don't like it when people change for no reason."

"You mean: you don't like it when boys stop looking at you."

"Ouch."

"Sorry. That came out wrong. That was mean of me."

"Do you think I'm like that?"

"No."

"Seriously! Am I?"

"Maybe a little. But . . . very little!"

Charlene went quiet, her hands pressed between her knees, her head hung.

"I upset you," said Willa.

"What do you think? I'm a vain, shallow person who needs to be the center of attention—but only just a little."

"I didn't say that!"

"Yeah, actually, you did."

"Well, then, I apologize."

"Right."

"They're boys. Single-minded, socially incompetent creatures. Like me, for saying that to you."

"Tell me how you really feel."

"Tell me I'm wrong."

"These two boys happen to be our friends. Friends don't ignore friends."

Willa lowered her voice. "We went over this. It's their plan. They are sticking to the plan."

"Yeah? Well, I don't like the plan." Charlene snorted. "Not that anyone asked."

"You didn't object earlier."

"I didn't know it was going to feel like this."

"Boys don't have feelings. They have plans. They have teams, schedules, and meals. You're giving them more credit than they deserve."

"You are in a funky mood."

"I get carsick. I want this trip over with." Willa paused, thinking carefully before she spoke. "Truth is: I used to love being a Keeper. But now? I'm not so sure it's a bad thing if they replace us."

"You can't be serious."

But Willa's expression said it all.

The bus's air brakes hissed and it came to a stop. Heads rocked back and forth.

Charlene used the tinted window as a mirror to check her face. "Vain and shallow."

"I did not say that!" Willa stomped her foot in frustration. "I am sooooo sorry, Charlene. Can we please just erase the past five minutes?"

Charlene nodded. But she didn't mean it.

* * *

The zip line training was done in groups of ten. The *Dream* team was split into two. Willa and Charlene's half headed up the mountain on a chair lift, followed by a hike to the steeper regions of what was now forest. The trail ended at the first zip line platform and a beautiful view of a long, treed ravine with what looked like power lines stretched across it at odd intervals.

The team leader repeated all the safety instructions, and one by one the adventurers were clipped on to the pulleys that would carry them. The first of the eleven lines was the longest—one thousand feet across—and the fastest: you would fly at speeds approaching twenty-five miles per hour. At the far end the line rose to the distant platform; working against gravity slowed the zip liner. Adventurers were cautioned to remain motionless near the end and to not pull on the brake for fear of coming up short and requiring help to reach the uphill

296

platform. But of course many people did not listen to the instructions. The first few people stopped short of the far platform and had to be hauled in, slowing down the process.

Finally it was Charlene's turn. She clipped in with the help of the platform leader, tucked her ponytail into her T-shirt to keep it out of the pulley, grabbed hold of the rope as instructed, and lifted her feet. She flew, wind singing in her ears. As the world dropped out from beneath her feet she screamed with glee and excitement. This was what birds must feel like, a kind of freedom she'd never experienced. The two pulleys whined on the double wires overhead; Charlene briefly closed her eyes, and then looked out feeling like an eagle. As she slowed and stretched her toes to reach the platform she cried out again celebrating her success.

The man helping her smiled widely. "You like?"

"O . . . M . . . G!" was all she could say. She couldn't wait for the next line. Charlene followed the path hacked through the woods, descending lower toward the mountain. The path twisted and turned past rocks and trees, and suddenly there appeared a second launch platform with an attendant. The helmeted people in front of her were lined up as they took their turns clipping in and riding. There were a great many smiles, including her own.

Willa arrived from behind, equally wide-eyed and thrilled. "That was amazing!"

Following the second zip line Charlene waited for Willa. The forest path was dark, despite the sunshine blazing into the ravine. She waited not for her own sake, but for Willa's, who was more of a thinker than an action figure. Charlene knew that if something gave her the creeps, it would terrify Willa—although Willa would never say so.

When Willa arrived, the gloomy path stole all conversation. They moved along, looking in all directions, jumping at the slightest snap of a twig. Weird bird calls and animal sounds filled the woods. The path stretched on, turning and twisting.

After another minute, it was clear to Charlene that something or someone was stalking them from uphill to the right. She hoped Willa had not picked up on it. She tested her theory by slowing down and speeding up. The sounds stayed right with her.

"I hear it," Willa whispered. "What do we do?"

Charlene waited for Willa to catch up. "You are going to run until you reach the next platform."

"I'll never keep up." Willa was not a particularly fast runner.

"I said 'you,' not 'we.' I'm going to provide a diversion."

"Meaning?"

"All you need to do is stay on the path."

"We're supposed to stick together." Willa added, "I'm supposed to be protecting you."

"Whoever, whatever that is, I'm faster. And I want to know what's up there."

"Are you crazy?"

"Color me curious, not crazy."

"Don't leave me!"

"On three. One . . . two . . ."

Charlene took off uphill, immediately swallowed by the forest.

Willa had never run faster in her life.

Charlene ran toward the last place she'd heard sounds. She believed she would find Greg Luowski tromping through the woods. It wasn't going to be Maleficent or the Evil Queen *running* through a forest in pursuit of them. It might be Mattie Weaver or one of the volunteer DHIs Wayne had recruited to help. It didn't matter; she wasn't afraid. Her confidence resulted from her own physical prowess—she could run faster, jump farther, climb more quickly and higher than most boys. Let someone try to catch her.

She moved as silently as a huntress, dashing through the trees like a wraith, pausing every few yards to listen attentively. *Who? What? Where?*

Finally, Charlene stepped out from behind a tree, took two steps, and collapsed to the forest floor, rolling up against a rotten log. All her heroic dreams of allowing herself to be chased were quashed by the distant sight of two figures approaching. Costa Rican, judging by their dark skin and hair.

But it wasn't their hair or physiques that frightened her; it was the camouflage clothing they wore. It was their bent postures as they paralleled the path. But mostly it was the military face paint that told her this was no game of catch-me-if-you-can.

These two were hunting; and they weren't after animals.

Charlene lay pushed up against the log, hoping they hadn't seen her. She listened for the sound of their footfalls, but the annoying prattle of an excited adventurer on the main path blanketed her ears.

"*That was amazing!*" One of the camouflaged figures—a woman—mocked in heavily Spanish-accented English.

Willa had said this to Charlene only minutes earlier.

The other figure—a man—shushed her.

By this time, the two were dangerously nearby. If Charlene tried to run, she would give them the advantage; if she stayed and they drew even closer, she was giving herself over. She held her breath.

The woman stepped over the log and crushed Charlene's hand. Charlene bit back the cry that wanted to escape. The man passed below her. The woman didn't feel the bones beneath her boot; she trudged onward through the forest.

The two crunched ahead, ten yards past. Now twenty. Charlene couldn't know for certain what they were up to: bandits preparing to rob tourists? Agents of the Overtakers? Security for the company running the mountain activities, *protecting* their guests, not stalking them?

She did not dare move until they vanished into the trees. Then she gradually followed, staying well back. Followed, even as the two caught a glimpse of the ship passengers currently on the path and broke into a jog. Clearly they had wanted to see only the two girls—Charlene and Willa. But Charlene revised this opinion as they hunkered down behind a giant upended rootball from a fallen tree, now with a clear line of sight to the path. They were awaiting someone else.

Charlene backed up gingerly and found her way back down. She waited for a family to come along and took the far side where the two who were spying would not be able to see her clearly. She moved in unison with the family, averting her head as they neared the section of trail she believed was under watch.

Ten minutes later, she caught up with Willa, who was waiting by the third zip line platform.

"I thought . . . I don't know what I thought," Willa said. "I thought something had happened to you." She said it too loudly for Charlene's comfort zone.

"Let's get across," Charlene said. "They can't follow us that way."

"They? Who? What'd you find out?"

"Later," Charlene said.

Once across the ravine, Charlene explained what she'd seen.

"So they work here?"

"Who knows? Some kind of security, maybe?"

"There's a lot of forest out here," Willa said. The mountains were nothing but green. "They could have crossed onto the property. They could have been hired to come after us."

"By who?"

Some fellow passengers approached down the trail.

"Later," Willa said.

Two hours later, smiling *Dream* passengers boarded the bus back to the ship, buzzing about their adventures on the zip lines. Their mood festive and excited, they shared photos and stories, laughter and cheers. Creatures of habit, most people sat in the same seats they'd occupied earlier, including Charlene and Willa.

From below came loud noises—coolers and equipment bags being loaded onto the bus.

Charlene cried out as Willa gripped her arm. Given all the noise and chaos, hardly anyone took notice but Charlene, who felt as if a tourniquet had been applied.

"That's not Philby." Willa released her hold as Charlene pried her fingers free.

The boy who boarded the bus looked surprisingly like Philby, but wasn't. It appeared to be a clever disguise. Coming down the aisle, this boy kept his hat brim low.

Willa came out of her seat to confront him; Charlene pulled her back down. The boy sat in the seat immediately across the narrow aisle. The hat brim lifted slowly. Both girls covered their mouths to stifle their shock. It was Kenny Carlson, the volunteer DHI, his face made up to look like Philby's.

"I can't find him," Kenny said. "I waited, but he never showed up."

"Who?" Charlene said sharply, not wanting the answer she felt certain she'd hear.

"Dillard."

"Dillard?" Both girls, simultaneously.

"Playing Finn."

"Playing?"

They waited for two older people to push past and find seats.

"Wayne's orders. We . . . Dillard and I . . . kind of detained Finn and Philby and took their places."

Charlene exhaled a sigh of relief, only to hate herself for it. Finn's gain seemed to be Dillard's loss.

"We've got to tell the Cast Member in charge!" Willa said.

"I did. That's why we're delayed. We were supposed to board thirty minutes ago. The staff is supposedly running all the trails looking for him. I guess it happens often enough that they have a system. Twisted ankles. That sort of thing. But I know where I lost him, and they're already past there."

"After the second line, before the third platform," Charlene said.

Willa gripped her arm again.

"How'd you know that?" a stunned Kenny asked.

The girls shared panicked expressions. Willa whispered dryly, "They're not going to find him."

Charlene said, "We're not leaving without him."

"The same guy told me it's happened before," Kenny said. "People get lost. When they find them, they drive them to the ship."

"They're not going to find him."

"Don't say that, Willa!" Kenny complained.

Charlene jumped up and fought the oncoming traffic to reach the front of the bus. Willa and Kenny watched as she spoke to the crew member leading the excursion. The exchange grew heated, Charlene's face turning scarlet. Charlene tried to leave the bus, but the crew member stopped her, turned her around, leaned in and spoke to her privately for what felt like a minute. Charlene's body language changed—her shoulders sagged, her head rocked forward. She trudged back to join them.

"We can't stay to look for him," she said. "The park is closing, and we're not allowed inside. If we miss the bus, we miss the ship. It leaves as soon as we board."

"So we just give up on Dillard?" Kenny sounded ready to cry.

"I wouldn't say that." Willa closed her eyes, trying to make sense of the plan already forming in her head. She smiled wryly. "We've been in other parks when they're closed."

22

"**Y**OU'RE BORING ME with all this tech stuff." Charlene shifted uneasily from the couch of the unused stateroom. "Can we, or can't we, cross over and try to find Dillard? And no more about DHI shadow and projectors and the difference between 1.6 and 2.0. Please!"

The *Disney Dream* should have been moving smoothly through the three-foot seas up the Pacific coast. There were still days at sea ahead, with stops in Mexico, and finally, Los Angeles. The Panama passage was nearing its end.

But the *Dream* was still tied to the dock in Costa Rica. The people in this room knew why: Captain Cederberg didn't want to leave without Dillard. The time was fast approaching when he would be forced to set sail in order to make the next port on schedule, but for now he awaited word from his shore party about the missing boy.

"It's complicated," the real Philby said.

"I still can't believe you guys went along with the switch," Willa complained.

"We didn't go along with anything!" Finn said, too

loudly. "They locked us in a conference room! They tricked us."

"Because Wayne told them to," Philby said.

"Why would he do that? How could he do that? How could he possibly put Dillard—of all people, Dillard!—in a situation like—"

"Because you're more valuable," Philby said.

"Dillard's a *person!*" Finn pounded the bed with his fist. "No person is more valuable than another! Wayne would never do that!"

Philby looked smug. "He did it. So we need to get past this. We need to *find* Dillard."

Finn spit out a word he never used. A hush hit the room. None of the Keepers had ever heard Finn swear. He blushed, but didn't apologize.

"We are not leaving Dillard behind," Finn said.

"Of course we're not," Philby said.

"So! Before you get started," Maybeck said, cutting Philby off, "can you *possibly* give us the DHI-for-Dummies version? Charlie's right: the *Mission: Impossible* thing is boring."

"It comes down to this," Philby said, looking disappointed and embarrassed. "I can cross us over here on the ship. We will walk off the ship and into DHI shadow."

"So we'll be invisible." Finn's voice rang with impatience. "That could be good."

"Correct. But it's also tricky. The network down here will not support 2.0, so we'd default down to 1.6. We can't just randomly go wherever we feel like; we have to stay within range of modems and cameras in order to—"

"B . . . o . . . r . . . i . . . n . . . g!" Maybeck made them all laugh.

"It's *dangerous*, okay?"

"And that's supposed to be something new?"

"Technically dangerous. Not physically dangerous. There's a difference. A moving ship. A dicey Internet connection. No decent projection system. I had about twenty minutes to research this. I need a couple of days."

"We don't have that," Finn said. "We need to make the decision. Go, or no-go?"

"I'm going," Kenny Carlson said. "I let this happen. No way I'm sitting around here."

"I could be of help as well," said Storey Ming.

"You'd have to be in the system," Philby informed her. "You'd have to be programmed into the system and that can take—"

"I am."

"The DHI server," he said, "not the ship's passenger manifest."

She gave him a look that caught and won the attention of everyone present in the room.

"You've been programmed as a DHI," Philby said, doubting her.

"Two point oh."

The silence that hung over the room was oppressive. Wayne having the foresight to program someone the Keepers had never met into the newest available system gave weight to the idea that the Keepers were going to be replaced by newer models at some point.

In fact, with Storey's announcement, that point suddenly seemed much closer than any of the Keepers had believed possible.

"We need you too, Amanda," Finn said, trying to change the subject while knowing he might be accused of favoritism or teased for his choice. "Because you can push."

"And you," Willa said, "because of your freakish strength."

No one had made a big deal about Finn's newfound abilities; he'd been glad for that, because even he did not understand them. He didn't have control of whatever it was; he didn't want to promise something he couldn't deliver.

"I don't know," he said.

"Finn's not going." Philby stood, arms crossed; defiant, anticipating an objection. "And no, Maybeck, not you either."

He allowed a few seconds for this to sink in. Rage washed through Finn. Philby, taking over as the leader. Again. He wanted so desperately to object, but kept himself in check.

"Finn's not going because whoever did this just kidnapped 'him.' We're not going to give them the real thing. They also went after you, Maybeck. As good as you are in a fight, you're going to sit this one out."

"We're going for Dillard," Finn said. Enough was enough. "And I'm in."

"You are not. Yes, we are going find and rescue Dillard. But I propose the following. First, Charlene is critical to the mission; she saw the two hunters in the woods. Second, Mattie will go with her—she's a stow-away to begin with; she won't be missed. If Charlene can identify either of the two people she saw, Mattie may be able to touch them and draw out information about where Dillard is."

"Mattie doesn't see the future." Finn tried to gauge the mood in the room. It seemed like the others were buying into Philby's plan; he didn't want to object, be outvoted, and look weak.

"No, but if Dillard, a.k.a. Finn, is mentioned, maybe this guy'll think something about where Dillard *is*, and that's all we'd need."

"Makes sense," Willa said.

Finn tensed. He was losing ground. "It's a bogus plan. The others can be returned and rejoin the ship. Mattie and Dillard can't. They're not DHIs."

"True," Philby said. "But Wayne can get us around that problem." He looked directly at Finn, who was steamed to hear of yet another secret conversation.

"Wayne has arranged for money to be left at the front desk. Mattie and Dillard are going to meet us in Mexico. The fishing boat they'll be on makes the *Dream* look like a sea slug. Finally, as Finn suggested, Amanda is the third piece. Her ability to push could come in quite handy. Three girls. I hate to sound sexist, but Dillard's kidnappers are also unlikely to see them as hostiles. That should give the girls at least a few seconds to get the jump on them."

The lack of even a murmur of discontent shocked Finn. Usually a plan was challenged up and down before acceptance. What did the apparent universal agreement mean?

His resentment of Philby—so recently dormant—built to where he wanted to say something—anything—to make Philby look bad. But he couldn't think of a thing to say. The urge passed, the fire died; but the coals lingered.

"An all-girl mission," Charlene said, making no attempt to mask her pride and joy. "I like it."

23

CHARLENE'S HAND FLICKERED and disappeared. When she tapped Mattie Weaver on the leg, the girl shrieked, and then faked a sneeze to mollify the surprised taxi driver. What caused Mattie's shriek was the empty backseat; a moment earlier, there had been two other girls sitting with her. With no technology to project their holograms, Charlene and Amanda had disappeared into DHI shadow a mile away from the ship.

Philby had explained it all—high speed modems, security cameras, laptops equipped with video. Charlene's focus was not when or how she and Amanda might be visible, but what came next. She was the appointed leader of this trio; it didn't escape her that this was an all-girl mission, the first in a foreign country. She'd only had one year of Spanish. A boy's life hung in the balance. Success or failure hung on her, fairly or not.

It made her think of Finn and all the times he'd led the Keepers, all the times he'd carried this kind of pressure so effortlessly. Until Charlene had felt the weight on her shoulders, she'd had no idea how heavy it was. Her admiration of Finn transformed into a jealousy of Amanda, the invisible girl sitting next to her.

The taxi jostled and bumped along the same poorly surfaced roads the bus had traversed earlier in the day.

By now, the *Dream* was out to sea, leaving Mattie landlocked and on her own. They all understood that if the holograms failed completely, Mattie was going solo.

"You all right?" Charlene asked, but no sound came out of her mouth. They'd hoped to be able to use cell phone technology for their voices. Perhaps they were out of cell range as well. Was the mission over before it began: one Fairlie against the foreign Overtaker force that had kidnapped Dillard? What chance did Mattie have without their help?

"Daa—a—ng it!" she said. Her voice! It sounded digital and supremely electronic, but it mirrored closely what she'd actually said.

The driver rattled off something in Spanish, swiveling his head toward the backseat. His eyes went so wide they appeared ready to fall out of their sockets. He had picked up three young ladies. But there was only one girl in his backseat. The taxi swerved toward the littered shoulder of the road. He gained control just in time, fishtailing the vehicle back onto the asphalt. Speaking a blue streak, which no doubt included a good deal of cursing, he aimed the rearview mirror lower. Then he crossed himself, fetched a medallion hanging on his necklace, and kissed it.

Charlene understood why: she could see her hand again. Her arm. Her legs. In all her DHI 2.0 hi-def brilliance. She had Philby to thank, but how had he . . . ?

Her eye was drawn to a small video camera mounted on the inside of the windshield, aimed into the backseat. If someone tried to rob or harm the driver, they would be recorded. Philby had caught the number on their cab, hacked the taxi's security system, and hijacked the camera's bandwidth to project both her and Amanda, who now sat next to her, looking equally real.

The driver—poor man—appeared to be suffering a stroke.

Charlene spoke the first thing that came to mind. "How much longer, please?" She tried again in Spanish. What she actually said was, "Time is long, please." But the driver got the message. He answered by pointing to the dashboard digital clock and seem to indicate twenty minutes.

Charlene smiled and leaned back. She'd have to remember to thank Philby if she ever got back to the ship.

* * *

The taxi dropped them off well short of Aventura's gate. Charlene did not want to announce their arrival. Mattie, who carried Charlene's iPhone, input the driver's number, making arrangements to be picked up in this same place if and when she called. All three girls thought the same thing at the same time: *With any luck, we'll have one more passenger.*

Charlene's and Amanda's DHIs had vanished and reappeared several more times in the back of the cab. Their images were fairly strong at the moment, thanks to the security cameras in use by the park. This was confirmed as they ducked behind a rock to discuss strategy, and the two girls went into DHI shadow. Their voices remained.

"We have two possibilities," Charlene's voice told Mattie. "The lodge here at the bottom of the mountain, and the cabin at the top." Philby's Google Earth reconnaissance had revealed only the two nearby structures for a very long distance in any direction. If Dillard had been nabbed, he should be found in one of them. If injured, or somehow left behind by the group *and* missed by the staff that had searched for him . . . well, that possibility didn't seem too likely.

According to Philby, the various cameras in use were not monitored in real time. Instead, they were connected to a VCR that dated back to the 1980s. If anyone broke into the compound, they would be caught on videotape, in grainy black-and-white. Fortunately, the same video system was being used to record televised

Costa Rican soccer games, which had given Philby a way to drill into the television's satellite system to determine its status and hijack the cameras.

What it meant for the girls was that no security personnel were sitting at a video monitor in the middle of the Costa Rican hill country awaiting a break-in. The girls were free to approach the compound however they wanted.

Entering proved easy. Charlene's DHI passed through the chicken-wire fence. Finding the front gate chained and padlocked, she located a side door, removed the wooden crossbar used to lock it, and let in Mattie and Amanda.

They faced three structures: two side buildings, small and dark, used for storage; the third, the main lodge where Aventura visitors ate lunch and shopped in the gift store. Big enough to hold several hundred people at picnic tables beneath a thatched roof, its open-air windows currently glowed with the bluish flickering light of a running television, a fact confirmed by the rapid-fire Spanish of a sports announcer.

A crouching Amanda stood cautiously and peeked inside. She held up a single finger as she sank back down, her back to the wall alongside Charlene who then signaled them to the distant storage hut. Her DHI passed through the wall and inside. She unlocked the door and quietly handed out four zip line harnesses and four pair of gloves, taken by Mattie.

"Helmets?" Mattie whispered.

"Please," Charlene answered.

While this was happening, Amanda went through the wall of the remaining hut. No Dillard.

Charlene panicked at the thought Dillard might have already been sacrificed.

They hurried to the bottom of the trail that climbed the mountain. Normally, park visitors ascended to the top by chairlift. The girls were in for a long, steep hike.

"What's wrong?" Charlene asked Mattie.

"I could have helped back there. If I'd touched that guard . . ."

"Then he'd have known we'd broken in. Unless we'd clubbed him on the head or something—not me! thank you—he'd have called or radioed or whatever, and we'd maybe never see Dillard again. Have no fear; you may get your chance yet. But first we have to find this other place and see what's up with that. If there's nothing there, then we go back to that security guy and do whatever we've got to do."

"These guys have done this a lot," Amanda told Mattie. "They've got a plan."

"It's just . . . one touch, and the things I know. The things I can tell you."

"As in, if a boy likes us?" Charlene asked, looking directly at Amanda while thinking of Finn.

Mattie looked at the two competing girls. "Let's not forget I spent two years living with Mandy and Jess."

The darkness of the trail quieted them. It was difficult to see, and using a flashlight was out of the question for fear of being spotted. The jungle was filled with unfamiliar sounds—hoots and howls, buzzing and flapping—that terrified all three girls; but no one was going to be the first to admit it.

Soon, Amanda and Charlene passed into DHI shadow, their images first sparkling, then vanishing all together. Their voices changed quality, but they could communicate with Mattie, reassuring her that they were right there with her. Over the hour-long climb, they took two breaks for Mattie's sake. One of the benefits of being a DHI, Amanda explained, was that projections didn't get muscle tired, need water, or get hungry. Sleep fatigue overtook them if their human selves got exceptionally tired—the result of slowed brain functions—but otherwise they were made for marathons.

Nearing the top, Mattie squealed as she walked through a thick spiderweb that stuck to her face and hair. She caught herself mid-cry and stopped, fighting off the sticky thread and feeling it like a net over her skin. She swatted at every itch, fearing there was some giant spider crawling on her.

"Wait here," Charlene's voice said. "I'm going to scout ahead."

"That was loud, wasn't it?" Mattie asked in a whisper.

"It wasn't quiet," Amanda said, "but there's so much weird stuff out here, I doubt it would be noticed."

"I'm sorry."

"I hate spiders. I'm right there with you."

"It was so much. Oh my gosh, it's disgusting." Mattie continued to pick at the sticky web glued to her.

"I don't even want to think about what's out here, animal-wise. Did you hear that thing grunting?"

"The snorting thing?"

"Exactly."

"I about screamed," Mattie said. "What was that?"

"I don't know, but it sounded big, and wild, and way too close."

"It can't hurt you, right? None of it can hurt you."

"No. But sometimes in shadow, you can still touch stuff. Do things. Even Philby hasn't figured that one out yet. Everything changed when they did this upgrade last year. Technically, we're still in beta. The Imagineers, the people who invented it all, are constantly chang- ing the software. We call it 2.0, but it's more like

2.6 or something by now. They're getting the bugs out."

"I hope that includes spiders."

The girls laughed together.

"I've never thanked you for coming," Amanda said.

"No big."

"It will be if you're caught."

"Not really. Everyone's terrified of me. All the docs and those soldier types. They make me wear the same gloves I wore when you were there."

"The ones that lock."

"Yeah. And they cover my face. All my skin. They have too many secrets, right? They know any contact with me, and I'll know it all. It freaks them out. That's the thing we should have figured out back when you and Jess were there. How much they fear us. We had all sorts of power over them that we never used. It's like you guys, the Keepers. By yourselves, maybe not so much—but together? Forget about it. I know that now. If the Fairlies could come together, if we could get past all the stupid jealousies about each other's powers and work together, there's no way those idiots could keep us locked up. We are way too powerful."

"Well, you won't have to worry about that."

"Won't I?"

"Mrs. Nash will take you in. She's a control freak, but mostly she's okay."

"You're not getting it, Mandy. I want to be caught. I'm good with it."

Silence.

"That freaks you out," Mattie said.

"Well, yeah."

"If I'm caught . . . when I'm caught, I'll be returned to Baltimore. To the facility. I can save those guys. I see that now. Until you, Jess, the Keepers, I didn't understand what we have."

"You're saying Jess and I should come, too. That we should all allow ourselves to be caught."

"I'm not. Just because it's right for me doesn't make it right for you."

"I never want to go back."

"It's good you know that."

"But it never occurred to me that we could break everyone out. They'd catch us. They always catch us."

"They haven't caught you."

"I'm pretty sure they know where we are. Mrs. Nash threatens to send us back all the time."

"Just because she knows about the facility doesn't mean the facility knows about you. You and Jess proved it's possible, to get out, to be free. And if you think about it, you know why."

"Because we stuck together." Amanda understood

Mattie's dream then. Her fantasy. But Charlene's arrival silenced any further speech.

"It's a ways up," Charlene's voice said from the darkness. "And I passed a sign that marks the park's border."

"It's not part of the park?"

"No. It's just a big house. Stone and wood. Some screened-in porches and screens on the windows. It's huge. And it's, I don't know, kind of fancy in a run-down way. Like it was fancy a long time ago. There were men's voices. Four? Five? More?"

"Were you visible?"

"Oh, yeah. Philby's got us powered up and projected. Security cameras, I think. We start showing up maybe a hundred yards away. Really clear pretty soon after. I didn't press it. All for one, and all of that."

Her comment drove home what Mattie had been talking about—that the Keepers worked as a team. Amanda thought of the five teens as individuals, hadn't given the team concept a lot of consideration, but there was no denying it. The Keepers did everything, big or small, as a group. Typically, the real problems arose when they were off on their own.

The invisible Charlene led the way for Mattie, with Amanda on guard, bringing up the rear. At the top, they passed the platform looming out over the ravine—the start of the first and longest zip line. It felt haunted, due to the loud jungle sounds. The constancy of the buzzing and humming of night insects made all the girls jumpy.

When Charlene's hologram began sparking and reappearing, Mattie fell back several yards, slightly afraid. The same phenomenon overtook Amanda's DHI. Pieces of the two girls appeared, disappeared, and reformed. An arm. A leg from the knee down. A torso floating in space. Then an arm attached to the torso and legs grew out of it, and there was the complete girl, walking, but shimmering in distorted squares of color like a television in a thunderstorm.

"That is so . . . awesome!"

"I thought you were freaking."

"No way! Wickedly cool."

"Quiet!" Amanda said. "We're too close!"

They huddled on their knees, still fifty yards from the building.

"Amanda and I will go first. You'll stay here and wait for my signal. I'm going to try to get a look at them so I can maybe see if either of the two who were in the woods are in there. If they are, we signal and you join us. Remember, they can't hurt Amanda or me. They can't catch us. But you? Different story. So the first thing is to keep you safe. If everything goes as we hope, then we'll go in. Or maybe we can lure one of the guys out so you can touch him. The thing is, you've got to be very smart about this, Mattie. You've got to know when to take off. Head for the first platform and get going. Don't wait. Call the taxi right away."

"But what if you need your phone? I'll have it. Besides, what if there's no time to tell you what I've found out?"

"Okay. Good point. So we'll have a code. Once you've read this guy, you will use one of two words: *Here*, or *Gone*. That's all Mandy and I need. You can fill us in on the deets later." Charlene held up a finger and listened. Jungle sounds. She whispered. "Maybe we'll have Dillard. Maybe not. About a mile down the road there's a sign advertising this place. Bring the taxi by there every half hour, but stay way away the rest of the time. Don't stop. Just drive by. You'll see us if we're there."

"Are you okay?" Amanda asked.

"I'm talking to a pair of holograms in the Costa Rican jungle. Do I have to answer that?"

"We've got this," Charlene said.

"The Keepers have faced way worse, believe me," Amanda said. "Like Charlie said, you've got to be very smart about getting out of there."

"If there's a reason for you to go in in the first place," Charlene said. "If not, no matter how bad it gets, don't play hero. Amanda and I can trick them. Don't fall for that."

Mattie nodded. Charlene turned toward the house, about to head that direction.

"Can I just say something?" Mattie's voice was no louder than a breeze in the branches.

"Go ahead."

"If I had friends like all of you . . ." She didn't finish.

Amanda placed her hand on Mattie's shoulder. Mattie twitched because she could *feel* herself being touched.

"You do," Amanda said.

* * *

The house was a one-story hacienda with terra-cotta Spanish roof tile and pale stucco walls. The open-air windows were wood-trimmed and screened. A large propane tank was concealed by a thicket of bushes. Solar panels reflected from the roof in the intermittent moonlight.

Charlene crawled on hands and knees, followed closely by Amanda. Being projections, their DHIs shone clearly, making them easy to spot. But without the telltale blue outline that had accompanied the 1.6 software, the two girls looked perfectly real. The only way to tell they were holograms would be for someone to try to touch them, something they had no intention of allowing.

Placing her back against the stucco wall, Charlene rose slowly until her head was alongside the window's opening. It amazed her that in this condition, she still felt everything as she normally would: sweat trickling down her rib cage, heart racing, breathing rapid and shallow. She moved just enough to peer inside, then dropped quickly, shaking her head. The two girls moved to the next window. Charlene tried again. She held up two fingers—two men. The next window showed the kitchen; empty. They dropped to their bellies and crawled past a back patio with two sets of sliding doors—a living room and a bedroom.

Through the bedroom window, Charlene recognized the Costa Rican woman from the woods, though she wasn't wearing her camouflage. Charlene dropped down alongside Amanda and closed her eyes to try to regain her composure. She put her lips to Amanda's holographic ear.

"Watching TV. It's her."

Amanda whispered back. "Door closed?"

"Yes."

"Just her in the room?"

"All I saw. Who knows?"

"Dillard could be in one of these rooms."

"I know. How easy would that be?"

"Too easy," said Amanda.

Charlene nodded. Nothing was ever easy. She tried to think up a viable plan to get Mattie in physical contact with the woman. The problem was that if Mattie made physical contact, then the alarm would be sounded, making it more difficult, if not impossible, to rescue Dillard. But without Mattie making contact with someone who knew Dillard's whereabouts, it was a wild-goose chase.

"First," she said, "we'll circle the house checking all the rooms. If no Dillard, then back here with Mattie."

"There is another way."

Charlene gestured for her to get on with it.

"I could push this woman," Amanda said, "and hold her while Mattie reads her and finds out where Dillard is."

"You'd waste your energy because she'd scream, and we'd be outnumbered."

"Not if we got her gagged, she wouldn't. You could do that, because the push won't affect your hologram."

"It'll drain you." Charlene had witnessed the effects of Amanda unleashing her supernatural force. "Who knows how long it could take us to find Dillard? And besides, we might need you to rescue him in the first place."

"It's an option," Amanda said.

"Okay. An option."

They circumnavigated the house, window by window. It took them ten minutes. They returned to Mattie in the woods.

"Nothing," Charlene told her. "No sign of him." She laid out the plan. Mattie would stay back in the woods, awaiting Charlene's signal. Amanda and Charlene returned to outside the patio bedroom, where, once again, the woman outlaw was seen watching TV from the bed.

Charlene waved for Mattie to join them. Mattie belly-crawled and reached them without incident. Amanda took Mattie by the hand and the two of them moved to the sliding glass door, the curtain pulled on the inside. Charlene slipped up the wall and gained a view of the woman.

Charlene nodded.

Amanda meowed. Extremely convincingly. She paused, and tried again, slightly louder.

Charlene watched the woman—five-feet six inches, incredibly fit, dark skin and short jet-black hair—slip off the bed and approach the patio door. The click of the lock. The door sliding open.

Mattie reached inside, grabbing the woman's wrist, and held on tightly.

"The boy," Charlene said in crude Spanish.

Amanda raised her right hand, palm out, while

lowering her head. She stared with a crazed expression. Amanda's push drove the woman's chin up and clenched her teeth so that her cry for help came out like someone choking on a fish bone. Mattie reacted physically, as if electrically shocked. She let go of the woman's wrist.

That proved to be the game changer. Amanda's pushing used enough force to keep the woman's jaw set; but once Mattie released the woman, that same force was enough to throw the woman off her feet and onto the tile. In that instant, Amanda's energy was no longer aimed at the woman, who managed to call out.

"Dillard's in her thoughts," Mattie panted, "but I didn't see where."

A man burst through the bedroom door. Amanda threw her push at him, pinning him. But a second man followed. The woman guard dove and tripped up Mattie, who tumbled back onto the patio.

Amanda's energy had to be tapped, Charlene thought. If she pushed again . . .

Charlene attacked the woman guard, pulling her off Mattie. The guard swung at Charlene, and froze as her hand swiped through the hologram. Charlene had witnessed this reaction before: the stunned incredulity that made no sense in a physical world—a fist did not swing through a person. It was impossible. The brain cannot process such information. It requires a second attempt before settling on a hypothesis.

As the woman wound up to throw a second punch, Charlene took her by the throat and pinned her to the tile.

"Where's my friend?"

The guard fought against a girl made of light. It was too much. Her eyes rolled into the back of her head, and she passed out, unconscious from fright.

Amanda threw the second man against the wall, but lost the first man in the process.

"To the left!" Charlene cried.

Amanda released the two inside, and—with a strength Charlene could hardly believe—pushed to her left, into the darkness of the patio. A man only Charlene had seen lifted to his feet and flew away from them. Amanda returned the force to inside the room, just catching a guard running at her. She staggered, nearly spent.

"That's him!" Charlene shouted to Mattie. "That's the guy!"

Mattie displayed nerves of steel. She stood and marched through the door. Amanda redirected her force, knocking the man down. Mattie grabbed hold of the man's ankle; her body shook.

Amanda couldn't do everything at once. Charlene

ran across the patio and shoved the guard as he attempted to stand. He kicked at her, but his feet did nothing but flop in the air. She shoved him again. He struck his head on a stone in the path and was dazed, blinking furiously to maintain consciousness. Returning to her friends, she arrived in time to see Mattie release the man's ankle; then Mattie fell back onto her bottom.

"Oh . . . no . . ." Mattie said. "We gotta get out of here."

"Run!" Amanda shouted, as she gave one final push. Both men and all the furniture in the room lifted off the floor and flew, slamming against the far wall. Amanda turned and followed Charlene and Mattie into the woods.

Charlene led the way, hoping her sense of direction was good. The guards would know the area far better than they. It was a footrace now, and all they had was the lingering hope that the guards would not think to bring harnesses with them.

"Dillard?" Charlene cried out, tormented at having failed in their mission.

"He's on the bus," answered Mattie. "The man was thinking about a zipper on a duffel bag getting stuck. A boy was in the duffel bag. The woman . . . she was thinking about the duffel getting to the ship."

"What?"

"I think Dillard's back on the ship."

"But why?"

"Don't know. Stones. A tunnel. Like the drawing. A monster. Different, but similar." She ran fast and easy. They helped Amanda, who was dragging. The kidnappers were closing fast.

"Similar how?" Amanda asked.

"Blood and death. The monster. The someone who's going to die? It's going to be . . . Finn."

Both Amanda and Charlene skidded to a stop at the same instant. They stared at Mattie. The sound of the guards grew louder and closer. Mattie ran past them.

"Come on!"

The other two girls started running again. The platform for the first line came into view as an angular shape. Then details could be seen: stairs, the two platforms. The girls hurried up. Charlene fumbled as she attempted to clip Mattie's harness in. It took too much time.

"Go!" She pushed Mattie off the platform. The girl flew out across the deep ravine, her flailing limbs like spider legs in the dull glow of the moon. Finally, she collected herself and moved even faster on the pulleys. The line whirred.

Charlene clipped Amanda to the line. Looking behind them, Amanda declared, "No time. Hold on."

She reached around Charlene's waist, and her arm passed through the hologram. "I need you solid!"

Charlene was too distracted by the approaching guard. She pushed Amanda off the platform, only to realize Amanda was right: no time.

Charlene dove off the platform, out into open space. The dark ravine yawned beneath her. She flew, light as a feather. As she stretched for Amanda, her friend sparked, spit photons, and disappeared. DHI shadow. Charlene witnessed her own arm dissolving before her. But she hit something soft and clung fast to it. Amanda's thigh.

An unseen arm scooped down and held to her.

Behind them, the first guard drew a pulley into place, and *without a harness* jumped off the platform, clinging to the pulley. He raced toward them.

Charlene realized that she and Amanda were slowing down.

"Our holograms don't weigh anything!" Charlene cried out. "We're not heavy enough to carry along the line!"

In fact, as the pulley and harness reached the halfway point on the thousand-foot stretch of cable, it glided to a stop. Behind them the cable pointed slightly up toward the platform they'd left; in front of them, it pointed up toward the platform that was their intended destination. They were stuck.

The guard flew toward them at breakneck speed. He was going to crash into the girls.

Amanda squeezed Charlene tighter. "Hold on!"

The guard never saw them. Even if he had, there was nothing he could have done about it. The collision hit him in a way it did not hit the girls because he'd had no warning. The pulleys clashed. The guard lost his grip on the pulley's chain.

He fell.

All the pulleys started moving now, driven by his added weight.

Charlene reached, practically dove, and grabbed hold of the guard with two hands. Amanda held Charlene, both invisible, both upside down.

The man rattled off something in Spanish that must have been cursing. Seen from a distance, he was suspended in midair, about three feet below the zip line. That's what his fellow guards saw from the platform. They began screaming. More than one crossed himself. The woman fell to her knees and clasped her hands in prayer.

Charlene tightened her grip as the man's wrist began to sweat. He was slipping from her grasp.

"I can't hold him," she said, her voice cellular and electronic sounding.

The man looked terrified. First, he was being held

from his death by an angel. Then the angel spoke. *English!* He'd always thought angels spoke Spanish.

The two girls rearranged themselves invisibly. Charlene slipped her legs around Amanda's middle and locked her ankles. "I've got it," she said.

"You sure?"

"You can let go."

Carefully, Amanda released her hold on Charlene, feeling the girl's legs tighten around her. With her hands now free, Charlene reached down and took the man's other arm. Together the girls grunted and pulled him higher. Charlene transferred her grip to his torso and waist. At last, he lunged and grasped the zip line. He hooked an elbow in the dangling chain, and released a lungful of air. Saved.

His eyes shut, his lips ran through a litany of prayer.

The girls began pulling themselves uphill on the zip line. Without any physical weight, the pulley moved easily.

After a moment, the guards on the platform began hollering at their companion. He came out of his prayers, saw the pulley moving of its own accord, shut his eyes, and began praying again.

The girls climbed steadily toward the waiting platform on the other side of the ravine. They unclipped and hit the down-sloping trail at a full run. Arriving at the second station, they saw the zip line bouncing. Mattie had crossed within the past few minutes. They clipped on and sailed across, still in DHI shadow. But again, without any weight, the pulley stopped in the middle, requiring them to pull themselves hand over hand to the exit platform. It took a long time.

The guards had gotten over their prayers. They were back on the hunt. As Charlene unclipped her harness, one of the guards was already flying toward them.

"I see you!" Amanda exclaimed.

Charlene looked down. Then at Amanda. They were fully projected again.

"RUN!"

They sparked in and out of DHI shadow on their way to the third station. More in than out, giving the man behind them a hard target. A rock the size of a fist flew past Charlene's face.

Flew far too fast to have been thrown by a mortal.

Overtakers? she wondered.

She stole a look behind her. A slingshot. Not the kind boys played with—surgical rubber strung between an aluminum Y—but the cloth-and-string variety that reminded her of Hercules and Bible stories and the Roman Colosseum. The man slung another. It came at them as fast as a rocket and passed through Amanda's head. Had she not been a DHI, she'd have been dead.

They talked as they ran at a full sprint, bounding over clumps of roots, skidding at turns in the trail.

"He's trying to kill us." Charlene was an Olympic runner.

"I noticed," Amanda said.

"You need to push him!"

"I'm not sure I can."

"You've got to try."

"When?" Amanda asked.

"When I say! Once you do, head down through the woods. The way we came up."

"But the—"

"I'll take care of the zip line," Charlene said.

"I'm not leaving you."

"Mattie needs you. I'll be right behind you. I'll be fine."

"I'm not leaving you!" Amanda shouted.

"Listen to me, Amanda. Push the slingshot dude and go down *on this side of the trail*. No more zip lines. We need to reach Mattie. She's ahead of us." They took two turns, like an S. "If they get her . . . She's the only one who knows what's going on with Dillard. I'm a hologram. What's the worst that can happen?"

"They want you," Amanda said, reminding her of Jess's drawing.

"You and I . . . they can't touch us! I'm fine!"

They reached the platform sooner than expected.

Charlene slowed. She glanced back at Amanda, trying to say with her eyes: *Now or never.*

Amanda turned, waited, and then threw out both palms. The approaching guard lifted like a kite and flew away, crashing deep into the jungle.

"Now, go!" Charlene scaled the platform. Amanda staggered off into the dark forest. Charlene slipped the harness off, clipped it to the pulley, and rocked the pulley back and forth, releasing it with all her strength. The pulley and dangling harness sailed out across the bottomless ravine.

A crunching behind her told her the pushed guard was returning. No time to get off the platform by the stairs; she'd be seen.

She looked off the edge of the platform that faced the ravine. It was straight down. About thirty feet below was a rocky outcropping. If she missed that . . .

Charlene took a deep breath.

She jumped.

The last thought before her feet left the platform, a thought that should have come a beat earlier, was: *One of you will die.*

* * *

Amanda's hologram was fully resolved by the time she caught up to Mattie near the bottom of the trail. She looked perfectly human; her voice was clear and capable of expression.

"Stop!" she called. Pulling Mattie off the trail she whispered, "They will have told the guard down here about us. He'll be waiting."

"But the gate. It's right there." Indeed, the way out was only twenty yards away.

"He's hiding. He's waiting."

"You don't know that! He could be in there watching TV."

"He's not."

Mattie was pale and trembling. In a state of shock. "What am I going to do?"

The ship had sailed. The reality of her situation registered: Dillard had been smuggled back aboard the *Dream*. Once Amanda and Charlene were returned by Philby, Mattie would be on her own.

"We're going to work this out."

"You are, sure! But what about me?"

"I need you to calm down, Mattie. These things . . . One step at a time. You get ahead of yourself and you get in trouble."

"Easy for you to say. You're going back to the ship."

"Right now, I'm getting out of this place. That's all that matters. That's the next step."

"What about Charlene?"

Amanda looked back up the trail. "No one followed us, so she pulled off, tricking them. She's a DHI. She's safe." Amanda didn't sound convinced. "By now they're working their way down the zip lines. It'll take them a while. A lot longer than it took us to get down, that's for sure."

"But where is she?"

"She'll be here any minute."

"And if she isn't?"

"She can't be more than two or three minutes behind. We've already spent most of that talking. We go, whether she catches up or not."

"You'd leave her behind?"

"Do I want to? No, of course not. But as long as she gets herself out of DHI shadow, she'll return with me. She'll be fine."

"But we won't know if she's out or in. Right? Not without seeing her."

"Mattie, I *really* need you to calm down. Take a deep breath. Chill out. We all make more mistakes when we're wound up."

"You're not my mother, Mandy."

"No, I'm your friend. And I'm Charlene's friend."

Mattie nodded. She drew a deep breath, held it and let it out slowly.

"Better?"

Mattie repeated the exercise. "Sorry."

"It happens." Amanda glanced back up the trail. "Come on!" she whispered aloud, not meaning to.

"You're worried."

"I'd rather we leave together. Of course I would. But we can't wait any longer. We're going now." She said this for her own benefit as much as Mattie's. She knew it made sense, but it felt wrong; and with things between her and Charlene and Finn being the way they were, it could look wrong, too. Mattie was right: Keepers didn't leave Keepers behind.

"You're worried about her."

"Charlie's strong. And clever. She'll be fine." Amanda took one last look up the trail. "Yes. I'm worried. Okay? But we're leaving anyway." Amanda led Mattie back onto the trail. "We're going to circle around to the right."

"But that's the opposite direction from where we came through."

"And it's not a direct route to the main gate," Amanda said. "We can't have two plans, Mattie."

"Okay. To the right."

"I'll be focused on what's in front of us. You will stay close. You will check behind us. But don't get distracted. If you see someone, you *do not talk*. You tap me on the back and then duck."

Amanda's hologram made no sound on the trail floor. Mattie snapped a stick, but from then on walked perfectly silently, gauging her every step. They came around the far side of the two storage sheds. Amanda peered around the corner, facing the pavilion nearly straight ahead. The main gate was to her right; the chicken-wire door they'd used to enter in front of her. It was thirty yards over to the door, all of it across wide-open space, with only a few clumps of flowering bushes in between.

She turned, tapped Mattie on the chest, and pointed to the ground, signaling, *You stay here.*

Mattie acknowledged with a brief nod.

Amanda slipped out of her zip-line harness and quietly eased it to the ground. She raised her finger to her lips to silence Mattie and stepped through the wall of the shed, disappearing.

Mattie nearly choked trying to keep quiet.

Amanda moved through the inside of the well-organized shed and paused at the corrugated metal wall. She eased her face forward a half inch at a time. If you'd been standing in the pavilion's courtyard picnic area and had happened to look over at the shed, you would have seen a nose suddenly appear through the wall. It was followed by a girl's forehead and eyes and chin. The face stopped. It looked as if it belonged to a ghost. Her eyes tracked right to left. The face disappeared.

Amanda saw him. He was sitting at the end of a picnic-table bench with what looked like a strange-looking cane on his lap, just out of view of where the path entered the courtyard. Had Amanda and Mattie not gone the long way around, they would have walked into this guard's trap. No, too short for a cane. With a thick rubber handle. Why rubber? Insulation! It was a cattle prod. He was set to zap whoever crossed his path.

That made things tricky for Mattie—even for Amanda. If she happened to be reaching for him with a solid hand and the shock hit her, it would disrupt her hologram. Maybe even fry her.

Amanda stepped through the wall and rejoined Mattie. Her voice was quieter than a breeze. "Wait for me. I'll call for you. Come when you hear me."

Mattie nodded again. Her face was white.

Amanda reentered the shed. She picked up a pair of spare pulleys, moved close to the shed door, and rattled them loudly. Paused. Rattled them again. She heard the door's metal hasp click. The moment the door cracked open, Amanda stepped through the wall and into the courtyard, now behind the guard. She shoved him from behind, throwing him into the shed, threw the hasp into place, and clicked it shut, trapping him.

"Now!" she called.

Mattie came running around the corner and into the open. The trapped guard was going nuts, trying to shake the door open. The girls reached the gate and ran out into the driveway as fast as they could.

"You called the taxi?"

"Yes!"

"Where is he?"

"Late?"

"That's bad. That's very bad."

They continued running as fast as Mattie's feet would carry her.

The sound of an explosion caused Amanda to look back. Not exactly an explosion: the guard had kicked down the shed's door. He spun in a full circle, spotted the girls, and hurried for the gate.

"We've got company," Amanda said.

"I didn't need to hear that."

What Amanda didn't confess was how much the multiple pushes had drained her. She was running low on energy. As if to mirror her feelings, her hologram flickered.

"Don't leave me!" Mattie pleaded.

"I don't have a lot of choice about it." Her left arm vanished. Her head disappeared and reappeared.

The man chasing them skidded to a stop, stunned

by Amanda's vanishing. In that moment, Amanda felt a kind of power swell inside her. She possessed a quality that could intimidate an adult she found terrifying. She tried to see herself: no arms or legs. DHI shadow. Again.

"I'm right here," she said, her voice cellular quality again.

The guard ran straight for her, eyes wide with fear and rage.

"Keep running," Amanda called to Mattie. She lifted her invisible arms and pushed.

Nothing. She'd missed. She was about try again when he closed the distance.

"Boo!" she shouted, just as he was going to run her over.

The man flew off the ground, screaming. He turned an ankle as he went down and slammed onto the hard road, its dirt surface compacted to cement by endless tour buses.

Mattie was now a small dot in the dark distance. The man rolled around, gripping his ankle and moaning.

Amanda didn't know much Spanish, but she knew a few key words. She sneaked up on the writhing man and whispered harshly, *"Vive el Diablo!"* The Devil lives!

He hollered again. Rolled away from her and off the roadbed, now tucked into a fetal position. He was going to need therapy.

Far away on the mountain, a girl screamed.

Charlene!

They should have never left her behind.

* * *

During the six o'clock hour, half the passengers attended the musical in the Walt Disney Theatre while the other half ate in one of the ship's three dining rooms.

Among the Keepers' cruise responsibilities was rotating each night to dine with a different family. Tonight, Finn had been assigned a table with a mom, a dad, and ten-year-old twin boys. At the next table, Philby was with two sets of parents and two good looking girls about his age. Some guys got all the luck, Finn thought bitterly. Was this Wayne's doing as well?

During the appetizer course—soup for Finn—a Cast Member, a young woman, arrived at his table.

"Finn Whitman?" She passed him an envelope.

"What's this?" Finn asked, accepting it. Typically, any note was left in a holder outside the door of your stateroom. A hand delivery had to be special.

She was college age, a little heavy, with sad, listless eyes. Not your typical Cast Member, Finn thought, though it had been a long day for everyone. She shrugged and headed off.

Finn opened the envelope. Inside was a typed or computer-printed card.

THE DIRECTOR OF SECURITY
REQUESTS YOUR PRESENCE AT 6:30 PM,
PER YOUR RECENT ACTIVITY IN ANIMATOR'S PALATE.

Finn gulped. *Per your recent activity . . .* As in: throwing a table across the room and destroying a wall?

The exchange had caught Philby's attention. Finn leaned out of his chair and passed him the note.

"Mind if I come along?" Philby said.

"I was just about to ask."

* * *

With passengers divided between eating and enjoying the show, the ship was like a ghost town. As Finn and Philby descended the stairway to Deck 1, the staircase lights sputtered, flickered, and died.

When the lights came back up a moment later, they were at half their original brightness, a gloomy amber.

"Do you always travel in pairs?"

They recognized her voice immediately, the knowledge followed by a wave of dread and terror. Maleficent rarely showed herself, and when she did . . . Finn and Philby had too many bad memories of those moments.

Exchanging a look, refusing to glance back and see the evil fairy, the boys continued down the stairway. They were careful not to run, not to instigate some action from Maleficent. She was powerful, but they'd beaten her before; she didn't scare Finn the way she once might have. They wanted to reach the landing where there would be more room and more choices for escape or even—did he dare think it?—victory.

Below them, on the Deck 1 forward landing, a second figure appeared: the Evil Queen.

A witch sandwich.

"No Chernabog," Philby whispered. "That's interesting."

"Only to *you*," Finn said. "But now that you mention it . . ."

Maleficent raised both arms, lifting her robe. She looked like a giant purple-and-black raven, but with a green face, pointed chin, and a long nose.

"There comes a time in every rite of passage," the evil fairy said in her clear but icy voice, "when one must confront one's demons. This is the moment between youth and adulthood. The dark passage. But you will never reach that passage, Finn Whitman and Dell Philby. For your time has come."

"Your magic is powerful," said the Queen from below. "Children should not play with fire. Sadly, you are neither children nor of age. You live in the middle kingdom, where views are never clear and trust is never certain. I envy you, if truth be told. I pity you as well. For in the end, it comes down to the person. The soul of the matter. We have transitioned, have we not? From one side to the next. From there, to here. And now, dear ones, you too will be given this honor, so that we may understand your magic better."

Finn and Philby were trapped. On any other section of stairway, they could have vaulted the banisters and escaped. But the final flight of stairs did not offer that choice.

"We need only a tiny favor," Maleficent said. "So much easier if you cooperate."

"So much easier," the Queen echoed.

Philby spoke calmly, like a man twice his age. Finn marveled at his composure.

"Beauty such as yours, fair Queen, should not be hidden. This wretch behind us—hideously foul, don't you think?—does not deserve to share the same air with loveliness such as yours. What does she want from you, do you think? Equality? Her? You may slay the two of us—helpless *children*—but beware the enemy within."

Finn spotted the opening. Just for an instant,

Philby's appeal to the Queen's vanity, his hints about competition from Maleficent, made the witch to take her eyes off the prize: she looked beyond the boys to the winged woman on the landing above. In that moment, Philby dove, a swan dive aimed at the witch below.

He heard the flutter of wings too late. Diablo—freed from his kitchen prison cell—struck Philby mid-flight. The smallish bird smashed Philby into the wall. He slid limply to the floor; the Evil Queen put her polished shoe on his neck and pressed down. Hard. Philby's face went red. She eased up, but not much.

"Return of the journal," Maleficent said. *"Now!"*

"I . . . ahh . . ."

"NOW!"

Finn looked between the two women. The Queen increased the pressure on Philby's neck. He was shaking his head no.

One of you will die.

"Okay! Okay!" Finn said. He gently slipped his Wave Phone from his pocket and called Maybeck. But all the while he was thinking: *If they need the journal, if they want to kill us, then they don't have Chernabog yet.*

"Listen up," Finn said nervously. "The safe combination is four-two-one-two." He gathered his courage. He would have to talk incredibly fast. He wondered if his newfound speed and abilities would translate to his voice. "Take the journal to the jogging track. Hold it over the rail. Wait for us. Drop it if we're not—"

He had done it: spoken faster than those guys at the end of radio ads. But Maleficent had him off his feet, held by the throat, her hand as cold as liquid nitrogen.

"Fix it," she whispered.

Finn could barely breathe—his throat was starting to freeze shut—but he managed to drop the phone. It bounced down the stairs.

"Curse you!" Maleficent cried, dropping him like a sack of sand. Finn collapsed to the stairs. "You obstinate, wretched little—" She raised her hands high, clearly preparing to end him.

Finn closed his eyes: *One of you will die.*

"Stop! You fool!" the Queen thundered. "We *need* him. We *need that journal!*"

Maleficent turned a darker, hideous green as she blushed, clearly not accustomed to being scolded.

"Up," the Queen commanded. "Both of you." She took her foot off Philby's throat. He rubbed his neck and sucked for air.

She addressed Finn. "We will go along with your plan, young man, but if I sense the slightest deceit, believe me, you will wish you were dead and buried."

"I believe you," Finn muttered.

Diablo landed on Maleficent's shoulder and stared cruelly at Philby.

Minutes later, they were on the jogging track, the evening wind driving warm sea air across the deck. A few stray passengers lined the rail looking out, some arm-in-arm.

One person was not studying the sea, but staring at the two women and two boys who came through the amidships doorway: Maybeck.

A bird took flight from the taller woman's shoulder, startling a few of the passengers. They immediately took this to be part of the evening's entertainment. Whispers went down the rail.

Ignoring them, Maybeck held the journal over the side.

"What now?" said Maleficent. She held Finn by the back of the neck.

"You release us and you both keep your hands at your side."

"You tell her, Finn!" a passenger shouted. A few applauded.

"He'll put the journal down on the deck," Finn said.

"Finn will join him," Philby said, taking over. "I stay with you. They will back away from the journal. When the Queen is close to the journal, you will release me. I run. The Queen gets the journal."

Maleficent considered the rules. "Agreed."

Philby caught Finn's attention and threw his eyes to the wall, where the shuffleboard equipment hung. Philby was a devious boy; it was everything Finn could do to stop from smiling.

"You hear any of that?" Finn called to Maybeck.

The boy shook his head.

"Journal goes on the deck. You kick it under the rail if they don't let us go."

Maybeck nodded and set the journal down.

Finn, who wanted to switch roles with Philby, knew better than to protest. He walked toward Maybeck. The Queen followed, a few steps behind.

Their audience grew significantly—the passengers seemed to be coming out of the woodwork. To them, it looked like an improvisation on an Old West shootout.

The Queen was now a step from the journal, practically drooling.

Maleficent held tightly to Philby, her grip cruel.

"Release him!" Finn called. He and Maybeck did the fox-trot; they took a step back and another away from the rail. "Do not move," Finn whispered to the Queen, who seemed ready to pounce.

Maleficent released Philby. He backed up toward the door slowly.

It was a five-person dance now. Maybeck and

Finn eased closer to the wall; the Queen bent toward the journal; Maleficent eyed the three boys, expecting trouble.

Finn didn't disappoint. He jumped for the wall, jumped farther than an Olympian, grabbed hold of a shuffleboard disc, squatted down, and shot it across the deck, knocking the journal beneath the rail just as the Queen's long fingers reached for it.

Philby and Maybeck rushed through the door, followed by Finn, whose speed made him nearly impossible to see. He was the last through the door, his eyes alight with victory.

The Queen shrieked, "KILL THEM!"

But Maleficent made no move. She was *smiling*—red lips, green skin, white teeth. A horror show.

Like an angel rising, here came Diablo above the rail, the journal's cover clenched in his beak, the rest of the pages dangling.

The Queen wound up to throw a spell. Finn dove inside, came to his feet, and ran.

"They got the journal!" he shouted as the three boys bounded down the stairs. "Diablo caught it!"

At Deck 3 they hurried toward the bow and the forward stairs.

"Where are we going, anyway?" Maybeck asked.

"Security!" replied Philby. "They're expecting us."

* * *

Poised precariously on a rock ledge thirty feet below the zip-line platform, Charlene dared not move, for fear of being seen. Having jumped from the platform, she'd also jumped into DHI shadow—invisibility.

As she reached out from where she was hidden, several of her fingers reappeared. For the ruse to work, every last guard who had pursued them had to ride the zip line to the far side. Only one guy had done so. After colliding with the empty harness that she'd sent ahead halfway out across the line, this man had shouted something back in Spanish. Whoever was on the platform above her—if anyone—had failed to follow down the line.

What any of it meant, Charlene wasn't sure. She was currently tucked in behind a plant with green leaves the size of beach towels, her back against rock.

The ledge was no more than four feet wide. Ten feet below was another ledge, and thirty feet below that yet another, like stair steps leading down into the dark slash of ravine. Her only hope of catching up to Amanda and Mattie was the trail on this side. But if she were seen taking it, she would lead their pursuers straight to her friends.

The only way to reach the trail from the ledge was to climb up to the platform, and until the man left the zip line he would spot her if she tried to do that. Presently, she saw him hand-walking back toward her, his ankles crossed over the line, moving like an inchworm.

What now? Charlene thought.

Climbing nearly straight up the rock should keep her in DHI shadow, but if not . . . Charlene wasn't overly concerned about her own safety; she was fast, strong, and a projection of light, impossible to harm. But Mattie was vulnerable. If she were captured, the Keepers would be missing two of their team members.

Decision time. The longer she stayed here, the longer Amanda would wait—no matter how detrimental to the bigger plan. Amanda was just too Amanda to leave without her. Charlene faced the rock and began climbing like Spider-Man, alert for both handholds and toeholds as well as her DHI reappearing.

Behind her, the guard continued pulling himself toward the platform.

Ten feet from the wooden struts, Charlene stretched her hand to grab a thick root sticking out of the mud wall and her hand sparkled to life. She quickly drew it down out of projection. The inchworm guard was close behind and moving fast.

She waited, holding on for dear life, the toe of her running shoe barely caught on a small jutting rock, her left hand clinging to a vine. She formed a plan.

As the guard neared the platform, two of his pals stepped forward to help him, their feet at the platform's edge.

Charlene timed her climb carefully. As the two leaned out, reaching for the man, she moved furiously, her DHI reappearing, first fuzzy, then solid. One of the two men leaning out spotted her, but too late. She grabbed the first leg she could reach and pulled. This man fell from the platform and wrapped his arms around the guard inchworming on the zip line. The second man tried to hold his partner back, but he, too, was pulled off balance. With the added weight, the zip line pulleys began to roll, and the three men, screaming for help, raced away over the ravine. Charlene hooked a knee, pulling herself fully up onto the platform.

The woman from the bedroom—fit as a ninja—stood there, blocking the stairway. She said something in Spanish that didn't sound particularly nice.

Charlene's DHI passed through her. The woman fainted, collapsing onto the platform.

Charlene took off running, her DHI dissolving and reforming, the darkness of the jungle engulfing her and driving her down, down, down the trail even faster. With any luck, she could reach Amanda, Mattie, and the taxi in time.

24

THE BOYS SPOKE AT ONCE. Uncle Bob tilted back in his chair. The monitors running behind him showed views of a quiet ship.

"First," Bob said loudly, shutting them up, "I did not send you this note." He rubbed the back of the card and tossed it onto his desk. "It was typed on a typewriter, not a computer. There are a total of two typewriters on this ship—they're only here in case the computers go down. Whoever sent this to you . . . well, it can't be many people. I can look into it. But, bottom line, you were tricked. So now we know who was in Animator's Palate. This is your second vandalism in three days. The company is going to take a dim view of this."

Philby held up a hand to stop Maybeck and Finn. "You must have it on camera."

"We have three kids on camera—Finn and two girls, one who plays lion tamer. We have a knife-throwing contest. You all are living on the edge."

"It's not a game!" Finn cried. "They were trying to kill us! You saw who was *throwing* the knives, I hope!"

"Off camera."

"Of course!" Finn shouted.

"Quiet down, son."

Finn glared. He was about to use the "dad" line Philby had used, but Philby cut him off. Again.

"You have cameras on your stairways. I'm sure you do," Philby said. "In case of lawsuits over people hurting themselves."

Bob's face revealed nothing.

"So, check out Deck 1 forward, maybe thirty minutes ago."

Bob pursed his lips. Barely looking at his keyboard, he called up a different four images on his screen. The upper right was black.

"That your doing, too?" he said, pointing to the blank quadrant.

"Oh, perfect," Finn said. "Do they make *any* mistakes?"

"And the jogging track, fifteen minutes ago? The same thing?"

"Same thing," Bob confirmed.

"And you think it's us?" Philby said.

"I'm told by the most reliable authorities that you, Mr. Philby, can hack just about anything. Some unsecured video feeds? Child's play, I would imagine."

The room went quiet.

Maybeck sat forward in his chair. "Okay, so check

it out: I get fried by a bolt of lightning. My boys get in a jam with Maleficent—the real Maleficent, not the pretty one. We're not asking you to buy this, because we're not selling, we're *telling*. There is stuff going down. Some of your own crew have been hypnotized. They're zombies. Bad zombies."

Uncle Bob nodded ever so slightly. Maybeck couldn't tell if his speech was having any effect, but continued determinedly.

"They're sending us fake notes. They're threatening our lives. Now, supposedly the five of us, as Disney Hosts, represent some serious financials for the company. Why else would they install us on your ship? Give us a free cruise? We make them money: as guides, with merchandise, video games, books."

"We're waiting for the movie," Finn added.

"And you're not going to do anything about these threats?" Maybeck said, sitting back and crossing his legs. "Seriously?"

A vein in Bob's neck was doing the Macarena.

"This is all going in an e-mail tonight," Maybeck said. "Maybe five e-mails."

"Are you expecting to turn your acts of vandalism into something I just excuse? Forgive?"

"We know you found the balloon, because you told us," Philby said. "It wasn't us."

"Animator's Palate was us, but in self-defense. I swear!" Finn said.

"Just now . . . maybe ten minutes ago . . . the Overtakers stole something that belongs to the company—"

"That was in our care," Finn said, interrupting Maybeck.

"And we need it back," added Philby.

Bob raised his hand. "Settle down, boys." He studied their faces one by one. "What do you know about a stowaway? And I want the *truth*."

"No idea where he's hiding," Philby said.

"But he's the one who gutted the hyena," Maybeck said.

"The what?"

"The . . . never mind."

"You stole the protein-spill cart," Bob said to Maybeck.

"Borrowed. Yes, sir."

Bob nodded. "Takes nerve to be honest with me, boys. I respect that."

"Thank you, sir," Finn said.

"*Not* what you've done. Not the damage you've done."

Finn started to object, but Philby stopped him, allowing Bob to talk.

"As for your safety, young man," Bob said to Finn. "It is and shall remain my top priority, just as the safety of every soul aboard this ship is my priority. As for your . . . escapades, yes, I'm in contact with Wayne periodically. Am I a 'believer'? No, I am not. But I'm willing to give you and him a certain amount of leeway, because when you work for this company as long as I have, well, you see things, hear things, that most people would think impossible. Also, because I do happen to believe in your cause: protecting Disney, keeping the experience 'magical, not tragical,' as Wayne once put it." He grinned. "Wayne's clearance is above mine. I'm not one to argue up the ladder."

The man's expression told them he'd revealed too much. He spoke quickly to cover himself.

"I'm going to give you a pass. We'll scratch the slate clean. I'm also going to endeavor to keep a closer eye on you all and make sure you remain safe, since you're of *such importance* to the company."

Philby glared at Maybeck.

"But for this, I'm expecting a little quid pro quo. A little tit-for-tat. Meaning I want to hear from you *before* you go destroying my ship again. Do we understand each other?"

Finn spoke for the three of them. "Understood. But—"

"Do not tell me you have to have the last word, because that is not going to happen in my office, young man."

Finn shut his mouth.

"Do you have something to say?"

"No, sir."

"That'll do." Bob motioned to the door.

25

"WHAT DID YOU SEE when you touched? What, exactly?"

The girls were riding in the back of a different taxi, the Aventura park now safely behind them. Or so they hoped. Apparently the driver of the original taxi had been too freaked by what he'd seen to return. Their current driver was a Costa Rican woman about the same age as Charlene's high school librarian.

"I told you guys, it's more a feeling. Quick little pictures sometimes." Mattie's face twisted in disgust. "You would not believe what people are thinking most of the time. Some of it is disgusting. What I picked up from that guy was his being all uptight about a zipper on a duffel bag not closing. There was a boy inside."

"Dillard," Charlene said. For all the excitement she'd felt, the burden of failure owned her. Leading a mission wasn't everything she'd thought it would be. They were going home empty-handed. No matter what they would say, Philby and Finn and Maybeck would view her as a failure. "Dillard was in the duffel bag."

"Being put on a bus. I'm pretty sure it was our bus.

The girl was all worried about the ship. And the guy, more jungle and rocks. He was desperate. Afraid. It was *daytime*. People spend a lot of time imagining what's coming. Don't ask me why, since they can't change it. But they do."

"Was Dillard there?"

"It's not a movie. I read their feelings, Charlene. There's a lot of love. Way too much hate. Hunger. Worry. Fear. Anger. People waste a lot of time."

The taxi snaked along the two-lane road; the girls sat in silence. Pretty soon, Charlene's and Amanda's DHIs hit interference, sputtered, and vanished. Mattie closed her eyes and tried to nap.

It was impossible.

With cell coverage restored, an invisible Amanda spoke.

"Why hide Dillard on the ship?" Frustration punctuated Amanda's digitally manipulated voice. "If they wanted Finn dead, they would have just killed him."

"Well, that's a cheery thought," said Charlene's.

Mattie's head tracked left to right to left like she was watching a tennis match.

"Maybe not," said Amanda. "They brought him back to the ship. If they haven't already, at some point they're going to realize it's not Finn. That can't be good for Dillard."

"I don't get it," Charlene said. "Why bother with all this? Why not just capture Finn on the ship?"

Mattie said, "Because if it happens *off* the ship, it's someone else's responsibility. No one's going to search the ship for someone who disappeared off the ship."

"They wanted the cruise to continue," Amanda said.

"We don't know if they still think it's Finn." Charlene sounded excited. "If we're lucky—if Dillard's lucky—the disguise is still working. And that means Finn can't be seen on the ship. If they discover they've been tricked, that won't be good for Dillard."

"Mattie," Amanda said. "We need to send Philby a text using Charlene's phone and have him tell Finn to stay in the stateroom, out of sight. He can't be seen by anyone. We'll have to smuggle him food and stuff."

"The boy in the duffel bag . . . he was alive," Mattie said. "Dillard was alive."

Charlene said, "Let's hope we can keep him that way."

Mattie took out the phone and began to type out a text.

* * *

The parting was not easy. Mattie repeatedly told them she'd be okay, but she didn't believe it. A teenage girl in a foreign country, headed for the boat to take her up the coast to Puerto Vallarta. Willa's passport. Charlene's iPhone. A fair amount of cash, and a credit card Philby had "borrowed" from his mother's purse. His mother wouldn't look for the card until she needed more cash from an ATM. She didn't use her plastic in foreign countries.

But it was still risky. Mattie and Willa didn't look perfectly alike, but in an odd way the red streak in Mattie's dark hair helped. If you took Willa and made her Goth, there was enough of a similarity between her and Mattie to believe a four-year-old photo.

Amanda discovered that her DHI could not cry tears. But still, feeling herself crying while a DHI was just another on a long list of things that surprised her about the hologram experience—like not feeling humidity and temperature change in the same way, and rarely if ever feeling hungry. But her heart could ache, as it did now, as she stood on a street corner beneath a tropical tree, the sound of car horns in the distance like coyotes crying beneath the stars.

"Do you think the passport will work?" Charlene asked.

"I think that's the least of her problems. You know how far it is?"

"But she'll beat us there?"

"Supposedly. But who knows?"

"Have a little faith!"

Amanda found Charlene's gung-ho energy annoying. She was all for optimism and courage in the face of danger, but a long boat ride up the coast for a sixteen-year-old girl carrying someone else's passport? Was it better than even odds that they'd ever see Mattie again? And how would they feel if she failed to make the rendezvous in Puerto Vallarta? What then?

"It was supposed to be her and Dillard traveling together. That made a lot more sense than her going it alone," Amanda said.

"Everything happens for a reason."

"But not always a good reason!" Amanda had had about enough.

"Since when are you a glass-half-empty type?"

Amanda reached out her hand. The Return would be an easier transmission if their holograms connected into a single graphics file.

"She should be requesting the return from Philby any—" Amanda failed to get the last words out.

She awoke in her upper bunk in Mrs. Nash's house. Before she fully opened her eyes, she ached to be back aboard the *Disney Dream* . . . with Finn.

26

INFORMED BY UNCLE BOB of the boys' visit to his office, Clayton Freeman walked with Rafina, a fellow security member from Rwanda. The breakthrough had come only moments before Bob's call. A child had spilled lemonade at a table with a view of the mammoth Funnel Vision screen. Clayton had jumped up to help clean it, but had stopped in the midst of laying napkins across the spill, his memory jogged: a string of successive drops stained the decking in a straight line.

The pattern was eerily familiar. And then, like a jolt, he had it: he'd seen the jogging path stained in a similar pattern.

Armed with two Taser stun guns, he and Rafina approached the forward jogging path's starboard curve, the spot where twice before Freeman had lost the stowaway.

Freeman had taken a forensics course in college. Fluid splatter had received two weeks of intensive study. These stains on the jogging track, like the lemonade, formed perfect little suns. Meaning they'd dripped straight down from overhead.

Freeman looked up.

A group of large pipes ran overhead, interrupted by two large metal cubes suspended from the ceiling end to end, each nearly the size of a refrigerator. The cube nearest Freeman carried dark stains running down its side.

"What is that?" Rafina asked.

This wasn't the first time Freeman had studied the upper area of the deck's tunnel; not by any means. But it was the first time he'd noticed a gap above the refrigerator-size boxes. He wasn't sure of the purpose the large steel boxes served—water tanks?—but they were clearly fixtures, permanent pieces of the ship.

The spills were not oil or pink hydraulic fluid. Not bird droppings or rust. It looked more like . . .

Soda.

For Rafina's sake, Freeman mimed his drinking from a can. He then signaled for her to be quiet, and she nodded.

Freeman concentrated on every detail of his surroundings. A slight scuff mark—faint scratches on the varnished wooden handrail—said it all. He motioned for Rafina to climb the wall, using the handrail as a leg up. He indicated his own eyes, wanting her to look into the narrow space above the piece of steel overhead. She nodded. He made fists, indicating she should be prepared for confrontation, pointed to himself and then the deck: he would remain down here. She understood.

Lithe and catlike, Rafina ascended the wall. In order to reach a particular handhold she needed to adjust her left foot—it perfectly covered the scratched area on the handrail. At this moment, Freeman knew he was right.

His search for the stowaway was about to come to an end.

As Rafina's head came even with the top of the steel box, pages of newsprint took flight from the opposite side, falling toward Freeman like giant confetti. He batted them aside. Food wrappers followed, as well as paper cups for soda. A large boy crashed to the deck. Freeman tackled him.

Rafina shouted down to him, her voice echoing.

"There's another one, on drugs or something," Rafina called down. "His eyes are open, but he's not moving."

"It's not drugs!" the other kid said, appealing to Freeman. "They did this to him. Zoned him out like that because he warned the kids."

"Who is 'they'?" Freeman asked.

"If you don't know that," the kid said, "I'd better talk to your boss."

27

WILLA MISSED THE MEETING, unable to get away from her mom's stateroom at such a late hour. Most of the parents had been off on their own for the cruise. Willa's kept a close eye on her late at night.

Philby kept looking around, as if expecting to see Willa.

Maybeck had been experiencing headaches and had gone to bed at eleven to get ready for the following day at Puerto Vallarta.

The *Dream*, "running behind schedule" due to delays in Costa Rica, was set to disembark guests three hours late, at ten thirty in the morning.

"Three steps," Finn said, holding up the copies of the pages from the journal and repeating what he'd said only a few minutes before. "The witch—that would be Tia Dalma. Step one." He raised one finger. "The key flower—Maybeck and Storey saw Tia Dalma doing a ceremony over before she picked it in the cave." A second finger. "And now Dillard. Just as Luowski and Mattie warned. A sacrifice. 'One of you will die.'"

Charlene wormed her hands between knees, tightly

pressed together. She looked ready to crawl out of her skin.

"It's not your fault, Charlene," Finn said.

"Easy for you to say."

"If we combine what Jess drew," the Professor said, coming to his feet in the small inboard stateroom, "with what Mattie felt up on the mountain, they pretty much match. Stone. Maybe a cave. Something dangerous."

"Chernabog," Finn said flatly.

"You'd think." Philby picked at a fingernail. It was a nasty habit he had recently developed. "I suppose no one's going to tell us if they found him backstage and locked him up or something. But if they had, let's face it: Wayne would know. Wayne would have told us."

"So, we know what they have planned," Charlene said, her face pointed to the floor. "What are we going to do about it?" Charlene seemed very dejected. The reality of the situation had sunk in.

The sound of defeat in her voice was so foreign, Finn found himself concentrating on the fact that it was really her. She blamed herself for Dillard, which didn't make any sense.

"We're going to stop it," Finn said.

"He's not a cat," Philby countered. "He doesn't get nine lives."

"He's a monster," Charlene said. "So maybe he gets more."

Philby snorted. "If they get us thinking we're beat before we really are, then they win."

"Look who's the cheerleader now," she said.

"They've got Dillard," Finn reminded him.

Philby countered, "They think they've got *you*. Kenny said the disguise wasn't perfect, but given the clothes and the fact they've never actually held you captive before, they may still believe he's you."

Finn thought: *Then he's dead.*

Kenny nodded from the corner. He looked like the kid going to detention. "It could go either way."

"So they have a hostage," Finn said. "And we know what they're planning."

"'Someone will die,'" Charlene repeated. "I really don't think we should have left Mattie! That was a bad plan."

"It was the only plan." Philby sounded defensive.

"It *didn't* work!"

"It helped!" he shouted. "Mattie empathized with two of them. We know more than we did."

"Yeah, right! She helped us, and now she's alone. Some friends we are. Some team!"

"The ones who are hurting," Finn said, "are Amanda and Jess. They got Mattie to come here in the first place."

"Do you *ever* stop thinking about her? Feeling sorry

for her?" Charlene raised her head just long enough to make Finn feel her scorn.

"So, what now?" Philby asked Finn in a mocking tone.

Was Finn supposed to capitulate and let Philby direct the next step?

"They're going to get off the ship," Finn said. "Either in Puerto Vallarta or Cabo. Unless these rocks and caves are in Disneyland, then it has to be one of the next stops."

"Agreed." Philby seemed to be taunting him: *Be as smart as I am.*

"They'll head to this place, whatever it is. They'll take Chernabog and Dillard. They brought me—or Dillard—back to the ship because there was more to do."

Philby nodded. He could be so annoying.

"The rise of Chernabog," Charlene said.

"That's such a drama-queen way of saying it," Philby sneered.

Charlene stuck her tongue out at him.

"The best move is for our DHIs to follow them. If we can even figure out when and how they're leaving the ship."

"They're creatures of habit," Philby said. "They will leave by the side of the ship away from the dock, the forward gangway. There will be a boat waiting. Just like in Aruba. Trust me. But it can't be our DHIs."

"No projectors."

"Gold star."

"We're supposed to guide the kayak trip. All five of us," Charlene reminded Philby, eyes moving to Finn. "If we're a no-show, the excursion crew will come looking for us."

"Yes," Philby said. "But once we disembark, we'll be logged off the ship by the computers. Security will be able to determine that we left the ship with the first passengers."

"And if the Overtakers leave the ship before we're allowed off?" Charlene asked.

"That would be smart of them, and bad for us," Philby conceded. "Good thinking, Charlie."

Finn raised a finger. "We can assume there will be projection in the town, just not out in the jungle." Philby did not contradict him. "We send Storey out as a DHI. She can jump through the hull, won't need to go through security at the gangway. Once out, she drops a rope—"

"A line."

"—or finds a ladder on the pier. We leave through the aft gangway door. We swim for it. Storey has figured out a way for us to get out of the water. Those docks are so high, there's no way we can do it without help."

"When the aft gangway door is opened, it will send a signal to Security. They'll check cameras. They'll see us." Philby sounded so confident.

"But not if you can rig it so they don't." Finn was testing his theory.

"Correct," Philby said.

"You understand we have only a slight idea of what the OTs are up to? Sacrifice. Reboot Chernabog. Charlene? Dillard? We also know they may want 2.0 and one of us in order to figure it out. We can't give them that. Stopping them is not an option, it's a requirement. Our purpose," Finn finished softly.

The only sound in the room was the faint hum of the ship's powerful engine, a slight, worrying vibration.

28

SURPRISINGLY, THINGS WENT according to plan.

It was almost as if Security served it up on a platter for Philby. He worked out an elaborate scheme to lure people out of the offices so he could get inside as his DHI and defeat the aft gangway alarm—only to watch an apparent emergency vacate the place like it was on fire. Philby overrode the cameras and the alarm easily. Finn and Philby hurried to the aft gangway door where they met up with Maybeck, Willa, and Charlene.

Having left all electronics behind, but keeping their IDs on them, they slipped into the water and swam to shore where Storey had left a line for them to climb, ingeniously located behind a large sign listing immigration policy for arriving passengers. The Keepers pulled themselves up to the dock, rolled, and hid behind the sign, undetected.

The pier work of unloading trash and loading mountains of food by forklift kept the crew and longshoremen occupied. Philby peered around the sign, gave a thumbs-up, and the five Keepers walked calmly through the warehouse to their freedom, avoiding the immigration station, which hadn't even opened yet.

Finn and Philby took up a location by an ATM that offered a clear view of Deck 11 and waited. Maybeck headed into the streets of Puerto Vallarta with Charlene, while Willa stayed near a taxi stand up the street with a clear view of the two boys.

Thirty minutes felt like several hours, but finally Storey appeared along the rail. She waved her arms. Philby waved back. She pointed forward.

"Here we go," Philby said. "The OTs are on the move. Same as Aruba."

Storey's final signal was cradling her arms and rocking an invisible baby—the sign that the OTs were carrying something: Dillard.

"They've got him," Finn said.

"Not for long, they don't," Philby said.

The sound of approaching motors caught their ears. They looked up to see Maybeck and Charlene riding scooters. The two pulled to the curb and indicated the spare helmets clipped to the seats.

"No way!" Finn said. "How could you possibly—?"

"It's Mexico," Maybeck said.

Charlene said proudly, "He told the guy renting them that he was twenty and I was eighteen."

"Turned out it didn't matter," Maybeck explained.

"You can rent them at fifteen or over. We have them for the day."

"What about Willa?" Philby asked.

"She'll take the taxi as planned," Maybeck said. "You going to climb on, or what?"

"You look stupid in that helmet," Philby said.

"Wait until you have yours on, Romeo."

Finn teamed up with Charlene; Philby with Maybeck. They rode up to Willa and filled her in. While her eyes betrayed her desire to be with Philby, she neither complained nor objected. To work their mission smoothly, the teamwork required of each of them overcame the rest.

Willa pointed out a rusted white van parked away from the *Dream* on the next pier. "I'm guessing that's their ride."

"Got to be," Philby said. "So one bike in front, one behind; and the taxi keeps the van in sight but never too close." He added, "Okay with you?"

A small boat pulled up to the pier near the van. None of them had noticed the crane until it lowered a sling toward the waiting boat.

"They're offloading something heavy," Philby said. "Something big."

"Him." For Finn, the one word rang out like the sound of a starting gun.

* * *

An hour outside of Puerto Vallarta, Willa realized she'd
run out of money. The taxi driver dropped her by the
side of the road. On the scooter, Charlene had lost sight
of Maybeck and Philby, the white van, and the taxi.

"Hey," Finn said into her ear, holding on to her
from behind. "Isn't that—"

"Willa's taxi!"

"Empty!"

Charlene sped up the bike, believing they'd reached
their destination. When they found Willa on the side of
the road, their spirits were crushed. Not only would they
now slow down further due to having three on the bike,
but any chance of closing the distance on Maybeck's
bike and the white van were dashed.

"We've lost them," Finn said.

"Maybe not," Willa countered. "The driver spoke
some English. And by 'some,' I mean very little. He
said the only thing out here is a stone quarry and some
ancient ruins. There's a trailhead. He said maybe ten
more kilometers."

"The quarry?"

"End of the road. Another five kilometers past
the trailhead. The early natives used the quarry
for their temple rock. They built a limestone road
from the quarry to the site. It still exists."

381

"I'd say his English was pretty good," Charlene said.

"He had a guide book. In Spanish, but there were pictures."

"A tourist trap?" Finn said.

"Not hardly. It was being excavated, but they ran out of money a long time ago. In the guidebook it's marked as the highest level of difficulty for hiking. There's no water, and it's not policed."

"That has Overtakers written all over it," Finn said.

When Willa failed to comment, Finn gave her a moment and then turned toward her. He'd given his helmet to her, so with the wind in his face he couldn't hear well.

"What?" he shouted. "Why do you look like that?"

"It wasn't just the money that stopped them from digging it up." Willa shouted to be heard over the complaining motor. "The site was apparently used for sacrifices. Human sacrifices. People thought it was haunted."

"Human sacrifice." Finn made it a statement. He leaned forward to Charlene. "Please tell me you can make this thing go faster."

* * *

Maybeck and Philby stayed well back of the white van, part by design, part by default.

Losing the van on the flats multiple times, they

were able to regain it on the jungle hills where the van struggled under a heavy load. Nonetheless, it was somewhat by chance that Philby spotted the vehicle off-road, penetrating deeper into the jungle.

He tapped Maybeck on the shoulder and pointed. Maybeck slowed the scooter and pulled to the side of the empty dirt road.

"What now?" Maybeck asked.

Philby looked back: Charlene was nowhere in sight.

"We can't wait for them," Maybeck said.

"No. And you and I have to stay together. So pull up to where the van turned in and let me hop off a second."

Maybeck did as requested. Philby clipped the chin strap of his helmet to a vine, leaving it hanging low where it might be spotted.

"Brilliant!"

Philby smiled. "That's why they pay me the big bucks."

It had become a common joke among the Keepers—their parents and guardians were receiving direct-deposit monthly performance fees in educational accounts to help fund a Keeper's college enrollment; the kids themselves never saw a dime.

A wooden sign sagged away from the road, its message faded and covered in vines.

"Not so sure about the bike," Maybeck said. "It's too loud."

"They could be miles down this road."

"Agreed. But they could hear us coming."

"That would make for an unpleasant welcoming party."

"As long as the . . . path"—Philby could hardly call it a road—"goes straight, and we can see the van's tracks out ahead, we can stay on the bike. We'll go real slow, so it barely makes noise. If we lose the tire tracks, we'll shut it down and walk until we know what's going on."

"Got it."

They rode ahead, eyes trained on the tracks left by the heavy van.

"Whoa!" said Philby after five minutes. The dirt trail narrowed, the jungle encroaching. "Nasty."

They climbed off and walked the scooter. The trail narrowed even further, barely wide enough for the two boys walking side by side. They formed a single file, Maybeck in the lead, pushing the bike. The crushed plants and vines indicated the passage of the van; tire tracks were no longer easy to see. It was darker here, the jungle blotting out the sun.

"I'm stashing this thing," Maybeck said. "It's a pain in the butt to push."

The boys leaned it behind a dead stump of a tree,

fifteen feet tall, easy to spot among the rest of the over-growth and well off the trail.

"This place is bizarre."

"It is," Philby agreed. "I think it's safe to assume they're heading to an ancient temple or archaeological site."

"If you say so."

"There were whole cities in these places a thousand years ago."

"Spare me the history lesson."

"I'm just saying."

"Well, don't. We shouldn't talk. I'll take the lead," Maybeck said. "Hand signals only until we know what's going on."

"You going to take your helmet off?"

"Oh, shut up!" He unstrapped the helmet and left it with the bike. As he did, he whispered, "What if the others see your signal but don't shut off their bike? What if they mess this up?"

"I trust them," Philby declared.

"Yeah? Well good for you. Me? I'll wait to make that call."

"You can't wait on trust. You either have it or you don't."

"Lose the professor thing, would you? We've got a monster to track down. And don't forget Dillard."

"Believe me. I haven't forgotten."

At that exact moment, the sky rumbled.

Philby looked up thinking: *What next?*

* * *

"What next?" Finn said, his eyes trained on the dark sky.

"Rain?" Willa said.

Charlene had spotted the helmet; Willa, the sign. Finn pointed out the depth of the single track—the scooter—explaining that it would only make such a deep impression if both boys were on it. They headed down the dirt trail, noticing how the jungle closed in from either side, choking off the route. Finally, with three of them riding, the scooter was spinning out too much. They parked it in the vegetation, ditched the helmets, and walked. When the rain came it drenched them like a fire hose, but it only lasted all of five minutes. Then the jungle felt like a sauna that had been turned up. Hot, sticky.

Mosquitoes whined by their ears, the girls swatting at them.

"I don't like this," Charlene said.

"Noted." Finn didn't like it either, but withheld comment. Troubled by the claustrophobic undergrowth and the lack of light—it felt like midnight!—he kept his fears to himself.

"The sign said something about religion," Willa said. "House of religion? I'm not sure."

"We don't know if it's important," Finn said, "until we get there."

"It could be miles."

"It could. So I suggest we save our energy with less chatter."

But it wasn't long until Finn lost sight of the bike track. He stopped the girls and told them to wait. Backtracking, he found where the track led into the undergrowth and, eventually, the other bike behind the tree.

"If this trail gets any smaller . . ." Charlene whispered. She didn't complete her thought. She didn't have to: the Overtakers couldn't be far.

* * *

Among the jungle cries, the buzz of insects the size of bats, and the noises of humans extremely close by, Finn picked out a cooing he identified as coming from Philby. Philby had cared for a wounded pigeon in seventh grade and had taught himself to coo like one, a bizarre talent that only his closest friends knew about. And though a pigeon's coo in the middle of a Mexican jungle might have caught the ear of an ornithologist, when mixed into the ongoing cacophony, only such a bird specialist would realize it had no place here.

Finn tugged on Willa's sleeve, stopping her. They'd been using hand signals for the past hundred yards, having heard voices. Now Finn pointed to their left.

There it was again: *coo-coo* . . .

Willa took hold of and stopped Charlene. The three carefully tiptoed into the undergrowth, following the call of a city bird a long way from home.

Maybeck and Philby had found a part of an old wall—a very old wall—made of refrigerator-size hand-carved stones stacked with exacting accuracy. Covered in creeping vines, flowering orchids, and giant ferns, the wall wasn't a wall at all, but the bottom flight of a tiered pyramid temple that had lost two-thirds of its upper structure to fifteen hundred years of hurricane winds and erosion.

With their backs pressed against the moss-covered third row of rock, and hidden by the vegetation, the boys held an elevated post looking down into a large flat area about the size of half a football field. Judging by the tall lumps of vegetation enclosing it, it looked as if it might have been a courtyard, surrounded by temples or meeting places. At its center was a massive stone, waist-high and five feet long, elevated on a platform of smaller stones. The platform and table had been cleared of vines and weeds. It stood in stark contrast to the wild, uncontrollable growth surrounding it.

Tia Dalma stood by the long flat rock, the journal open in front of her. Maleficent paced nearby. The Evil Queen leaned against the van, scowling, a large duffel bag at her feet. Four men—ship crewmen who Maybeck recognized as OT Zombies—struggled with a towering horned gorilla.

Chernabog. As nasty and terrifying a creature as Finn had ever seen. His skin crawled as though he were covered with leeches.

"He's huge," Maybeck whispered. Given the jungle sounds he could have shouted and not have been heard. But Chernabog had stunned him to silence.

"He's disgusting," Charlene said. "Eew! Is that a bull's head?"

"And bat ears," Finn said.

"Eight feet tall at least," the professor said clinically. "Possibly ten. A living monster."

"We've got to get out of here," Willa said, her words hanging in the thick air. "He's . . . worse than anything we've ever seen."

"And then some," said Charlene. "Do we really think we can help Dillard against *that* thing?"

"We don't leave yet," said Philby.

"The three steps," said Finn. "A witch, a key flower, a sacrifice. It's about Chernabog. We were right."

"Yeesh!" Willa said. "They're going to take him out of torpor!"

"Tia Dalma," Philby said.

"You give something that . . . evil even more power," Willa's voice was hollow, "and it's over."

"Son of Frankenstein," Maybeck said.

"Dillard doesn't possess any powers," Charlene said. "So maybe it won't work."

"We're not Wayne! We're not going to let them kill him to find out!" Finn said, too loudly. Tia Dalma raised her head.

"Freeze!" Philby hissed.

The Keepers did not move, did not breathe. It felt to Finn as if the voodoo priestess was looking him directly in the eye, but somehow she didn't see him.

He could feel her straining to hear above the constant sounds of the jungle.

She called over to the Queen, who raised her thin arms and stepped out into the courtyard.

The jungle went instantly silent. Every last living thing stopped singing and buzzing, moving, breathing. Only the leaves, dripping the remnants of the rain shower, could be heard.

Finn's heart threatened to tear a hole in his chest. If it pounded any louder the OTs would hear.

Bit by bit, nature's sounds returned. First a whisper,

then a wind, and finally a storm of all God's creatures.

"I know that symbol," Willa said softly. Pointing across the courtyard to an exposed rock, she drew attention to a large face chiseled into the rock. "It's *sa-ja-la*. Technically, it means subordinate lord."

"How about not so technically?" said Charlene.

"Under lord."

"As in lord of the underworld?" Finn said.

"More like four-star general instead of a five-star," Willa said. "A title of importance but not the highest importance."

"Is that a cave?" Maybeck said, referring to the huge black opening alongside the rock in question.

"An entrance to the temple," Philby said. "Possibly, a burial crypt. These things had all sorts of secret rooms and tunnels, same as the Egyptian pyramids."

"Square stone tunnel, I'll bet." Finn was about to pull the folded e-mail with the scanned image of Jess's dream out of his pocket when he thought better of it. It would make too much noise.

"Lord of the underworld," Charlene whispered eerily, stuck on Willa's definition.

"They picked this spot carefully," Finn said. "There must have been other ruins and temples in places like Aruba and Costa Rica."

"It's the table," Maybeck explained. "My uncle Jim

works in a processing plant—a slaughterhouse. They have tables like that, only theirs are metal. You see that line all around the edges?"

"The border," Charlene said.

"It's not decoration. It's a drain system. See the hole to the right? You put a jar under there and collect the blood."

"That's disgusting!" Charlene protested.

"No," Maybeck said. "That's part of a sacrifice. Kill the animal, drink its blood."

"Eew!" Charlene went shock-white. "Can we change the subject please?"

"The ancient civilizations didn't kill animals," Willa said. "They killed—"

"People," Philby said. "Human sacrifice."

Finn spoke faintly. "We were right. 'One of you will die.'" His eyes fell on the duffel bag at the Queen's feet. When they'd talked about it, it had felt more abstract. Dillard, posing as Finn, was in that bag. And he was going to die.

"Are you telling me Dillard's blood is going to be Chernabog's power drink?" Maybeck had a way with words. "For the record, I'm now disgusted as well."

"What's with the sun?" Charlene said. "Why's it so dark all of a sudden?"

Finn had noticed the darkness during the brief

storm, but Charlene was right: if anything it was actually darker now.

"Oh dear." Philby said, checking his wristwatch. "It's the solar eclipse."

The four others stared at him. He looked into each of their faces.

"What? You're going to tell me you didn't know about the solar eclipse? It's May twentieth." He looked for some spark of recognition on their part. "A total eclipse. Extremely rare. Arizona to Panama is the best possible viewing. As in: a jungle in Mexico." He studied his watch again. Fiddled with it.

"In eight minutes it's full. A total eclipse. We've got eight minutes to save Dillard."

29

"THE GIRLS WILL CAUSE a distraction. You two," Finn said to Maybeck and Philby, "will grab the duffel. I'll try to get the journal, so this can't ever happen again."

"What kind of distraction?" Willa asked.

"Don't take any stupid chances. Just make a bunch of noise and take off for the highway. We'll you meet you there."

"Nothing stupid," Philby repeated.

"Are you two on again?" Maybeck asked.

"Shut up!" Willa said. But she didn't deny it.

"Six minutes," Philby announced.

"One thing to keep in mind," Willa said, holding everyone together for a moment longer. "This thing is part Minotaur." She meant Chernabog. "In Greek mythology, Theseus leads the Minotaur into a labyrinth. The Minotaur is trapped and can't find his way out."

"Get to the point!" Maybeck said.

"I'm getting to the point," Willa said, pulling a lock of hair behind her ear nervously. "The point is, historians say it may not have been a labyrinth, but a palace or *temple* with a lot of rooms." She was looking at the black hole alongside the symbol chiseled into the rock. "If that's an entrance . . ."

"The under lord," Philby said.

"Keeper of the underworld," Finn said, repeating what he'd said earlier. No one dismissed it this time.

"If we can lead him in there," Willa said, "who knows? Maybe he never comes out."

"And maybe we get eaten alive trying," said Maybeck.

"Five minutes," Philby said.

* * *

Finn missed Amanda. About to take the risk he was about to take, he felt a hole in his chest and once again regretted making her hate him, even for a moment. Those moments, he thought, had been wasted.

He'd circled around to the side of the cave entrance. In front of him: Tia Dalma, Maleficent, the Evil Queen.

Chernabog.

Finn felt woefully ill-prepared to battle such forces. He had gained new strength—unexplainable strength— and speed, but he had no real control over it. It was like stepping into a cockpit where you didn't know what the buttons were for. He was unpracticed, unpolished.

He wished for Amanda's ability to push. One shove

from her, and the witches and fairies, maybe even Chernabog with his wet black nose and black, hideous eyes, would be thrown against the rocks. Dillard would be rescued. They could steal the van and be on their way, leaving the OTs behind.

But Amanda wasn't here.

But *he* was here: where he'd never wanted to be. In a Mexican jungle, the survival of his friend depending upon him.

Tia Dalma turned a page in the journal. She nodded and raised her right hand, then placed it across her chest.

Chernabog walked ploddingly toward her. The ground shook. Finn's animal instincts told him to run.

This thing was more than a monster. It was a creature; a bull/bat creature with huge eyes, a wet snout, and the pointed nose of a bat broken by sharp saw teeth. Granted, it behaved as if drugged; but if anything, that enhanced the threat.

Tia Dalma barely looked over at the beast. Finn couldn't see her face, but he could hear her mumbling.

The Evil Queen unzipped the duffel bag. In the gloomy darkness of the eclipse, Finn would have sworn it was his twin coming out of the bag.

Dillard's hands were bound behind his back. His eyes were crazed with fear.

Dillard had once begged Finn—*begged* him—to allow him to become a Kingdom Keeper. Finn had gently turned him down. Dillard was not cut out for it.

Apparently Dillard had convinced Wayne otherwise.

Finn briefly closed his eyes. He hated Wayne at that moment.

A few milliseconds passed—more like a blink. But in that fraction of time, Finn attempted to summon the speed and strength he'd demonstrated intermittently throughout the voyage.

Caw! Caw!

Diablo. Finn knew the bird's identity before he spotted the raven, because like Philby's pigeon cry, that particular birdsong had no place in a jungle. Perched near the Evil Queen, Diablo clung to a vine over the empty duffel bag.

Exactly where Maybeck and Philby were hiding.

Maleficent walked in that direction: toward the Evil Queen and Dillard.

Chernabog marched for the sacrificial table.

Finn couldn't breathe. The beast grew bigger with every step. The four crewmen backed up, sensing something awful.

Where were the girls and their distraction?

Willa was a genius. Rather than stand up and shout

or do something overtly obvious, she and Charlene slipped in and out between the rocks on the far side of the courtyard. A girl's leg appeared and then disappeared.

Maleficent signaled the four crewmen, who dashed off in pursuit.

With any luck, Finn thought, the two girls were sprinting toward the road by now. For a moment it looked as if Maleficent would pursue them as well, but her nasty crow continued signaling—for all Finn knew the thing was talking to her. She moved toward Dillard, toward where Philby and Maybeck were hiding.

It had to be now.

Finn darted toward the stone table like he was going for the prize in Capture the Flag. Tia Dalma, distracted by sight of the girls and by Maleficent's swift crossing to Diablo, never saw Finn coming. He careened into her, throwing her to the ground. He reached for the journal.

His legs were trembling. But it wasn't his legs; it was the ground, as Chernabog dragged himself toward the table. The beast was clearly at half speed; Finn didn't want to see him supercharged.

Up close he was a hideous combination of wild bull, rabid bat, and human giant. Drool leaked disgustingly from his partially-open mouth, which was lined with hundreds of triangular teeth. His coal-black eyes, so bloodshot as to look otherworldly, locked onto Finn. He grunted, his nostrils snorting fluid.

"Hey, buddy," Finn said, backing up, the journal tucked under his arm.

Chernabog swiped out at Finn, his reach extraordinarily long, his black, bear claws coming incredibly close. Much closer than Finn thought possible.

A fireball ripped through the air by Finn's left ear, sounding like a jet engine at takeoff. The surprise of it pushed Chernabog back and off Finn.

Maleficent took a step toward Dillard. The Evil Queen stepped out of the jungle, dragging Maybeck with one hand and Philby with the other. The boys were conscious but dazed.

"Stop!" she called to Finn. "The book, young man. Put it back on the table, or your friends die."

Tia Dalma clawed herself to her knees. Her eyes played across Finn like a meat inspector's. She was going to end him.

Willa and Charlene had broken from the plan, doubling back. Out of the corner of his eye, Finn saw them dip into the mouth of the cave entrance that bore the pictograph.

Cackling evilly, the Evil Queen pulled a vial from her cloak and force-fed Maybeck and Philby its contents. The boys slumped to the jungle floor.

Dead? Asleep?

"The book!" she cried out.

Both furious and terrified, Finn returned the journal to the stone table. But something in him snapped as it clunked to the stone. He raced toward his fallen friends. Maleficent badly misjudged his superhuman speed. Her first two fireballs missed.

Seeing more power in Finn's emotions than anything with which fire could contend, she wave a crooked finger at Dillard and drew the boy to her.

Finn was three steps from Maleficent when the two girls screamed.

A cloud of fruit bats flew from the mouth of the cave. They were the size of flying squirrels. They swirled around the courtyard like smoke escaping a chimney. A black fog, so thick that wings licked the faces of everyone gathered there, forcing them to recoil.

All but Chernabog, who spread his arms in welcome. The bats formed a funnel over his head and spiraled up into the dark sky.

Chernabog roared so loudly Finn would have sworn the trees shook. *And this thing's at half speed?*

Maleficent crossed her arms in front of her face to shield herself. Taking advantage of her distraction, Finn attacked Maleficent, grabbing her from behind and spinning her in the direction of Tia Dalma just as the witch doctor threw her arm forward, intending a curse for Finn.

Maleficent buckled over. Finn kicked her to the dirt and kneeled by Maybeck's side.

A fireball grew from Maleficent's palm. Finn abandoned Maybeck and struck the fairy's arm, sending the fireball in the direction of the Evil Queen, whose cape caught fire. The burning Evil Queen dove to the dirt and rolled.

Chernabog roared yet again.

The moon slipped fully in front of the sun, blotting out all light.

The fallen Maleficent, writhing from the pain inflicted by the curse, looked to the sky.

Tia Dalma had Dillard by the throat. She produced a large knife—bone or ivory—from her waistband and leveled its blade across Dillard's throat. She pulled on the blade, cutting Dillard's neck, spilling his blood.

"Stop!" Finn shouted. He couldn't bear it. Couldn't allow it. It was worse than anything he'd ever imagined.

To his surprise, the witch doctor paused.

"Me, for him," Finn said. "You would much rather have me."

"Blood is blood, lad," Tia Dalma said in her lilting voice. She could have been talking about vegetables in the grocery store. "He," she indicated Chernabog, "is not picky."

Finn saw an exchange of some sort between the Evil Queen, who guarded Maybeck and Philby, and Tia Dalma. Tia Dalma's hand tightened on the knife handle. Chernabog bellowed and snorted, waiting by the stone table.

The bats descended in a swirling blanket, engulfing the beast. The vortex of flapping wings shifted across the terrace, throwing up a tornado of dust that consumed Finn, Tia Dalma, and Dillard.

Blinded, Finn shielded his eyes. He fought forward, swiping at the bats with his bare hands, knocking them aside.

They lifted.

Tia Dalma was hauling Dillard toward Chernabog and the stone table. "Coming, my lord." She stretched out an arm to pull the open journal closer.

My lord. The words registered with Finn.

Finn dove and rolled, leaping to his feet in time to catch Tia Dalma's back-stretched arm as she wrestled to lift Dillard onto the table.

An excited Chernabog snorted and stomped. The ground shook.

Finn yanked Tia Dalma's arm and knife back a few inches, away from Dillard's throat. The witch doctor released Dillard, leaving him laying half-on, half-off the sacrificial table. Finn redirected the knife, turning her wrist so the tip of the blade faced her, surprised by her formidable strength.

"You . . . should . . . have . . . taken . . . me," he said. "I would have gone willingly."

"For the King!" the witch doctor said, reversing the tip fully toward Finn.

Anger flashed through Finn, making him ten times as strong. He and Dillard had played at Knights of the Round Table using palm tree fronds as swords, battling for the virtue of princesses and the valor of the King. How *dare* she know that! How *dare* she quote that?

It gave him the final blast of strength, the pump of adrenaline he needed. He bent her wrist—snapped its bones—and plunged the knife into her chest.

Finn relished the shock in her eyes, the way he felt her resolve flag. There was something else in her eyes as he twisted the blade within her: betrayal? How could she possibly accuse him of such a thing?

The life went out of her eyes.

The bats swirled.

Dillard sagged on the end of the knife.

Dillard.

Not Tia Dalma.

Finn looked at the table. The witch doctor lay there,

arms crossed over her chest, laughing coldly.

Dillard looked down at the knife, then into Finn's eyes. *Betrayal!* Finn should have known! He pulled out the knife. Dillard collapsed and fell, eyes open. Tears ran down his cheeks. If he was crying, he was alive!

"The bloodshed of friendship is so much thicker," Tia Dalma said, off the table now and catching Dillard before he hit the ground. She lifted Dillard's hand, which hung limply in the air.

"Life is because of the gods; with their sacrifice they gave us life . . . . They produce our sustenance . . . which nourishes life."

Chernabog leaned forward.

"Nooooo!"

Finn punched Tia Dalma in the face with all his strength. Her head snapped back and she collapsed, unconscious. Before he could think, Finn pivoted and broke Chernabog's grip on Dillard, putting himself between the beast and his friend. He jumped straight up and landed, squatting on the stone table, facing Chernabog. He waved the knife.

The beast swung, but to Finn it registered as slow motion. Finn ducked the blow, but lost the knife. He rotated and kicked out, connecting with the beast's chest. It was like kicking a wall.

Chernabog dropped his fist like a hammer. Finn

lurched aside. The eight-inch-thick stone table cracked with the blow.

The beast's jaw opened and snapped at Finn's head, narrowly missing. Finn backed up and fell off balance. He tumbled into the dirt, the table between him and the beast.

Chernabog roared, pounded down angrily on the table, and split it in two.

The knife flew up, spinning tip-over-grip. The beast snatched it out of the air. It looked like a toy in his hand as he brought it to his maw and licked the blood hungrily from the blade.

Dropping the knife, Chernabog raised his head toward the ever-lightening sky. His flesh rippled as he seemed to grow, or swell, or increase in some indefinable way. A chrysalis in catharsis—a butterfly's drying wings ready for flight.

The demon—no longer merely a beast—gazed down at Finn and cocked his head.

Finn reacted primordially. He grabbed for the fallen knife and plunged it into Chernabog's thigh.

Chernabog roared in pain. The jungle canopy shook. Startled birds erupted upward.

Finn scooped up Dillard and ran for the tunnel entrance. He could see death flicker behind Dillard's eyes with his every step.

"Don't you leave me!" Finn told him, his own tears starting now.

Dillard's eyes floated open. He stared up at Finn, who could not take his eyes off his friend.

"Don't . . . you . . . dare," Finn said.

"'If you don't take a chance,'" Dillard said, a weak grin sweeping his lips, "'you don't have a chance.'"

"You're a Keeper. Always a Keeper!"

Dillard's eyes brightened, then eased shut; and Finn felt the life leave his friend's body. It was sickening and magical, disgusting and vile.

Finn cried out.

Chernabog followed the sound, the knife still in his leg. He'd tasted the boy's blood. He wanted more.

Finn caught sight of the writhing Maleficent, distant now, still under Tia Dalma's twisted spell. The dark fairy managed to squirm to her knees.

"He awakens!" she called out.

Finn carried Dillard's body into the dark tunnel.

Behind him the jungle erupted in a deafening chorus of savage sounds: hissing, licking, sucking. Finn felt the world driving him deeper into the tunnel.

* * *

"Psst!"

Finn stopped, but the trembling of Chernabog's

feet pounding the ground from behind gave him chills. There was faint light flooding through joints in the overhead stones, just enough to see, but not clearly. Two shadows stepped forward.

Finn recognized Charlene's voice. "The tunnel splits ahead."

"And again after that. It's a labyrinth," Willa said, "designed to defeat tomb robbers."

"Like Escher's Keep," Charlene added.

"You're saying we can't go in?"

"It's designed so you never come out."

Chernabog plugged the far end of the tunnel. He crouched and heaved himself forward, narrowing the distance.

"But if I could find my way back out," Finn said. "If you two took Dillard and hid in one tunnel while I led *it* down another . . ."

"You can't," Charlene protested. "Seriously, you can't."

"But if I could find my way out and he couldn't?" Finn hoped to appeal to Willa's sense of challenge, to Charlene's sense of adventure. He understood what perhaps they did not: the four of them were not getting past Chernabog. They had to come up with some kind of plan. "I need a string. A really long string."

Charlene tore her shirt and pulled at the frayed

ends trying to start a run of thread, but it wasn't going to work.

"How are you with spiders?" Willa asked.

Finn could barely see her finger pointing out a delicate spiderweb.

"I don't love them," he confessed.

Chernabog was close now—too close.

"If you squeeze a spider gently, it lays its silk."

"I don't think I want to know that," Finn said.

"You follow the silk back," she said. "He . . . *it* isn't smart enough to do that."

"You're crazy!" Charlene protested. "What if it breaks? Or runs out?"

Clomp! Clomp! Chernabog was no more than twenty feet away.

Finn widened his eyes, admitting more light. He saw the large black spider, the size of a lemon, at the lower edge of the web. He cringed, thinking of actually taking hold of it.

The image of Dillard's eyes, of the light slowly going out of them, flashed through his mind, strengthening his resolve. Finn held his breath and snatched the spider from its web. It wiggled in his hand. He dropped it.

Willa scooped it up and returned it to Finn.

"You're set," she said.

"Protect him," Finn said.

"Go!" Willa said. "We can handle it. Go!"

"Good luck!" Charlene added.

"Nothing stupid," Willa said, quoting Philby.

Finn squeezed the hairy spider. He felt sick to his stomach. But Willa was right—as always. The silk played out like a whisper of silver thread. Finn stuck the end of it to the nearest wall.

A giant hunchbacked troll in the form of Chernabog stood twenty feet from him. The demon sniffed the air. And again.

It had poor eyesight, Finn realized. Chernabog not only didn't fit in the tunnel, but he could see only a few feet before him.

Finn dragged his running shoe across the stone floor to make sure Chernabog followed him and did not head toward the girls. The beast sniffed the air again. If he sensed Dillard's blood . . . Finn made sure he heard him, made sure to lure him in his direction.

Chernabog grunted and lunged forward with surprising speed and agility, his hand—the size of a catcher's glove—swiping the air mere inches from Finn's face.

Attaboy, Finn thought.

Giving the spider a gentle squeeze, Finn touched the silk against the wall of the left tunnel and continued deeper into the darkness.

Chernabog followed.

30

THE CREATURE WAS a quick learner. He was moving faster now in his pursuit.

Finn arrived at another Y in the tunnel—the third since he'd left the girls. This time he faced descending stairs and more darkness to his left, level and light to his right. He touched the spider silk to the wall, and descended.

Chernabog was no climber. His cloven hooves slipped on the stairs and kicked Finn, sending him flying. Finn held on to the spider, but landed awkwardly, spraining his right wrist while attempting to break his fall.

Chernabog swiped at Finn, connected, and plastered him to the wall.

Finn dropped the spider. It scurried away before Finn could recover it.

The beast struck out again—a cat toying with a mouse. He sent Finn to the bottom landing, then slid down the stairs after him.

His head aching, Finn tried to navigate the darkness. There was no light at all. It sounded as if Chernabog was groping around in the dark for him. With each blow, the beast loosened the rocks. Sand and dirt rained down. Dust spread. Finn coughed.

Some faint light seeped through.

Chernabog roared. The tunnel shook. Finn covered his ears. Chernabog lowered his horns and lunged at Finn but missed as Finn dove to his left into a pile of bat guano.

Finn spit the disgusting taste from his mouth and crawled away from the beast in a crab-walk. He needed to take advantage of his smaller size, agility, and speed; he also possessed an enormous reserve of anger-derived strength eager to be released, a power that filled him to bursting.

Standing, Finn darted left to right, causing Chernabog to slug the stone wall with his fists and groan with each miscalculated blow. The blows were delivered with the force of a pile driver, cracking the rocks and undermining the thousand-year-old construction. An overhead stone dislodged several inches.

In the dim light, Finn saw Chernabog more clearly. If he'd been a child before the ceremony, he was a man now. His grotesque head, all bull and bat, looked massive, a pink tongue dangling from his jaw. He kicked out and caught Finn, smashing him into the opposing wall.

Finn's hand fell onto another hairy spider.

Grimacing, he picked it up, squeezed, felt for the silk.

Chernabog pivoted and roared. Finn crawled through the beast's parted legs, elbowed the beast on the backs of its knees. Chernabog kneeled, and Finn drove his right elbow like a spike into the back of the bull's neck. It was like hitting brick, but the thing cried out and fell forward. Finn kneed it in the spine, forcing it to arch its back; he then dropped another elbow. Knee, elbow. Knee, elbow. With each blow, Chernabog sagged farther forward.

Finn Whitman, defeating a giant.

The beast threw an elbow of his own. Finn hit the wall so hard, he couldn't see. The spider tried to escape. Finn touched its silk to the stone and hurried deeper down the tunnel. Another hit like that would be his last.

This tunnel was narrow and low-ceilinged.

Finn put some distance between him and Chernabog, but clawing and scratching sounds told him the beast was moving.

With each lunge forward, Chernabog's back worked against the ceiling stones, unsettling them. More sand and dirt rained down, clouding the air.

Chernabog's growls grew increasingly strained and vicious. Finn touched another spot of spider thread to the wall, wondering if he'd be alive to follow it out.

He entered a wide but low chamber off which ran

three additional tunnels—each in the center of a wall, just like the one through which he'd come.

The chamber's floor was sticky with mud.

Chernabog approached.

Finn froze. Which tunnel?

He chose the middle, touching the spider silk to the stone.

In the dark, he ran face first into a wall. Trapped.

A dead end tunnel about ten feet long. If Chernabog pinned him here, he'd be torn limb from limb and eaten.

Chernabog burst into the chamber, swinging his clublike mitts.

The chamber offered him more room than a dead end. Finn charged out to face the beast. Needing both hands, he dropped the spider. It scurried away. Finn felt a sharp pang of loss.

How many times had he crushed a spider? How could he suddenly miss one?

Chernabog faced him, panting, lips still stained with Dillard's blood.

He swiped.

Finn ducked. He spotted the knife protruding from the beast's leg. Lunged for it.

Chernabog caught him on the side of the head. Finn saw stars. Staggering to the side, he planted his hand into the gooey mud. Another blow. Finn collided with the wall, the wind knocked out of him. A tunnel entrance to his right offered escape, but Chernabog maneuvered to block it *and the others.* The beast cocked its head, seemed to be considering whether to end Finn or toy with him for a while.

Somewhere inside, Finn knew he still had untapped strength. His head spinning, his chest aflame, he lacked the will to find it. In the battle of the boy against the beast, the beast had won. Finn hung his head.

Chernabog's hoof moved and crushed the spider. His spider.

Killed so easily.

Like Dillard.

It came from somewhere deep inside, like lava to a volcano, venom to the snake. His muscles swelled, his mind knotted. Finn charged. He hit the beast in the gut, drew the knife from its thigh and heaved it over his head. As Chernabog bent forward from the pain, the knife entered his chest. The beast roared so loudly, Finn's ears rang.

This time Chernabog yanked the weapon out and threw it across the chamber where it shattered against a wall. Finn ducked instinctively from the flying pieces.

Wild with rage, the beast tried to force itself to standing.

At that moment, the roof caved in, unleashing a

torrent of water. Chernabog slashed at the flow, not understanding it. In lashing out at the ceiling, he further ruptured the precarious seam between stones. Water gushed down, filling the chamber. Finn floated off his feet, slapping the surface to remain buoyant. He spun in the water. Which way was out? All four walls, all four tunnel entrances looked identical. He tried to recall Chernabog's movements. Hadn't he crossed the chamber diagonally? Was that where he stood now, fighting against a fallen rock that was pinning him?

Only one tunnel led out to the jungle.

Finn treaded water frantically. The pinned beast heaved. More water gushed down—a river now—but Chernabog had freed himself.

Finn had to pick a tunnel; there was no time.

Then he spotted it: the water was quiet at the mouth of two of the tunnel entrances—*because they were dead ends.* Two others had water spilling into, and filling, the tunnels. One of these two he'd come through only moments before.

He only had one chance. He guessed it was the tunnel immediately to his right, the one farthest from . . .

Chernabog stood beneath the waterfall coming through the ceiling, reaching out and pulling at it as if it were fabric. *He's scared of water,* Finn realized. The beast was fighting the water, screaming, thrusting his horns into the flow and swinging his great paws. He was consumed with fear.

As the water rose, Finn swam underwater for the tunnel. Should Chernabog look over, he would fail to see which tunnel Finn chose.

Echoing from behind him came the guttural, bubbling sounds of a monster near drowning.

Finn hurt all over as he walked. He slipped and fell, stood again with great difficulty. The speed of the water rising lessened. Finally he was out of the water altogether.

He combed the stone surface to his right, desperate to find the silk thread. Maybe the water had pushed wind ahead of it; maybe the absence of silk didn't mean he was moving *deeper* into the tunnels. If he only had more light; it was dark as pitch in here. How was he supposed to see something thinner than a human hair?

Finn thought back to DHI version 1.6, when he'd been able to briefly turn his human self into a hologram. That particular phenomenon had surprised even Wayne and the Imagineers. The upgrade to 2.0 had stripped him of that ability; again, no one understood why or how.

With the water rising again at his ankles, with the sound of Chernabog thrashing in the flood, Finn came to a realization. The trigger for "*all clear*," as they'd called the 1.6 phenomenon, was to lose your fear. Not hide your fear, not cover it up, but lose it. Completely.

What if the ability had been within the 2.0 upgrade all along, but the rules about losing one's fear had changed? Everything else in 2.0 was *enhanced*. Why not *all clear* as well?

Losing one's fear wasn't enough. What was more than losing one's fear?

How could losing his fear be more than losing his fear completely?

Chernabog roared. There was no doubt: he'd freed himself. *And he was coming closer.*

"*To resist her power is futile. With her you must lose yourself to win.*" Wayne had said that before abruptly changing the subject.

Not lose yourself, you idiot! Finn chastised himself. "*Lose your* self."

Your identity. Your ego. All sense of "you." A deeper place than fear.

He closed his eyes and blocked out all sound—only to realize that to block something out, he had to be something. If he was something, he was self. He tried to think of a physical description for "nothing." His thought jumped from *thing* to another; but any *thing* was not nothing: no-thing. He had to imagine no-thing.

Space. Black. Cold. Silent. No gravity. Finn put himself there: into space, consumed by its full emptiness. Its no-thingness.

His head felt light; in fact, he didn't have a head. Or arms. Or wet feet. He opened his eyes.

He was glowing. Not like 1.6. No blue outline around his hologram, but a hologram just the same. And a hologram that emitted a faint amount of light—just enough to see a single bluish thread of spider silk stuck to the wall.

*　*　*

Willa looked up at the steep cave wall, and imagined easily how she'd climb up. The grips, the crux . . . The one sport where I top Charlene, she thought wryly.

"Charlene, I'm going to hide up above. But for the record, I still say this plan sucks. You shouldn't be going out there alone."

"Of course I should. I'm fast. Superfast, as a matter of fact. You think those middle-aged freaks can possibly catch me?"

"Tia Dalma swapped herself with Dillard, you twit! We don't know what they're going to do next!"

"I'd love to debate you," Charlene said. "Actually, not, because you'd win. But we don't have all day. We need the van, and we need the boys in the back of the van. Do you have a plan? No? Because I do. So that's our plan: mine."

"We just can't mess up," Willa said softly.

Without meaning to, both girls looked back at Dillard's body, his bloodless face haunted her. They had carefully propped him in the shadow of a column near the tunnel opening, making sure he couldn't be seen.

Shaking her head, Charlene stepped into the stone corner near the main tunnel entrance to the labyrinth and looked at Willa expectantly. Willa sighed.

"The minute you're out, I'll climb up."

"Promise. Do as I told you," Charlene hissed, and peered outside.

Maleficent was squatting alongside the sitting Evil Queen, whose clothing was still smoking but no longer in flames.

She couldn't make her plan too obvious. The witches were far too smart and cunning for that. It had to be subtle, but it had to be quick: Willa wouldn't be able to hold herself for long, no matter how good a climber she was.

Charlene sprinted across the open terrace and hid behind a rock near the sacrificial table. Tia Dalma still lay on the ground. Wanting to win the attention of Maleficent and the Queen, Charlene ran a zigzag pattern toward the unconscious boys, made a point of appearing to reconsider, turned, and headed back to the tunnel.

Maleficent threw a weak fireball and missed. Charlene entered the tunnel. Her fingertips found the crevices between the stones that Willa had pointed out.

As the two witches entered the tunnel, Maleficent formed a fireball and rolled it ahead as a torch.

"My Lord's prints!" the Queen said, pointing to the cloven hoof marks heading to the right.

Maleficent lit another fireball; held it at shoulder height.

The ball nearly burned Charlene's face. Both girls were now stuck to the ceiling, pressed between the walls, directly above the two Overtakers. The flames threatened to set Charlene's dangling hair on fire.

Maleficent hurled two fireballs. One into each tunnel.

In the flickering light, Charlene saw Willa about to fall. Her hands were ashen white.

Come on! Charlene willed the two witches. *Move!*

As if hearing her, Maleficent and the Queen headed quickly down the tunnel to the right.

There had been no hoofprints on the floor of the entrance; Charlene had scattered the dust so that Willa could be drawn to the prints and then wipe away her own, leaving only the hoof marks. Maleficent and the Queen were entering uncharted territory.

The two Overtakers first threw shadows, then nothing at all. Gone.

Willa lost her hold, rolled over in the air, and landed like a cat on all fours. Charlene released her hold and landed quietly.

"We did it!" Willa choked out as a whisper.

Charlene could not rid herself of the image of Dillard's still body.

"Dillard," she said. "The boys! The van."

Together, the girls carried Dillard into fresh air, fighting back tears.

* * *

A shimmering silver thread of spider silk hung from the stone. For Finn, it looked like parade bunting, worthy of a brass band with trumpets and cymbals. He thought he might have kissed the spider if it had still been alive.

Finn followed the silk. Used his newfound 2.0 *all clear* to light up his way when necessary, he took a corner to the right. It got easier to invoke each time he tried.

At the end of a tunnel to his left—not the tunnel

he was following—he saw yellow flickering light. Fire!

Two figures walked past the tunnel's end, visible for only seconds: Maleficent and the Queen.

In a parallel tunnel.

The firelight grew faint.

Finn settled into *all clear* and reestablished he was following the silk road.

To his left, more light! The two had turned around and were heading his way. Finn reacted too quickly, stepping back instead of forward. Trapping himself instead of freeing himself.

No. He would not allow them to push him back the way he'd come. Finn lay flat on the stone and belly-crawled across the intersection. He was back on his feet and halfway up the tunnel when a giant shadow formed in front of him: his own. Maleficent had rolled a fireball as a searchlight.

"You!" she said, in a voice shrill and brittle.

Finn ran several more steps before sliding to a stop. He spun around.

Me! he thought.

How long was he going to run from Maleficent? How many years had it been? Cowering. Afraid. Always on the defensive.

Now, Chernabog was on the run. And a friend was dead.

Just the thought of Dillard made it hard for him to breathe.

Finn could run, or he could stay and stop this woman and her kind from killing his friends.

She threw a fireball. Halfway to him it slowed perceptibly. Finn dodged it effortlessly, marching toward her now, one confident step at a time.

31

DIABLO FLEW DOWN the tomb tunnel, aimed squarely at Finn's head. But in his current state, the bird of prey came at Finn more like a butterfly. Finn reached out, pinched its wing between his fingers, spun it like a stadium towel, and delivered it into the tunnel's stone wall. Knocked unconscious, the raven fluttered to the floor.

Maleficent wailed, as if some part of her had gone dead. Finn continued his march through the dying flames of several fireballs.

I will not fear you. I will not be intimidated. Bring it on.

Maleficent's eyelids fluttered shut; her lips moved almost imperceptibly. Her neck began to elongate disgustingly; her arms, held out to her sides, thickened.

In a normal state, Finn would not witness the stages of her transfiguration, only the change itself. But with time slowed to a crawl, the woman grew limbs, her chest and body widened and grew scales, her long chin became a dragon's snout.

Just as it had been too small for Chernabog, the stone tunnel was too small for a dragon—Maleficent's anger had misguided her. She'd misjudged.

A green dragon, on folded knees, plugged the tunnel. It scrambled forward, cried, twisted, but could not move.

The Queen was hidden.

The dragon opened its mouth.

Finn's slow-motion world allowed him to turn and dive for the fallen raven, Diablo. He held the bird out as a shield—*a sacrifice*—making sure the dragon could see the crow as he advanced one cautious step at a time.

The dragon wiggled, could not move. It cocked its head, then roared so intensely the tunnel's stones shook. Sand fell.

But no fire from the dragon's mouth. Maleficent would not burn her precious Diablo.

As Finn continued his advance, Diablo in front, the dragon's limbs began to shrink, its head changed shapes. Maleficent was returning to form.

But in Finn's time-shifted world, he charged, dropped Diablo at the dragon's feet.

He closed his eyes and willed away all thought, dropping into *all clear*.

Her transformation continued.

So did his.

He'd never tried this feat, but there was always a first time. Dillard's voice returned in his head. *"If you don't take a chance . . ."*

Finn spoke aloud. "You don't have a chance."

Eyes shut, mind calm, he plunged his hologram hand through the transfiguring flesh at the base of the dragon's neck. His eyes popped wide open, and he felt his "self"—he felt Dillard's self.

He lost his DHI, his arm and hand solid *inside Maleficent.*

The dragon wailed, a shrill, deathly cry. Flames rolled down the tunnel ceiling from a mouth half-human, half-dragon.

Finn pulled with all his strength, creating a fist-size wound.

The fire abruptly stopped.

He stepped back as this creature—half-woman fairy, half-green dragon—curled in on itself, blood flowing in great quantities from its neck.

As the dragon-woman's eyes began to pale in the dwindling firelight, Finn remembered the same light leaving Dillard's eyes. He cried out in agonized victory, turned and walked away as Maleficent choked and coughed wetly, gasping for breath that wouldn't come.

The Evil Queen was a speck of dark, fleeing him, into the tunnel, *away* from any hope of finding the entrance.

Finn found his silver silk adhered to the wall. He collected it so that others could not follow.

Home . . . he thought.

32

A STONE-FACED FINN drove the white van, careful to obey the speed limit in case there were any police patrolling the Mexican back country. They had covered Dillard's face with a rag, unable to look at him. Maybeck's and Philby's sleeping bodies were stretched out, the girls on either side of them. Willa was crying.

Tia Dalma was gagged and blindfolded, both wrists and ankles bound tightly. It had taken three of them to lift her into the back of the vehicle.

Charlene looked ready to choke the witch doctor. They'd covered her head with Dillard's bloody shirt so they didn't have to look at her either, and so she couldn't aim a spell at them.

"Don't do it, Charlie," Finn said. "She's for me."

"What are we going to do?" Willa sobbed. "It's like the Syndrome. You get that, don't you? Both Philby and Maybeck are under a spell! They're . . . gone."

"Dillard's gone," Finn said in a brutal monotone. "Philby and Maybeck are still breathing. They can still be saved."

"We'll get them onto the ship," Charlene said.

"We'll figure something out. Maybe Wayne can help. The Imagineers?"

Finn started to speak, but at the mention of Wayne his voice broke. He shifted in the seat and was poked by something in his pocket. He reached in and came out with a piece of the broken knife blade that Chernabog had shattered. It had found its way into his pocket as he'd ducked from it. He could suddenly feel the knife sinking into Dillard, the knife he'd held. He stopped the van, rolled down the window and threw up out the window. His hand was back on the gearshift when Willa called out.

"Wait!"

Finn couldn't think, he couldn't feel. He wanted to blame it on going *all clear* so often in the tunnels. He knew better. He pocketed the chip of the blade.

Willa said, "It was the Queen, the Evil Queen who did this."

"So what?" choked out Charlene.

"The Queen made them drink a potion, like with the apple in Snow White."

Charlene was with her. "OMG! Snow White. The Evil Queen. The apple."

"And that means . . . ?" Finn asked.

"The seven dwarfs drive her to the mountaintop. The lightning. She goes over into the . . . Then the prince . . . Don't you see? True love's—"

"Kiss," Willa said, finishing it for her.

Charlene looked paralyzed. "Fine for you, but what if it's not . . . true?"

"The story, or do you mean—?"

"If it's not real love?"

"What are you two suggesting?" Finn said, impatient.

Willa addressed Charlene. "I don't think it has to be forever love, just *true* love. Real love. Honest love."

"You think?" Charlene said hopefully.

"No. I *know*," Willa said. "True love isn't reserved for weddings and ceremonies. It's from the heart. That's all it has to be. All it ever is."

Charlene tried to contain the tears streaming down her cheeks. "Well then, we have to try."

Another nod.

Finn interrupted. "What are you—?"

"Shut up!" Willa called to the front seat.

"Not just any kiss. It has to be—"

"Real."

"Yes."

Charlene looked into Maybeck's face. She saw kindness. Felt warmth. Sorrow. Joy. Laughter. Frustration. Concern. Envy. Light-headed fear at the thought of losing him.

As Willa leaned down toward Philby, Charlene bent and kissed Maybeck.

33

"THE DOCTOR GAVE YOU something to wake you up," Uncle Bob said as Luowski's eyes began tracking the two security men in the room. That included Clayton Freeman.

"We need your cooperation," Freeman said.

"Where . . . am . . . I?" Luowski said.

"Aboard the *Disney Dream*."

Clayton Freeman cupped his hand whispered into Bob's ear. "You see his eyes? I swear they were *green* when I took him into custody."

Bob's astonishment bordered on disbelief.

"You came aboard *illegally*," Bob said.

Clayon shook his head, trying to keep Bob from being so stern with the kid who was clearly delirious. "We will be more lenient than the Los Angeles Police Department. We're taking you off the ship in a matter of minutes."

The kid looked totally lost. "The witch," he mumbled, as if remembering something for the first time.

"You are a stowaway. You can go to jail for that," Bob said.

Freeman stepped closer to the boy on the exam table. He talked to him confidentially. "The witch. What did she say? What did she do to you?"

"Oh . . . give me a break!" Bob roared, but Freeman quieted his boss with a sharp look.

Luowski said, "I was supposed to get one of them for her. I wouldn't do it. She . . . got . . . me. Instead."

"Maleficent," Freeman said.

Uncle Bob was about to burst a blood vessel, he was so mad at Freeman.

Luowski nodded. "Bigger than she thought."

"What's bigger?" Freeman asked, leaning in. The boy was speaking so softly that his voice was barely wind from his lips.

"There . . . are . . . others," the boy said.

"Who?"

"Homeless . . ."

"What? Who?"

"An . . . army."

The kid's eyes rolled in his head and his eyelids fluttered shut.

"What'd he say? What'd he say?" Bob asked.

Freeman looked at his boss, back at the kid, and then to Bob again.

"I think he said there's going to be a war."

34

IN THE BRIGHT SOUTHERN California sunshine, three young people stood at the rail of Vibe's deck on the *Disney Dream*—two girls with a boy sandwiched between them. Charlene, Finn, and Willa.

A moveable walkway connected the amidships gangway leading to the terminal, ferrying hundreds of passengers from ship to shore.

A girl with red-streaked hair stood less than five feet away, also looking out. She'd been aboard the *Dream* when a banged-up white van had pulled up to the ship in Puerto Vallarta. She smiled at the three of them.

A drone blimp advertising the Disney Channel floated in the sky.

"If I didn't know better, I'd say that blimp was following us," Finn said.

"Oh, no!" Charlene said.

The other two looked at her.

"A kid in the lounge. She said her friend *saw us on TV*. That it was scary . . . I thought she was talking about a three sixty-five."

"But those weren't scary." Finn looked up at the blimp.

"That's exactly what Charlene said," Willa said. "What's going on?"

"Two point oh," Finn said. "Reality TV."

"W . . . h . . . a . . . t?" Willa looked pale.

"Remember the new contracts they had us sign when they installed the upgrade?"

"A formality," Willa said. "My mother called it a formality."

"My parents, too," Finn said. "But then there's . . . that."

He pointed at the blimp.

"They're filming us?"

"They've turned us into a reality TV show."

"We don't know that!" Charlene said.

"Ah, come on!" Finn said, "We're the real-life *Hunger Games*! It'll be the most popular show *ever*."

"They would tell us!" Charlene complained.

"And we'd start acting, and they don't want that. They want us as natural as possible."

"As if this is natural!" Willa said.

"No kidding." Finn took his eyes off the blimp. "Like it matters. We'll know soon enough." He pointed out at Los Angeles.

"Well, even if they are filming us, it's not all bad.

We've got to focus on the positive," Willa said, attempting to encourage Finn. "Maleficent could be dead."

"She *is* dead," Charlene said.

"No matter if she is or isn't, they'll never find their way out. Chernabog is trapped, maybe drowned. They brought their most evil monster, and we defeated him. Them. We beat the Overtakers, Finn. They're finished."

"You know what they say about evil," Finn said in a gravelly, flat voice. "You end it one place, it pops up in another."

Charlene shot him a disapproving look. Finn's resulting expression of fatigue and sorrow said it would never be over for him.

"They're keeping Dillard on ice," Charlene said, "you know . . ."

"He's dead," Finn said. "I killed him."

"You shouldn't have told them that," Willa said, angrily. "That was a stupid thing to do."

"It's the truth."

"It's a crime. You'll be deported."

"Extradited."

"Whatever! Tia Dalma killed him. Not you."

"You think a judge'll buy that?"

"We *won*," Willa said.

"Too great a price," Finn said.

"There's another possibility." A new voice.

The three turned. Philby and Maybeck walked out onto the deck. The girls swallowed them in leaping hugs.

"Which is?" Willa asked, linking arms with Philby.

"Since you're all so deeply worried," Maybeck said, interrupting. "We passed our physicals. No side effects for the second day in a row."

Finn proposed his theory about the blimp and the reality TV show. Philby just laughed. "You need some rest, man."

Willa squeezed Philby's hand as the five lined up against the rail, looking out in the far distance at the rather flat Los Angeles skyline.

"What other possibility?" Willa asked Philby.

"You ever heard of plea bargaining?" Philby said.

"I have nothing to bargain with," said Finn.

"Not you. Tia Dalma."

"You lost me."

Philby reached into his pocket and pulled out a crude-looking hand-sewn doll. "This was found on Tia Dalma."

The doll, dressed clearly as a boy, had a pin stuck in its chest. Charlene gasped.

"What if this represents . . . what if this is Dillard?" Philby said. "You handled the knife, sure. But what if Tia Dalma handled you?"

Finn rubbed his finger over the head of the imbedded pin.

"What if we offer to let her go in exchange for her removing that pin?"

"Let her go?" Finn was aghast.

"Is that even possible?" Charlene said hopefully.

"What's the one thing we've learned from all of this?" Philby asked.

Maybeck answered. "Anything's possible. Everything."

A flicker of life returned to Finn's dull eyes. "You think? But how? When?"

"Soon," Philby said. "But if she's released, we need the team full-strength."

Maybeck said, "We need to relax. We need a cruise!"

They laughed together, all shaking their heads at once.

"We need a couple of days in Disneyland," Finn said.

No one contradicted him.

"I love Disneyland," Charlene whispered.

Down the length of Deck 11, a crewman was spraying the ship's deck with a garden hose, working the runoff into a channel drain than ran beneath the railing. He politely moved the five Keepers aside with his spray.

"Hey, there!" an adult voice called from outside the

terminal. The kids looked eleven stories down, each spotting a parent, or in Maybeck's case, his aunt Jelly. Finn saw his mother next to Philby's. She was waving frantically, her face filled with joy and excitement, her eyes blue in the bright sun.

Finn covered his face, not wanting the others to see his tears.

The blimp turned toward the ship and sailed closer.

"Let's get out of here," Philby said.

"Not just yet," said the crewman, twisting the nozzle shut. The voice was old, but steady. Eerily familiar to all of them.

Wispy white hair escaped the ship's cap he wore. As he lifted his head, the cap gave way to the face beneath its brim, and an all-knowing, white-toothed smile.

In unison, the Keepers gasped.

ACKNOWLEDGMENTS

The Kingdom Keepers series is a team effort, and a complicated one to try to get right. For those Disney enthusiasts who spot mistakes, they're entirely on me. The parks, cruise line, and publisher extend to me every possible resource to try to keep things accurate and exciting.

Special thanks to Disney Cruise Line's Karl Holz, Jodi Bennett, Christiaan Abbott, Sherry Roth, Clayton Lyndsay, and Captain Henry F. Andersson for giving me access to their amazing ships. As always, to Chris Ostrander and his team for the Synergy. To Alex Wright and all the Imagineers, including Joe Lanzisero, for their help with exploring the ships and the Imagineers' vision of how to do things (at sea) differently!

More down to earth, thanks to my editors Genevieve Gagne-Hawes and, at Disney Books, Wendy Lefkon; Dan Conaway and Amy Berkower at Writers House; Matthew Snyder at Creative Artists Agency; Brooke Muschott, my incredibly knowledgable intern; and Nancy Zastrow and Jen Wood for endless help in the office and on the road.

Don't miss the next adventure:

KINGDOM
KEEPERS
THE INSIDER

BOOK SEVEN

1

SHE HAS BEEN CALLED MANY THINGS: the Black Mamba, Calypso, Tia Dalma. And worse. Much worse.

The scratching of rat claws on stone at her bare feet is accompanied by the disturbing squeals of the rodents as they stream past. Consumed by the darkness of the tunnel, she shuffles forward, her toes stabbing into the void like a cockroach's antennae.

Her stubby fingers feed twine from the ball she carries. Slowly she plays out the lifeline, measuring the ball's diminishing diameter with a slight pressure of her left thumb. It is the third such ball she has knotted, one to the other, in as many days.

The string now stretches more than fifteen hundred feet behind her—nearly a third of a mile—as it winds through the unmarked turns and dead ends of the Devil's Labyrinth, the name she has given this seemingly endless underground maze. Carved from caves by an ancient civilization believed to be long extinct, the interconnecting subterranean passageways might have once connected temples or burial monuments, might have provided safe harbor from hurricanes or served as death traps for exiled citizens, prisoners, or the sick and elderly. Her torch burned out twenty minutes and two tunnels ago. She has considered going back, chasing the twine to the daylight, but what would be the point? Though she cannot see in the dark, Tia Dalma is not without her ways. She has her voodoo, her visions, is able to direct wormholes through reality to sense Danger, Desire, and Death—the three Ds.

She does so now, but detects only the worry and scurry of the rats and a looming menace that hangs like a stink. Bad things have happened here. Evil stains these walls. Where some would feel fear so intense as to set teeth to gnashing, this woman warms at the very thought.

Getting close now.

A slight breeze, fainter than the breath of a bumblebee bat, flutters the two mole whiskers on the underside of her chin, tickles her tattooed eyelids with delicious warmth, fills her dilated nostrils with the fetid odor of moldering organic matter. Proof of life. Somewhere, perhaps far from her current position, perhaps as near as the other side of a two-ton slab of rock, something lives. Or it once did. Candidates include blind wolves, dead snakes, dragons, or bubbling gases from the corpses of sacrificed animals stacked like cordwood two thousand years earlier. Tia Dalma picks up on it with the instincts of a bloodhound. Won't let it go. Sniffs the air loudly as she pursues the frail thread of decomposition.

The twine uncoils as the ball spins on her fingers. Even a maze as complicated and devious as this must contain compromises, secret passageways connecting one to the other, hidden exits, covert companionways. This whiff of decay is her first encouragement. But it proves fleeting, no more than a temptation to hurry her forward to the fraying end of her rope, where she stops, eager to press forward even without the connection back.

Not daring to release the twine, she stretches her body, pushing her fingertips as far as she can reach, tickling the dark with pointed purple nails like a relay runner reaching for the baton. It is a risky business, this, for she could inadvertently release the stretched string and send it recoiling from her, elusively difficult to relocate. Divorced from the certainty of survival, a person could go mad in such darkness.

But Tia Dalma is no person. If she were, she would prove herself less susceptible than most: she's mad already.

Once again the fetid, rank odor of rot overcomes her. It comes from stone rubble to her left caused by a cave-in. She approaches and begins to dig, driven by a gnawing suspicion that whatever corpse is causing this foul report it is meaningful to her, pertains to her. This thought causes a spike of energy, determination and—dare she admit it?—apprehension.

The digging is surprisingly easy. She pulls a stone loose only to cause a small rockslide. The grave comes open for her. A few more rocks is all and—

She gasps as her fingers touch not rock but scales—large scales, the size of dinner plates, but with the rough texture of giant fingernails. *Dragon scales,* she realizes. She howls into the dark like a lone wolf. Maleficent transfigures herself into a dragon—*or did,* Tia Dalma realizes. No longer. In her mind's eye she can see the willful boy who trapped and killed one of the greatest practitioners of black magic ever to live.

The boy who did this!

A second haunting cry reels though the catacombs. It's a high-pitched complaint tinged with pain and anger, morose grief, and agonizing uncertainty. There should be others even if the one is lost. The Evil Queen. The Beast. Tia Dalma has made it her charge to collect these principals and rebuild. No battle is without losses; no army survives with all its generals. Hope is ephemeral, defying her wish to hold on to it. Who needs hope when there is hate to take its place? Who needs even hate when there is an attack planned for later this same night many, many miles to the north? An attack set to bring the Kingdom to its knees?

Still, she will not let go of the hope or the twine. She twists it in her fingers as she reverses direction, begins collecting the twine around itself, the ball in her hand growing thicker as it directs her back along a route well traveled.

2

THROUGH THE WINDOWS, an image. At first, the
Security guard—appropriately named Bert; he looks like
a Bert, and was even named for the character of Bert
in *Mary Poppins*—can hardly believe it. Here? At this
hour? Waving to him like they're old friends?

Bert glances at a photograph on the interior wall of
the same man, much younger, standing with Becky Cline
and Mickey Mouse at the grand opening of the Disney
Archives. They call him a Disney Legend. In the courtyard terrace outside, this man's palm prints and name
adorn a ceramic-tile plaque on a pillar supporting the
trellis. A child prodigy, he worked with Walt Disney
himself, helped design Disneyland and later, Walt Disney
World, overseeing the creation of attractions. He was a
founding member of what would come to be called "the
Imagineers"—those people whose job it is to have vision.

He is old now, his hair white as cotton, but his
ruddy face is youthful and full of surprise. Bert feels
better just seeing him out there. Wayne Kresky has the
power of personality, of confidence and willful joy. It
almost looks like he's glowing.

Wayne motions for Bert to unlock the door. Later, this will strike Bert as odd; surely Wayne possesses every key, every code needed to access any building anywhere in the Disney kingdom—so why signal for Bert's help?

But Bert does not hesitate. Who is he to deny Wayne Kresky anything? It might as well be a royal prince making the request. As Bert moves toward the door, he is once again struck by Wayne's charisma. Against the backdrop of night, the man appears cloaked in incandescence—almost shimmering.

Bert bumps the door's push bar and heaves it open with his hip.

"Good evening, sir."

"I have business to attend to. . . . Do you mind?"

The two sentences seem—somehow—prerecorded, like two different pieces of dialogue edited together. But Bert is overcome by the man's presence. Wayne Kresky, here! Bert doesn't stop to question anything about the situation. Hindsight will help others fill in the blanks. For now, the Security man is awestruck. Albert Pujols or Kobe Bryant would have less of an impact upon him than Wayne Kresky.

"Of course!"

"The Archives."

"I was just looking at the picture of you and—"

Wayne's face is devoid of emotion as he pulls the

door farther open and blocks it with his foot. It's an aggressive act: so unexpected, it stops Bert's cold, in midsentence.

"Welcome to Walt Disney World!" Wayne says in a theatrical voice different from any inflection he's used thus far.

Bert thinks, But this is Burbank. South of here is Anaheim, home to Disney*land*. Disney *World*? Why did he say that? Can the old dog no longer hunt?

Just above the courtyard, a string of specks appears in the night sky. If this wasn't Southern California, Bert might think they were snowflakes. Fireflies, perhaps. Hummingbirds. The specks grow in size and proximity quickly—they are flying, flying fast, straight toward an openmouthed Bert, whose expression changes now from wonder to dread. Not snowflakes. Not hummingbirds. If he didn't work for Disney, he would have thought, *Not possible!*

The first three or four come into focus: brooms, brooms with buckets—the nemeses of Mickey in his role as the Sorcerer's Apprentice. Flying brooms. No, not flying—the brooms are carried by ghosts, the ghosts followed by demons and monsters, hollow-eyed, horrid creatures from unseen graveyards, decayed and fetid, so grotesque that Bert averts his eyes, recoiling from the procession as they swoop under the courtyard's trellis and flow inside the building as if driven onward by a ferocious wind.

"No!" Bert hollers. "Please! No!"

But who's to hear? A demon hovers over him, gray and toothless with the shriveled, sunken cheeks of a two-thousand-year-old mummy and eyes like wrinkled dates. The demon points the bony nub of one long, skeletal finger at Bert as the he floats lower . . . lower. . . .

Bert shrinks into a tight ball, moaning in terror. The finger pokes him.

And then . . . blackness.